ODYSSEUS

THE RETURN

Valerio Massimo Manfredi

ODYSSEUS

THE RETURN

Translated from the Italian by Christine Feddersen-Manfredi

MACMILLAN

First published in the UK 2014 by Macmillan
an imprint of Pan Macmillan, a division of Macmillan Publishers Limited
Pan Macmillan, 20 New Wharf Road, London N1 9RR
Basingstoke and Oxford
Associated companies throughout the world
www.panmacmillan.com

ISBN 978-0-230-76935-9 HB
ISBN 978-0-230-76937-3 TPB

First published in Italian 2013 as *Il Mio Nome è Nessuno: Il Ritorno* by
Arnoldo Mondadori Editore S.p.A., Milano

1 3 5 7 9 8 6 4 2

A CIP catalogue record for this book is available from the British Library.

Typeset by Ellipsis Digital Limited, Glasgow
Printed and bound by CPI Group (UK) Ltd, Croydon, CR0 4YY

Visit **www.panmacmillan.com** to read more about all our books
and to buy them. You will also find features, author interviews and
news of any author events, and you can sign up for e-newsletters
so that you're always first to hear about our new releases.

To Christine

ἀμωμήτῳ ἀλόχῳ

Neither Laestrygonians nor Cyclopes
Nor bitter Poseidon will you ever meet
Unless you carry them within your heart
Unless your heart raises them before you

Constantine P. Cavafy, *Ithaka*

1

TROY WAS STILL BURNING.

A huge storm of fire raged. Blazing shafts plunged from the heavens with a deafening roar. The shades of fallen warriors still screamed their outrage amidst the smoke and flames; restless, anguished souls, teeming now at the gates of Hades. Troy would burn for days and nights, until she had turned to ash.

The glare of the fires guided us back.

Two men from each ship swam to shore, struggling against the strong current. They anchored the vessels to land by tying them to the solid oak stakes they drove into the ground. I ordered them all to wait aboard as I set off towards the city; no one was to go ashore for any reason. *I still wonder why I didn't stay with my men that night, why I went back to the scene of deceit and slaughter. I don't have an answer.*

I could see, from on high, the ships of Agamemnon and the other kings who had chosen to remain. They were anchored at the sterns, their prows facing seaward – so they were on their way as well. Perhaps they'd understood that there were no sacrifices or hecatombs that could make amends for the horrors we'd committed. All that innocent blood spilled.

I found the road that led to the city, passed between the scorched jambs of the Skaian Gate that we'd believed to be impregnable, walked up towards the citadel. I arrived just in time to witness the unimaginable: the horse I myself had built was collapsing, at that very instant, devoured by the fire. It had taken the flames this long to envelope the horse, so tall it had once towered over the city and the palace. It crashed to the earth in a vortex of sparks and white smoke. Its head was last to dissolve in the blaze.

I heard, or thought I heard, the echoing shrieks of those the fire had consumed. They were gone, but their dried blood still clogged the cracks in the road. I continued to ascend, until I reached the vast porticoed courtyard where the sanctuary of my goddess still rose. The roof had caved in, and the blackened pillars now stood alone like silent guards.

I went in.

The sanctuary was empty. The pedestal where the glittering statue of Pallas Athena had stood was empty. The powerful idol had vanished. Who had taken it? Who would have dared to do such a thing?

The Achaians, perhaps?

I, myself?

Had my mind erased this completely? Is this what had dragged me back inside the walls of sacred Troy? Questions without meaning and without answers that could not stop me from wandering like a spectre among the charred ruins. The rain sizzled and hissed as it met the flames that still burned with accursed energy. In the end, exhausted, I made my way back down to the battlefield. There was a strange, unreal light in the air, a luminescent vapour that transformed the objects around me, making everything unrecognizable. I found myself suddenly at the wild fig tree, without realizing how I'd got there. The familiar grey trunk, the green leaves, the bark so often wounded. I leaned against it and felt the scars of the immortal tree at my back, the only living thing remaining in the devastated field. I slumped, bone-weary, and fell asleep.

It was the moon that woke me. It led me back to the promontory, lighting my path and then the high yards and sleek flanks of my ships. At dawn, a strong land wind scattered the clouds and carried the smoke out to sea, clearing the sky above us and leaving it luminous. We cast off the moorings then, pushed the ships out and raised the sails. The wind steered us towards the coast of Thrace.

I knew those lands well. I'd gone there often during the long war to buy the wine that had so often consoled us during our many sufferings and gladdened our banquets. A strong, sweet wine that we diluted with water so it would last longer. It certainly wasn't a job that required a king. Any of the merchants who had pitched their tents outside our camp could have seen to it, but it was a job that I liked. It made me feel alive again. I would walk through the fields, watch as the wine was poured out, have a taste, haggle over the price. Sometimes I would be invited to lunch, and I could linger at the table with the vine-dressers. It felt like I was home again, in a way.

Now we were at sea, finally, and we were never going to turn back.

How did I feel . . . tears fell from my eyes. I looked back and remembered my comrades, the friends I had lost, all those who would not be returning with us. And I looked forward, counting the days that separated us from our island home. It didn't seem real. I was starting to think again like a man who inhabits his own house, grows his own crops, tends his own flocks. I let myself imagine joyful events: embracing my parents, the little son who had never known me . . . Penelope, who I had so keenly desired on all those long sleepless nights . . . We would lie together in the bed I had built and after we'd made love I would gaze at the beams over my head, breathe in the scent of the olive trunk, the scent of my wife. We would have so many things to tell each other, under the covers that my mother had embroidered . . . And Argus? Was Argus still alive?

I thought of painful things as well: facing the families of my fallen comrades, listening to their inconsolable weeping, offering them the share of the booty that was their right in exchange for a son's life. The news of our endeavour would have travelled from mouth to mouth, from village to village, from island to island and I would be making my return as the absolute victor, the destroyer of cities, the man with the mind who had plotted unimaginable stratagems. The trophies of my victory would be hung from the walls of my palace: embossed shields, bronze panoplies, baldrics of silver mail with gold and amber buckles that would astonish my father and all the visitors who came to call . . . But I couldn't think any further than that. So many years of ruin and grief had taught me that you can't make plans. The future is inscrutable; the gods are often envious of our happiness and enjoy watching us suffer. Only my goddess loved me, of this I was certain, but not even she could bend destiny.

Then we sighted land and in no time I was thinking like a warrior and predator again. It was like a disease, lurking deep inside me; after all, I'd done nothing else for ten years. I found myself pondering the thought that all the booty I carried with me was surely not a sufficient token of my great glory. My people would be expecting much more of me.

From the sea we could see a city up on a hill and its inhabitants could probably see us. It was defended by a wooden palisade and had gates of stone.

'Let's seize it!' shouted my men.

They were like me. They knew they would be putting themselves in danger but they didn't care. Perhaps they were already craving carnage, terror, violence. After all, this was the land of the Ciconians; they were Thracians and allies of Priam. It was only right for us to attack them. I ordered my comrades to take up arms and we put ashore. The men of the city must have been far off, in the fields or at pasture with their flocks. No warriors came out to challenge us. It wasn't until we had crashed through the main gate using the mast from one of our ships that we saw a single living soul. A hasty assembly of about a hundred men stood against us. We easily overcame them and poured into the city.

Before long, the city of Ismarus was put to plunder and its most beautiful women were rounded up and dragged off. I walked into one of the richest houses and found a man who appeared to be terrified. He fell to his knees and begged me not to kill him. He wore the headdress of a priest and I spared him. In exchange he gave me a big skin full of wine, the best he had. The same fine wine that I had brought back to the battlefield so often for the banquets of the princes and kings.

We loaded up the booty and I ordered the men to set sail immediately, but many of them had gathered on the beach and had started drinking while others had slaughtered and quartered a few sheep and had lit a fire. The strong wine and the women had gone to their heads. They simply would not listen to me; they were no longer the obedient, disciplined warriors I was accustomed to, I realized bitterly. I feared that it wouldn't be long before they reaped their punishment. I went back to my ship alone, ate a cup of barley toasted on the brazier at the stern, and drank some water.

Eurylochus approached me. 'They've suffered for ten years,' he said, 'and they've always obeyed you, fought with great courage. They've lost more than two hundred of their comrades. Don't begrudge them a little celebrating. Haven't they earned it?'

'No one deserves to enjoy what he can't afford. They're acting like fools and they'll pay for it with their lives. Is any amount of revelry worth such a risk? Listen, don't you hear anything at all? And those lights, up there on the hill, can't you see them?'

Eurylochus strained his ears and scanned the darkness. A distant roll of drums . . . fires up on the heights. News of the fall of Ismarus was flying from hill to hill, from village to village.

We would soon be attacked and, in the meantime, my brave fighters and daring sailors were turning into a bunch of drunks, incapable of standing up straight. Fog fell over land and sea and I remained wakeful all that night, a solitary sentry.

The grey, cold dawn roused me from a brief, fitful slumber and what I saw unfortunately confirmed my fears: thousands of Ciconian warriors were streaming down the hills, heading our way. I shouted out an alarm and I kicked my men awake. As they came to, they began to understand what was happening. They stumbled to their feet and into their armour but had no time to eat. I drew them up in front of the ships in close ranks as I had so many times in Troy. The enemy were just a couple of hundred paces away from us when they lunged forward at a run and pounded our formation like waves of the sea against cliffs. Hard as it was for me to believe, my men resisted the attack; they were holding their own, shield to shield, shoulder to shoulder. I tried several times to lead a counter-attack from the centre, in the hopes of frightening the enemy and routing them, but to no avail. As long as our strength held up, I knew we could manage to maintain our position but by afternoon, exhausted and hungry as we were, we started to lose ground. We had nothing but our ships and the sea at our backs. Where could we go? How could we hope to save ourselves?

I ordered one crew at a time to push their vessel out into the water, climb aboard and take up oars, while all the others protected them on land. Once on board, they would be able to cover their comrades still on foot with a fast, steady rain of arrows until all the men could get back onto the ships. My battle plan worked, the men resisting until the last ship had gained the open sea. But by then more than forty of our own had been lost to the enemy.

The sun had set. Eurylochus approached me and asked if we could give the final salute to the dead who had been abandoned unburied. It was traditional to shout out each man's name ten times. I replied: 'Thrice will be enough. They don't deserve such an honour from us. They died as fools.' It was my way of not crying.

A STORM was in the air and it was getting very dark now. I took the lead with my ship, sailing close to the coast to avoid the freshening north wind. When I thought we had distanced ourselves sufficiently from the land of the Ciconians, I gave orders to haul in the sails and to row to shore. We dropped anchor forward, keeping the bows pointed towards the sea, and moored aft. I allowed the men to bivouac on the beach and to eat their only meal of the day, with sentries posted all around and close guard shifts established. We ate without speaking, because the loss of so many comrades was a dull ache in each of our hearts. Many men had tears in their eyes.

At the end of our meal, I decided the route we would take: we would go south, passing between Lemnos and Scyros and then between Euboea and Andros to reach Cape Malea.

'We'll sail both day and night,' I said. 'I don't want what happened today to repeat itself. Each helmsman will ensure that the brazier at the stern of his ship remains lit at all times. I want to be able to count the vessels one by one at any hour of the night.'

We all returned aboard the ships to sleep, leaving only the sentries on land. We rested rather well, all told, and halfway through the night the wind even seemed to die down, although the sea remained rough.

Thoughts crowded my mind. I didn't dare hope.

Would my goddess come to my aid? Or was I at the mercy of Poseidon? Every drop of water, every creature and every weed, every cove and every gulf was his. I prayed in my heart that he might show us clemency and allow us to see our homeland and our families again after so many long years. At dawn we cast off the mooring lines and weighed anchor. We launched the names of our fallen comrades to the winds, three times for each one of them, and when the last echo was lost in the distance, I couldn't hold back any longer. I went to the highest point of the prow as the other ships followed mine away from the shore and shouted out the triple cry of the Ithacan kings. I cried out as loudly as I could, to be heard over the wind whistling among the shrouds: 'To Ithaca, men! We're going home!'

They answered in a single voice with the same shout, pounding their oars on the benches. Our true return voyage had begun. If the gods and the winds helped us, we would moor at the great port at the seventh dusk.

As the day wore on, we spied the hills of Lemnos to our left. At times during the war, on a very clear day, we could make out their outline from the slopes of Mount Ida, where we would go with the woodcutters to chop trees. The clouds were moving quickly through the sky but they were not massing, and my most expert sailors felt that this was a good sign and that fine weather would accompany us.

Sailing the open sea at night was a risky choice, but the desire to return was so strong in each of us that no one dared oppose my decision. All six of the ships following mine sailed at an equal distance from one another in an oblique line, so that each could see both the ships in front of and behind their own at any time.

By the following midday, Scyros, the island of Pyrrhus, appeared before us at a considerable distance. We sailed past, leaving it to our right without attempting to go ashore. I had dark memories of that place. I wondered where the savage warrior was now, that brutal, bloodthirsty youth who would spare neither an old man nor a babe in arms. How would Peleus, king of Phthia of the Myrmidons, welcome his grandson when he returned preceded by such ill fame? I turned and watched at length as the island slowly vanished behind the billows, until the sea became purple and the air damp and cold.

The moon finally appeared among the clouds. It was white, and cast a long silvery wake on the broad back of the sea. I imagined the other fleets that had already set forth over these waters. The hundreds of ships of Menelaus Atreides, of Nestor the Knight of Gerene, of Diomedes Lord of Argus. And Helen . . . where could she be? What was she thinking? Who was she thinking of?

Sinon was sleeping wrapped in a blanket behind me, nestled in the coils of rope like in a serpent's embrace. Without him, our trick would never have worked: he, small, practised liar. I smiled. Sham victim, feigned fugitive.

I didn't fall asleep until Orion was nearly touching the surface of the waves. In the distance, towards Asia, the sky was whitening. Eurylochus had taken my place at the helm. I slept in the shadow of the sail until the sun was high in the sky. My first thought when I awoke was for the men I'd lost, and I couldn't understand why we had risked our lives for such meagre booty and a few skins of wine. Such an insignificant battle, against a trifling twin to Troy, against mere shepherds and hunters, could have been fatal for us: we, who bronze-clad had fought a hundred battles against the most powerful warriors in all Asia! I tried to force those unhappy thoughts from my mind but serenity escaped me. I could not push away those dead, abandoned, unburied comrades on the beach; the winds, so strong, that I could neither control nor tame; the last obstacles that I knew would be approaching, looming between me and my island, my wife, my son, my parents.

Later that day a little bay appeared on our right and I decided we would go ashore before facing the straits between Euboea and the island of Andros. The men had been fighting the wind and the waves all night and all day. I had to let them rest. Mine was the first ship to beach. One after another, the others followed, making a complete turn so that our sterns were facing the shore.

We had touched the land of Achaia, after ten years.

The men fished. They found some big pieces of driftwood, lit a fire and roasted what they'd caught over the embers. It smelled inviting and I sat down on the dry sand with my comrades to participate in the frugal banquet. Those who had wine shared it with the others and it warmed our hearts.

Food had never tasted so good to me. I thought of when, under the walls of Troy, the other kings had made fun of us islanders, calling us fish-eaters. Only a few days had passed since we'd taken the city, but they seemed like months. The memory of the furious fray around the wild fig tree was fading like a bad dream before dawn. The day was slowly coming to an end although the wind showed no sign of dying down, and the foam on the sea still blossomed whitely on the crests of the waves crashing against the rocks.

When our hunger had been somewhat satiated, some of the men began to sing. It was the hour of remembering. Distant images, forgotten for years, came to lap at our minds like waves reaching across the beach. The man that I'd lost sight of, in so many years of war's din and bloodletting, was coming alive in me again, with feelings, emotions, hopes. But I knew well that our journey was not yet over: what still lay ahead was a treacherous passage, fraught with difficulty and danger.

Cape Malea!

'Let's sleep now,' I said. 'A difficult day awaits us tomorrow.'

I stretched out in the shelter of a rock, covered myself with my cloak and tried to rest. At my side, the sword of Troy reminded me that the past never dies, and can return to strike at any moment. All night, the wind rushing through the bushes and the high boughs of the trees kept me half-awake. I rolled first to one side and then to the other while sleep eluded me. Finally, just before Dawn lit up sea and land, I was able to find some rest. My aching limbs relaxed and I dreamt that I was alone on a deserted beach. The place was immersed in silence. I could hear neither the roar of the sea that never sleeps nor the shrieking of seagulls. But all at once I heard barking and saw a dog running towards me. He jumped all over me, whimpering with joy.

'Argus, Argus!' I shouted, 'it's you!' And I petted and caressed him, my heart swelling with affection for my faithful friend. He hadn't forgotten me.

Then I woke up.

The men had found blackberries among the bushes, ripe cane apples, pine nuts and almonds, along with a great number of enormous asphodel bulbs which they'd roasted over the embers.

We ate them all, because we knew they would completely abolish our pangs of hunger.

The time to set sail had come. We got onto the ships and turned them south. Mine was the first to reach the open sea.

I knew of the hazards that awaited us in the narrow passage between Euboea and Andros. The speed of the current and of the wind, already very high, would only increase in the strait. I had the sail taken in and the oars lowered into the water to better manoeuvre the ship and check her speed. The sun was already high when my vessel exited again into the open sea. I counted the ships behind me as they moved forth on their skewed line like a herdsman counts his heifers when he brings them back to the fold from the pasture. They were all there, and I was greatly relieved. I had my crew raise the sail again and watched as this manoeuvre was repeated in the same way by the rest of the fleet. By dusk I could see Cape Sounion, but I didn't approach the land for fear of the reefs. Had Menestheus already arrived at Athens? Had he already gone to the sanctuary to thank Poseidon by offering a sacrifice? Perhaps he was up there watching our passage over the foaming sea . . . We continued south as the sun began to decline on our right over the mountain peaks. The wind was freshening again. I rushed to the ropes with Eurylochus, Perimedes and Antiphus the helmsman. We had to control the speed and direction of the ships and calculate the time that separated us from the most difficult passage yet to come. Was it best to seek a place to land before it got dark and set off again the next morning, or proceed at a faster clip, continuing through the night, in order to get to Cape Malea and double it as soon as we could, leaving the obstacle behind us once and for all? I thought this was the better strategy. We would navigate by night with the braziers lit, watching the stars to stay on route and taking into account the strength of the wind and its direction. We would shorten the sail by half. The others, behind us, would only need to follow our example. As soon as we came within sight of the cape we would dismast and pass beneath the high promontory by the strength of our oars alone, then come back up the other side.

It was a well-conceived plan and I could already see it happening in my mind's eye. I could almost feel how the speed of the wind would drop off as soon as we passed the cape, how the air temperature would become milder, the waves of the sea calmer. Our next stop would be Pylos, that sheltered, welcoming bay. Nestor would greet us and have a great banquet served up . . . I was beginning to let myself think of Penelope: was her heart still faithful to me? Did she love me still? Ten years seemed a terribly long time . . .

But the wind, instead of dropping, increased in intensity. The sail ripped and we had to replace it, with enormous difficulty. None of us slept all night. We didn't move from our posts. We kept scanning the heavens and consulting each other about the decisions to be taken. All at once, the sky became covered with high, thin clouds and the stars disappeared. From that moment on, our eyes were fixed in the direction of the shore, straining to see a light, a farmhouse, a shepherd's shack, to reassure ourselves that land was indeed close and that we weren't being blown off course. But all we could see was darkness, all we could hear was the voice of the sea that never sleeps. I trained my gaze to the east, then, to our left, awaiting the first sign of dawn with growing anguish. The only sight that comforted me was when I looked back and saw, in that utter darkness, the braziers of my ships tracing an oblique red line of fire on the water.

When the sky lightened, it held no stars nor moon. Above us was only a pale void. The wind was colder and stronger: we were in the middle of a storm. I was seized with dread: the gods were pushing me away from my destination!

I was shaken by the voice of Antiphus, full of sadness. 'Wanax,' he said, 'where are we?'

No matter which way we looked, we saw nothing. The headland of Cape Malea, which must still have been out there somewhere, was invisible, distant, lost to us. I had hoped, dreamt, for so long of my island my house my family. They felt so close I could have touched them. I was reminded of the day that my father had taken me out into the open sea, to the point where all lands vanish. The sea had stretched out before me then, extending infinitely in every direction, while the sun pounded down on us, its rays calling up sprites of light that danced on the still waters.

The sea, all around us, was empty.

2

WHAT WERE THE MEN ON the other ships thinking? That I'd made a mistake? That the king of Ithaca didn't know how to get them home?

My heart was burning in my chest like a firebrand. I would talk to them when the moment came, after we had landed. The position of the sun soon told me that we were heading south, fast. I had never navigated in those waters before and I had no idea what to expect, but the wind raged on, swelling the sails, ripping them to shreds at times. We had to change them time and time again. Black clouds galloped through the sky and pelted us with heavy rain. No one would have been able to change course, not even by striking the sails and manning the oars. The sea rushed tumultuously in a single direction, her high, grey waves boiling with foam.

'Land!' shouted Perimedes. 'To starboard!'

'Cythera,' said Eurylochus. 'I've seen it many times. The wind is pushing us further away.'

And so it was, unhappily. No force could have challenged the wind and the waves. We sailed in this way for nine days and nine nights of tempest, without ever stopping. My comrades could not fish as they had become accustomed to doing, by throwing out nets or casting out lines with barley kernels soaked in water as bait. We had very little food left. I was eating my heart out with pain, rage and despair.

On the tenth day, the wind dropped all of a sudden and the sea calmed until it became a shiny bronze plate. Slivers of light slipped around the ships, their dark profiles beaded in the deep blue.

I hoisted the signal for assembly and the ships gathered together, all within reach of my voice.

'Have you lost any men?' I shouted.

'No, *wanax*!' replied the commander of the second ship.

'No, *wanax*!' replied the commanders of the other five, one after another.

'Neither have we!' I said. 'We're all still here and this is good luck indeed after such a storm. Now put your backs into the oars and we'll forge on. Land is surely close by. There are birds in the sky and you can smell it in the air.' An odour of unfamiliar herbs. But we could see nothing. A thick mist had risen in front of us and we were surrounded by water on every side. I signalled to the helmsman to head into the mist that hovered above the sea. The others followed us.

Never before and never again have I felt the way I did at that moment. *Alone, afraid, cold and my heart was empty, as if my blood and every other humour had been drained from my body.* The way a man feels when he collapses to the ground pierced by a spear or the sharp tip of an arrow, as his life escapes, streaming, out of the wound. How often I'd seen it! I seemed to be caught in a dream, of the kind that fills you with anguish. One knows that the visions of the night are false imaginings, insubstantial, and yet the suffering they inflict on your heart could kill you. I called out to my comrades: 'Eurylochus! Antiphus!' Why couldn't I see anyone? Could I be alone on my ship? Who was at the oars, driving it on? I could see the prow slip forward, cleaving the water which fell to either side without making a sound. I could see myself running back and forth in the mist and yet I knew full well that I was standing still at the bow, scanning the impenetrable fog. What was that disc of pale light fluttering in the mist? The moon? The sun? Shrieks. Birds scattering, terrified. Splashing. Who, what, had fallen into the still water? Was this a portal into some other place? Was I alone? The other ships, where were they? Elpenor! Antilochus! Euribates, where are you all? Answer me, it's your king who's calling! I could see someone passing by . . . a shadow nearby, slipping away, walking. Who are you? He didn't turn. I turned. He disappeared. Athena, where are you, where are you? You're hiding! Why won't you come out?

How much time passed? I don't remember. Hours, days . . . Waves lapping, water whispering. Suddenly a shock to my heart, like the blow of a dagger. I shouted so loudly that my throat bled and then . . . I was out!

Land before me, sea behind me and the wall of fog, thick and smoky. The waves then, finally, the lapping at the shore, the scent of earth, tongues of sea lengthening onto the glittering golden sand. Now I could see my comrades rowing, striking the sail. Hadn't they heard me shout out? Couldn't they see my mouth bleeding? I washed it out with seawater. My throat burned.

'We'll moor aft!' I ordered. 'Drive the stakes into the ground, drop anchor forward! Antilochus, on me!'

He ran over: '*Wanax*, look!'

One of our ships was emerging from the fog at a certain distance. It looked like it was coming from Hades: half was in the light, the other half invisible. The men looked like ghosts.

Another, further east. Both spotted us and joined us. Then no more. We waited and hoped for a long, long time.

'Where are the other ships?' I asked Eurylochus.

He looked bewildered.

'Where are they?' I insisted. 'They were so close. We all made it through the storm, all the ships had assembled, I spoke to the crews. You all heard me.'

'We heard you, king.'

'Then how could we have lost four ships with all their men?'

Eurylochus shook his head: 'You know as well as I do. We were in a dark place.'

We disembarked. What land was this? Who lived here? What

language did they speak? There was a wide sweep of tall grass and patches of sand here and there. Towering palm trees swayed in the morning breeze. In the distance, a grove of tamarisks. And creatures we had never seen before. They looked like little hairy men, with tails. Shiny eyes, piercing and unsettling. They squawked, they screamed, they jumped from one branch to another.

'Monkeys,' said Eurylochus. 'Among all animals, the ones that resemble us most. Disagreeable things. Clever, bold and rude. I sailed as far as Crete once to buy some terebinth oil and an old beggar had one.'

'Send out men to look for water and food,' I ordered. 'A party to the east and one to the west. Tell them to come back as soon as they've found what we need. The others will drop the nets and try to fish. In the meantime, start a fire. Everyone will keep his arms at the ready.'

They all fanned out and I stayed close to the ship. As I looked around, I realized that nothing looked familiar: the air was different from the air I'd always breathed, the rays of light appeared to be shed by a different sun. The atmosphere was close, suffocating and time seemed to stretch out immensely. The thought of the ships and comrades I'd lost was unbearable.

A shout startled me and I saw Elpenor making wide gestures from up on a sandy rise at the end of the long beach, to the west. I ran towards him.

'*Wanax*, look!' he said when I was close enough to hear. I turned around. In the distance, perhaps a thousand paces from us, were the rest of our ships. Beached stern to, all four of them.

'Follow me,' I ordered. 'But don your armour first.' Elpenor and the group of men with him set off with me on foot. I sent one of them back to warn the others not to move. They were to wait for us where they were until we returned.

When we reached the ships we found no one inside. We searched them one at a time without finding any signs of violence or disorder. The oars were in their rowlocks, the sails had been taken in, the steering oars tied to the rails. The trunks full of Trojan plunder at the prows were undisturbed. The only sound to be heard was the sea pounding untiringly against the keels and the wind whipping the shrouds. The rest was silence.

'But . . . where are they? Not hunting or looking for water, they would have left someone on guard. They haven't fallen into the sea because the ships have been left in perfect order and secured with their anchors forward just as they should be.'

I saw terror in the men's eyes. They could face any kind of danger, but the unknown or unexplainable filled them with fear. Had our comrades been kidnapped, carried off? By harpies, by fog demons?

'Listen to me,' I said. 'It's nothing like what you're imagining. Here the ground is rocky, but if we go inland it's grassy. We'll search for traces of their footprints and follow them until we've found our mates. Keep your weapons at hand. We don't know what land this is or who lives here.'

As I was speaking, the man I'd sent off to the ships came running back. I told him about what we'd found and that we would soon be setting off to search for the missing men. He was to go back and tell his comrades to put out to sea, bring the three ships around to the stretch of beach where the empty ships were at anchor, and moor them there. A single set of guards would suffice for all of them.

The man, a fellow from Zacynthus who had always fought bravely under the walls of Troy, replied: 'I will do as you say, *wanax*, but if there's someone else who can carry out your order I'd prefer to come with you.'

'No,' I replied, 'but I appreciate your courage and your loyalty. Next time you'll be at my side, but go now and do as I've asked.'

As he ran off again, we started up the path leading inland. On our left stood a hill topped by a high plain. Its slope was crossed by a stream of clear water that flowed through a luxuriant green field on which animals with pointed, doubly curved horns were grazing peacefully. The coats on the beasts' backs had black stripes. The other creatures I could see lumbering in the distance looked gigantic, truly frightening in size.

I'd never seen anything like them, and never would again for the rest of my life. I was beginning to understand why I'd had to cross that mist. I felt that I had crossed an invisible threshold and entered a hidden, secret land where everything would be different, where anything could happen. Although my heart was heavy with thoughts of our missing comrades and our failed return, my eyes were wide with astonishment upon seeing these wondrous creatures. I understood how big and how marvellous the world was, and I was sure that my adventure and that of my companions would be no less exciting than the voyage my father King Laertes had undertaken with his comrades on the *Argo*.

We marched all day, following footsteps that were evidently those of our men, who wore boots. The other footsteps had been left by bare feet.

'They've been taken prisoner by savages!' mused Antiphus.

It was difficult to believe that. If they were walking alongside men who were barefoot, perhaps these were people unfamiliar with the arts of cultivating the soil and melting metals, who lived on what nature gave them. How could such people capture men who fought clad in bronze, armed with spears and swords? What's more, our men were numerous. From the footsteps, more numerous than the others.

'There's only one explanation,' I replied, 'our men followed these people out of their own free will. Look: the prints of the boots are everywhere, they're mixed in with the others. If they were prisoners they would be in a column at the centre, with those who had captured them at the sides, in much greater number.'

'Are you saying they simply abandoned the ships with all that plunder aboard? How is that possible? The spoils which justify ten years of war and the loss of over two hundred of our comrades? I just can't believe that,' replied Antiphus. 'What reason could they have had to do such a thing?'

'A reason worth leaving everything: the ships, the treasure, their weapons. And perhaps even . . .'

'What? What else?'

I could not answer. Too bitter would have been my reply. Sorrow choked off my voice, the word on my lips raced back to stab my heart.

We made our way in silence, warily. Late that afternoon we found traces of a bivouac, ten or so campfires already extinguished, with the remains of a meal that many men had consumed: animal bones and enormous eggshells. Eurylochus picked one up and turned it in his hands. 'The Phoenicians paint these and sell them on the islands and . . . look, down there, see, they're laid by those gigantic birds. See them? The Cretans call them camel-birds.'

We followed his pointed finger and saw a dozen whitish-brown feathered females and a large male with magnificent black plumage. Our eyes could scarcely take in all they beheld. In that land of wonders, time had stopped at the golden age. Vast herds of animals grazed near and far, thousands and thousands of them. They belonged to no one and hence to everyone. And the trees were laden with fruit of every sort. In the distance, storm clouds rose and lightning bolts streaked from the sky to the earth as columns of rain poured down to quench it. A boundless land . . . How small our own world was, compared with this! The sinking sun was an enormous globe, much bigger than ours, much redder, setting the entire horizon ablaze from one end to the other. We pushed on until late that night, when we had to stop and rest. I left four men on guard; they were relieved halfway through the night by four others. In the darkness we heard the roaring of lions, the shrieking of unfamiliar birds and other noises we could not identify . . . sometimes close, sometimes distant.

The dawn was not hindered by any obstacle: no mountains, no cliffs. The light rose like a powerful breath: uninterrupted, diffuse, the colour of water. Then that infinite land awoke: flocks of thousands of birds flew into the breaching sun, the galloping of vast herds made the ground tremble beneath our feet. Even our gods felt very small and far away.

On their tracks again, we continued our long march until we came upon a line of low, rolling hills. Once we reached the top, we realized that we had arrived.

Below us a wide green valley with a small lake at its centre was surrounded by thousands of palm trees. At the valley's edges were vast fields of crops and plots of land densely planted with flowers as red and fleshy as fruits. In the distance were hills of sand that looked like mounds of gold dust. Houses stood here and there, shacks covered with bundles of dried grasses. Ropes made of braided grass were rolled into coils at the edges of the fields. Children swam in the lake and splendid dark-skinned women walked by completely naked, with high hips and slender legs.

Almost all of the men were assembled at a vast space at the side of the village, grouped around a red stone monolith. They were playing instruments, flutes and drums, and singing.

And there were our comrades.

'What shall we do?' asked Eurylochus, who never left my side. 'I say we attack. We're slightly outnumbered but we're well armed and they're not. If they have weapons, they'll be inside their houses. We'll free our men and return to the ships.'

'No. There's no need for arms,' I replied. 'We'll leave our shields hanging on our backs, as they are now, our swords in their sheaths and the spears pointed downward. The most difficult thing will be to convince, or force, our men to leave.'

Eurylochus nodded and we made our way down the hill. We were noticed almost immediately because there were so many of us, a small army, but no one seemed frightened. They only stopped singing. We were careful to show no signs that we intended to use force against them.

I smiled and bowed towards them, turning to seek out the one who might be their chief. Then I greeted my own: 'Hail, men.'

'Hail, Odysseus,' they replied. They were calling me by name as if I were one of them, an equal.

'We found your ships empty and abandoned. We imagined that you were carried off by force and we came searching for you, but I can see that's not what happened.'

'No,' one of them admitted. 'We weren't dragged off by force. They convinced us.'

'They don't seem to speak our language,' I observed.

'We had no problems understanding them,' said another.

'How?'

He took one of those red flowers from a basket: 'Taste this and you'll understand.'

I shook my head. 'I'm glad that no ill has befallen you. We'll go back to the ships now and return home.'

'Have you taken a look around, king of Ithaca? Have you seen the grasslands, the animals and birds, the sunsets and dawns? Have you noticed that no one carries weapons? Do you know why? Because there's nothing to steal or plunder. Food is abundant – there's enough for everyone. The women are beautiful and skilled in the arts of love and the children belong to everybody; they swim and play in the lake, run happily in the fields. The men sing and dance and tell stories every night. Stories which we'll learn to understand in time ... That's another thing there's an abundance of here. See? Everyone has time here. It's never too early and never too late. You can sleep by day and stay up all night with one of these radiant beauties, the colour of burnished bronze.'

'What about your wives? The girls who've been waiting for you all these years? Your children, who were still babbling when you left them. Why aren't you thinking of them?'

'We're dead for them, Odysseus. Dead, understand? The girls we were betrothed to will have found other husbands, our children were too young then to remember us now; it's as if we never existed for them . . . For ten years we've gone into combat almost every day. We've done nothing but kill, wound, slaughter. Our hands are soaked with blood and the screams of the dying never leave our ears . . .

'Is it easy for you to sleep at night, brave, cunning Odysseus? Well, it wasn't for me. I couldn't sleep. I was surrounded by ghosts, shrieking spirits. They bit away at my heart.'

He held out the flower to me again. 'With this you forget everything, understand? Everything.'

'Even our homeland?' I challenged him. 'Her fragrance? Her forests and sea?'

'Certainly! That as well. Do you really think that after having lived as we did for as long as we did, we can return home as if nothing had ever happened? Hoping to find that nothing has changed? Return to what? To our women, who will have gone off with someone else? To our parents who've grown old waiting for us? To our children, who won't recognize us? Do you think that the blood and carnage of our nightmares won't find us there?

'Our land is here, Odysseus, where we've found peace and oblivion. Oblivion, king of Ithaca, understand? Oblivion . . .'

'Burn the ships,' said another, 'and join us here. We'll be happy together, and together we can forget.'

I drew my most trusted men aside. 'They're under the effects of a powerful drug,' I said. 'How else could they forget their homes, their parents, their children and their wives? We have to get them away from here at any cost, as quickly as we can. The others, back at the ships, will already be worried about us.'

'It won't be easy,' said Antiphus. 'There are so many of them and they seem set on staying.'

'I've seen many coils of rope made with dry grasses. We'll use it to tie them up, one by one, and we'll drag them back if we have to. As soon as the effect of the drug contained in those cursed flowers wears off, they'll go back to being themselves again, you'll see.'

We waited until night fell, when everyone had lain down to rest. Our comrades, who had no homes to go to, were stretched out on mats near the fire, and this made our task much easier.

'Let's wait a little longer,' I said. 'They've eaten many of those flowers. If we wait for them to take effect, the men will be deeply asleep.'

When their breathing became heavy and they all seemed to have fallen into a dead slumber, I signalled to my men and we began, swift and quiet as ghosts, to tie their hands behind their backs, ring the rope around their necks and then fetter them one to another.

One of them awoke and cried out: 'What are you doing? No! No! We don't want to go. Leave us here!' He tried to rouse the others: 'Wake up! Wake up! They're taking us away!' But by this time they were all tied up and we began to drag them away from the clearing. We'd done a good job, but nonetheless I had twenty armed warriors draw up on either side of the column. Those posted at the front drove them forward and others made sure that no one escaped at the rear.

As we began to climb the hill, we saw the dark-skinned in-habitants of that land leave their shacks to watch what was happening. The moon shed a bright glow and we were all clearly visible to them, and they to us. They did not try to come closer. Our bronze armour glittered in the light of the moon. They stayed where they were but they began to sing. A long, sad lament with two different tones: the subtle, clear voices of the women and the deeper, more intense ones of the men. *I'll never forget it as long as I live.* Perhaps that was their way of saying goodbye to the men to whom they'd offered hospitality in such a magic and marvellous way, in their boundless, timeless land. They watched them being dragged away like animals snared in nooses and they wept for them. Their song became shriller and more penetrating, like a funeral wail for people who were going to their deaths. That's what I heard, and so did my comrades, walking silently with their spears in hand and their shields on their arms. The others, stumbling along with their wrists and necks bound, seemed to understand the meaning of those voices and when any of them raised their faces to look at me I saw them streaked with tears.

We walked all night without ever stopping and all the next day, resting only to regain our strength and drink. We never said a word to our unhappy comrades nor did they ever speak to us, but I could see that they were beginning to look reality in the face again and that they were bitterly bemoaning what they had lost.

3

I HAD TO LASH THE MEN we'd saved to the oars and to the rowing benches, and I put my most loyal comrades in command of the ships we had found abandoned: Eurylochus, Euribates, Antiphus and a few others, all armed to the teeth. Then I gave the signal to set sail.

I didn't want to linger a moment longer in that place. The fascination of that mysterious and magnificent land had wormed into my own heart and I wanted to stop any of the other men from becoming ensnared in the tantalizing world of the flower-eaters. My desire to return home was what was keeping me alive. I would not give up trying for any reason in the world, nor would I allow my men to give up. I was the one responsible for their lives and their futures. I was duty-bound to bring them back to their parents, who were surely wasting away as they tried to keep alive the feeble hope of seeing their sons again. I had taken these men to war and I had already lost too many of them on the bloody fields of Troy; I could not lose any more on our return journey.

I often asked myself whether news of the fall of Troy had reached the land of Achaia. Some of the warriors had certainly made their return. Had the news flown from Pylos to the shores of Ithaca and the rooms of my palace, raising the hopes of Penelope and my son Telemachus? Were they waiting, watching? *Wait for me, I beg of you, wait for me! I'll come back, as I swore I would when I left, to you, my bride, and to you, my son.*

The wind was driving us elsewhere. Where, I couldn't say.

The sun seemed to perch at the centre of the sky for an endless time, only to dive like a flaming meteor into the horizon. The night stars seldom sparkled, often hiding behind the clouds, and it seemed more difficult every day to get our bearings.

I tried to inspire the confidence of my comrades. I wanted them to believe that I knew which direction we were sailing in, but the sea just became wider and more deserted day after day. I realized that since the storm had driven us away from Cape Malea, we hadn't ever encountered another ship, not even a fisherman's boat. The world had changed. I couldn't recognize the sky and the sea and they didn't recognize me. My goddess wasn't speaking to me, never appeared to me. Perhaps her gaze hadn't been able to penetrate the wall of fog that separated our world from the one we'd found: a world so unlike our own, peopled by pure, innocent, unarmed men.

We sailed all that day and the next. After the sun had set, we prudently hauled up the sail halfway, as the lookouts at the bow searched for a landing place while scanning the darkness for possible hazards or traps. We didn't want to spend the night at sea. The moon, which had been guiding us, hid behind the clouds and a thick fog enveloped us. There was no light anywhere. We lit some torches, using the braziers, and tried to lighten the choppy surface of the sea. I ordered my men to haul the sails in completely and to proceed with the oars. We called out to one another, from one ship to the next, so we could stay in touch and not lose heart. Then, all at once, the sea flattened in front of us.

'Look! We've entered a sheltered place,' I said to Eurylochus. 'Behind us you can hear the sound of the waves breaking, but it's smooth as oil in front.'

'A natural harbour of some sort. Can you see anything?'

'No.'

The torch I was holding went out, but we continued on slowly in the thick fog and absolute darkness until the ship's keel grazed the low, sandy ground of a beach. A god had guided us there: there was no other explanation.

'Come forward,' I shouted to the other ships following ours. 'We've found land!'

One after another, the ships were brought ashore, bows scraping the beach. The men laid their cloaks out on the sand and fell asleep. The air had changed; it was warmer now, and not so humid. The clouds had thinned out and the dim light of the sky revealed low, dark hills. The place seemed uninhabited. I untied the comrades who we'd rescued from the land of the flower-eaters.

I spoke to them. 'I had to do what I did because you weren't yourselves any more. You seemed to have lost your minds. I am responsible for your lives. We've lost too many comrades already. I could not find it in my heart to tell your parents that you had refused to return, uncaring of their pain.' There was no answer from them. Their dark silence made my heart ache. They were acting as if they'd lost the only good thing remaining in their lives. But everything was strange that night: the fog, the darkness, the sounds . . . Later we heard distant cries, hoarse growling, like hungry lions roaming in the blackest night, but different in some way, almost human. None of us had ever heard anything like it before.

We awoke when Aurora rose to illuminate sea and land. I looked around: my comrades were getting up, one after another, gathering together, speaking to each other. There were still a great many of us; we were still an army. With the light everything looked different, more natural, and I realized that we were beached on a low island, fertile, but not cultivated. There were a great number of wild goats and the vegetation was abundant.

I walked all the way around the coast and saw that the mainland was close. It was vast, covered with luxuriant bushes and trees. I ordered my comrades to take their bows and arrows and to hunt goats on the island. I would go to the mainland with the crew of my ship.

The men tried to dissuade me. They asked me to wait until we had feasted on meat roasted over the embers, and the strong red wine that still filled our jars. But my desire to explore the vast, unknown land before us was greater than any hunger. I wondered who inhabited it: were they men who respected the law and feared the gods, or violent, ferocious savages who only obeyed those stronger than they were? Even if we were to meet up with the latter, I was not worried about any danger. The night before I'd fallen asleep thinking of Penelope, of my parents and my son, trying to imagine what he might look like now. I had not been at all frightened by the dark, moonless night, the unfamiliar, fog-covered land. Every sound, every smell, every stone on that island roused my curiosity. It made me realize how great the world was, how much the gods of the origins had created and how little we knew. How much I could have learned in ten years, if I hadn't spent them fighting under the walls of Troy, breathing in nothing but dust and the stench of blood in that thin strip between city and sea!

I set sail in the afternoon with my crew after we had prepared and loaded the ship. I left Eurylochus in command of the others, who would wait on the island for our return. I brought some of the men who had been among the flower-eaters with me, hoping that activity, and perhaps a bit of adventure, would shake them out of their lethargy. We pushed off and crossed the strait that separated us from the mainland. As we approached, we could see that the land was rich with vegetation but there were no traces of villages or even houses. The only feature of note was a cave, half hidden by trees and bushes, near a promontory.

We went ashore at a small bay that lay beneath a high cliff, nearly a mountain. We took a skin of wine with us to offer to the inhabitants of that land, if there were any to be found, in order to win their favour. The buzzing of the cicadas was the only noise to be heard. We found no other boats, no nets. There were no leafy shelters to protect us from the summer sun, the winter rain or wild animals. *Sometimes I still ask myself whether I really lived that adventure; whether I felt what I felt and saw what I saw* . . . We spotted some grapevines, but they were wild as well, with clusters of big, hard, sour grapes. One of the men who had scouted forward reported that he had found a dirt path. We followed him. *This is the way that the story returns to my mind every time. It is thus that the images infest my dreams, forcing me to wake up soaked in cold sweat.*

We arrived at the entrance to the cave that we'd seen from the sea. And here we finally saw signs of human life: the space inside was divided into pens which held lambs and goats. Everywhere there were big wheels of cheese resting on drying racks to age. But all the objects were enormous in size: the jars full of curdled milk and whey, the axes for chopping down trees . . . Who could be living in such a place? No sooner had my comrades taken a look around than they became spooked and insisted that we grab anything that was worth taking and run back to the ship. But it was too late.

We heard the bleating of a big flock and a footstep so heavy it made the earth quake. A pile of long tree trunks was dumped through the opening to the cave as if it were a bundle of sticks. Wood for the fire. I could see the panic on my comrades' faces. At the door to the cave stood a hulking black shape without features or expression. A giant.

We dashed to the deep recesses of the cave, looking for a place to hide, but it wasn't long before the lord of that dreadful place decided to light a fire. The flames blazed up, illuminating the entire space, and it was impossible to stay hidden. But even more impossible to stay still. The monster noticed some of us moving, and with a sort of roar (*was that the bellowing voice we'd heard the night before on the island?*) asked us: 'Who are you, foreigners? Sailors or pirates? Where is your ship?' *I was in a peculiar state, of understanding with different ears and seeing with different eyes, in which one of a myriad of possible realities becomes the only one in a mere instant and excludes all the others.* Terror gripped me because the light had made his face visible now as well. He had a single eye beneath his brow which glowed like an ember but stared fixedly in a vacuous way. His hair was long, bristly and uncombed, his chest was enormous and his arms shaggy, his bare feet were caked with the dung of sheep and goats. He let off an intolerable stench.

Without coming too far into the open, I replied that we were the survivors of a shipwreck and that we'd entered to ask for help and hospitality in the name of the gods. *Athena . . . why wouldn't you speak to me?* He burst out laughing, a thunderous laugh that ended in the hoarse snarl of a vicious beast. When I understood it was too late. He grabbed two of my comrades, one in each hand. He crushed the first in his fist. The crunch of bones breaking rent my heart. He flung the other one against the stone wall so hard that the man's brain spattered our faces. He devoured them both. *The sound of their raw flesh being chewed up in his open maw makes my blood boil even now that I'm so cold . . .* We watched in horror as his beard became soaked with blood.

I alone, I believe, had realized which of us were gone – who the monster had seized to grind between his teeth. It was two of the men who had tasted the red blossoms. They had gone stone still at the sight of the giant and it had been easy for him to snatch them. They hadn't even tried to bolt away or to slip into one of the cracks in the cavern walls. And this thought brought tears to my eyes. They had experienced a different way of existing, free of anguish and troubles, and my tearing them from this sweet oblivion had killed them.

I'd wanted them with me, thinking they would help me explore a new land, meet peoples and animals unknown to them, face danger if necessary . . . and that this would suffice to pull them out of their stupor and indifference. I was wrong. And yet, even as the cavern echoed with the belching of the monster who had stretched out to sleep, I wasn't sorry I'd done it. I was certain that a man worthy of his name would not give up his memories, forget the faces of his wife and children, reject the land where he was born. Only a coward could leave all that behind in exchange for a life without purpose or meaning. But I was tormented by the ignominious end they'd come to, by the thought that their remains would be digested and expelled by that fetid creature. Deprived of funeral honours, the flames of a pyre and the final rites. Horror gnawed at my heart.

That was the worst night, so atrocious that sometimes I think it was a nightmare, one of those that can kill you because it's more real than reality is. In those unfamiliar lands, different beyond any imagining, I'd become accustomed to the thought that what I had once considered reality no longer existed; it had been replaced by a turmoil of feelings and passions without beginning or end, without place or time. Possible and impossible became one and the same thing, and time became like the route of a ship that, having lost its bearings, sails in a wide circle while the helmsman believes he's following a straight course because there is no land in sight and the stars aren't shining and everything is shrouded in fog.

We spent the night there. My comrades clung to one another in fright and dread and I was certain they were cursing me, in their hearts.

I, alone, gripped my sword. I wanted to slip up on the monster and stick it into his neck all the way to the hilt and then twist it to cut off his airways and make his blood flow and fill his gullet, but I knew that if we killed him we would perish as well. That's why the cyclops could fall asleep without worrying about us. Once we ran out of food, our last day would soon follow, because there was no way out of the cave. The entrance was sealed off with an enormous boulder that not even the strength of one hundred men would be able to budge. The only other opening was a hole at the top of the cavern that the smoke rose out of, but it was too high up. Unreachable. It was then that my mind came to my aid, or perhaps it was the goddess Athena who inspired me, without letting herself be seen or heard. The one thing I could be sure of was that my thinking was much more wide-ranging and complex than the monster's and that I could find a way to render him incapable of harming us but not deprive him of his strength: without it, we would never again see the light of day or breathe in the open air.

I crept near my comrades then and said: 'Don't lose hope. I'll save you all.'

'How's that?' said one of those who had eaten the red flower. 'There's no way to escape.'

'Yes, there is. He can only look in a single direction. We have to split up so that while he is looking one way, the others can flee. All we have to do is survive until tomorrow night.'

I managed to convince them to get a little rest. I watched over them as a father watches over his own children. In my heart I was plotting the ruin of the cruel monster who had scoffed at the laws of hospitality and scorned Zeus himself, the protector of all guests. I prayed in the deep silence of the night: 'Great Zeus, you who keeps wayfarers and guests from harm, allow me to avenge the horrible deaths of my comrades! They escaped the perils of war in the bloody fields of Troy only to die an abominable death in this savage land.'

My prayers said, I slumped against the stone wall of the cavern, in the shelter of a crag, and tried to get some rest, without abandoning myself to sleep.

I was jolted wide awake by the voice of the cyclops, muttering as he tumbled from his bed, and the pounding of his footsteps as he neared the back of the cave. The ground shook under his feet. I saw my comrades' eyes fill with terror again, but they acted as I had urged them to, separating into two groups. At first, things went as I had predicted. The cyclops was forced to turn his head from one side to the other constantly and he could not seize any one of the men, but then he became enraged by the situation and turned his entire attention to one group alone, driving them into a corner.

Their eyes wildly sought me out, but at that moment I was as helpless as they were. The giant snatched up two of them and ripped off their limbs one by one as they screamed in horror, and then he devoured their mangled trunks. These two had eaten of the flowers as well, and the effects somehow still lingered in them. They had remained isolated from the others, frozen with fear. I could not hold back my tears. They ran down my cheeks as the heart in my chest howled like a rabid dog.

Once he'd finished his meal, the wild man, his round eye staring, separated the lambs from the sheep and then removed the enormous boulder and stood at the opening so none of us could get out. Only the sheep were allowed through, led by a large ram. When they had all scampered out, on their way to grassy pastures, he followed, wedging the big boulder behind him. We were plunged into darkness again, save for the ray of light streaming in through the opening in the ceiling.

I gathered my companions and said: 'Listen to me. We're all sickened by what we've seen, but I promised that I would save you and I will keep my word. You must promise to obey me, to do what I order you to do. We're still an army of Achaians and we can win against a miserable beast that feeds on human flesh.' That is what I said, but my mind was empty. I could not devise any strategy for escape from the horrible fate that seemed to await us all.

I cast my eyes about, desperate for a solution, and made out, leaning on the wall of the cavern, part of the trunk of a young olive tree, a side shoot that had grown as straight as a spike and had been chopped off so that a tool could be made out of it, or a walking stick. I hadn't noticed it before, although it must have been there. An olive tree . . . sacred to you, goddess of the green eyes, daughter of Zeus, Tritonia. There, in the darkness before me, I felt I could see the helmet covering your head, the cuirass and aegis on your chest. It was you who gave me the suggestion, who inspired me. The olive tree is yours, your gift to all of humanity and to me. I who love and venerate you.

'Take that tree trunk!' I ordered. 'I want it stripped of its bark and scraped smooth as the handle of an oar. I'll take care of the tip.' Thus work began: the men cut off the smaller branches and removed the bark, working swiftly. Waiting idly for death to take them had made them feel like sheep, not men, while a task that needed doing gave them hope. I unsheathed my sword and set about sharpening one end, with great care. I shaved off small chips first, like a carpenter with his plane, then used my knife and a pumice after that to make the surface perfectly smooth, capable of piercing deeply without the least friction. The longer and sharper I saw the tip becoming, the more intensely my heart savoured the thought of revenge.

When we'd finished, we put the sharp-tipped stake back in its place and covered it with the dung of the sheep and goats.

'Now all we have to do is wait,' I said.

'Wait for what?' exclaimed one of my comrades, another one of the flower-eaters. 'For him to devour another one of us?'

I drew close. I knew his parents, who lived on Same but had land on Ithaca as well. His name was Trasimachus.

'I know what you're thinking, my friend. You're thinking that I'm exposing those of you who ate the red flowers to danger in order to get rid of you, but you're wrong. I saved you from the void. I brought you back to the ships so you could return to your parents who are still waiting for you. You, just like everyone else. I've lost too many of you already. It's you who desires death, even if you don't know that. The cyclops can sense it. Do you know why he has a single eye? Because his mind isn't big enough to command two. But he can smell weakness like an animal. And he strikes, without mercy. Now listen well to what I'm saying. Do you see this stake? We're going to drive it into the monster's eye and make him blind. Then we'll take advantage of his strength to open our way to freedom.'

'That's not possible! He can even hear us breathing. How can we get close without him jumping to his feet and slaughtering us all?'

'I'll worry about that, but I'll need your help. You are the man who will decide all of our fates. I'll take aim but you'll be right behind me. You'll be the only one able to see the direction of the stake and you'll direct the men standing behind you, helping me to thrust the sharpened trunk.'

He took a step back. I could see the bewilderment in his eyes.

'Why me? I'm not capable of it,' he protested. 'I'll make a mistake and ruin everything.'

'Because you're the one who has the strongest reason to do it. You have to avenge the companions who sought oblivion with you, and prove to yourself that you can gain command of your life again.'

'No,' he replied. 'I can't. Take someone else.'

'As you like,' I said.

The other comrades were gathered around me and listening attentively. I could see hope and rage in their eyes, and I thought that we would succeed. All that day we practised every move, every step, every gesture. I explained when they would have to hold their breath, when they would have to let it out all at once.

'Think of when you draw your bow,' I told them, 'and then of when the enemy you've pierced with your spear crashes to the ground in front of you and you yell out in victory.'

It was dusk when we heard bleating and a heavy step approaching the cave door. It filled us with dread. The boulder rolled inwards and the cyclops let his flocks in. The big ram came first, then the sheep and the lambs behind him. Their hulking shepherd opened the pen where the suckling lambs were kept and each one ran to seek out its own mother. When all the animals were back in their folds, the cyclops turned to us. I had no hopes that he'd be feeding on cheese or mutton. He would finish off all of us first.

He grabbed another two of my comrades, the first he could get his hands on. He killed them by dashing them against the walls of the cave, smearing the stone surface with their blood. Then he dismembered them both and ate them greedily. The time had come for me to act. I took the big wooden tub the cyclops used to curdle milk and filled it with the wine we'd brought from the ship inside a sack made of oxhide. It was the wine we'd carried off from Ismarus, sweet and strong. I held it out to him.

'Now that you've eaten human flesh, drink!' I said. 'You'll like this. It's called wine!' I exclaimed.

The monster approached and I saw his eye, as big as my own head, observing me. I did not tremble. I knew the life of my companions depended on me. Really, it felt no worse than when we were hidden in the belly of the horse and I heard the voice of Laocoon, the priest of Apollo, calling for the Trojans to set fire to it. The giant stretched out his enormous, hairy hand and seized the bowl, bringing it to his mouth. I watched as he gulped down the foaming red wine and my heart laughed inside my chest, because he was acting like a fool and he would fall into my trap. The monster let his voice be heard: 'Give me more, it's good!' He banged the empty bowl down on the ground.

I gestured for my comrades to fill it again. Then we withdrew to the back of the cave, divided into two groups. The cyclops bent down, picked up the bowl and drained all the wine out of it without spilling a drop.

He belched loudly and then turned to me. 'I've never tasted anything so good in my whole life. I've had my fill of sheep's milk and goat's milk but this drink is worthy of the gods. You haven't told me your name yet. Tell me what you are called so I can repay you for your gift!'

I looked at the back of the cave, at its centre, at the empty space between the separate groups of my comrades, and I saw a shadow, on the wall, of an erect figure with spear in hand: Athena! *You were back with me again, wanaxa, and all my fears dissolved. How had you found the way to slip into that godless and lawless land?*

'Beware!' echoed a voice inside my heart. 'Where there is the sea, there is Poseidon, who embraces all there is.'

I had to answer, and the goddess inspired me, I'm certain of it. 'You wish to know my name? I'll tell you my name. My name is No One. Everyone calls me No One.'

'All right, No One, then I will eat you last. Let that be my guest-gift to you.' He burst into thunderous laughter.

'And you?' I asked then. 'What is your name?'

'Polyphemus,' he replied. 'Because my fame is, and always will be, great. My father is Poseidon who surrounds all lands. He conceived me with a mountain nymph, Thoosa.'

Those were his last words for the night. He lay down on his bed of sheepskins and for some time he seemed to be staring at one of the two groups of my men, the one on the left. I signalled them to move about so they would attract his attention while I beckoned the other group to join me.

'Do we have any more wine?' I asked them.

'Another tub full,' they answered, 'if he should wake up.'

'He won't wake up,' said Trasimachus, the man who had refused to help me drive the stake into the monster's eye.

I turned to look at the cyclops. He would belch now and then, and a reddish stream dribbled from the side of his mouth, a mixture of wine and blood that made me sick. When his breath had deepened and his body relaxed into unconsciousness, I gathered all my men around the fire, adding branches to stir up the flames.

'This is the most auspicious moment to act,' I said. 'Bring the stake here – we'll harden the tip in the fire.'

'Maybe it's better to wait,' said Trasimachus, the flower-eater.

'He's deep asleep now. Things could change later.'

'Nothing will change,' he replied. 'I added the essence of the red flowers to the wine. We have all the time we want.'

'So you never stopped.'

He bowed his head and did not answer.

'Do you mean to help me now?'

'I have helped you, and now I will grind that stake into his eye. I will avenge my companions.'

'Let's go then. After we've struck, we'll all have to run for shelter. The pain will drive him mad.'

The tip of the spike was red and the rod hard and compact

as the best olive wood. We seized it and approached the monster, climbing up on an outcropping that rose over his bed. I had taken a brand from the fire to light our way. When we were directly above the cyclops I signalled to my men and we lowered the burning stake until it was hovering directly above his eye. I glanced at Trasimachus and he nodded back. He was ready.

The cyclops turned in his sleep, then lay on his back again. The red tip was coated with a thin layer of ash. I gave a signal and the stake was lowered. Now the point was just a hand's span from his eye. I laid the firebrand on the ground. I raised one hand and kept the other solidly on the stake.

'Now!' I shouted. All my comrades moved as one and the tip descended at the same moment in which the eye opened. There was no expression in it; it was blank and staring, as yellow as the eye of a cetacean from the ocean depths. The red-hot tip sank into his eyeball and, with the help of Trasimachus and the others, I ground it in. His lashes caught fire and blood gushed forth in streams, sizzling in the flames.

'Go!' I yelled again, and we scattered in every direction, seeking shelter in the hiding places each one of us had already chosen. *I'll never forget that blank, astonished expression: the eye of a fish. I realized then that what he told me must have been true. That he was the son of the blue god, the lord of the depths.*

Polyphemus lurched to his feet with a piercing scream. He pulled the spike out of his eye socket, which looked like a black hole, and flung it away, yelling so loudly that the walls of the cavern shook. He was calling for help. Then he started making grabs for us, fumbling all around, knocking everything over, destroying the pens of the animals who scattered everywhere, terrified. But the tremendous pain overwhelmed him in the end and sapped away his energy. He fell to his knees and moved his hands from his head to his brow, moaning.

Time passed. Voices could be heard outside.

'What's happening, Polyphemus?'

'Has someone attacked you? Thieves? Have you been robbed?'

'Who has hurt you?'

Other cyclopes, similar to him in size and savagery.

'No One has hurt me!' he shouted. 'No One has attacked me! Help me!' he roared like a wounded beast.

Long moments of silence. We kept completely still and held our breath.

'If no one has hurt you, then there's nothing we can do for you! It's a plague that only the gods can cure. Pray to your divine father for help. Try to rest. Tomorrow you'll feel better.'

Their footsteps faded into the distance and my heart laughed in my chest. I savoured the taste of revenge.

The flesh-eating monster wept and wept, all night long, but I thought of my comrades buried in his stinking bowels and I could not rest. I still wanted to hurt him any way I could, more than I already had. But I repressed the seething rage in my heart because my work wasn't over. For a long time he slumbered, seeming nearly dead, but then he would wave his arms and legs around wildly hoping to snare us in case we'd moved close to get a better look. But I made sure that the men stayed as far away as possible and let no one approach him.

Dawn finally showed her face and a ray of light poured through the ceiling to illuminate the cavern. The cyclops stumbled slowly to his feet, groaning, so that his bulk completely blocked out the light streaming in from above. His dark shadow covered us all. The sheep and goats had begun to bleat more and more loudly, because they were hungry and thirsty. They were used to going out to graze when the sun rose.

Moved to compassion for his flock, the monstrous shepherd groped around until he found the boulder that sealed the entrance to the cave and he moved it. Light flooded into our prison, the tomb of all our hopes. It was I who had opened the cavern door, my mind that commanded the arms of the colossus.

As the sheep began to move out, the cyclops lowered his

hands to make sure that we were not trying to slip out among them. He patted each animal, recognizing it by its fleece.

I had assembled my men and told them the plan I'd devised for their escape. We took the ropes made of palm fibres that were lying about the cave and with the help of Trasimachus I trussed the sheep together three at a time and then slung a man under the belly of each middle one. I bound Trasimachus as well, and then watched them all slip out from between the giant's legs as he let his flock through.

I was last to leave, hidden under the belly of the big ram, clutching his wool. I realized that this was the fulfilment of the prophecy my mother had made when I'd returned from my first hunting party with grandfather Autolykos; I felt sure I could follow my companions out. But this was instantly cast into doubt when the cyclops recognized the ram and began stroking him gently: 'How is it that you are last to leave, dear old friend? You would always run out first to lead the sheep to pasture and today you are the last. Are you sad for your master, who can no longer see the light of the sun?' His hands lingered on the deep fleece and more than once his immense fingers brushed my own. My heart trembled thinking of the fate that would befall me if he caught me. I would not even have the time to grasp my sword and slay myself; he would make sure that I suffered all the agony that a man can suffer at the hands of the most cruel of torturers. This time my anguish was even more acute than when, from a crack in the hollow belly of the horse built by Epeius, I spied the fiery torch held by Laocoon, priest of Troy.

But he allowed the ram to pass and I finally let myself drop to the ground. I got up and hastened to join my companions who were waiting for me. We ran down the path that led back to our ship. When we reached the seashore we embraced one another in tears. For me they were like brothers or sons for whose lives I had long feared. The joy in my heart was great because I had not failed them; I had snatched them from an atrocious death. I'd returned them to the light of the sky, the scents of the earth, the colours of the sea. The last to embrace me was Trasimachus, the man who had eaten the red flowers.

'You've given me back my life, *wanax* Odysseus. And now, my king, take us home!' he said. I grasped him tightly and could not hold back my tears. One after another we all boarded the ship, myself last, and we cast off the moorings. My crew were bent hard over the oars, so anxious were they to leave that accursed land. At the prow, I was keeping a watchful eye on our course when I spotted the cyclops at the top of a cliff, leaning on a tree trunk the way a shepherd leans on a staff when guiding his sheep. My shipmates had seen him as well and were rowing with all their might to distance the ship as quickly as possible from the shore.

But I could not hold back, at the sight of the monster who had held us in his thrall. I yelled: 'Cyclops!'

My voice echoed like thunder on the sea.

He heard me and wheeled around to try to understand where my voice was coming from. My comrades implored me to keep silent, in vain.

'Cyclops!' I shouted again. 'You disrespected the sacred laws that protect guests by devouring my comrades and you've paid the price for your savagery. If someone one day asks you who blinded you, tell him that it was Odysseus, son of Laertes, king of Ithaca, destroyer of cities. It is I who took the light from you!'

My words infuriated him. With brute force, he ripped off the peak of the mountain he stood on and hurled it into the sea. The huge rock fell just in front of our prow, raising a huge wave that pushed us back towards land. The men were terrified that the threat we had just escaped would engulf us again. They set to their oars with renewed vigour, but Polyphemus flung out another and even heavier boulder which just missed the ship, landing in the wake of our stern. The billow it created pushed us out on the open sea and towards the island.

I could hear the giant's voice in the distance. He was imploring his implacable father, Poseidon, to avenge him, but his words could not touch me, not yet, so great was my joy at that moment for having freed my friends and delivered them from a horrible death, and so deep was my grief at seeing the still oars and empty benches on my ship. The taste of the vengeance I had just inflicted was strong and bitter. Not even the blue god who the giant claimed as his father could heal him.

I let out the triple cry of the kings of Ithaca, shrill as the scream of an eagle.

4

THE ECHO OF POLYPHEMUS' ranting rang in my ears for the whole stretch of sea that separated us from the low island and stuck in my heart like a freezing blade.

When we went ashore on the island, we learned that our comrades had been struck by foreboding when we failed to return. Eurylochus had readied a strong combat unit with archers and heavily armed warriors to set off for the mainland in search of us. But the great exultation that greeted us soon faded when it became clear that a number of the men who had set out with me were no longer with us. In so many years of war the bonds between the men had become very deep. They'd always protected one another on the battlefield and every fallen comrade represented a wound in their hearts that wouldn't be healed. It was like they were all members of the same family.

The men had not whiled away their time in our absence – they'd hunted, and captured a good number of wild goats. They were divided up, and we included the sheep we'd managed to carry off from the cyclops' flock. In all, the crew of each ship were allotted ten animals, with eleven for me, out of respect.

The cyclops' curse still sounded in my heart. I dragged a fat sheep to the seashore, skinned it and burned the thighs and the best parts in sacrifice to Zeus, in the hopes that this might ward off the ill omen that chased me over the waters as I escaped from that cursed, lawless land peopled by creatures without respect for gods or men. I thought of Calchas, of what he'd said to me that day long ago under the wild fig tree of Troy. I wished he were present, so he could tell me whether the god was pleased with my offering, or disdained it. I could not tell on my own. *I sacrificed the animal for nothing, I know that now, but then I still nourished hope.*

When I returned to our camp, the men had butchered other sheep and goats, opened jars of wine and lit fires to roast the meat. We ate and drank until sunset on the sand still warm from the rays of the sun. Everyone was quiet. Those who had encountered the cyclops wanted to forget and the comrades who had stayed on the island sensed that something awful had taken place but didn't have the courage to ask. Little by little, as time passed, as I breathed in the scents of land and sea, watched the stars glittering in a clear sky, listened to the bleating of the kids tagging along after their mothers as they wandered the fields, I could almost forget what had happened. I even had a brief, fleeting sensation that nothing had happened, nothing at all. That I'd dreamed it all up. Perhaps I could even believe that; I'd understood by then that things were true if we believed them. My thoughts went back to my adolescence . . .

'Atta, when I was at grandfather's house, I saw the goddess Athena.'

'Sleep, my son.'

What would King Laertes my father have said to me at that moment had he been present? If I told him: 'Atta, a giant with a single eye in the middle of his forehead, as tall as a pine tree on Mount Neritus, devoured six of my comrades'?

'Sleep, my son.'

Yes, sleep, heart of mine, sleep if you can.

'What happened to the men who are missing?'

The voice was Eurylochus'.

'Ask the others. I'm tired. Too tired, understand? Tomorrow we'll leave here – we have a long voyage ahead of us. We have to get home, and do you know why? Because even on this side of the wall of fog we crossed – *When had that happened?* – the sun rises in front of us and sets behind us. When we reach Ithaca and we enter the great port, when we have mourned our dead and embraced our loved ones, all of this will vanish. For always, like a nightmare at the rising of the sun.'

Eurylochus said no more and walked away. I stretched out on the sand and covered myself with my cloak. Distant in the night, on the mainland, I heard a groaning like that of a dying animal. A long suffocated wail. A shrill wind whistled back from the sea.

AT DAWN, we loaded the ships with everything that the land could offer us, especially reserves of fresh water. We drew up along the shore facing the mainland. We called out the names of our fallen companions ten times each, and then each crew of men boarded their own ship, went straight to the rowing benches and took up the oars.

We sailed into the open sea and my ship once again led the others. A brisk, hot land breeze pushed us north and west. There was no way to fight it. We sailed for days and nights as the wind shifted eastward and gained in intensity. Elpenor was at the helm of my ship and Eurylochus was checking the tautness of the rigging and the direction of the sail. A great sadness gripped my heart because I knew that we were getting further and further away from our homeland and because I mourned for the comrades I had lost. If only I had left them in the land of the flower-eaters! They would still be basking in the rays of the sun. Instead they wandered in the gloom of Hades, lamenting their lives lost. I thought I had been acting for their best interests, but the gods and fate decided differently from what I intended.

It was a little after midday when Eurylochus approached me: 'Why won't you tell me what happened to the men who didn't return with you from the mainland?'

I had been hoping that he would not ask again, that he would understand that the memory of what had happened was too bitter for me to recount. I had to answer him this time, and I told him the whole story. If he didn't hear it from me, he would have heard it from the others.

'You have nothing else to say to me?' he asked again when I had finished.

I knew what he meant. 'If you already know, why are you asking me?'

'Because I want to hear it from your lips and I want to know what awaits us.'

The wind was getting stronger and bellying the sail, the mast was groaning under the stiff gusts. All of the beams were creaking. The men dipped their oars into the sea only when they thought it would lessen the strain of the helmsman.

'The monster shouted out a curse. He invoked Poseidon, asking him to prevent my return.'

Eurylochus looked down to hide a scowl. I didn't have the heart to tell him the worst. But what I told him then had the ring of truth. 'He cursed my name,' I said, 'but as you know, my friend, my name . . . my name is No One!'

Eurylochus smiled and so did I. This meant that my comrades had not repeated quite everything. On the third evening of our voyage, the wind started to drop off and to shift slowly westward. The setting sun was, in fact, directly in front of me, and the foaming sea was dark as wine. The light that flooded the ship made it look as if it were made of copper.

Eurylochus approached me again. 'What is that?' he asked.

'What are you talking about?'

'Down there, look at that line of white foam. The waves, they seem to be dashing against something.'

'An island?'

'That's what it looks like. Or a peninsula, perhaps. What shall we do?'

'Go ashore,' I said. 'It's always best to have as much fresh water on board as we can, and the men can eat fresh food, although we're not running out of what we have. We're strong. We can defend ourselves in the face of danger, and the mass of land doesn't look that big. Give orders.'

Eurylochus didn't wait to be told twice. He ordered Elpenor

to veer slightly north towards the line of foam, which could now be seen much more distinctly. The men put their backs into the oars to help the manoeuvre. The foam was turning pinker as we watched, and the wind getting weaker until it had died down almost completely. We struck the sails and rowed towards the shore in a semicircular formation.

As we approached, an astonishing vision appeared before our eyes. The sea was covered with floating stones, so close to one another that they seemed to be an extension of the land. Behind them we could see tall walls made of bronze or copper and, beyond that, a column of smoke slowly rising towards the sky. A deep, loud rumble sounded like it was coming from the bowels of the earth. An island, floating on the sea.

We looked at one another, wondering what to do. Recent memories made me wary of braving danger in an unknown land, but this place was clearly inhabited, and we could not avoid meeting the local chief or lord, whoever that might be.

I ordered the ships to remain at the mouth of the port and had a boat take me to the shore. I spoke with Eurylochus before leaving: 'You remain here with the rest of the fleet. I'll just take a few men. Don't approach land until you hear from me. If by dusk tomorrow you hear nothing, turn your prows to the sea and continue on your own to Ithaca. You will assume command.'

We embraced because we didn't know whether we'd ever see each other again, and I went ashore with the men I'd chosen. We walked towards the wall, which was reflecting the last rays of the sun. There were no other ships in the port, no houses along the path leading to the wall, no flocks at pasture. We were armed under our cloaks and I told my men to be ready for anything.

We finally arrived at the city gates. The doors were carved with figures of fantastic, unfamiliar animals. At the centre was an eight-pointed star, with four long points and four shorter ones alternating. From inside came the sound of flutes and cymbals, as if a celebration were under way, with singing and dancing. The air was completely still. Not a puff of wind, not the slightest breeze. I found it very odd to be on an island without feeling the wind's breath. I remembered my youth on Ithaca well: every afternoon, whether it was winter or summer, the wind would pick up and swiftly cross the channel between my island and Same, ruffling the forest leaves with a thin breeze that soon became blustery, and could turn very cold in the wintertime.

I knocked with the pommel of my sword and waited. Just a few moments passed before the tall doors began to turn on their hinges and opened wide. We entered cautiously, hands firmly on the swords we held under our cloaks, and proceeded towards a deserted courtyard, following the sounds of merrymaking, which seemed to be coming from inside the palace. There were no guards, no warriors, nor were there any weapons hanging from the walls. They were decorated, instead, with ornamental objects: masks of unknown creatures and of men and women with unfamiliar features. Fanciful figures, symbols perhaps, cast in gold and silver surrounded them. The men walked behind me, murmuring low-voiced at the wondrous things on view. The light of the day was quickly fading but another light in front of us filtered from under a solid bronze door adorned with friezes of gold, silver and red copper, polished to a high sheen.

That door also fell open before we could make a move, letting us in to a big hall with tables prepared for a feast. At the head, on a silver throne, sat a strong-limbed man, not yet old despite the thick head of smooth white hair that shone like silver framing his face. All around him, reclining on couches covered with linen and purple fabrics, were young men and women, drinking wine from magnificently crafted glittering cups.

'Welcome, foreigners!' he said to us. 'Come forward. Here you will be treated well.'

My heart leapt in my chest. What a difference from the atrocious welcome of the savage cyclops! Well, he'd got what he deserved, in the end, and although his curse dogged me I was not sorry that I had blinded him and condemned him to a lifetime of darkness.

Servants immediately added places at the table close to the throne for all of us, and when we had satiated our hunger and thirst for good wine, our host asked us to speak up: 'Who are you, my guests? Where do you come from? What has brought you here? Not many men have ventured this far.'

I spoke, as I always did, and as always I did not tell the whole truth: 'We are Achaians. We were returning from the war after having destroyed the walls of mighty Troy, but a strong gale dragged us far off course. For nine days and nine nights the storm tossed us on the sea. Then the wind let up and the waves carried us to your island. May the gods give you health and prosperity in exchange for your hospitality.'

'Are those your ships that wait at the entrance to the port?'

'They are. We did not want you to imagine that you had pirates at your gates.'

'You did well. I have no weapons, as you can see, but I can count on much greater forces, and that's why anyone who dares to come here with hostile intentions pays a high price. But send one of your men, now, to tell the others to join us. Here they will find water and food; they will have nothing to worry about. The news of the fall of Troy has reached our ears. Tell me about it, I pray you, for my curiosity is boundless, and my sons and daughters will be glad to hear your story as well.'

We stayed for one long month at the court of Aeolus, his wife, and his sons and daughters, all united in marriage amongst themselves. Every day, as evening fell, the king invited us to his table, ready with a thousand questions for me about the war, its bravest heroes, our most daring endeavours. He never tired of listening to my stories and I never tired of telling them. This is how a guest repays the hospitality he receives, by recounting events that the master of the house will never be able to see or experience in person. I could feel his interest becoming keener day by day. He asked about Hector and Achilles, about Great Ajax and about the king of Achaian kings, Agamemnon. At times he even clapped his hands like a child when I began my tales.

The strangest thing was that he never asked to know my name, as was the right of any host with his guest. Nor did I tell him who I was. He called me his 'guest' or his 'dear friend' and that was fine with me. One evening it was I who bid him to speak: 'Oh lord who reigns over this island, I would like to ask you some questions, for I am always desirous to learn that which other men do not know.'

'Speak, then, and I will answer you.'

'From the moment we arrived, I have never felt a breath of wind. How is this possible? I have never seen an island without wind, although the islands are quite numerous in my homeland and I have visited a great number of them.'

'I shall tell you why: I am a tamer of winds and I have power over them. This power has been given to me by the gods. They know well that I have never abused this gift.'

'I had imagined as much,' said I, 'and I would thus appeal to you for that which lies closest to my heart. My companions and I have suffered greatly under the walls of Troy and on our voyage at sea as well. Our greatest desire is to see our home again, the land where we were born and where we have our houses and our families. On this unfamiliar sea we despair of finding our way. Help us, I beg of you, tell us how we can find our home again.'

The lord of the winds smiled: 'I will be glad to do so, because I have much enjoyed this time with you. Prepare for your departure and tomorrow I will join you at the port.'

We took our leave, rendering homage to him and to the queen, and returned to our ships. I was happy because I felt that the end to our troubles and tribulations was near. Would we have to cross the wall of fog again? Would we return to familiar waters, recognize the invisible paths of the sea?

The next day, the ships were ready, loaded with food and water, and the men were sitting at the rowlocks, their hands gripping the oar handles. When Dawn tinged the sky and the sea foam pink, Aeolus, the lord of the winds, appeared on a litter borne by eight servants. Next to him was a well-sewn skin, its mouth closed with a silver chain. He stopped in front of me: 'Listen well to what I am about to tell you, even if it seems impossible to believe. In this bag, I have trapped every unfavourable wind that could push you off your course. The only one I've left free is Zephyr, which blows from the west. All you need to do is steer straight and you will arrive at your island.'

I never took my eyes off Aeolus as he spoke. I was careful not to miss any tiny movement of his face or his lips, any change of the light in his eyes, and it seemed to me that, after having pronounced the last word, a shadow crossed his features. It was barely perceptible, and yet his mouth seemed to twist into a mocking, or perhaps pitying, smile. I swiftly told myself that I was imagining it, because my heart wanted to believe completely in his promise. When I thanked him I had tears in my eyes. His servants stowed the big sack, made of a single bull hide, under the planks at the stern of the royal ship, my own, and I went aboard. I had the signal for departure hoisted and the horn sounded once, twice, three times.

The fleet made a wide circle inside the port, then my ship ventured out into the open sea and behind us the other ships, sailing in an oblique line so that I would never lose sight of any of them, by day or by night. My eyes turned back to seek out Aeolus, the tamer of winds, and the walls of his city reflecting the light of the sun. I left a lookout at the bow and went to the stern so I could govern the steering oar myself. All day and all night.

Is it possible for a man not to sleep? Even as an entire day elapses, or two, or three? One would say not, but if you keep your thoughts anchored to the tasks you attend to, every strain becomes bearable. You continue to tell your heart: do not sleep, heart of mine, hold out, you're already within sight of your island, you can already smell the scent of myrtle on the breeze. Your ship has already been sighted from the high palace on the mountain. A procession is being prepared to come and meet you. Your standard has told them that the king is back. Your son is leading the procession, garbed in blinding bronze, and behind him is

*the queen his mother, your bride, even more beautiful than when you
left her . . .*

Stay awake, stay awake, stay awake. I trusted no one, perhaps
not even myself. I didn't want any unexpected event to surprise
me, didn't want to let destiny or some god play a trick on me.
The most dangerous was not Poseidon, even in his wrath. The
worst was Hypnos, the sleep who is brother to death. He swirled
around me, tried to seduce me with the never-changing sing-
song pounding of waves against the prow. I envied my men as
they stretched out on the rowing benches at night and, covered
with their woollen cloaks, slept.

I wouldn't have thought it possible that a man could go for
two days without sleeping. And yet three, four went by. The
wind was as monotonous as the waves, always the same, blowing
and singing the same song with the same voice. I forced myself
to keep thinking that with each passing hour I was that much
closer to having my desires come true. That bitter nostalgia
that Penelope had once sung about in Sparta was about to end.
But even that gentle voice was turning into a tedious, formless
refrain. Sleep, the twin of Thanatos, wanted me to surrender,
wanted me to crawl under the benches in exhaustion, oblivious
to my surroundings, so that he could freely command my
destiny. 'But I am Odysseus son of Laertes, king of Ithaca,
destroyer of cities and I will not yield.' Thus I sought to inspire
strength and pride into my weary heart.

Every now and then, during the day, I would allow myself a
moment of watchful rest, certain that I could never fall asleep
under the blinding sun, with the screeching of the seagulls, given
my obligation to lead the fleet. I'd learned to sleep while awake
and to remain alert in my sleep, calling on my goddess, who I
hadn't heard from in such a very long time. The men couldn't
understand what I was up to. They thought that I had lost my
faith in them or that folly was fogging my mind.

'Why don't you try to sleep for a short while. What is this
delirium?' asked Eurylochus. 'You've always trusted me with the

steering oar, and I've never given you anything to complain about.' But any voice that spoke to me in that way was the voice of the god who wanted to put me to sleep and deprive me of my return, and I became even more strongly convinced that I could not surrender, could not allow anyone to touch the helm.

Four, five, six days passed. I was performing a miracle, something that no one before me had ever succeeded in doing. The longing for sleep turned into pain, becoming sharper and sharper. Pain that did not help me stay awake, but only hurt me; my heart, my eyes, my mind. At night I could hear the harpies cawing from the yard at the top of the sail. They were perched up there, rapacious, just waiting for me to fall asleep so they could tear me apart. How often I drew my sword! The boundaries between day and night, wakefulness and sleep, madness and reality, no longer existed, and this generated a weary anguish in me that weakened me without disabling me, annihilated me without killing me.

I spent the seventh and the eighth day in the same way. I ate often, but in small quantities so as not to burden my stomach nor weigh down my eyelids. I could not become accustomed to my condition. The brief snatches of rest seemed to help at first, but then seemed to make me even drowsier. The smell of land was wafting out to me or perhaps I was already asleep and dreaming. The last night was the longest and the most difficult. I felt tormented, and the men watched me with eyes full of dismay. They didn't recognize me any more; I had become a stranger to them.

On the ninth day, just before dawn, I saw a dark mass on the horizon and the outline of a mountain that I could not have mistaken for any other on earth.

Ithaca.

My island, her fragrance, her colours, her surroundings were for me like the body of the bride I had so long desired. My eyes, red from such inconceivable strain, filled with tears and the salt burned them. I would soon touch the stones and sand, the rocks, the bushes . . . I would see my son.

For a moment I thought it was a dream, as the dawn showed her rosy fingers behind the dark mass of the mountains. Then I plunged into total unawareness.

When I opened my eyes, a storm was raging.

5

I COULDN'T BELIEVE WHAT I was seeing: my fleet, at such a
short distance from the destination we had so long desired,
was being pushed away by the violence of the wind and sea. I
shouted to be heard over the din of the storm: 'What happened?
Where are we? Why didn't you wake me?'

Only the howl of the wind answered me. The men were
racing back and forth on the ship. Elpenor was clutching the
handle of the steering oar at the stern but could barely hold it
steady, so great was the force of the breaking waves. Massive
amounts of water were pouring into the hull and the men at the
oars were struggling to steady the ship, so she would not tip
sideways into the waves. The sail had been partially, but not
completely, taken in, a sign that the crew had been surprised by
the storm. My eyes fixed upon the big sack, no longer stowed in
the hold at the stern and secured with strong ropes, but flapping
from one side of the boat to the other. The silver chain that
closed its mouth was gone. Desperation seized me, but what was
happening left me no time to speak with my men. I had to save
the fleet and guide it back to calm waters; the rest I would take
care of when the time came.

We sailed for many days and nights. I never moved my eyes
from the long slanting line of fires that signalled the presence of
the other ships. Then, just like the first time, the winds stopped
blowing almost all at once, a thin mist hovered over the flat sea,
and the air was filled with silence.

Little by little, above the mist, the peaks of an island appeared and then a plume of dark smoke rising towards the sky. Walls and houses of bronze were next, and then a palace encircled by bastions made of a greyer, more opaque metal. It advanced slowly towards us, cleaving the fog, and the waters opened into two waves tipped with white foam. The gods had helped me! The wind had carried me back to the floating island of Aeolus, tamer of storms. We had become friends: he would help me again.

As I made ready to go ashore, signalling to the rest of the fleet to remain at a distance, a voice thundered from above: 'How is it you're back, king of Ithaca? Hadn't I closed up all the contrary winds in the skin and left Zephyr alone free?'

His voice had changed. The charming sovereign of the island, who had hosted me for a month of banqueting with his children, the sons and daughters who were married to one another, now spoke with an incredibly powerful and rather threatening tone. The air trembled, the sky rumbled.

I replied: 'Noble lord, hear my words! I manned the steering oar for eight days and eight nights without ever closing an eye, for fear of being surprised by the unexpected. On the ninth day, when I was finally in sight of my island, I fell prey to sleep. When I awoke, the storm was raging against us and the winds brought me back here. The skin that you had given me was open. I beg of you, in the name of hospitality: help me once again, close up all the foul winds in the sack and allow Zephyr to carry me home again!'

Silence fell again, heavily. The voice of the tamer of winds tore through the still air: 'Leave now, and don't ever dare to come back! If you did not succeed in reaching your island with everything that I did for you, this means you are an abominable being, hated by the gods. I will not help you and thus turn the gods against myself. Get out of here, I said, forever!'

At that moment I understood, as if lightning had struck me, the meaning of my name. I was not he who hated, but he who aroused hatred. I had never before fully felt the curse inherent in my name. The inextinguishable hate of a god pursued me.

The words of Polyphemus, which I had tried to drown at the bottom of my heart, surged back then, clear and strong: '. . . may he return late, a broken man! All his companions lost . . .' Until that moment, I'd forced the words he'd used to petition his father out of my mind, pretended to myself that I hadn't understood them.

I gave orders to bring the ships about because we had no choice – the wind was blowing in that direction. I would act as if the worst had not happened, I would not surrender. I would fight with everything I had to get my mates and my ships back to Ithaca as soon as the wind changed direction. Then I sank to the aft deck, covered my head and my face with my cloak, and wept.

I left the island with a heavy heart. I couldn't help but ask myself what had happened when I was sleeping in that slumber that resembled death. Perhaps my shipmates had loosed the chain that closed the neck of the large skin, imagining it contained sparkling treasure and precious gifts. I thought of Aeolus, the tamer of winds: did he truly have the power to trap them all in a sack? Or was it a way to make me believe that he did? I remembered the words I heard once from a sailor who had brought my father back to Ithaca from Iolcus after the expedition of the Argonauts. He told me: 'There's a point, very far west from here, where all the winds cancel each other out, resulting in a perfect calm. The problem is that it doesn't last very long. The way it ends is that one of those winds, but only one, starts to blow again. If it blows east, you'll find your home and your family. If it blows in the opposite direction, you'll find yourself lost in unknown places that very few have ever made return from.'

Then the weather cleared up. The sun shone in a cloudless sky and a warm wind began to prevail, pushing us north and west, but my comrades seemed rueful and tormented. For two more days, we never spoke about what had happened. In the end it was me who brought it up, with Eurylochus, Elpenor, Euribates and all the others: 'I found the sack open. I don't want to know what happened when I fell asleep, because my anger won't change things. Whatever it is you did, there's no remedy for it now. All we can do is remain together and use all the resources of our minds and bodies to fight off ill fortune. What I want to tell you is this: the winds starting blowing against us because that is what winds do; we all know that winds change. And that's all. Nature acts in every moment of every day and every year of our existence on this earth, while the gods act only now and then, and always remain hidden. We conquered Ismarus, we overcame the temptations of the red flowers, we defeated the cyclops, that bloody monster, and we were about to reach the homeland we have been longing for. Destiny decided differently, but we must not lose heart. I'm asking you to believe in me, because my only aim is to get you back home. I promise that I will share the spoils of war with you. You will not return to Ithaca empty-handed after so many long years. But only after we've entered the great port of Ithaca.'

I believe my words rallied them; at least, they went back to work with renewed vigour. After four more days and four more nights of sailing we came within view of a craggy, lush land, covered with red, yellow and blue flowers and deep-green foliage. The sea bottom beneath our boats was strikingly visible as the waters took on a light blue and then an intense green colour. It reminded us greatly of certain parts of Achaia and this touched our hearts. On our left was a small island connected to the mainland by a narrow sandy strip, which led to a wide arching beach so white that its sands sparkled like silver. There was also a larger island, shaped like the head of an arrow, joined to the mainland by a slightly wider stretch of sand mostly covered by shrubs. Dolphins leapt out of the sea, accompanying our ships. On either side of us, schools of iridescent silvery fish slid through the water like a festive procession leading the fleet ashore. The seven vessels sailed in a straight line at a short distance from the coast. There was no danger: the water was transparent as air, and the sea bottom was perfectly visible. When we had passed the second peninsula a wide channel opened to our right, leading inland.

'What shall we do, *wanax*?' asked Eurylochus.

'We'll enter the channel. It will probably take us to a safe, sheltered harbour. We need water and food. Perhaps we'll be able to hunt here, and pick wild fruit. I don't see any inhabitants along the coast or any other signs of danger. But keep your weapons ready – the bows foremost, then the spears and javelins. When we land, a few of us will venture out unarmed, knowing that the rest of you are behind us, ready to defend us with the same rage and swiftness you showed under the walls of Troy.'

They obeyed and relayed the alarm status to the rest of the fleet. Each ship responded by flashing shields. I watched with pride as they attached quivers full of arrows to the rails. As I kept watching, they drew their bows and hooked the bull-tendon strings. Their chests were fitted with shining bronze cuirasses and their legs with greaves.

Their shields hung from the rails: the sun reflected by the water lit them up, one after another. *My ships . . . I can still see them gliding over the shining waters. Slim, perfect, powerful cetaceans.*

Each of them had a lookout posted at the top of the mast. They scanned the slopes of the high, rocky banks of the channel. We made our way forward in complete silence until a point where the channel seemed to end but, as I approached, I saw that there was another narrower passage that led to a second basin: a marvellous, perfect haven. A spring gurgled nearby, and flowed into the harbour.

I signalled for the others to follow and they did so, one after another, slipping into the well-sheltered pool.

There were no ships moored there, but many large boats filled with fishing gear. On the heights above us, tall, solid stone towers were scattered here and there, with parapets at their tops. My fleet was arranged in a semicircle facing the coast. I chose three of my men, Cephalonians all, as scouts; they lowered themselves into the water, which was shallow enough to allow them to walk ashore.

'Go and see if there is a city nearby,' I told one of them, our herald, 'and if possible find out who governs it. Perhaps they will be able to tell us where we find ourselves, and the route we must follow to return home. We're travelling through a remote region that none of us knows.'

I watched as they reached the shore and approached the spring. A girl soon walked up to them. She was very beautiful and wore a bright gown of multicoloured wool, with golden necklaces and glittering pendants on her ears. She was carrying a jar on her head and had come to the spring to draw water. The men seemed to be conversing with her. It was only then, when I saw them next to her, that I realized how tall she was. Gigantic.

The girl raised her finger, pointing to something behind the hill. The men waved and signalled to us that they were going to follow her.

Eurylochus came up to me: 'I don't like this place. It seems deserted and yet it feels like someone is watching us from those towers up there.'

'If they are, they'll see that we have no hostile intentions. We've made no show of arms. We've just sent out a few men, who've asked a girl for directions. We'll wait for them to come back. Don't worry – they'll return soon.'

We waited all afternoon for our comrades to come back. Euribates and Elpenor put out fish-traps and nets. The sea bottom was crawling with shrimps and crabs bigger than any I'd ever seen before. I sent a few more men to shore to collect reserves of fresh water. They filled jars at the spring and passed them from hand to hand in the low water until the last man of the chain hoisted them aboard ship. Standing in the water had the odd effect of distorting their proportions, so that the part of their bodies outside the water seemed long and their legs short and stubby.

When we'd finished laying in the stores, it was time to prepare for spending the night. It would have made sense to go ashore, light fires and cook a meal and then stretch out on the sand to sleep comfortably, but something told me that Eurylochus was right.

'We'd better stay on the ships until our men return. It will be safer.'

I had just said this when I heard shouts coming from the area where the spring was. Two of our men were scrambling down the slope that led to the sea as fast as their legs could carry them.

'We have to get away from here!' they were yelling. 'Fast! Fast!'

They dived into the sea and swam swiftly to the ship of Perimedes, the chief of the Cephalonians, who quickly pulled them on board. I drew up with my own ship so that it was nearly touching theirs. 'What happened?' I asked.

'Laestrygonians! Fierce, gigantic savages!' replied the herald in a ragged voice. 'They got our shipmate, cut him to pieces and devoured him. It's a miracle we got away.' Their eyes were filled with terror. Gasping to catch a breath, they were sobbing like children. And these were my tough, seasoned Cephalonian warriors. I didn't wait an instant, and shouted out: 'Let's go! Head east! We're getting out of this trap! Row, row, row as fast as you can, set to it!'

These words were not out of my mouth when an incredibly loud noise rent the late afternoon silence. I saw an enormous boulder rolling downhill along one of the gullies carved out by rainwater. It was picking up speed at a tremendous rate as it fell. A short rise at the bottom of the long slope gave it the lift it needed to go sailing through the air. It fell square on one of our ships, breaking it in two. Screams of pain and despair echoed behind us but I shouted for my men to keep rowing. There was no time to stop or try to save the crew flailing in the frothing waves.

Another boulder appeared at the rim of the crater that

crowned the high cliffs encircling the harbour and, as if pushed by invisible hands, started rolling down towards us. Then another, and another, and yet another: it was a frightful sight and the din was terrifying. One after another, the ships were struck, broken, smashed, reduced to shapeless wrecks. The sea was covered with splintered planks and ruined gear. The beautiful, agile ships that had braved so many a violent storm had been destroyed and the clear, calm mirror of our hidden haven was thick with blood and dust, strewn with corpses, wounded sailors and survivors who were desperately trying to swim to shore. That was when we learned what the boats were for. Giant brutes boarded them clutching harpoons, and steered them through the water, spearing anyone who was still alive as if they were fish. They pulled the bodies on board and took them to shore. It wasn't difficult to understand what they were going to do with them, given the reports of the men who had already met up with them.

I found myself alone, with my ship and my crew, outside the port. I had lost the entire fleet that had followed me to Troy, which had departed from the port of Ithaca so many years earlier amid blaring bugles and fluttering standards. Unhappy companions of so many battles, of so many adventures! I wept bitterly. My shipmates wept for them, an endless stream of tears. I couldn't stop thinking about those who I had forced, against their will, to leave the land of the flower-eaters, the land of oblivion. They would still be alive, enjoying seductive pleasures, free of any worries. If not happy, at least untroubled. Now they were only dead meat, butchered for the meal of ferocious savages.

WE DIDN'T STOP until we got to the open sea, out of reach of their boats, and then we dropped anchor. I was desperate for help, for advice, but my goddess was silent! It was no use invoking her. Regardless, in the silence of my heart, I prayed with agonized intensity that she light a tiny spark, no matter how small, in my mind, so that I might understand.

It was dark above us and below us. The sea was a sheet of bronze and the moon was new, but all at once the light ignited inside me and I understood everything with a clarity that stunned me.

What had happened was exactly the same as in the land of the cyclopes, although ending in a very different way. Then, as now, we had reached a perfect port where the waves were utterly still and a group of us went inland to reconnoitre. One of our men here had been ripped apart and devoured by a gigantic creature, and several of our comrades suffered the same fate in the cyclops' cave. But this time, the aim of the brutes was frightfully precise, and the boulders that were thrown struck our ships and sank them. All the ships but mine. The message was clear and it was evident who had sent it to me: the god of the abyss. The blue god with his seaweed locks had finished what his son, blinded by my own hand, had not succeeded in doing. Smashing my vessels, sending ships and crews to the ocean depths.

Terror flooded my heart. One single hope: if Athena had lit that light in my mind so that I could clearly understand the significance of the events, perhaps she would also try to show me the way out. In that part of the world, where the sea knew no bounds, Poseidon was so strongly present that she could not appear to me, not while I was awake nor while I was sleeping, not as an ethereal mist, not in disguise. What she could do was stimulate my mind to understand and see clearly the designs of the gods, to seek a way to escape, to find the path that Fate had prepared for me, for Fate was stronger than the gods themselves.

That was the saddest night of my life, because I had never lost so many of my comrades before, not even on the bloody fields of Troy. I wept until dawn brightened the horizon, until the stars in the sky paled and vanished in the growing light. Like the other survivors, I remembered our dead companions in silence, shedding bitter tears, distilled by pain, into the water of the god who was our enemy.

At the hour when the sun appeared I glimpsed an enormous

dark shadow gliding under the surface of the water, which rippled as it passed. Was it the god of the abyss, alongside my ship? Was he studying the keel, strong and well made, but fragile against his infinite power? Was he already planning how and when he would destroy her?

Perhaps, and yet my heart did not want to surrender. Because I had something that the powerful god of the seas and the ocean did not even know about: my fear of death and my boundless love of life, not only my own but that of the others, of my ship-mates, my friends, my distant wife, the child I had never seen grow up. I would fight. I would fight to my last breath, even more furiously than I had under the walls of Troy. And when my time came, I would face Death by staring into her empty eyes.

I spoke to the lord of the depths, that shifting shadow under my keel: 'Oh god of the blue locks, you have heeded the prayers of your son, who I myself, Odysseus the son of Laertes, blinded. But where were you when I watched him pull the limbs off my comrades, grind their bones between his teeth? I listened as he belched up their flesh while he snored, that revolting bloody monster. What should I have done? Waited until he devoured every last one of them? What I did wasn't enough – I should have ripped out his heart and eaten it. It was my right, the right of a guest violated and offended, a right that your brother, the great Zeus himself, holds sacred.

'You took many lives yesterday in exchange for a single eye put out, the lives of brave men. Each one of them had a house, a wife and children, and had fought with courage for years and years under the walls of sacred Troy, always dreaming of the day he would return to his distant homeland. None of them will ever return. But I will bring my shipmates back home, in this royal ship of mine that still holds the treasures of Troy. When I meet the parents of those you killed I'll tell them how and by whose hand their lives were spent, so that they may raise a mound on the seashore and sacrifice victims to their shades. They will finally find peace, you can be sure of it. I do not know what will become of me, because it's impossible for a mortal to escape the wrath of a god as powerful as you, but Fate is a veiled divinity, stronger even than the gods. I will seek my destiny in every corner of land and sea, I will follow my path to its very end and not even you will be able to stop me.'

The black shadow slithered down to the depths of the sea and vanished in the dark. I gave orders to weigh anchor and loosen the sails.

WE SAILED for days and nights, drinking the water of the Laestrygonians contained in big jars at the stern. Then one day, at the first light of dawn, Perimedes, who had climbed to the top of the mast, sighted land.

It was a long promontory that extended into the sea right in front of us, covered with a thick blanket of shrubs and bushes. Here and there an oak could be seen, and there was a dense wood of tall oaks further inland. We all lined up at the bow, but there were no cries of joy as there would have been had our fleet been with us. We were alone, and we stood silently gazing at this unknown land, until the ship touched sand at the beach.

We all disembarked and I gave orders for all the men to don full armour, since I didn't want one more comrade to die a defenceless victim. After we had ensured that the ship was solidly anchored we began to walk and headed to the highest point of the promontory. From there we could see a wide, deserted gulf and, beyond a brief stretch of sea, a small island. It was very beautiful and completely forested. Eurylochus approached me: 'Look,' he said, 'down there, past that clearing. Smoke!'

He was right. A slender column of smoke was rising from a spot where the forest seemed thickest, just beyond a clearing. Flocks of birds soared from the trees, white wings wide. Their shrill cries were muted by the distance. A single house stood on the entire island. We could spy no further signs of human presence, nor had we seen any on the mainland, where we had anchored the ship.

'Who could be living in a place like that, *wanax*?' asked Euribates.

'Maybe a shepherd. He might use a raft to take his sheep to pasture,' replied Eurylochus.

'There's no trace of any other structure,' I said, 'as far as the eye can see.'

I could feel irresistible curiosity growing in me. I had to go. I wasn't thinking of the dangers that might be lurking there, I wasn't considering that Poseidon in his wrath might have devised a way to do away with us once and for all. I said: 'We'll return to the ship and then we'll go and see who lives on that island. We're armed, and still numerous, but we'll take no risks. We have to understand where we are and how far we are from Achaia. We've been sailing blindly for too long, without a route. We have to search for someone who can help us.'

My shipmates nodded in agreement and together we returned to the ship and cast off the moorings. Each man took his place at the oars. The sea was calm enough and the sky was luminous. Once again, the world opening before our eyes seemed to be free of dangers. We went ashore on a wide, completely deserted, sandy beach. There was not a single human footprint, but traces of a great number of seabirds. The waves were barely visible, but they curled over the sand for a very long way.

We secured the ship and, one after another, set foot on dry land. I assigned six men to go with Eurylochus to discover where the smoke was coming from, and then to come back and tell us.

'It won't take you long. As you've seen, a man could easily walk the entire perimeter of the island in half a day. Do not stop for any reason. We've suffered too much grief already. Come back, and remember that every moment of delay will cost us anguish and worry.'

Eurylochus promised that he would obey my orders and he

set off on foot with his men. They soon disappeared into the thick growth of myrtles and wild olives.

When the echo of their footsteps and their chatter died away, the deep silence was broken by a song. A clear, melodic voice. The voice of a woman, as sweet as that of a bride sitting at her loom.

6

WE WAITED UNTIL LATE AFTERNOON, but nothing happened. They did not come back. When evening drew close and we still didn't see them, I reasoned that they'd been invited to stay for dinner and a cup of good wine. Nothing bad could come of it. They had already suffered such unspeakable pain, what else could possibly happen?

We waited the next day as well, but when I saw they weren't returning I decided to go and look for them. They knew we would be worried. I'd made them promise to return as soon as they could. In any event, even if he had decided to enjoy the hospitality offered, Eurylochus would have surely sent one of the others back to tell me, given that it was such a short distance.

'Wait for me,' I told the others. 'Do not move from here, I'm going alone. If by nightfall I haven't returned, leave. Weigh the anchor and get away from here. Imagine that I have embraced each one of you, like brothers, before you set sail.'

Elpenor regarded me with an odd smile. The light skipped across his eyes, causing them to glitter with golden specks. 'Come back soon, *wanax*. I don't think we're going anywhere without you. We've been together too long.'

I smiled back and then set off with a long stride. I crossed a thicket of low bushes first and then a stretch of sand that must have been carried there by the wind that blew between two high cliffs. I then entered a forest of centuries-old oaks, advancing cautiously, with my hand on the hilt of my sword. The wood was strangely quiet. The trees were still full of leaves, but I could hear no birdsong or the fluttering of wings. Not even a cricket chirped to disturb that deepening silence.

All at once, I became aware of a sensation I knew well: a sort of tremor under my skin, a sudden chill in my heart and the certainty that someone was near. Just then, a voice made me jump. My sword sprang into my hand.

'You won't need that here.'

A beautiful youth, with the sun in his hair, was sitting on a boulder a few steps away from me. He was holding a flower.

'Do you live on this island? Is that your house with the hearth smoking?'

'Not really. I come and go. It's a tranquil place, this. Hardly anyone ever passes by but the few who do never leave.'

I drew closer. 'What do you mean by that?' I asked.

'Just what I said. Why, does that seem strange to you?'

'No, if it weren't for the fact that I mean to stay for a short time and leave again as soon as possible.'

'Why such haste?'

'I want to know where my men are. I sent them to search for that house and they never came back. Do you know anything about that?'

He smiled.

'And there's something else I find strange about this place,' I added. 'It's warm here, and yet there's always a wisp of smoke rising from that house.'

'They must be cooking something. Perhaps they're expecting guests. Perhaps they have guests.'

Cold terror seized me. My mind filled with monstrous, ferocious creatures who feed on human flesh. But a voice sounded in my heart: 'That's not the danger.'

'Who are you? Can you tell me your name?' I insisted.

'I'd better not. But there is something I can do for you.'

He pointed at a plant not far from us. It wasn't too big and it had tough, leathery leaves: 'Take it.'

I grabbed hold of it and yanked with all my strength but it wouldn't pull free. I unsheathed my sword.

'No, you have to pull out the whole thing.'

'I can't.'

'It's easy, look.'

He reached out a hand, closed it around the tuft and uprooted it easily. He shook the dirt off, letting it fall on the ground, and held it out to me. 'This plant is special,' he said. 'It's called moly. Have you ever heard of it?'

I shook my head.

'You have to eat the whole root before you go to that house. It will protect you.'

'It isn't poisonous, is it?' I asked.

'On the contrary. Go now, follow the smoke.'

'Thank you. I'll do as you say. Farewell.'

I set off.

The voice sounded again, behind me: 'Don't ever part from your sword.'

'I never do,' I replied, turning.

There was no one behind me.

I cut the root into pieces and ate it. It tasted like bitter almonds, and dripped a sour juice. I went forward, following the swirl of smoke that I could see above the tops of the trees. I'd gone a good distance; it seemed as though I must have crossed the entire island, from one side to another. I finally reached a clearing and then suddenly heard the distant, suffocated roar of a lion. I knew it was a lion because I'd heard them in the land of the flower-eaters and I'd spotted one prowling outside the village. A lion! I drew my sword. But other voices were joining the roar now: howls, snorts, growls, hisses, as if a slew of wild animals were roaming the island. Birds of prey, enormous reptiles. I felt my skin crawling and my heart froze in my chest. What was this place? Where had my world disappeared to? Had I lost it forever?

Just a day ago, as I was climbing up the promontory with my

men, it almost seemed as if we could have been on Ithaca and now, instead, it felt like each step I took was distancing me from reality, from the things that had a familiar meaning, from the shapes and sounds I'd learned to recognize on my island since I was a child. I thought of the years of war, of all that blood. I had endured privations, wounds, horrible losses, but I recognized the places I found myself in, the voices around me. I laughed and I cried. But since I had passed the wall of fog and reached the land of the flower-eaters I had lost my mind, and my heart was prey to wild imaginings. Events seemed to hang between doubt and unreality. As I crossed the clearing, I felt those same strange sensations again, but I was beginning to understand (or was it vain hope instead?) that my journey had a destination, albeit an unfamiliar one, and that it was about to be revealed to me.

After I'd crossed another stretch of forest, I found myself at last in front of the house with the smoke rising from its roof. It was close to sunset, the hour in which the sun enflames the sea. There were the animals whose cries I'd heard, locked up in big cages made of thick reeds or bronze bars. I saw the lion, pacing back and forth, incessantly roaring, an enormous grey-green lizard with a pointed tongue, a snake I'd never seen before, as thick as a man's neck and all coiled up on itself. I could also hear the grunting of pigs and the deep bellow of a wild bull.

How could I go forward? How could I find my companions? I suddenly heard the voice of one of them in my ear, like a breath: 'Wanax . . .'

'Where are you?' I cried out. 'Speak up, where are you?'

I shouted, more loudly: 'Where are you all?'

The animals calmed, fell silent. The snake pulled in its pointed tongue and laid its head down on the bottom of its cage.

A woman's voice startled me, coming from behind me: 'Who are you looking for, foreigner?' I spun around.

It was difficult to believe what I was seeing: her hair was violet and her eyes shone with a changing light whenever she shifted her head. The eyes of a dragon, of a quivering deer, of a greedy hawk . . . Her gown hung luminous from her shoulders in a myriad of tiny pleats, whispering of the wind, of the foam of the sea. From her stomach down, it divided into infinite filaments and with every step slipped between her perfect thighs, revealing smooth, ivory skin.

I replied: 'Who are you who speak my language?'

'We all speak the same language, haven't you noticed?'

'I'm looking for my men. Have you seen them?'

She moved in front of me. 'Men? No. I've seen no one. But come, there's a shady garden inside the house, the sun won't burn us there. Many flowers grow within, and their scent is inebriating. You must be hungry, foreigner, you look like you've been walking a long time.'

She turned and I followed her towards the house. We entered. Her feet seemed to barely skim the floor made of marble as blue as the waves of the sea, with black and gold streaks. Ceiling beams of cedar wood rested on top of tall columns. From each hung a wicker cage with intensely coloured songbirds inside. Their eyes were bright, curious. 'Foreigner foreigner foreigner,' they sighed.

A garden opened in the middle of the house, a fountain gurgling softly at its centre. Plants bowed over the water, flowers, flowers everywhere, of every marvellous colour, releasing a sublime scent made up of infinite fragrances.

She offered me a chair and sat down opposite me. Sitting on the lush green grass was a large bowl of embossed gold, with a thin alabaster cover. She opened it and, using a silver ladle, filled a smaller cup for me. 'Take this,' she said. 'With this you'll eat, with this you'll drink. I prepare it only for my most honoured guests.'

'There's no reason to honour me.'

'For me there is, foreigner of the smiling eyes.'

My gaze was unwavering. I brought the cup to my lips and drank slowly, in small sips, without ever hiding my eyes behind the rim of the cup.

'What is your name?' I asked her. She regarded me as if I were an alien creature, who eluded her understanding. She took a stick and tapped it on my shoulder.

'Won't you tell me?' I insisted.

She touched me again and now I saw incredulity on her face.

'Nothing is going to happen,' I said firmly.

She seemed dismayed, but then instantly gave me an enchanting smile. 'Now that you've had some nourishment, won't you come upstairs with me? That's where my bedroom is.'

I smiled back, as I swiftly drew my sword from the sheath at my side and pointed it at her throat. 'No more smiles, lovely *wanaxa*?'

'You don't know what you're missing. You would slay a body that could give you infinite pleasures never experienced by any man on this earth?'

'Without a moment's hesitation.'

'Why?'

'Because I want my men back. That's why I came. What have you done with them?'

'They entered my house. They surrounded me and looked at me greedily, like pigs, full of obscene lust, ready to lay their hands on me. Now they're out with the pigs. Didn't you hear them grunting out there?'

I pushed the blade against her throat. A tiny pressure and her blood would spurt out to stain her white breasts and beautiful gown. I gave the golden cup a kick, and the liquid inside spilled out onto the ground. 'My men!' I shouted.

She understood that she had no choice. 'Follow me,' she said, and walked towards the door. We reached a pig enclosure. There were my men, naked, in the mud and excrement, snorting and rolling around with the swine. Tear filled my eyes, so great was the compassion I felt for them.

'Free them,' I said, and then the tone of my voice changed: 'I beg you.'

· She listened to me. She took her stick and touched their

filth-smeared backs, one by one. One after another they got up, realized what had happened, what they had become and, overcome with shame, they wept.

'Go to the stream and wash,' I ordered. 'You're repugnant. Look for your clothes and run to the ship. Tell Elpenor that you've seen me and that I'm in no danger.'

The lady of the island approached me and said gently: 'My name is Circe. I've always lived in this place, so distant from any other. Who are you? What is your name? I don't know you, and yet I've always known that a man immune to my spell would come here one day.'

'I am Odysseus, son of Laertes, and I reign over the island of Ithaca. As we were returning from war, a howling gale drove us far off our route and dragged us into a world unknown to us. I could not have imagined that such a world existed. But now, *wanaxa*, know that I come in peace and that I respect your house and your person. The stick you hold did not turn me into an animal because I've always been a man, at every hour of the day and night, before other men and before women. You see, I trust in my mind and in the thoughts, versatile and complex, which the gods have graced me with.'

'Tell your men they can all come here. There will be abundant food for them, pure water and wine. You can all stay as long as you like.'

I followed her and a big dog with long fangs lay down at her feet and licked them.

'Was he a man as well?' I asked her.

'Yes, as faithful as a dog. Too much so. You're seeing him now as I see him, but he's still a man, look closer.'

The dog had disappeared. The dark-skinned man standing in front of me had downcast eyes and his arms crossed over his chest.

'What do you mean by that?'

'Here nothing is what it seems. But even Odysseus needed help in order to face me.'

'I just needed to believe in myself. A youth in the woods gave me the roots of a plant to eat, as a defence against your spells. But I was sure, from the moment I set off, that nothing would be able to bend me. It was that belief, not the plant, that made me resistant.'

'You have the gift, Odysseus. Like me . . . and very few others.'

I thought of Calchas. He too had used the very same words under the wild fig tree. I still remembered him whispering into my ear and what I, at the same moment, told him.

It was quite dark when the men I'd sent to the ship returned, including Eurylochus. They wouldn't come close to the house; they hung back, at the edge of the clearing, watchful and uneasy. The animals' cries and the memory of what they'd just gone through were still too fresh in their minds. I went out to them and tried to convince them to come in with me, but they insisted on staying where they were, at least for the night, and I didn't want to force them. I stayed with them for some time and even had food brought to them, which they didn't touch.

'You needn't worry,' I said to them. 'No ill will befall you now. You can post armed sentries all night, sleep with your swords at your sides, and tomorrow, when the sun rises, you'll see that I was right. I'll come back here unharmed and perhaps then you'll follow me to the house of Circe, the lady of this place.' Some of them looked away, confused, but not Eurylochus. I embraced him and whispered into his ear: 'Yours is the command. Make any decision you feel necessary, but do not fear. Tomorrow you'll see me back here at first light.'

He exchanged my embrace, vigorously, and stood watching me from the edge of the clearing until I turned and raised my hand when I reached the house of Circe.

When I entered it was lit by lanterns, but empty. Only the scent of unfamiliar flowers wafted between the columned hall and the secret inner garden. I heard a sound coming from the upstairs chamber, a song as light as a morning breeze. I went up the stairs, following the voice, until I found myself at the door to a room: the space inside seemed infinitely big and the melody hung in the air like the scent I was breathing. Circe lay on a purple bed, which rested on a tree that came up from the garden below. There was no floor. The branches were decked with big red leaves and dozens and dozens of fleshy white flowers that gave off the gentle scent I'd smelled. Circe was naked: only her long hair veiled her breasts.

'Isn't this the bed you've been desiring for so long?' she asked me.

'This tree didn't exist when I entered the garden.'

'True. It grew while you were talking to your men.'

I nodded. 'I see. Nothing on this island is what it seems. Not even you, I imagine.'

'Not even me,' she replied, 'but what does it matter?' She held out her arms to me. 'Come, son of Laertes. I've been waiting for you for such a long time. I knew that you would come, and that my spell would not break you. Don't be afraid. Walk on the branches of the tree; any one of them leads to my bed. Choose any one you like.'

I hesitated. The flowers made me wary and so did Circe; I couldn't believe that she had given up. But I was tired. I'd suffered too much pain, too much loss and I longed to abandon myself to a woman's caress. High-waisted Circe with her proud breasts and long hair that swayed around her body. I pulled off the baldric that held my sword and hung it from one of the branches. Her arms drew me in. Her love was like pure wine. I lost myself in the dark magic of her eyes.

When I awoke, she was sleeping next to me on a bed of carved wood with sheets of white linen. My sheathed sword lay on a floor made of a semi-precious, ochre-coloured stone. I looked at her: a young maiden, immersed in serene sleep. Dawn was lightening the horizon and I went to seek my comrades. They greeted me with joy. The sentries were toasting bread over a fire, topped with cheese they'd cut with their swords.

'Eat with us, *wanax*,' they said, smiling. I took my place next to them as the others began to awaken. The birds saluted the rising sun with their song, the sea curled lazily along the long golden beach; the island woke up with us and everything seemed familiar to our eyes.

'See, Eurylochus? Nothing happened. We're all well and we've found a marvellous place to rest in.'

Circe welcomed them graciously and accepted them all as her guests. The place was as beautiful as any we had ever seen and as one day turned into the next, we felt at ease, at home, almost. Time passed without any of us really noticing. My men fished, hunted, inspected the hull of the ship, replaced the parts harmed by the storms and the lashing waves, mended the sail. But I felt uncomfortable with them, because I was the only one among them enjoying something they could only dream about: the graces of a woman of stupendous beauty . . . if she was a woman at all.

One day, near the end of autumn, I was stretched out in the shade of a palm tree when she came up and sat on the sand next to me. 'Time has flown. It seems like yesterday that you arrived.'

'Nothing is what it seems on this island. That's what you told me, remember?'

'That's right,' she replied, and she ran her fingers through my hair, slowly. 'You'll leave, won't you?'

'Yes. I have to take my men home, as I promised them when we left for Troy so many years ago. They yearn for their homeland and they are sad at heart.'

I realized for all that time I'd been able to forget the words of Polyphemus, and that I was able to remember fondly the men I'd lost to the Laestrygonians; no longer were they bloody, restless spirits in my mind.

'I imagined as much. I've always feared this day. I'll remain here alone. I'll walk the beach endlessly by day or toss sleeplessly in my bed at night . . .'

'Perhaps other ships will arrive, attracted by the plume of smoke that always rises into the sky from this island . . .' I said. 'But why must you stay in this house?'

Her eyes were shaded with melancholy when she answered: 'Each one of us has a debt to pay. Even you . . .'

'Even me,' I replied, 'and I can't wait to see the end of it.'

'I know . . . Can't you forget?'

'How can I? I'm responsible for my men. I've already lost too many of them. But you, my divine friend, you who have a greater gift than anyone I have ever met, can't you tell me what you see in my future? Will I ever get back? Will I see my island again and my family, will I take my men home with me?'

Circe touched my lips with her fingers. 'Is knowing the future what you really want? Isn't it better not to know what awaits us?'

'No, I have to know. I'm tired of living in doubt, in uncertainty.'

'What you want to know is a secret guarded by the Moirai. They are cruel, vindictive divinities, and I can't help you. There's only one man who could, but he's not among the living.'

'Who is he?'

'Tiresias, the seer. He could tell you, but he is imprisoned in implacable Hades, and if you want to consult him you'll have to go to where he is. You'll have to call up the shades of the dead.' She looked away from me, as if trying to hide the feelings in her heart.

'Can't you teach me how?'

'Oh, king of Ithaca, what terrible things you ask of me on this luminous afternoon! But if you really want me to, I will teach you.'

'I do. And if you do this for me, you'll always have a place in my heart.'

She sighed. 'Push your agile ship into the sea and sail due west until you reach the shore of the deep Ocean. You will see a cliff as white as silver with a cave beneath it, and there you will go ashore. Use your sword to dig a ditch one cubit wide by one cubit long. Cut the throats of black-coated victims, and collect their blood in the ditch. Scatter handfuls of flour, the best, and honey, to attract the idle ghosts . . . and then you may invoke the pale-headed dead. Call them again and again, and they will come to you . . . in great number.'

The sun was hot and radiant in the centre of the sky and I felt cold chills. Lovable Circe, her long hair like waves of the sea, continued: 'Hold them off with your sword. They'll still be afraid of it, even if they can't die twice, and allow only Tiresias to drink the black blood of the victims. Then he will speak to you, and tell you the whole truth.' She fell still and her head dropped as if succumbing to a mysterious weariness.

'Thank you,' I replied, 'for not being deaf to my pleas. I will always hold your memory dear in my heart.'

'Remember,' she said, 'it is a terrible thing to meet the shadows of the dead.'

'I know.'

'Can't you stay a little longer? The autumn is almost over. The force of the wind will build, and churn up foamy waves on the sea.'

I lowered my head without answering.

'You cannot. I see. Then, if thus it must be, if I will have to mourn forever, alone, the days and nights I have spent with you, make me never forget this last night that we'll be together. I'll pray for the sun to remain as long as he can in the land of the Ethiopians and keep the night darker and longer for us so we can have our fill of love.' Her eyes shone, damp, the colour of deep water.

7

THE MEN EXULTED WHEN I announced that we would return to
the sea. The life we'd been living was a great relief after what we
had seen and suffered on our last voyage, but they were already
bored with it and were ready to set off. I, instead, was thinking
of how I would tell them about the change in our destination
and how they would react to my words.

They started to work vigorously on preparing the ship. The
lady of the island was very generous with us: she gave us food in
great quantity, wheat and barley as well, jars filled with strong,
heady wine, smoked meat and baked breads. We drew pure
water from the stream, filling more jars and loading them on the
ship.

They were all happy, but my eyes were on the beautiful
wanaxa of this strange, mysterious island who had been feeding
us for almost a year. I watched her, a silent shadow, as she walked
down the low hill that rose over the port. She observed us as we
bustled around the robust hull that had faced so many adventures and would perhaps face many more. She was suffering, I
think, imagining the solitude that awaited her for long days or
months or years.

She disappeared as suddenly as if she'd vanished into the air,
and in her place stood a ram black as night and next to him a
sheep, black-fleeced as well. I understood. The victims to be
sacrificed to the Lady of Darkness at the mouth of Hades. It was
time to depart. I loaded the animals onto the ship as my mates
took their places on the rowing benches, ready to pound the sea

with their oars, eager to start the voyage that would take us home. The ship pulled away from the coast, the prow turned towards the open sea.

But soon a cry rang out from the shore: 'Wait! Wait for me!'

Polites! So great had been my comrades' haste to set off that we hadn't counted ourselves.

'Fast, jump in!' I shouted. 'We can't stop. The current is pushing us away.' Polites dived in and swam with great vigour as we raised the oars out of the sea, using only the steering oar to keep on course. We hoisted him onboard, dripping wet.

'Elpenor!' he said. 'You forgot about him as well. He's dead.'

I grabbed him by the shoulders. 'What are you saying? Where is Elpenor?'

'There!' he shouted. 'There, where the house is. He's dead, he's dead! We have to go back and bury him!'

Eurylochus caught my eye as he awaited orders. I replied: 'We can't. The current is too strong. It would be too complicated to turn back. The crossing that awaits us is already difficult enough. Turn around, look at the island. See how far it is already?'

Polites bowed his head in resignation, but there were tears in his eyes.

'How did it happen?' I asked.

'I don't know how it happened and I don't know who did it,' said Polites, still panting. 'I was gathering up my clothing and my arms to come down to the port, since I could see from the house that the ship was ready, and I yelled out to tell him it was time to leave. He called back to let me know he'd heard me, and so I started walking. When a few minutes had gone by and he hadn't joined me, I turned back, calling his name, but he didn't answer. Then I found him. He was lying on the ground, dead, with his neck broken. I knelt down next to him. His face was still rosy coloured, his skin still soft, there was still a bit of warmth left in his limbs. It looked as if he were sleeping.'

'Why?' cried out my heart. 'Why, just a moment before we

went out to sea?' Elpenor was the youngest of us all, and he'd never stood out for his courage or daring on the battlefield. A modest lad, but reliable, and dutiful. Why hadn't I noticed his absence? The news of his death wounded me deeply. Another part of us had disappeared. The gods and destiny were hacking away at us, a little at a time.

I shouted out: 'Was it you?'

Was I thinking of Athena, or of Circe? I had no answer because there was no answer, as there had not been for any of the comrades I'd lost first on the fields of Troy and then on the serpent-shaped back of the unsleeping sea. Simply, his fate had caught up with him.

'I closed his eyes, but could do nothing else,' Polites said. 'We owe him funeral rites, so that he can enter the house of Hades. I beg you, *wanax*, let's turn back. He was my friend.' All at once I heard the cries, the growls, the roars of the animals living around Circe's house.

'We can't,' I replied. 'I won't risk the lives of the living for the funeral of a dead man.' Polites dropped his head and hid his face between his hands.

We continued on our route and, as my shipmates raised the sail, I watched from the stern as the island slowly disappeared. In the end all I could see was the plume of smoke rising from the house. Circe, sensuous and loving. I couldn't bear the thought of not seeing her again.

The wind was blowing from the east and the crew was sick at heart over the loss of their friend. He had escaped years of war, the bloodthirsty cyclops, the savage Laestrygonians . . . to lose his life on a calm morning in a tranquil place on a remote island, far away from other men like us who live on bread. I feared that their despair might overwhelm them, and I realized I must speak to them before that could happen. I had never needed them as much as I did then.

'Comrades,' I said, 'before we left, Circe taught me how to call up the shadow of wise Tiresias from the kingdom of the dead. She has urged me to go to where he is, to consult him, and I cannot disregard her words if we hope to know what future awaits us.' I looked them straight in the eyes as I went on. 'Look, men, the wind is blowing from the east, as if to manifest the will of the gods. That's why we shall sail west until we reach the Ocean. There we'll find the white cliff that marks the entrance to Hades.'

My shipmates were staring at me in green, unreasoning terror.

'I'll make my way there alone – you'll wait for me on the ship until I come back,' I continued. 'And that will be the start of our return. I promise you. Men, prepare your hearts to be strong and patient. A grim place awaits us, covered with shadows by day and by night, in the summer as in the winter. A cold wind blows constantly – the earth and sky resound with sighs and groans. But you must not despair: you will have accomplished a deed that only the greatest heroes can boast of. Few are permitted to explore the extreme confines between life and death.'

I'm sure they were thinking that I'd completely lost my mind. They were weeping as if I'd condemned them all to death. I tried to light the spark of courage in them, I swore by the earth and the sky that I would bring them back to the land of the living. And in the end I convinced them to accompany me on that endeavour, the most arduous and exhausting that I would ever face in my lifetime.

We sailed west for days and days, crossing the entire sea, until we reached the current of the river Ocean that surrounds all lands. From there we pushed on, following the coast as we drew nearer and nearer to the kingdom of darkness. The passage of time lost all meaning, for the days were ever shorter and the nights longer and darker, until daytime was nothing more than a dim, leaden prelude to dusk. The stars hid from our sight and only the dark line of the shore continued to guide me towards the realm of the dead.

We finally spotted a tower, high up on a cliff surrounded by jagged pinnacles. Dismembered wrecks were lodged on the algae-green rocks below. We'd reached the land of the Cimmerians, as Circe had predicted. They were the guardians of nothing. Their city was built of black stone on a desolate, craggy mountain surrounded by gusts of billowing fog. We sailed past the cliff and the menacing tower and once again we found ourselves manoeuvring amid rocks as sharp as keenly edged bronze while the sea churned around us. We thwarted many a fatal crash by using our oars to push free of looming rock ledges. Finally, after a long struggle, from the top of the mast one of my men signalled that he had sighted the tall white cliff. Soon we could see it as well: steep, rugged, plunging into the sea. A ghost in the fog. I had my men strike the sail and we rowed in towards the coast. Our path was still strewn with reefs and cutting rocks, grey as iron, but our line of approach finally became wider and the swelling of the waves diminished until it had vanished completely. I led the rowing then with a slow rhythm, so the keel would not fracture if we struck a rock. We finally touched ground and the prow glided into heavy black sand. I jumped onto the shore. I had my cloak and my sword and nothing else. My men handed over the victims to be sacrificed, lowering them alongside the ship: the black-pelted ram, a huge animal with great curving horns, and the black-fleeced sheep, both destined to be offered to the divinities of Hades.

I walked along a muddy path. Fetid vapours rose all around me, the dank breath of Erebus. I reached the top of a rise and, before descending the other side, I took a look back at my ship: all I could see was the mast, swaying in silence. The sea was quiet as well, and very still. Before me opened a dark, barren, flat, desolate valley. Then, as if out of nowhere, the path filled with footprints, hundreds, thousands, a myriad of children's, women's, men's tracks left by an infinite army, all of them defeated by the Chaera of death. I had found my way.

I followed it for . . . I don't know how long. I was cold, getting colder and colder, my thoughts condensed into small gasping puffs. All at once, an enormous cavern welled open before me: it descended into the bowels of the earth. I had reached my destination.

I knelt, and used my sword to dig a hole one cubit wide and one cubit long. I seized the ram by its horns and cut its throat, and then did the same with the sheep. I let their black, steaming blood flow into the hole. The moment had come. I called up, with a long song, the pale heads of the dead. And they came to me: mothers who held in their arms the babes who killed them in the struggle of being born, old men with vacant eyes, young men in bloody armour, dead before their time, done in by a sword or a spear or a bitter arrow. The sadness in their eyes was infinite. I was gripped by icy terror. Although I had prepared myself to meet with the dead, what I saw was unbearable: the purest, sharpest despair.

I recognized a youth: a purple mark crossed his forehead.

'Elpenor! You! You've already arrived in the house of the dead? How swiftly you came. You got here faster on foot than I in my ship! What sorrow to see you here among the shadows of the dead!'

I wept as I beheld him, for I could clearly see his features, the look in his eyes. I gasped as I understood that what seemed real to me was but a shadow.

'How did it happen?' I cried. 'You so often avoided death at the hands of the enemy in battle. How did you meet with such a senseless end?'

'Any death at my age is senseless,' he replied, and dropped his head as if trying to conceal his forehead. He was ashamed.

'I was drinking. I was drunk. I'd gone up to the terrace of the house where the sea breeze was cool. A grapevine had sent its shoots to cover a wide space with its shade. I fell asleep, deeply so. When my friend called out to me, I woke suddenly, my mind in a muddle. I didn't know where I was and I put my foot forward to start walking. I fell headlong and my neck snapped.' He was weeping as well, tears of air and cold vapour. 'I beg of you, when you return, search for what is left of me and put it on the pyre, and when you have gathered my ashes and buried them, raise a mound on the seashore with my name and sacrifice victims to me so that the lady of this black place will allow me a little peace!'

Drunk. He died drunk. Why? Didn't he have abundant meat and bread, a beautiful, hospitable house on a marvellous island laden with every kind of game? It wasn't enough, I knew that. His nightmares had never stopped tormenting him. He had tried to banish them with wine, like his lost comrades had with the red flower of oblivion. There was no escaping the nightmares of war.

'I will, Elpenor. I will immolate the best animals in my herds, and I'll burn the thigh meat as well, to appease the lady of the Underworld.'

He fled, sighing.

Many other sorrowful spirits were thronging around the hole where the victims I'd sacrificed were still dripping blood, but I held them all back with my sword, shouting: 'Keep away! Keep away!' The sword frightened them. They knew well they could not die a second time, but they remembered its power to take life.

And it was then that I saw, among the others, the sacred prophet: spent-eyed Tiresias, the famed seer of Thebes who had revealed that his city had been suffering the scourge of the gods because its king, Oedipus, had killed his father and married his own mother.

He neared me, sensing the smell of blood, the blood that gives life.

'Pull back your sharp sword,' he said to me, 'and let me drink if you want to know your destiny.'

I stepped back and thrust my sword back into its sheath. Tiresias bent down and drank deeply of the blood. Life surged into him, colouring his empty shade.

He said: 'You seek a smooth return, Odysseus, but the god of the abyss will render that return most difficult, for you blinded his son and humiliated him pitilessly. You will return, late, a broken man, alone on a foreign ship, having lost all of your ship-mates, and you will find your home invaded by arrogant men who squander your wealth and court your wife. All of them you must extinguish, either openly, with your slashing bronze, or stealthily, with deceit. And not even then will you be able to enjoy your sweet wife and your dear son.

'You will depart again with an oar on your shoulder,' he continued, 'and you will journey over the continent, travelling so far that you will meet up with men who do not use salt to season their food. They know nothing of the sea, nor have they ever seen crimson-cheeked ships or the oars that make them fly. This is the sign. You can't mistake it: when a wayfarer asks you if the oar you carry on your shoulder is a fan used for winnowing grain. You will plant the oar into the ground and offer sacrifice to great Poseidon: a bull, a boar and a ram. Only then will you be able to reign in blessed peace over happy peoples. Death will come to seek you only when you are exhausted by serene old age. She will come for you softly, from the sea.'

Tears streamed from my eyes. I wanted to scream, to vent my rage against the god who punished me solely for having defended myself. Why did Poseidon insist on persecuting me? Because my mind had found the way to prevail against a bloodthirsty monster, because I sought revenge for my comrades who had been slain and devoured? But I knew the truth: a mortal is never allowed to challenge a god. I implored Tiresias then: 'I beg you, prophet, foretell another destiny for me, a better one, because this one breaks my heart and pains me beyond any comprehen-sion. Give my comrades, at least, a means for escaping this fate!'

The prophet, moved to compassion – if a ghost can have feelings, although he no longer has a heart – pronounced other words: 'You will sail east after leaving this dark place and you will not find shore until you reach the island of Trinacria, where the herds of the Sun who sees all from above have their grazing ground. If, despite your great hunger and suffering, you do not touch them, you and your men will reach your destination. If, instead, you lay a hand on the calves, then I predict ruin for your ship and your shipmates. Even if you yourself are spared, you will arrive late at your homeland, a broken man. More I cannot say.' He melted away like the fog.

Tiresias had vanished from my sight, and yet I could not return to the ship and my men. I felt a force that kept me rooted there, a presence that infused my heart with thoughts and emotions that I'd long forgotten.

'Mother!' I called out suddenly. 'Mother, are you here?' Echo, in that moment of pain, repeated my words endlessly.

'Yes, my son,' sounded a voice in my heart. 'What are you doing here, beneath the dark shadow? It is terrible for a living man to enter the kingdom of the dead.' And then there she was, standing in front of me.

'Mother!' I cried, weeping. 'What brought you to the thick gloom of Hades? Was it Artemis, who struck you with one of her arrows? Or did a disease slowly consume you?'

'No, son, it was neither Artemis, nor a slow, fatal illness, but the longing for you, my beloved son. The terrible desire to see you once again took my life.'

'And my father?' I asked. 'Is he living, still? Does he still enjoy his privileges as king? And Telemachus? Do our people respect him?'

'Yes, son, your father is still alive, but he has retired to the countryside and lives alone with an old servant who cares for him. In the winter he stretches out on the ashes still tepid from the hearth, and in the summer he lies down on a bed of leaves wherever darkness catches him. There he sighs, his heart aching for you. Of Telemachus you can be proud: he is a handsome young man and well respected by his people. They all call upon him to administer justice.'

'And my bride? Is her heart still faithful to me? Or has she found another man and married him?'

'She is faithful, my son, but she does nothing but weep, day and night, for she suffers great humiliation in your house, as she pines for your return, and you . . . you never return.'

I drew close, so great was my desire to clasp her to me, but my hands returned empty to my chest. 'Let me hold you,' I implored, 'Mother, let me hold you.'

I thought I saw a tired smile on her bloodless lips. 'You cannot, child, there is nothing here you can embrace. A pyre burns flesh and tendons, dissolves bones; the soul flies away like a light puff of air. It is only your desire that makes me visible to your eyes. Leave this desolate place, I beg of you, escape while you still have time.' These were her last words to me before she dissipated into the dark aura, taking her place again among the multitude of ghosts of men and women mowed down by the Chaera of death.

I fell to my knees and wept. I sobbed like a little boy at the thought of the anguish that had killed my mother. So many memories flooded my mind, from the happy days of my childhood when I would ask her to tell me about my father. As I had just now, but for very different reasons. In my mind's eye she was garbed in precious gowns, the daughter of Autolykos. She was like a goddess when she had sat on the throne of Ithaca. Now she was nothing but a fleeting shadow, dissolving in the darkness of Hades . . . and my father, the hero Laertes: I saw him lying on a lowly bed of ashes like a beggar, and my heart split in my chest. I finally raised my head again and then, in that multitude of dead souls, my eyes, full of tears as they were, discerned other spirits, but only those that my heart desired.

The first to appear was Agamemnon, the great Atreides, a dark frown on his face and a horrendous gash across his neck. I was incredulous; I could not believe he was dead. 'Oh glorious Atreides!' I said. 'What brought you to this place of tears? Were you shipwrecked as you returned from Troy? Or killed in some hostile land where you were seeking rich plunder or women?' He recognized me and came close. He moved to embrace me but his arms, once so strong when they swung the heavy sword and bore the great shield, had lost all their force. I could not feel them at all on my body. He was surrounded by a host of bloody ghosts: the comrades who had always guarded him, shielded him in battle; those who never left his side under even the most relentless attack. The tremendous truth began to worm its way into my mind.

'No,' he replied, 'wise Odysseus, valiant companion of so many battles, it was no storm that took my life, nor savage warriors protecting their land and their women. It was murder. It was my own wife who armed the hand of her lover Aegisthus.'

I could not help but recall his terrible, cruel sacrifice of Iphigenia, his own daughter – an innocent victim offered so that the greatest fleet of all time could set sail, so that our endeavour could commence. Perhaps he no longer thought of it, or perhaps he had buried the memory in the darkest depths of his soul. All he could remember was the wrongs he had suffered, the plot and the massacre, his wife's betrayal.

'As we made our return to Mycenae,' he started again, and his voice sounded as dark and deep as bronze sounds when it is pounded, 'fires carried the news from hill to hill, from mountain to mountain, all the way to the palace. The lookouts posted up on the tower of the chasm saw the flames and announced our arrival. When we entered the gate of the two lions, it creaked on its hinges and our chariots thundered down empty streets, past the silent tombs of the ancient Perseid heroes. The whole sky was dark, for the new moon shed no light, but the palace was not: it was bright with torches burning to celebrate our victory. Surely enough, the news of the fall of Troy and kingdom of Priam had already reached them. My wife had prepared a banquet. And it was there, like a bull at the trough, that I was slain by the axe of Aegisthus. But that was only the start of the carnage! My comrades were slaughtered as well, one by one, like swine. The floor smoked with their blood. Our bodies lay sprawled among the overturned tables and all around the great bowl brimming with wine . . .'

Terror gnawed at me but *wanax* Agamemnon, shepherd of heroes, hadn't finished: 'Odysseus, you've often seen warriors come to a bloody end, whether in the fury of the brawl or in fighting hand-to-hand, but even you, inured to the horrors of war as you are, even you would have shuddered. Your heart would have wept at such butchery. As I lay dying, with nothing to push back the bronze axe but my bare hands, I finally spied my wife, proud daughter of Tyndareus, Clytaemnestra. She turned her back to me and left the room. That bitch lacked the heart to close my eyes as I descended, groaning, to Hades, or even to close my mouth with her hands. If she could commit such a monstrous crime, against her legitimate husband, who among us can ever trust his woman again?

'You who have yet to make your return, trust nobody! Say one thing but hide the rest. Keep your intentions hidden until you are sure that your wife is not plotting against you. But surely you, Odysseus, need not fear, because your wife is Penelope, daughter of Icarius, a wise woman who will have remained faithful to you. When we left, she had a child at her breast who now has certainly taken his place among the warriors. You will have the immense joy of seeing him a grown man. You will feast your eyes on him, clasp him to your chest . . .'

He sobbed, Agamemnon, *wanax* of heroes, and sighed. 'I will never be able to embrace my own son. I never saw my boy grow up. I don't even know what has happened to him. He must still be alive. I haven't seen him here among the dead. Perhaps he's been taken in by one of the other kings, my brother Menelaus in Sparta or Nestor on Pylos . . .'

We wept, facing each other in that still, dark air, in that world of regret and heartbreak. And it was then that I saw rise before me a sudden, appalling sight: the shadow of Achilles!

He hailed me. 'Odysseus, glorious son of Laertes! My brave, reckless friend: can nothing stop you? How will you ever be able to think up something more foolhardy than this endeavour? You've dared to enter Hades, the kingdom of the deceased.'

I trembled. He was a frightful vision indeed, dressed in the armour he had been wearing when he killed big-hearted Hector. But it wasn't real: there was no gleaming metal there, only its likeness. This was how he imagined himself, and it was thus that his spirit formed his image. But as I looked closer I could see the bronze was turning green, from being long abandoned, and I thought of that brilliant sunny day I'd gone with Nestor to Phthia of the Myrmidons to plead with Achilles to join in the war with all the other princes of Achaia. I had succeeded in convincing him and was so pleased with myself for having accomplished the task. And now, what was this thing in front of me? Who was this grey ghost speaking inside my heart? Why had such a bitter destiny been created for humankind? So deep was the sadness in his eyes that I thought I might find words to ease his melancholy; that I might speak to him as I did that day we walked in the woods, followed by his wondrous, unharnessed horses, Xanthus the blond and Balius the dappled. What a fool I was.

'Achilles, most glorious of us all, most valiant, I've come here to learn my destiny, to question the prophet Tiresias and learn from him how I can get back to Ithaca. I have suffered greatly since we left the shores of the Troad. As I tried to make my return, I was swept up in a storm and dragged off course for many days and night. When the wind quit, we found ourselves abandoned in an unfamiliar world populated by monsters and by fierce, savage peoples. I have lost all my ships. I have seen my comrades massacred, slain like beasts at the slaughter. I have not yet reached my homeland. The gods have not yet had their fill – they sport with me and amuse themselves by inflicting every sort of suffering on me.

'Do not grieve that you are dead, Achilles. I myself have desired to be so many times. When you died, we raised a gigantic pyre. Three hundred heavy-footed warriors escorted you there! Your glorious armour shone bright on your body. The flames rose high enough to scorch the vault of the heavens. We all filed before the blazing fire and one by one we tossed in locks of our hair, our belts, our silver-studded baldrics, our bracelets, even our rings with the seals that preserve our names. Then we raised a gigantic mound over your ashes and we sacrificed to your wrathful shade: an infinite number of victims, bulls and rams and men, prisoners bound by chains. Still now, a fire burns there day and night. Any sailor who passes along the coast of Asia sees those inextinguishable flames and says: "That is the tomb of Achilles, that magnanimous, valiant man whose shout alone was so powerful that entire armies would flee upon hearing it."

'What do I have to look forward to but suffering and despair? When my time comes, my body will lie forgotten on some deserted beach. You, instead, will always have power as you do, even here, over the pale heads of the dead.'

I fell silent and the hissing of Erebus, that deep, infinite lament, was the only voice in the darkness, until Achilles spoke: 'Do not praise death, Odysseus, my shining friend. I would rather be a slave for the poorest and most miserable of men on the luminous earth than reign over the dead. Life is the only gift, the only treasure, the only magnificent adventure. I lost it for a mere moment of dazzling light, and I will spend eternity mourning it.'

Around him thronged many thousands of other ghosts, fallen warriors, and their faint voices sounded like birds chirping in the dark or bats squeaking. Only one of them, huge, majestic, stood apart and stared at me mutely with eyes of fire. I recognized him instantly and felt my heart wither in my chest: Ajax! Invincible Ajax, bulwark of the Achaians. It all came back to me, the shame and dishonour, the despair of the humiliated giant, the cruel, inevitable death that was his destiny.

I called out to him: 'Ajax! Not even dead have you given up your anger over that cursed suit of arms! It was taken from you unjustly and given back to you too late. What a terrible misfortune for us! Because of that armour, the Achaians lost our greatest tower of strength. The way you left us was the font of immense suffering for me, for all of us. I beseech you, believe me: I would have given my life to bring you back. But your fate had already been decreed by the gods and I could not undo what had been done. Please, join us, speak to me, let us console each other, set aside our woes. Forget your grudge, I beg of you.'

I implored him, but he gave no answer. He turned his back on me and melted away into the multitude of weeping ghosts, dissolving into the fog.

8

THEN, IN AN INSTANT, it all disappeared. All that was left was the mouth of the cavern, spouting forth dense vapours with an acidic stench. The faces of my lost comrades, their words, their regrets: had I dreamed it all? And yet the cold I felt was real, and real was the grey, icy rain that penetrated into my bones. Most real were the words of Tiresias, the Theban prophet. I remembered them then as I do now: they pierced my heart, my mind, like needles. The offspring of other words which I'd heard from the cyclops, from Calchas, from the mistress of wild beasts on that remote island: late and broken, late and broken, late and broken! But I was still alive, wasn't I? Still putting one foot in front of the other on a muddy path under rain-swollen clouds. Distant thunder greeted my return to the world of the living.

Not a blade of grass, not a flower, not a ray of sunlight, not a living being around me. Or rather, nothing but a toad, a misshapen creature, that I saw scuttling down the path that had led me to the kingdom of the dead, croaking his hoarse protest against the wickedness of nature. When I got to the point where the footprints of the dead began, or ended, I looked to my left and there I saw the city of the Cimmerians on the black cliff, glowing like burnished metal in the flashes of lightning. I thought of my cry, the triple war cry of the kings of Ithaca. I'd raised it from my ship as I was leaving my island, I'd hurled it at the phalanges of warriors brawling under the walls of Troy.

And now I howled it into the storm. It was louder than the thunder, than my fear, than my bitter melancholy.

I thought: 'Why didn't I see the shades of Hector, or Priam, or little Astyanax? Perhaps the lady of the Underworld wanted to spare me the sight of a decapitated trunk holding his own head in his hands, or a man stripped of his skin, stripped of his face, unrecognizable . . . or a rock-battered, mangled infant.' I could no longer even call up an image of the enemy we'd defeated. We'd wiped out their bodies and their souls.

Then I started humming the lullaby that my nurse would sing to me as a child to put me to sleep. The song was a balm to my aching heart, and as I pushed forward it gave me strength. I got to the top of a hill and from there I could see my ship. My mates had stretched the sail from one end to the other, bound it fore and aft, and like chicks under the wings of their mother hen they were sheltering from the storm, keeping each other warm by staying close. Around them the white-rimmed waves lashed out at the jagged cliffs.

One of them saw me and yelled out: 'Wanax!' And the others started shouting as well, their voices joining in one by one. By the time I reached the shore, they had thrown out a line. I grabbed on to it and entered the water, advancing one arm's length after the other, walking through the grey, gelid sea until I found the flank of my ship. My comrades hoisted me on board, carried me to shelter under the sail, rubbed me dry with a cloth and covered me with a cloak. I was livid with cold, and trembling.

When I looked at them, I saw my own face reflected in their faces, like in a mirror of bronze. I saw stupor, fright, incredulity. Although the rain was crashing down over our heads, an overturned shield stopped the fire of the brazier from going out, and the warmth it gave off slowly started the blood flowing through my veins again. I threw the cloak over my shoulders, went to the bow and saw that the wind was blowing in the opposite direction to the one we had sailed in on.

I ordered my men to run up the sail, to take their places at the oars and to turn the prow seaward. I unsheathed my glorious bronze sword and sliced the hawser in two with a single blow. Perimedes and Eurylochus moved to man the steering oar. My ship left the shelter of the rocky shore and took to the open sea, advancing swiftly under a billowing sail.

We travelled all night, riding the foaming current of the great river Ocean, the next day as well and then the night after that. As time passed, the air became milder, the waves relaxed into long curved lines, light filtered through the clouds and finally the sun appeared, dazzling us with blinding reflections and heat that finally banished death from my clenched limbs.

'What did you see?' Eurylochus asked me. 'Did you really meet the shadows of the dead?'

'I saw what I went to see. I met the unhappy souls of our fallen comrades. My mother is dead.' I could feel the tears running down my cheeks.

He didn't dare ask me anything else, seeing the pain I was in. Until evening fell. Then he started up again from where he had left off: 'Was our future revealed to you? Will we return home? Will we see our wives and children?'

His hand was clamped down hard on my arm.

'Yes, but only if you all obey me, if you do everything I order you to do. If I'm not obeyed, it will mean the ruin of the ship and of all of us. We must act as one. If only one of us were to survive, he would no longer be a man; his life would no longer have any purpose, would it? Terrible trials await us still, without a doubt. But what can rouse fear in men who have sailed the livid Ocean through the lands of eternal night, in men who have dared to question the pale heads of the dead?'

Eurylochus asked no more, but raised his eyes to the stars, to the bear that guides the way north – she was behind us. He seemed deeply discouraged. He had certainly expected a blow-by-blow telling of what had happened after I'd been swallowed into the Underworld.

I simply couldn't give him what he wanted. It was too painful for me to dwell on what I'd experienced – I could not bring myself to relive that world of death. All I told him was to steer straight until we reached the inlet to the inner sea. From there we would begin our journey home.

My days and my nights were filled with the trials that awaited us. I dreaded the thought of arriving at the island of Trinacria, finding the pastures of the Sun who sees all from above. Would we be able to resist our hunger? Would I be able to bend destiny? 'Late and broken' were the words that sounded continuously in my heart.

We sailed east for many days and I continued to hope that we would reach a point where the world of the impossible would give way to familiar places, recognizable lands. I longed to find my goddess again. Would I hear her voice anew, would she guide and protect me?

I still hadn't understood how vast that world was.

It was quite early one morning, while I still slept at the stern under my cloak, when Perimedes' hand roused me from slumber: '*Wanax*, there's something strange going on. I can't understand it. Look!'

I got up and walked to the ship's rail. 'I don't understand,' I replied. 'What is it?'

'Look at what's happening,' he said. 'There's no starboard wind, none at all. The sea is calm. And yet the ship is being dragged in the opposite direction. Even if I hold the steering oar fully to the left, it doesn't matter. I cannot oppose whatever's pulling at us.'

It was true. An unyielding force, as if a strong crosswind were at work.

I was determined to thwart it and stay on course. I gave my men orders to drop all oars into the water on the right side of the ship and row with all they had on the left side. A futile effort: it was impossible to change course.

'Look!' said Perimedes again. 'Smoke!'

I felt a sense of growing presentiment. Could the smoke be coming from Circe's house? We were soon to find out that it was. The outline of an island we knew well appeared distinctly at a short distance from the promontory where we'd first landed. That mysterious force was dragging us all the way to the port where we had once moored the ship and, as we drew closer and closer, I saw her.

She was standing on the height overlooking the port and was holding out her arms. It looked like she was calling us in. We manoeuvred stern-first into port, the way we chose to approach the shore whenever possible so we'd be ready to head back out to the open sea at a moment's notice.

I jumped onto dry land and at that same instant Circe turned her back to me and started walking towards her house. I gave my shipmates a look. None of them seemed eager to join me.

I said: 'Men, I'm going to follow Circe. The mistress of this place has certainly called us back to her island for an important reason and I must discover what it is. In the meantime, stock the ship with water and go hunting. Cook the meat and smoke it so that it will last longer. The rest of you will check the ship plank by plank to make sure no damage was suffered during our journey to the mouth of Hades. When all your work has been completed, search for Elpenor's body and place it on the pyre. Raise a large mound over his ashes, plunge his oar into it deeply, as he asked me to do, and make ritual offerings to his spirit.'

The men all set to work as I started down the same path I'd followed the first time we'd landed there, the path that led to the home of the lady of the island. Circe ran out to greet me and wrapped her arms around me, pulling me close.

'Did you call up the shadows of the dead as I bid you?' she whispered. 'Did you meet the spirit of the Theban prophet?'

'I did,' I replied.

She released me and looked into my eyes, satisfied that I had told her the truth. 'I never thought that you would succeed. Or that you would return,' she said.

'And yet you urged me to go . . .'

'I thought that if there was a single man in the world capable of succeeding, it would be you. I don't want to know what Tiresias told you.'

'Then why drag my ship back to your island? We had already said our farewells, and I never thought I'd see you again.'

'Because there is a thought that obsesses you, a thought that won't give you peace. And I know that I alone can help you understand why.'

I wasn't expecting such words. My mind was confused. I suddenly feared, no, I was certain, that I'd dreamed up everything; that I'd never left her island, or perhaps never even left Ithaca. But then I looked around: there were trees, there was a house, there were clouds in the sky and butterflies on the flowers, and food on the table, and wine. And a woman of resplendent beauty standing in front of me.

She took me by the hand and led me to her bed. It was no longer perched on the branches of a tree with big white flowers, nor did it stand on a floor of red stone. There were soft carpets everywhere and the big bed lay upon them. It had neither feet nor a frame, but was soft, woollen, covered with linen and big pillows.

'Make love to me,' she said as she stepped out of her gown.

I was no longer in control of myself. And she hadn't even touched me with her stick! She embraced me, lay on top of me, she pulled me into a whirlwind, plunged me into an abyss, held me in her thrall amid the clouds of the sky. We went on making love until evening fell. I fell asleep in her arms and when I opened my eyes again it was night.

'Eat,' she said. And there before me was a table heaped with bread, honey, fruit. Time went by. 'Are you tired?' she asked me.

'No.'

'Good. Now that you've eaten, prepare yourself to take a journey. With me.'

I was lost again in her look, her smell, her hands, so long and slender. 'A journey? Where?'

'You'll see. Get up.'

The wind rose, the leaves rustled on the trees and then the wood, the meadows, the stream, everything disappeared. We were on the battlefield. Behind us the camp and the ships, before us the city, the walls, the towers. The Skaian Gate! Chills and acute pain were what I felt.

'Where are you?' I whispered.

'With you. Remember? That night you entered the walls of Troy for a second time, looking in every way like a Trojan warrior, but with a long rope coiled up, hidden in the inside of your shield. A clever scheme . . .'

'It's not true.'

'No? Come. I'll show you.' The wind that had carried off Circe's house, the entire island with its woods and stream, was now blowing even harder, pushing clouds of dust down the deserted streets of Troy.

'Can't you see your footprints in the dust? Only you walk that way.'

'It's not me.'

'You know very well it is. You just wanted to forget and you've succeeded. There you are, in front of the ramp. That's where you agreed to meet Diomedes. He entered from a side gate on the northern wall. There he is, dressed as a Trojan as well. We're almost at the highest point of the citadel. Down there is Priam's palace. The sanctuary is this way. Can you see it? That's you, dropping from the roof on a rope. You climbed up on the side where the colonnade is, where the guards couldn't see you.'

I was split in two. I was the warrior lowering himself into the sanctuary and I was the vagabond observing the scene alongside Circe. She started to speak again and her voice was strange, distorted, because, I realized, I was hearing her from far away and long ago.

'Look, you're coming out on the rooftop . . . And now you're using the rope to lower something to the ground . . . Diomedes is grabbing it. You know what it is, don't you?'

I did not answer.

'You do know, Odysseus, you know very well. It is the Palladion, the statue of Athena that makes the city that possesses her invincible. You are carrying her off so that Troy can be defeated and destroyed.'

I turned towards Circe and the metallic light in her eyes froze me. Her look was like a slashing sword. It was she who was having visions, *now I am certain, those rapacious eyes were seeking out* what I was not capable of seeing.

'I wanted to go home,' I said in a low voice.

'And they wanted to survive.'

'The strongest wins. That's the law.'

'Or is it the most crafty? Now you know why Athena won't speak to you any more.' Her words pierced me like a dagger of ice. 'You committed a sacrilege against her by profaning her image.'

I shook my head incredulously. Part of me did not want to believe what the other part of me was affirming: 'The night of the massacre I saw with my own eyes that Diomedes was running from the sanctuary. I remember it well – he was carrying something close to his chest.'

'And from that moment on, you talked yourself into believing that it was he who had profaned the sanctuary, ignoring what you knew you had done. Forgetting, you became oblivious to your sacrilege.'

A thunderbolt exploded over our heads and we were back on the island, standing in front of each other in the middle of the night, listening to the silence.

Circe stared into my eyes again with tremendous power. No one could resist her.

'Now you know. Don't forget what has been revealed to you. Tomorrow you will set off again on your voyage. More trials await you. Any of them can destroy you. You will reach the rocks of the Sirens. Their song is gentle and very sweet, but it carries death.'

'I'm not afraid of any rocks. I've come back from the mouth of Hades.'

'It's not the rocks that can destroy a man like you.'

'What, then?'

'The truth.'

'Which truth?'

'The one that can kill you.'

In the bottomless silence that surrounded me, I heard the shrieks of a griffin: the sun was about to rise.

Circe spoke again: 'Then your ship, the last one remaining to you, will have to pass through the narrows. On one side and on the other deadly perils await you. You will have to decide. Whatever choice you make will mean death for your companions.'

The tears which I had been barely holding back welled up and poured, hot, from my eyes. How much more would I have to go through? How much pain, how much anguish? I had crossed the threshold of the gates of Erebus – what could be worse? Or had my daring to walk among the dead provoked even greater ire from the dark powers?

'I have nothing more to tell you.' The light in her eyes went out like a flash of lightning vanishes from the night sky, but as the glow of dawn spilled into the house, colour and life and feeling flowed back into her gaze.

'This is truly the last time, son of Laertes. When you have crossed the threshold of this house, I will never see you again, but you will remain forever in my eyes and my heart. Of all those who the sea has cast up onto these shores, of all those who audaciously landed their ships here, you are the only one I will remember in the long silence of midday in the summer, on springtime nights laden with mystery, on those sad autumn evenings when the cranes abandon their nests and fly off to distant lands, in the whistle of the winter wind that raises white foam on the waves. Only the sound of your name will live in my heart, Odysseus of the myriad thoughts, patient and fearless, small, indomitable mortal.'

She looked at me with infinite tenderness – mistress of wild beasts, enchantress, most beauteous among the women of the earth and the goddesses of the heavens. And she wept.

I LEFT WITHOUT a kiss, without a caress, mindful that I would never have the strength to go back to my shipmates had I lingered a moment longer. I crossed the threshold and began to hear the cries of the animals inhabiting that place – souls in torment. I returned to my comrades and saw that they had completed the burial of our worthy friend Elpenor, sad spirit of Hades. They had raised a high mound over his ashes and into it had plunged the oar that had been his to grip when he would sit at the rowing bench and hasten our ship on her journey to the unfaltering beat of the oarmaster's drum. Ten times we shouted his name, trusting that our voice would reach him in the nether world, land of the blind, among the pale heads. The wind carried it away, far away, over the cresting waves.

WE TURNED the prow west and a steady, stiff wind sped us on our way. Once the sail had been hoisted, the men rested, after pulling the oars on board and laying them out under the benches, along the bulwarks. Only Perimedes was sweating as he manned the steering oar, keeping the ship true to her course, even with the glare of the sun in his eyes. In the afternoon, the shadow of the sail covered him and he was able to enjoy the sea breeze. All we could see was water in every direction, no matter where we trained our gaze, but I would have been a happy man had not so many thoughts been occupying my mind. Circe's words nagged at me. I had no way of knowing when the time would come for danger to raise its foul head. How close were we to the Sirens' lair? My eyes fell upon a finely crafted wicket basket full of the combs left behind after all the honey had been squeezed out of them. Only the wax remained. An idea suddenly occurred to me: perhaps I would be able to brave the voice of truth without it killing me.

We sailed for days and nights with fair weather and a hot sun – the rigging hummed in the wind like the strings of a lyre. There were times when I told myself that Circe had certainly been mistaken, or that she had said those words to persuade me to stay with her and give up on my stubborn plan to return. This was my most ardent hope, although it didn't help to distract me from her predictions.

What tormented me the most was the notion that I had profaned the image of my goddess and that I had vexed and offended her. The very thought was poisonous to me. It made me feel completely alone and defenceless against treacherous, even deadly forces. But I had no way to go but forward. It was like when my ship was being pulled to Circe's island: I realized that I had no choice and no power to avoid any of the trials that she had foretold.

And thus one day, I can't remember which, we came within sight of a little archipelago made up of small islands. Nothing apparently grew on them, nor did they seem to be inhabited. Bluffs of bare rock, with a few bright-green pine trees. One of these was enormous. The roots snaked down through cracks in the rock, and great birds perched upon it, still as death on the gigantic branches. A distant melody, soft and unutterably sweet, drifted towards us from the cliffs steeped in the sea. Sirens! No one else could live on such barren crags in the middle of the sea. The wind, that had accompanied us so far without ever faltering, dropped all at once and anxiety flooded my heart. We passed close enough to one of those small islands for me to make out heaps of skeletons and corpses half devoured by animals and seabirds, a horrid sight! I had no doubts.

I picked up the basket with the wax and kneaded it in my fingers until it became soft and easy to shape. I was already talking to my men. 'Listen to me!' I shouted. 'The ordeal that awaits us will be terrible to endure, but it is one of the last. I've been warned by an oracle: these are the islands of the Sirens. The bones and bodies you see on those rocks belong to sailors who were drawn in by the melodious, enchanting song that no mortal can resist. They ended up dashed against the cliffs and now their bones shine white on the bottom of the sea and on these rocks. They will never see their families or their homes again.

'I will not let you run this risk. I will put this wax into your ears so that you will not hear them. But then you will have to lash me to the mast. I have to listen to their song! I have to hear everything the Sirens say. It may be crucial to knowing what awaits us. My mind may crack. I may beg you to untie me, order you, even, to loosen the ropes that bind me to the mast. You must not obey me. On the contrary, you must tighten the knots that hold me. Do not be moved by my tears or frightened by my screams, no matter how heartrending they are. My voice may change, and my face as well. Do not listen to me. Do not look at me. It won't be me you are looking at, but some dark force speaking to you through my mouth. Row, row with all your might, make the foamy sea boil, get as far away as possible and only when you recognize me again as the man I am will you untie me.'

My comrades obeyed. They allowed me to stop up their ears and then they lashed me tightly to the mast using the knots that seamen know. Inextricable. The ship continued to advance with Perimedes at the steering oar, keeping us on course. I could feel the twist in the hull in the tremor of the mast base under my feet and I could see the archipelago nearing on my right, the crags and pines rising from the frothing sea. The melody became more audible as the ship was slowed by a strong cross-current which I could sense from the increasing pressure of the mast against my back. It was a subtle, penetrating song, sweet at first but then sharpening into an intense, agonizing tone. As the voices came closer, they turned into a chorus, winding around each other like the threads that form a rope. Finally, when the giant pine tree was bending over us, the voices became a single voice.

The voice of my wife!

It was Penelope singing, among those threads of song, a melody of infinite melancholy, one I knew well: 'End the sting of nostalgia, bring him home to me!'

I did not bend. I knew it was my own heart singing and no one else; the voice of my longing to rest in the arms of my queen after so much suffering. But then the song splintered and other voices accompanied Penelope's. There was Circe, and Helen . . . and the voice of a woman I had imagined dead: poor, tortured Andromache . . . and two more voices that I would not know, and love, until much later. They were sublime. Each was clearly distinct but they joined into a single sound, something I knew was impossible. I began to understand the song: it was the song of my adventure as a man, a king, a husband, a father, a friend, a son, an enemy, a hero, a coward. It was the song of my past, present, future life . . . and what I understood was so painful that it tore shrill screams from my heart. I wanted to kill myself. I begged my companions to untie me, to loosen me from the knots that kept me bound to existence, much more than merely to the mast of my ship. *I saw myself as I am now! Now that I walk in the deep snow talking to myself to keep my soul clenched between my teeth. Now that I suffer unspeakable, cruel, infinite sorrow. Now that I taste bitterness without end nor limit . . . I who saw the pale heads, I who spoke to the ghosts of great Ajax, of Achilles, of Agamemnon, I who shed scalding tears before the grieving shadow of my mother.*

I wanted to die.

To die so completely that not even an empty image wandering around the blind world of Hades would remain of me. I wanted to be no one, nothing.

Nothing did they spare me, those beautiful, alluring voices. The sharper the dagger is, the deeper and more deadly the wound. I understood, in that extreme, wondrous song the whole meaning of the curse contained in my name.

Then my comrades unbound me.

9

'WHATEVER CHOICE YOU MAKE will mean death for your companions.' These were the first words that surfaced in my mind when my men untied the ropes that kept me lashed to the ship's mast. Circe, announcing the narrows that I would have to navigate, with equally deadly danger on both sides. Where were they? When would we meet with them? Many a narrows had I passed in my day: between fear and duty, love and honour, friendship and gain, the world of the living and the world of the dead. I'd passed between jagged cliffs, unassailable walls . . . but those awaiting me would be the most terrible. I could feel it.

The sun shone high in a clear sky. A seagull was perched on top of the mast and the wind ruffled his feathers. There were no signs left of what we'd been through. The men had taken the wax from their ears and their eyes darted out over the glittering blue waves as the wind urged the ship south. Only I felt a tremendous weight, a welling sadness that wasn't coming from nowhere. It was coming from the voices ringing inside my heart. I hadn't dreamt them; they were real.

We sailed all that day and the whole night as well, keeping the brazier alight at the stern and all eyes alert at the prow. The moon rose from the horizon as the second watch was beginning and it lit our way for a while with the wake of silver it cast on the water, before being veiled by thin clouds. It was the middle of the night when I thought I heard a slight whisper of oars and I saw, or perhaps thought I saw, a ship much larger than mine passing silently in the other direction, no more distant from us than the flight of an arrow. A dark but perfectly clear shadow, the ghost of a torn sail fluttering in the air, the white foam curling at the prow as it sliced through the waves. Then the ship was swallowed by the darkness. Who was passing in the night?

On our entire journey, we'd never crossed paths with another ship. We'd seen only wrecks, ships foundered and crashed against reefs. We had always felt alone and abandoned, as if we were navigating the sea of a strange and unreal world. Never, after crossing the wall of fog, had we found a city inhabited by men who eat bread, with a port, a market square and a sacred enclosure dedicated to the gods. Never had we seen a single emporium crowded with merchants of many races intent on selling and exchanging their wares. And I had never again felt the presence of my blue-green-eyed goddess . . . now, after what Circe had told me, I despaired of ever finding her on my path again. I mourned her and tortured myself for having lost her.

We sailed on for many a day and night without ever encountering anyone or anything. Only once, in the dark, did I see a mountain looming, edged at its top with a sinister red light. A low rumble seemed to come from deep within it and it flashed streaks of fire. My world seemed further and further away, while anguish seeped into every corner of my heart. One day, before dawn, Eurylochus turned the helm over to Euribates, one of my strong Cephalonians, and came over to me.

'You were the only one among us to hear the song of the sirens. Is it something you can tell me about?' my friend asked.

'No. I can't. Don't ask me to summon up its memory. I'm trying to banish it from my mind because it stops me from thinking, from deciding, from hoping. All I can tell you is that their song was very sweet. Sweet enough to drive you mad with the cruelty of its words. A contradiction that was, that is, insufferable. Heart-breaking. The only hope I still hold is that it wasn't true . . . or that it wasn't the only truth.

'Listen to me, comrade. I believe that once we reach familiar waters, everything will change. We will win back the power to bend fate, to ward off bad omens with the force of our minds and our arms. Here, in this strange world we've stumbled into, everything is difficult, harsh, hostile. I'm afraid that terrible trials may still lie before us, but you must help me. If, when it comes time for the final test, you support me and convince the others to obey me, perhaps we can still save ourselves. We'll finally be able to point the prow east, towards home, and stay on course. The ship will obey the helm and the oars, distances will let themselves be measured and we'll be able to count the days that separate us from land. From our land.'

Eurylochus regarded me with an imperceptible scowl, but he didn't say a word. Maybe he thought I'd gone mad. Perhaps not even my faithful friend believed in me any more. This thought wounded me but I never stopped seeking out his help. Days went by. Often we would sit talking, exchanging memories. Stories of when we were children and free to roam through the forests and swim in the sea. 'Do you remember our first voyage to the mainland?' I asked him.

He did. We recollected the days and the hours, our songs, our words, our dreams. It helped to remind us that we were alive and real, that we could think of the future, that we would win in the end and that, at the end of our long journey, we would return to our world. We would go back to the life we'd had before we left for war.

Eurylochus' voice interrupted my thoughts: 'Look! Land!'

I looked at the sea instead because I'd realized that our speed was increasing although the wind was not getting stronger. My heart jumped in my chest. Danger!

The voice of Sinon rained down on us from the top of the mast: 'Whirlpool on the right! Reefs on the left!'

'It's happening,' I thought. What Circe had predicted. Unavoidable. Whatever decision I made I would lose my companions. How many of them? This I did not know. I ran to the bow and shouted: 'Haul in the sail! Man the oars!'

Then I trained my eyes forward: the crashing sea was

wedging itself, as impetuously as a river in flood, between the two horns of the strait. Any attempt to override the current I felt tugging at the ship was unthinkable. The whirlpool to the right was created by an enormous flow of water smashing into a promontory. The crags on the left jutted out around a cave whose curved vault we could see emerging from the sea.

'Give orders for the prow to hold to the centre!' said Eurylochus.

'No,' I answered. 'If we stay in the middle we'll be sucked into the whirlpool and the ship will be swallowed up with everything in it. We'll bear as far left as possible without grazing the reefs. That won't be easy but if we try to stay in the centre it'll be the end of us all.'

'Helm right! Left oars dead in the water, right oars at full force!' I shouted to make myself heard over the roar of the whirlpool and of the waves pounding at the reef, seething with foam. The men all pitched in to execute the manoeuvre. Sinon scrambled down from the mast and went to his shipmates' aid at his oar. The ship began to heel left under the thrust of the oars and the helm as my comrades on the right side bent their backs, rowing with all their might, but then the turbulent current drew us in towards the reefs and the cave. The mouth of the cave was hidden behind a curtain of spray and mist and we couldn't easily make it out, but we stayed on course because the roaring vortex on our right terrified us even more.

We were enveloped all at once by a dense cloud: the water was everywhere, blinding us. I suddenly heard blood-curdling screams as enormous tentacles lashed at the ship's deck and snapped several of the oars in two. I saw my shrieking comrades writhing and twisting, tossed high above our heads, before they disappeared. Their shouts were louder than the crashing of the breakers, their desperate pleas for help were swallowed by the mouth of the cavern, bristling with points as jagged and sharp as the teeth of any monster. Then the force of the current prevailed over the surge and, roaring, it dragged us away and out of the straits. When the thick wall of foam and spray had dispersed, the ship finally slowed its course and we found ourselves in the open sea. The bucking waves calmed as we drew away from the straits. Towards sunset we stopped in the middle of nowhere.

Eurylochus' voice shook me out of my dazed state: 'We lost six men.'

'What was it?' I asked as if I was just waking from a nightmare. I didn't recognize my own voice.

'A . . . monster,' replied Eurylochus. 'It was a monster with seven heads.'

I said nothing. I walked down my ship, counting the empty places: Sinon . . . Polites . . . Eurynomus . . . Leucippus . . . Kresilas . . . Anticlus. I was shattered, but I would not let it show. They were watching me, my men: panting, crushed by exhaustion, terror, grief. My tears mixed with the salty drops of sea on my face.

'Men!' I shouted. 'We have overcome a dreadful trial! We have survived the invincible current, the ravenous vortex, the massacring monster! We have lost six brave companions, but they will live on in our hearts. We will weep for them when we touch land and when we return home we will raise mounds in their honour, one for each man on his island of origin. Their memory will never be lost. Poets and singers will tell of their adventures and their sacrifice. Their faces, their smiles, their voices will be forever with us. Once again, men, we have not allowed the forces of these terrible places to take the upper hand.

'I was forced to make a decision that broke my heart. A choice between risking the lives of our men or losing the whole ship with everyone on it. Their sacrifice has allowed us to live! And now there is one thing we can be sure of – only one final test awaits us. Then, men, we will return home. We will embrace our wives and our children, we will see the land where we were born, we'll watch as smoke rises from the rooftops of our homes.

'Now, establish a new order on the rowing benches, space

yourselves out. Replace the broken and damaged oars. We'll make new ones when we find land and trees. We will carve them with the bronze of our swords.

'Only this I still ask of you – obey me, no matter what I order you to do or prohibit you from doing. Obey me and I will take you home! I swear it on the head of the son I haven't seen since he was an infant, and on everything I hold most dear and precious. Your endeavours will be glorified for centuries to come, and all those who see you or, many long years from now, come upon your tombs, will pause, and say: "This was one of the comrades of Odysseus, son of Laertes, the destroyer of cities. He survived monsters and tempests, the savage cyclops, unimaginable ordeals. He made it all the way to the threshold of implacable Hades, alive, and he never forgot his homeland."

'And now, loose the sail!'

I let out the triple war cry of the kings of Ithaca and the ship, thrust by the wind, moved out, solid and quick, her bow ploughing the blue swell of the sea that never sleeps.

WE SAILED around in a wide circle on the current that was still carrying us, then struck out south, turning west and then north again. We were headed to the land of Trinacria where we would find the herds of Helios, the Sun who sees all from above, grazing. That was what Circe had foretold and it was there that we would face our last trial.

We landed in a beautiful bay where a spring of clear water flowed. The first thing we did when we went ashore was to celebrate funeral rites for the companions we'd lost. They would thus be free to join the other comrades we'd lost in battle or in our long wanderings and, sad as they must be, they would none-theless find company in that blind and melancholy world and perhaps even a bit of consolation.

When the sun had set, we built a fire and gathered around it to eat and to partake in the wine that cheered our hearts. We had just enough wine left for this last meal together, the last of all the jars Circe had filled and stowed aboard. We lingered there on the shore until late that night, speaking in low voices, and I wondered whether a god could be watching the glow of our small fire from the height of the heavens. Might he not even decide to help us? I poured an offering to my goddess, because I could not stop myself from searching her out. When weariness descended on my eyes and I felt the desire for sleep, I lay down on my cloak and dozed off with a heavy heart, because I had no idea when my tribulations would end.

The next morning the sun awoke us as it rose from behind the hills, but very soon a stormy cloud advancing from the south obscured it. At first, the warm air drew the dampness of the night from our limbs, but then, as the hours passed, the wind grew stronger and we had to run to the ship and push her to the shelter of a sea cave, where we managed to moor her. We slept on the ship as the wind raged and howled all that night. Only towards morning did it begin to die down, although strong, hot gusts kept blowing from the south for days, suffocating us. I understood that the relentless wind, blowing contrary to the direction of our destination, was the lethal sign of our last test. A god was imprisoning us on that land. We could not even have escaped by rowing the ship out. We were down six strong rowers and without them our strength could not hold out – the southerly Auster would drive us back to land.

After ten days of this, our food stores ran out. Luckily, the fresh spring was providing us with plenty of cold, clear water. We would even go for dips at times to cool ourselves off, but no sooner were we out when the heat overwhelmed us again. As the days passed, I noticed that the spring water had begun to diminish and that the current was slowing; soon we had to start filling the jars to ensure our supply.

In the mornings and towards evening, when the heat abated, some of us would walk along the shore in search of fish, crabs and shrimp, while others went inland to gather roots, fruit, berries and tubers or to lay traps for birds, but they always came back with meagre pickings. As the days and nights passed, our bodies became leaner. The muscles which had made our blows in battle so lethal and our oars so powerful were wasting. By day we roamed the desolate land like ghosts, at night the screaming wind kept us from sleeping. Then one morning, just before dawn, we heard the sound of bells in the dark and before long a whole herd of cattle and gigantic bulls with long curved horns appeared. But there was no herdsman.

There it was, the final test! The herd of the Sun. Untouchable. Deadly.

Some of the men were already getting up and closing in on the mysterious creatures. We were all famished. Alarmed, I stopped them and woke all the others. I spoke as they gathered around me: 'Everything that Circe predicted has happened: we have encountered the Sirens and the fatal straits, the monster and the maelstrom. We've survived, although we have had terrible losses. If these prophecies of the *wanaxa* of that remote island have turned out to be true, you can be sure that this last ordeal will prove to be as terrible as she foretold. It is the last, but most dreadful.

'Another man has warned us as well, in no less dire terms. When I summoned the prophet Tiresias from Hades, he told me that if we so much as lay our hands on these animals, who are sacred to the god who sees all from above, death for us all, and the destruction of our ship, will be the consequence.'

I did not have to add anything else. They seemed to accept my words, but Eurylochus exhorted them as well: '*Wanax* Odysseus, our king, has revealed the truth to us. If the Theban prophet, the blind man who once saw, and still sees, what is invisible to other mortals, announced our ruin and that of our ship if we touch these animals, it means that if we stay away from them, we will be saved. It is said that no man can resist hunger's terrible pangs, but we must.'

'Search everywhere for asphodel bulbs and eat them. That will ease the cramping of your stomachs,' I said. 'They'll give you no sustenance but at least you won't suffer. The wind will change direction. It may happen just a moment before our deaths, but it will change, and call us back from the gates of Hades. We will set sail again. Our ship will drag nets that will fill with fish. We will roast them on the brazier at the stern and we will regain our strength. Nothing and no one will be able to stop us. We will point the prow east and we will make it back home! I swear it. You'll tell your grandchildren one day about what you went through . . . your extraordinary adventures, your heroic perseverance, and they will listen enchanted. Resist, my comrades, friends, brothers! Do not allow your spirits to be shaken! The strongest among you will help the weakest, the bravest will encourage the fearful and console those who weep. No one will be left to die, no one will be left alone. All of us, all together, will cross the threshold of the impossible on our ship and we will find our sea, our sky, our horizon.'

They listened with attentive expressions but their eyes betrayed wariness. I could not understand what they were feeling at that moment, what was going through their hearts. But they obeyed me. They did not approach the herd and I fervently hoped that the animals would leave as quickly as they had un-expectedly appeared. Instead they stayed. They never moved, but grazed now and then on the scraggly shrubs growing between the rocks and the sand. They never lay down to rest. Their imposing, massive bulks never lessened, as if they were feeding every day on the lush, tender grass of a fertile meadow.

I tried to think of a way of scaring them off, of chasing them out of sight of my men who were dying of hunger, but I didn't want to touch them or hurt them. I didn't know how far the prophecy went. How jealous was the god of his herd? How closely was he watching? Would he tolerate the approach of a mortal?

Days passed thus, and nights. There were no fish left in the sea, no bulbs in the ground, there was no more water from the spring and the hot sky sparkled like a bowl of bronze. I was desperate enough to drag myself to the top of a promontory overlooking the sea. My face turned to the blinding globe, I cried out: 'God who sees all, look at me now! I'm here on the island where your herd is grazing. It was not our will to land here. The current that carried us was to blame, the wind that drove us on. We have suffered all that men can suffer, let us leave! We've shown our respect, but we're dying! Extinguish your fire, curb your torrid wind, send us rain, drive away your cattle . . . let the wind blow in our favour! I beg you! I implore you! Listen to me! Heed my words!' I burst into tears, fell to my knees and pounded my head on a sharp stone until blood spurted from my forehead. I offered him my own blood.

I had no more tears. My voice was gone. I was stripped of strength.

I began walking, to return to my men, but my suffering was destined to never end. What I saw as I approached cut me like the blade of a sword. The men had attacked the herd. They had brought down two animals and there they were, sitting around a fire, devouring the meat. From their flesh-stripped carcasses I heard lowing so loud and deep it sounded like thunder. The sound was deafening . . . or was I merely imagining it?

My eyes spun around and I saw Eurylochus dragging himself up the craggy hillside. He was wounded. I ran to his side.

'It all happened so fast that I couldn't stop them. They flew at me, knocked me down, kicked me, brandished their naked swords. They seemed possessed by demons. The beasts did not move a single step – they simply collapsed to the ground under the men's blows. I shouted at them to abstain from eating the meat, in the hope that the god would spare them. In vain. It was Perimedes who answered me, with a crazed laugh: "At least we'll die with our stomachs full!" and that's when I gave up. Forgive me, forgive me!' He was sobbing.

I helped him to his feet. His face and his right arm were bleeding. He had fought them. To no avail.

My shipmates feasted all night long, gorging themselves on

the meat. Eurylochus himself got up at one point and went close to the fire.

'Stop,' I told him. 'Don't go.'

'What difference does it make any more?' he asked, and snatched a piece of meat out of the flames, sinking his teeth into it greedily.

'You'll see,' said my heart, but no word issued from the shelter of my teeth.

I prayed again to my goddess, still hoping, forever hoping, that she could hear me. I called her name, I implored her to give me a sign of her presence. Nothing. I went aboard my ship and stretched out under the rowing benches, wrapping myself in my cloak. Finally, exhausted with fatigue and hunger, overwhelmed by the feelings crowding my heart, I fell asleep.

The sea breeze and a cold chill awoke me. The wind had picked up and the sail was flapping and smacking the mast. My shipmates were waking as well. They gathered up their cloaks and filed silently aboard the ship, one after another with heads hanging low. The herd was gone. All that remained were the two carcasses, jaws agape in mocking grins. I waited until they were sitting at the rowing benches before I walked to the prow and shouted at the top of my voice: 'Why? Why?'

A fish, a small tuna, flipped onto the aft desk as I was casting off the moorings. Its tail and fins were wriggling as it tried to jump back into the sea. I skewered it on my sword, gutted it and put it to roast on the brazier. I sat in a corner and ate it all myself without offering even a bite to my men. I did not open my mouth for days and days. Eurylochus took care of governing the ship, giving orders and appointing shifts. Everything seemed to be going well: the wind was stiff and steady, blowing east. Sailing was a pleasure, but I knew that the end was near, I could feel it. Tiresias' words echoed in my ears: 'I predict ruin for your ship and your shipmates.'

After six days of navigation and of silence, the storm blew in.

A cloud as vast and dark as the sea itself galloped at us,

blotting out the sun almost instantly, then a bolt of lightning tore through the black sky, flashing on the horizon like an enormous fire arrow. Thunder crashed above us and a gale whipped up the sea, raising huge, roaring waves tipped with livid foam. The ship was struck violently on its side and listed so sharply that it nearly overturned, but then swung upright and began to ride the waves, plunging into sudden vortexes and swiftly climbing sheer walls of dark water. The men were flung from one side to the other, fore and aft. Some, thrown against the benches and flanks by the terrible force of the storm, their limbs shattered, laboured to drag themselves across the bilge. The hull groaned, twisting from one end to the other like a wounded cetacean. I rushed to reach the helm, gripping the rail tight as I made my way, to go to Perimedes' aid.

'Will we make it, *wanax*?' he shouted to make himself heard over the winds that carried away his words. 'We'll make it, won't we?'

'We will make it, helmsman!' I replied, shouting even louder. 'We'll make it as we always have. There's no storm that can sink us!'

No question could have been more foolish, and yet I understood what my helmsman was trying to tell me. He wanted me to know that he had disobeyed me out of desperation, like all his comrades, that exhaustion had done them in, but that I was still his king and the high commander of the ship, and that he would go all the way to Hades with me, braving monsters, demons, gods and tempests.

A wave as high as a mountain struck the left side of the ship. It swept away the benches and crashed into the mast, which collapsed onto Antiphus' head, killing him. It slammed down into the keel, snapping the beam in two and snatching away Perimedes who was still shouting my name. It plunged straight into the heart of the hurricane, dragging my helmsman with it, where the harpies, monsters of windstorms, were waiting to tear into him with their talons. The ship's prow flooded with water and sank, dragged down by the gold and silver of Troy – accursed plunder! I saw nothing, I had no sense of where I was, I was swallowed into the depths and tossed out again without understanding why, until I realized that I was clinging to a piece of the mast of my ship. I had heard her cry out as she was going down, cracked in two. That's right, because ships have a soul and a voice and when they sink they salute their commander with a last mournful wail before dying.

10

I DO NOT KNOW how long I spent at the mercy of the waves and the wind, how many blinding bolts struck the sea around me. I was enveloped in terror and burning anguish, knowing that I had lost all my comrades. I had watched as my perfect ship, in splinters, sank into the abyss. There was nothing around me but darkness. My salt-scorched eyes could no longer distinguish anything but masses of water surging over me, one after another, with roaring crashes. Water was everywhere outside and inside me: it penetrated into my mouth and nostrils, it cut off my breath. I was sure at every moment that I was drowning and that, sucked into the sea's deep gyres, I was on my way to joining my shipmates in the abyss.

All at once, I saw a piece of the ship's keel beam surfacing near me and I tied it to the mast with one of the leather stays still attached to it. Then I hoisted myself up onto that unexpected refuge and hung on to it with all my strength. I would not give up, would not surrender to the cruel blue god, my ruthless enemy. He'd have to come out of the sea himself to get me.

Perhaps the god heard my challenge because I soon realized that the current was heading towards the narrows where I had lost six of my men and this time it was dragging me into the whirlpool. This certainly meant the end for me. The fast current caught the mast and the beam that I still rode, clinging to them for dear life, and began spinning me faster and faster, closer and closer to the centre of the vortex. The water pulled at me with such force and speed that I could see all the way down to the black sand of the sea bottom. At any moment I would be dashed into the maelstrom and would become, after all my struggles, food for the fish.

And yet, as I was about to close my eyes and prepare for the end, I spotted a branch, belonging to an age-old fig tree, that was stretching out over the whirlpool. Just as the abyss was about to suck me into its depths, I rose to my feet on the keel beam and made a leap. I managed to catch the branch. It cracked. I grabbed the one next to it, obstinate in my unwillingness to leave this life. From there I tried to heave myself up onto a bigger branch but my muscles were cramping and my strength was going. I looked beneath me to see that the whirlpool had closed up. The water reversed its current and the keel beam of my ship was spat to the surface. I let myself drop and swam with desperate force until I could grab the mast and the stay of entwined leather. I pulled myself up until I was sitting astride it and seized the broken fig-tree branch that had fallen with me, using it as an oar, following the current that now, since its direction had reversed, was pushing me into the open sea.

Every time the sea let me catch my breath I cried out for help. I shouted to men, to gods, to monsters. I don't know why but I still hoped that my goddess could make out my voice in the din of the tempest; that she would hear me and that the heart in her chest would be moved to help me.

Finally, after days and nights, a ray of sun broke through the clouds.

All around me the sea extended all the way to the horizon. Infinite, smooth. I saw nothing but water, and the wind, once again, was driving me away from my home. I don't know how I managed to keep on top of the mast. I was cold, hungry, thirsty, there was not a muscle in my body that wasn't hurting, but I was sitting on a piece of the ship which had faced so many dangers with me, soaked with the sweat of my comrades. I would die before I left her.

The current and the wind took over and pushed me on day after day. I was caked with salt and I couldn't even keep my eyes open any more. The sun burned my back and my shoulders and covered them with blisters. I was skin and bones. I was sure that my time had come. I was about to die. The blue god had spared me only so he could inflict a slower and more painful death. I began to let myself go.

WHEN I OPENED my eyes it was dark. I thought I was in Hades but my hands were touching sand and pebbles, my nostrils smelled the fragrance of earth.

I sat and then struggled to get to my feet. I was barely able to stand. I turned my back to the sea and could not believe what I was seeing: lush plants laden with ripe fruit, fruits that I'd never seen in my whole life. I ate and drank until I was no longer thirsty or hungry. Then I collapsed, exhausted, and fell into a deep sleep.

The rays of the sun woke me. The reflections of the water were dancing on the leaves of the trees looming over my head. A brightly feathered bird looked over curiously as he hopped along the shore, a glossy green serpent slipped slowly down the rough bark of a centuries-old tree. Where was I? In a place inhabited by men who eat bread or in a lawless, uncultivated land without villages or cities?

The sea lapped at my feet with a long, warm caress. That same dreadful, thousand-souled monster, ruthless and frothing, that had broken my ship and killed all my comrades.

The memory of them surged into my mind, their faces, their hands grasping the handles of their oars or their spears, men of infinite resources, valiant warriors, bold sailors, tireless. I had taken six hundred of them with me on twelve ships when I was leaving Troy and I would never bring a single one of them back home with me, if I ever returned myself. I would have no booty to divide up among the families who had lost their sons. I had nothing to offer to their memory. All I could do was shout out their names. I called out to them in a powerful voice so they could hear me all the way in the dark house of Hades, then I pushed the keel beam tied to its mast out to sea, my only gift for the men snatched away by the storm. I watched for a long time as it drifted away.

I built myself a shelter for the night using the knife that was still buckled to my belt, an excellent bronze blade crafted by a smith of Corinth for my father. I cut the trunks of young trees and made stakes to drive into the ground, and I used palm branches to make a roof. I even made a small door so that wild animals could not enter while I slept.

The next day I set out to learn what I could about this place, walking along the coastline so I would never lose sight of the sea. When darkness overtook me, I spent the night in the shelter of a rock with my knife at my side, ready to jump to my feet if I had to. Years of war had taught me to feel the slightest movement of the air. I saw nothing recognizable about that place – it was the same sensation I'd had on Circe's island and in the land of the cyclopes. The sea, I guessed, had carried me far, far west, perhaps not far from the point where it mixes with the waters of the river Ocean.

I walked on for many hours but my exploration was still not complete. I stopped to light a fire and to eat some of the numerous birds' eggs I'd found at the edge of the forest. I was getting stronger, but with every step I took one thing became clear to me: I would never get over the loss of all my men. *No joy, perhaps not even embracing Penelope and Telemachus, could ease the distress I felt, that deep sorrow that still pains me today. The words of Laertes would never leave me: 'A king is the father of his people.'*

The next day I crossed the northernmost area, where I found wild rabbits and tubers, along with fruits and nuts of different kinds that I'd never seen before. I wouldn't die of hunger. I would cut myself a fishing pole, and make a line by braiding my own hair. The curved thorns of a plant I'd found with beautiful yellow flowers could be used as hooks. I would craft a bow for hunting from a pliant branch. Plant fibres could be stripped and twisted to fashion a bowstring and I could make arrows by sharpening the slim, hard reeds that grew on the shore with my knife. I spent the second night and the third in makeshift shelters: caves and crevices that I happened across. I never saw a hut or any object crafted by human hands, I never met a woman or a man. Nonetheless, every now and then, I sensed an invisible presence as if someone were watching me. It wasn't my goddess, surely. I didn't get that sensation of a chill that made me shiver.

How would I be able to build a boat so I could set out to sea again? Certainly not with my knife alone. I needed something more like an axe or a saw. Difficult, but not impossible. The only thing I wasn't lacking was time.

At the end of my journey, as the sun was setting on the fourth day, I ran across the shack I'd made. In my heart I had hoped that that would never happen. I'd hoped that I was on part of a larger land mass, not a prison surrounded by the sea. I had met no one on my travels and had seen no trace of a human presence, but I wasn't ready to give up and I decided I would go inland to see if there were any inhabitants to be found. In the following days I scoured the island from different directions. I saw no trails that had not been made by animals, no villages, no buildings of any kind. Not a human footprint.

I was alone.

That had never happened to me before, in my whole life.

Those days taught me that it is better to face dangers, worries, even suffering, while surrounded by friends and comrades, than accept the inertia and tedium of complete solitude. At that point, I had no one but myself to count on, on my strength and on my wits. I would have to find a way to build a boat, load it with food and drinking water and then wait for a westerly wind to take me home. It was said that the blue god would go off to the land of the dark faces when the weather worsened in our lands and on our seas. I would have to decide which was the greater danger, taking to the sea alone or risking Poseidon's wrath once again.

Perhaps fortune, or Fate, or my goddess, would guide a ship to the island where I found myself . . . I would ask to be taken on board, I could offer water to drink, food and nourishing plants in exchange. But I'd never sighted another ship since I had crossed the wall of fog – I'd only ever seen the ghost of one and I wasn't even sure of that. In any case, I would not sit and wait, *I know what it means to have no one to talk to*. One way or another, I'd go to sea.

SOME TIME LATER, returning to my shelter after having visited the last unexplored part of the island, I found the shack almost destroyed. The palm branches were scattered everywhere, only the bare stakes remained. And yet there had been no strong wind or other signs of a storm. The weather was fine, it always was; the sun shone but it didn't burn. It had only rained once, at night. I'd listened to the raindrops pattering on the palm leaves, but I hadn't got wet at all. As I was falling asleep I felt like I was in my own bed among the olive branches with Penelope, under the covers smelling of sweet lavender, listening to the rain on the roof.

It must have been some animal.

I rebuilt my little house, tying the branches to the stakes more securely and fixing the stakes to poles which I drove deeper into the ground. Then I turned my attention to making a bow and some arrows, along with a rough quiver made of wicker, and a bag to wear on my shoulder, fashioned from braided palm leaves. I was ready to go hunting and I set out for my first foray, which lasted a whole day. I returned that evening with a rabbit, one of those birds with the garish feathers and long tails, and three stork's eggs. They could have been the makings of a small banquet, but I had no wine, no bread, no olive oil, nor anyone with whom to exchange a word.

Hard not to cry.

I don't know why, but I had taken to counting the days I spent on the island by making cuts in the bark of a wild fig tree. A milky fluid seeped out, and after a day or two, a small scar was formed: one, two, three, four . . . Fifty-three.

I was getting used to being alone. Sometimes, when the sea was rough, I went up on a rocky promontory and shouted to be heard over the crashing of the breakers; other times I ran along the beach and scared seabirds into flight. I'd made myself a sling and I'd learned to use it well. I had plenty of time to practise. When the sea was flat, I tossed white stones on the surface of the water, counted the skips and calculated the distance. None of those activities amused me or gave me pleasure, but they quietened my incessant brooding and shut out the thousands of images of my past life. The sounds, the screams, the clamour, the rustling. The whispers. A mortal silence would descend into my heart, while everything around me was alive and had a voice, noise, music, colour, light.

Days afterward, I discovered that the little shack I'd built had been wrecked again. But this time . . . there were footprints on the sandy soil. Why now and not then? What I saw upset me and countless thoughts went through my mind. I followed the prints: they were small and quite distinct, left by the bare feet of a boy or a young woman. They vanished when they got to the smooth, sparkling beach. When I lifted my eyes, I saw a figure sitting on a flat black stone that emerged from the sea where the waves died out. But all I could see was a black silhouette against the light of the sun.

I approached slowly, a hand on the hilt of my knife.

A woman. A marvellous beauty, golden hair, eyes the colour of the sea. The veil that covered her was liquid as water, shiny as the sun.

'Why are you destroying my house? I have no other shelter.'

'Don't you want to know who I am?' Her voice was like a girl's, fresh and silvery.

'No mortal woman could find herself in a place like this, alone on a wild island at the ends of the earth, looking as perfect as a flower in its first bloom.'

'You know how to recognize a goddess, then.'

'How long have you been watching me?'

'Since you arrived.'

'Why, *wanaxa*, have you not appeared to me before?'

She smiled. 'When you got here you were horrible to look at, thin and dirty. I waited until you had your strength back and I could see whether you were handsome or not.'

'What about you? Are you what I see or is it a trick?'

'I've chosen this semblance to be pleasing to you. I'll be thus for as long as you're with me.'

'I beg you, *wanaxa* of this land, don't mock me, for I have suffered long and hard, on land and at sea.' I did not tell her that a powerful god was persecuting me – she didn't need a new reason to reject me.

'I am Calypso, daughter of Atlas, and I inherited this island from my father. And you are Odysseus, king of Ithaca, destroyer of cities. Your fame has reached this remote land.'

She descended from the gleaming black stone and walked towards me. The waves that were ebbing and flowing wet the hem of her gown. She took me by the hand and led me to a place I had never seen, although I was sure I'd explored every part of the island.

It was a cave in a small promontory jutting into the sea. Above the cave grew plants of all kinds, many of them blossoming in yellow, pink, white and bright-red flowers. The branches cascaded down all around the entrance.

'This is my house,' she said.

'This is a trick,' I replied. 'It wasn't here before. I covered every bit of this island and I never saw it.'

'It's always been here. It's you who didn't see it.'

I didn't want to contradict her. It's not good to contradict someone much more powerful than you.

She stepped in front of me and entered first. I followed her and was taken aback by the wonder of what I saw. The bottom was covered with dry sand, the rock walls shone with shades of red and ochre. A strange light fluttered all around, dancing on the walls. There was a little pool to one side with water so clear I didn't notice it until it rippled as I walked by. The rock ceiling was studded with large quartz crystals that reflected the light in myriad ways and colours. At the centre, close to the pool, a square boulder rose out of the sand. It served as a table, with wicker chairs placed around it.

'I see you receive guests,' I said.

'Never. It's only to give me the illusion that I'm not always alone here.'

I thought of Circe. What destiny had befallen these perfect, incomprehensible, immortal beings? I thought for a moment that they must be the last denizens of an ancient race that was dying or perhaps the first of a new race that hadn't yet formed.

'Is that why you brought me here? Because you want some-one to keep you company when you sit down to dinner?'

She smiled and continued to the far end of the cave. There she showed me her bedchamber. A bed of flowers. Resting there must be like lying down in a spring meadow, I thought. She took off her gown of water and sun and lay upon the flowers. I took off what was left of my own clothing and lay down next to her. At first Calypso was tender, so delicate that I could barely feel the touch of her hands, but then she became stronger, vora-cious. Her embrace was so fiery that I didn't think I could bear it. But how to slip free from the embrace of a goddess? When I entered her, penetrated her womb, I felt like I was dying, being devoured, sucked of every sap of life. I felt I'd lost my words and my sight. I'd become a part of her. I had no mind or thought, I was delirium itself. In her I melted like snow in the rays of the sun. I could not perceive the confines of my body, couldn't hear the beating of my heart. Then everything vanished.

That act of love was an act of annihilation. I understood now why Circe had wanted me in her bed instantly, and how my refusal had saved me from total slavery. But here I hadn't happened upon that youth with the sun in his hair who gave me a warning and a magical herb to make me invincible. Here I had melted, like metal in the crucible, in the embrace of Calypso, the goddess hiding on the island at the ends of the earth.

From then on I became a single thing with her. I don't know if it was love or what it was. I only know that the attraction between us was so strong, so intense, that it verged on violence. For years she was my only desire, my only obsession; and I was that for her. I had been transformed: never had I been so strong, so acute in perceiving what was happening around me. The air I breathed, the smell of the island – the flowers, the sea, the grass, the sand, the forest – was the scent of her. She was the island and the sky above it and the sea that embraced it. The entire island was our alcove and only sometimes did we make love in the cave, on the bed of flowers. Wherever desire seized us, the island was our bed, a drape of soft linen beneath us.

And yet I had not forgotten Penelope.

Often, when the moon rose, even while the goddess, my mistress, squeezed me between her ivory thighs, my heart escaped my panting mouth and cried out to my distant bride. When, exhausted, I would collapse onto the sand like a castaway and Calypso, naked and lunar, left me there, I would weep silent tears, turning my head towards the shadow of the night.

At times she would disappear, without a word, without a reason, vanishing like fog when the sun rises, and I would go mad. I'd search for her everywhere, run down the beach, across the forest, through the stream, shouting her name like a lunatic. When that happened I would curl up in my old shelter at night. I didn't dare search for the entrance to her cave, for I knew that I would never find it, no matter how hard I looked.

My heart turned to stone, my eyes burned, the sky and the sea grew red. The birds cawed out horrible shrieking songs.

Then, as she had gone, she reappeared. Sitting on the same

smooth stone where I'd first seen her, or strolling along the stream picking flowers, or taking a small flock of sheep to pasture, dressed as a shepherdess. She would give me a look and I was enslaved again. But as time passed, as dilated and immeasurable as time had become for me, I found a way to make her understand that there was part of me that she would never be able to conquer, a part of my heart defended by a bronze wall. A part of my heart that would never let her in. I was sitting on a reef in the middle of the sea. I had swum there and I was waiting for the moon to rise from the waves. She appeared suddenly, walking on the water.

'What are you doing here?' she asked. 'What are you thinking about?'

'Of my wife. My son. The friends I lost, those who are buried in faraway Asia and those who sleep on the bottom of the sea.'

She seemed not to understand my words and not even my thoughts. They were foreign to her nature, such feelings.

'Forget them,' was her answer. 'If you saw them again you'd be disappointed. You've built up images in your head that aren't true. Your wife is no longer the seventeen-year-old you left. The long wait has sapped her. Her tears have lined that lovely face, wrinkled the eyes and the mouth that once set your senses on fire. Your son is no longer that soft, babbling infant that aroused such tenderness in you – you wouldn't even recognize him if you saw him. And as far as your comrades go, they can no longer see you or hear you. They have turned to ash, or the fish have feasted on their soft flesh; there's nothing left but bones, nothing left to recognize. Forget them as well. What are these memories good for?'

'For nothing. That's why I need them, why I hold them so dear to my heart. For you life has no value; it has no limits, no start or finish. Nothing can affect you, nothing can change you. I know that my own life will end, sooner or later, and that's why I love every instant of it, every puff of wind, twitter of a bird, whiff of a wild rose. Every dawn and every sunset are different, each wondrous and stupefying to behold. That's why I want to see my son again. Even if he were awkward and ugly, he would be no less dear to my heart. You see, I begot him loving his mother when she was in the splendour of her youth, a moment as fleeting as it is precious.

'I want to see my father, who lives alone, stripped of his dignity. He was Laertes the hero, shining warrior, powerful king, and now sad old age grips him and he has no one to care for him. Why do I long to see a hoary old forsaken man? Because I'm his son and I have his blood in my veins, and it is to him that I owe this life, with all its horrors and wonders, its sorrows and its crazy joys. He inspired me with the insatiable desire to see things for myself, to love and to hate and to dream, and to seek out the distant lands that lie beyond every horizon. I long to see my mother as well but I can't – she's dead.'

'How do you know that? Mortals aren't allowed to know such things.'

'Because I called up her shade, and many others, from Hades. I travelled to a desolate place beneath the white cliff on the shores of the river Ocean that encircles the earth and there I found them. I tried to embrace her, in vain. My arms returned empty to my chest. I wept many tears.'

Calypso was gone then, following the silver wake that the moon cast on the sea. Her transparent veils fluttered in the breeze.

Now and then, as the days became shorter and the wind of Boreas descended shrieking all the way to our blissful island, she would take me with her inside the cave, where there was always an abundance of food and wine. She had me lie next to her in the bed that changed with the changing seasons: it was big now, and soft, with warm covers of purple wool. We clung to one another, watched as the surf crashed at the mouth of the chamber and listened as the rain beat down on the rock that covered the entrance, filling the crags with puddles and soaking the sand. Her lips were tender, her skin warm, her breasts soft against my chest. At times like those an infinite sweetness surged in my heart, sad memories vanished and so did my longing for distant Ithaca. Only the present counted. That was how a god lived: there was no past, no future, just an infinite, continuous present, like a sky that is always clear, a sea always calm, rippled only by tiny whispering waves.

'I thought,' I said, 'that the weather was always fine here; that it could only rain at night to nourish the earth and to water the thirsty plants and trees.'

'That is so,' replied Calypso, 'but I know that you mortals also need the storm, the raging sea, the screaming wind. It's only thus that you appreciate clear skies and a soft breeze.'

'So it's you moving the waves? Raising spray to the heavens and dashing the breakers against the cliffs?'

She smiled. 'It's not difficult for one like me. But Poseidon, the blue god, can do much more. He could uproot the entire island with a single blow of his trident, if he chose to.'

'Does he know I'm here?'

'Certainly, and he knows about you and me. Many creatures see us and we cannot know who they are. Not even I can. He gets his news from them whenever and wherever he wants.'

'Poseidon . . . is my implacable enemy. Aren't you afraid he'll take out his anger on you? It wouldn't be the first time.'

A bolt of lightning sent a blue flash into the cave and into her eyes; they were closed. 'For now he's content to know that you are a prisoner here in my arms. He knows you have no way of crossing the sea.' Thunder exploded.

'Why don't you kill me and bring an end to all this?' *But even as I spoke, I thought with terror of the blind, eternally wretched world of Hades.*

'Because that's not what's destined. Even we have to obey Fate.'

Whenever she was near me, I watched the light in her eyes and the expression of her face closely, looking for signs of feeling, for a skip in the beat of her heart. Had I truly been given the fortune of living with an immortal goddess? Would it feel this way to be close to Athena? Would she have the same unchanging scent, the same silvery lilt to her voice, the same perfect skin?

One night, while she was sleeping, I lay my ear on her chest, between those magnificent breasts. I wanted to hear the voice of her heart. It was deep and powerful as the thunder that rumbled over the distant mountains, yet her breath was like the breeze on a spring night and smelled like violets. When I lifted my head I saw that her eyes were open and looking at me.

'What makes you different from me?' I said. 'That's what I'd like to know.'

'If I have a heart like yours? What runs through my veins? If I could live without breathing or without sleeping? Is that what you mortals want to know about us?'

I did not answer. I felt confused, sad, discouraged.

'We're very similar to you. We have everything that you'd like to have but can't. I can't tell you any more than that; it's not allowed. Perhaps the sirens would have told you had you asked them, but they told you other things instead, didn't they?'

I nodded. *Other things.*

'The only way to understand is to become one of us. Only then will you know. I have this power. I can give you immortality, stop your time, now. Think about it. I would like to live with you forever and ever . . .'

I DON'T REMEMBER *when all this happened.* Whether months or years passed between one night and another; whether I became older in all that time or if my limbs grew stronger and more flexible. I know that my heart became heavier and heavier as the scars multiplied on the trunk of the wild fig tree.

Then, one day, I saw her sitting alone inside the cave. A beam of light caught her in its glow and an orichalch pitcher beamed like a star on the little table in front of her. I turned to the sea because I thought I'd heard the beating of powerful wings.

When I looked back at Calypso, sitting at the opposite side of the table was the youth with the sun in his hair; he had appeared out of nowhere.

11

I DID NOT GO IN. I didn't want to disturb an encounter whose very nature excluded me. I went to sit on my reef in the middle of the sea. The tide was low enough for me to walk out with the water at my waist. I sat there watching my shadow, which the sun kept lengthening over the sea as it descended towards the horizon. How could it disappear in the west only to reappear in the east after the night had ended? And why did its path become longer and longer, only to become shorter and shorter? Perhaps because the steeds that drew the sun's chariot ran more swiftly or more slowly on their fiery charge? Only divine horses could measure their power so perfectly that light and shadow always expanded and retracted in such a constant manner.

I'd never asked anyone about that, neither Circe nor Calypso. Perhaps not even they had the answer. I turned just once towards the cavern as the sky was blazing with the colours of the setting sun. I saw a seagull flying out. She was still there, alone. The youth with the sun in his hair was gone.

Calypso came and sat next to me. Her shadow stretched out on the water next to mine.

'How often will I come here to watch the sea, how often will I call your name, Odysseus!'

'Why are you saying such things?' I asked as she came closer. I could feel the heat and the scent of her body.

'A messenger of the gods came to visit. The great father Zeus has ordered me to let you go.'

'What does that mean? I could have left whenever I wanted to. I could have built myself a raft.'

'You would never have succeeded unless I let you. Didn't you know that? But now the time has come. I had so hoped that the gods had forgotten this island and me living on it. Someone surely interceded on your behalf. These things never happen by chance.'

'My goddess!' I thought in my heart, but no word came out of my mouth.

'Yes, her. She's jealous,' replied Calypso without making a sound. And then she made her voice heard: 'But come now, come with me. The tide is very high.'

She embraced me and rose in flight. She held her arm around my waist and we ascended together, turning as if we were dancing. We crossed the sea and flew over the island. I could see it all: the coves, the spiky rocks climbing towards the sky, the flower-filled valleys, the torrent that ran down the mountainside in a cascade of white foam and a mist of colours, as if the rainbow gaze of Iris the messenger were crossing it.

'Was it she, colourful Iris, who brought you the message?' I asked Calypso.

'No, it was another messenger,' and saying thus, she began to spin and our dance became closer, faster, more inebriating. I saw beneath me infinite flocks of birds seeking shelter for the night. I heard their calls as we passed through the red clouds of twilight. We cut through their swirling paths like a kite diving after its prey. I could never even have imagined such a thing. Then she let me fall. I plunged downward, the current of the air so strong it felt as though it was tearing out my hair, and then Calypso appeared close to me again. She looked into my tear-filled eyes and we rose up together. Our lips sought each other and our bodies did as well, with infinite, ardent force. We were enveloped by the ambrosial sweetly scented night. The rays of the stars wounded me like swords. And the creature I was embracing was miraculous. She let me fall again. It took my breath away, the wind whipped my tunic against my back so hard that it hurt. Then Calypso carried me up again. We soared through the leaves of the trees like the wind, the scent of the air redolent of soil and sky.

We fell again, and she let go of me. I couldn't feel her any more, couldn't touch her. She would not hit the ground. Nothing was impossible for a god. I would die.

I WAS LYING on the bed next to her. She was nude, golden, shot through with light.

'We made love all night,' she said.

'I dreamt that we were flying through the sky, over the river, above the trees, among the stars . . .'

'I wanted you to feel what it's like to be immortal before you sail towards death.'

'Are you saying that the gods are allowing me to leave so they can kill me at sea?'

'I only want to say that you're mortal and every day brings you closer to the end.'

'How much of my time have I spent here on this island?'

'Seven years.'

'Seven years?'

'Haven't you counted the cuts on the trunk of the wild fig tree?'

'I can't count them any more. The scars left by my blade have clotted into a single wound.'

Thus I had drawn closer to death. Without knowing it, without counting the days, the months, the years. The gifts of the gods, even the most beautiful ones, are always paid for in tears.

'Rest now. You have a long journey ahead of you.'

And so I slept there, next to her, inebriated and exhausted. I knew that my leaving would not be painful for her. The lustrous gods never weep; they are happy unto themselves. I, instead, found myself free to begin thinking again like I used to. Of the past and of the future, of food, water and the wind in my sail.

Calypso helped me. I found logs lying on the beach, ready for me to use, cut from a tree with lightweight wood that I knew would float well, along with tools and long ropes made of palm leaves. I bound the logs together, working eagerly, sweating like a craftsman eager to finish his work before the master comes looking for it. I cut a square block of cypress wood with the axe I'd found, made a hole in its centre and secured it to the middle of the raft as a base to support the mast. Then I cut the ends off the logs in decreasing order on either side of the central one, which I left full length, and assembled them to form a kind of prow. I split other logs, fashioned planks to form the sides, and then drove wedges cut from the cypress tree between the planks to secure them in place.

My mind went back to when I had built my own wedding bed snugly between the branches of an olive tree, to my youth and the hopes I had then, and a sadness flooded my heart, but I was not sorry about what I had done in my life. I'd experienced what no man before me ever had, I had visited unknown lands, met the shades of the pale dead heads. I had loved and hated. And yes, I had kindled tremendous hate as well, and perhaps would do so again if I survived, but I had left my mark on land and sea, *I, son of a small island, son of a bitter destiny.*

Then I loaded up the supplies that lovely Calypso, who remained hidden from me, had left on the beach: water, strong red wine, foods of every sort and honey and fruits and tubers and more rope and wood and cloth. I fashioned a yard and hung it from the top of the mast, and then attached a sail woven by the goddess of the cave. I sweated for four days without ever stopping and on the fifth day my work was done.

The time had come to say farewell.

I found her standing before me, in all her sublime beauty. She looked deeply into my eyes and advised me to always keep the stars of the Bear and the Herdsman on my left as I sailed, without ever losing sight of them. I could not make myself meet her gaze; it was like looking at the sea from a high cliff a moment before jumping into the void.

'Divine Calypso . . . it is love that I've felt for you every day and every night that I've spent on this island. If I were a vagabond, a man without ties, I would stay here with you until you tired of me. You can't understand what I feel because you are an immortal goddess and you need no one . . . but I must return, I have to see my family and my home again. My heart drives me to do so.'

'I do understand. For as long as you've been with me, I've lived in your time, not in my own, which doesn't exist. I've loved your eyes that change colour when you smile, your lies, even, and your marvellous stories, the words that sounded like spring rain on the flowers and on the waters of the sea . . . I would follow you, if I could, on this raft, over the crest of the wave, wherever the wind carries us.'

I thought I saw tears glittering in her eyes and liquid pearls falling down her perfect cheeks. I know that's not possible, because the gods do not weep. But she wanted me to believe her, and nothing is impossible for the immortals.

THE WIND was favourable and it swiftly distanced me from the island but we kept our eyes on one another, I from my raft and she from her stone in the middle of the sea until the broad back of the never-sleeping sea rose to hide us from each other's sight and separated us forever.

My boat slipped over the waves much more quickly than I could ever have imagined. The sky was clear and the wind constant. I had taken my fishing line and hooks, as well as a string net that I dragged behind the boat from a rope tied to the oarlock at the helm. I pulled it in every now and then and found scores of fish wriggling inside, bright and silvery. I ate them raw because no fire could have remained lit so close to the water and the spray of the frothy waves. I always kept a firm grip on the helm, by day and night. When the urge to sleep overwhelmed me, I would lash the oar to its lock and lie down on a little platform I'd built at a corner of the raft. There I kept the covers that Calypso had given me, there I would close my eyes and rest, but only for the briefest time before returning to my place at the oar. When darkness surrounded me on the infinite, deserted sea, my gaze would turn to the Bear and the Herdsman in the sky, as Calypso had ordered me.

As the days passed I became increasingly weary. My limbs ached and my eyes burned as if they were full of sand, but I tried to keep them open as long as possible so a sudden storm would not take me by surprise. When, exhausted by my long vigil and the strain of handling the raft alone, fatigue got the better of me, I'd let myself sleep but I never allowed myself total unconsciousness. I was sleeping but aware at the same time. For as long as I could manage it.

Once, in a rare moment of complete abandonment, it felt as though I were walking down the beach on Calypso's island and I heard her voice in my heart. She was saying: 'Poseidon, the blue god, will soon make his return from the land of the burnt faces.'

I jerked awake and understood my goddess' secret warning: with the return of the spring, Poseidon would leave the company of the Ethiopians. He'd enjoyed the hospitality of those simple, innocent people over the winter months, as was his wont, but now he was likely to be on his way back to his own sea. Would he spot me? Would my tiny raft attract his attention? I went straight to the helm and released the steering oar from its lock so I could govern it with my own hands. I grasped the yard line in my left hand to be able to turn the sail into the direction of the wind. I'd used my knife to carve a notch in the mast for every day gone by. Seventeen cuts that formed no scar on the dry wood.

I had been sailing for seventeen days and sixteen nights with the same, constant wind and I had never sighted a single ship or boat. As I scanned the horizon in the hope of making out some sign of human presence, I thought I could see the outline of a land mass emerging from the waves. An island or the extreme tip of the continent? My heart started pounding. Could I put my misadventures behind me? Was my ill fortune ending? After all, hadn't the prophecy proved true? Here I was returning late and broken after losing all my comrades. What else could my implacable enemy possibly want from me?

Alas, I was wrong. His ire was not yet spent.

At first I heard the sound of distant thunder, a low rumbling. Then a black cloud started to advance from the north, on my left. A sudden burst of wind made the mast groan and creak in its base. It made a quarter-turn and the sail swung almost fully in the direction of the wind. The raft veered to the right, the left side rose from the surface of the sea, the right sank and water flooded inside. Although I had taken such care to bind the logs tightly, they started knocking against one another.

The sea swelled, the waves whipped up higher and higher, lightning tore through the black cloud that covered the sky and thunder crashed over my head with a deafening roar. Night descended black all around me and I knew I was lost. My heart shouted: 'This is the end! I'll never manage to save myself this time. It would have been a thousand times better to die on the fields of Troy, fighting under the sun with my comrades of a hundred battles, clad in blinding bronze. The gods trifle with me!'

I yelled out, into the furious sky and sea: 'Come on then! Kill Odysseus! What are you waiting for? You have wind, lightning, thunder, billows! Don't you have the guts? I'm alone, naked, nothing but a puny man. You've taken everything from me, take my life! There's nothing else left.'

The titanic forces were listening. A gust of wind arrived screaming, flew from one cresting wave to the next, sliced through the foam and sent it spraying like thin mist into the black air. It hit the sail full force, cracked the mast and carried them both far off like a winter leaf in a stormy night. A swell came rushing in, tall as the walls of a fortress, crashing into the raft and disintegrating it. The logs burst apart, with only a few ropes holding them together here and there.

I was thrown into the sea and sank into a vortex that dragged me down deeper and deeper, into an abyss of darkness and silence. I could not make my way to the surface. I was losing my senses and any notion of my existence. And yet, some mysterious force breathed life into my limbs, my arms moved, grasped, reached, stronger and faster, until I burst out of the whirlpool.

I spat salty water, floundered, found myself once again in the terrifying roar of wind and sea in the eye of the storm. As I was pulled upwards by a gigantic wave, I saw below me what was left of my raft and I began to swim with all my strength to reach it. I grabbed the last remaining side rail and hoisted myself aboard. Four logs were still held together by the ropes and pins wedged into the wood, and I caught my breath. I breathed in deeply, waiting for my heart to slow its furious pounding.

I do not know how much time passed as the wreck of my raft, without a steering oar or a mast or a sail, was carried away on the seething waves. I had no idea of where I was. Tossed in every direction, I felt that my bones were surely broken. I was bleeding everywhere and my skin was scraped raw. Then something happened that left me so astounded I forgot the fury of the hurricane. From the water shot a black coot, like an arrow loosed from a bow. It alighted on the railing. The wind ruffled its feathers, white at the neck, and promised to blow the bird away at any moment. That tiny creature resisted as though it had the claws of an eagle. In its beak was a length of lightweight cloth. A voice sounded in my heart: 'Wrap it around your loins and throw yourself into the sea.'

My goddess, finally!

I tried to get closer, pulling myself hand over hand along the railing and shouting: 'It's you!' I stretched my fingers out towards the water-soaked cloth. As soon as I touched it, the coot let it go, rose up in flight and then dived back into the water. It disappeared.

'What did you say?' I shouted. 'I'm to throw myself into the water, with this? Is this a trick?' I stayed on the raft, biding my time, watching and waiting until I could make out the stretch of land that I'd spotted in the distance before the storm had come. I understood that what my heart had heard was the truth. My goddess had shown me the way and given me help to get there. The little that was left of my raft took the full brunt of a violent wave and shattered into pieces. I dived into the sea and swam for some time under water. I needed to hide, to vanish. My enemy had to be convinced that revenge had been served. I would emerge now and then only to dive back under. In doing so, I could see that I was getting nearer to the coast.

When I was rather close, I became alarmed first by the churning sand on the seabed and then by the sight of a wall of rock bristling with jagged points, pinnacles and sharp spurs. I realized that the sea was dashing me against a reef. I'd be cut to pieces. So my trials were still not over. I was very close by then, too close. A wave a bit stronger than the others flung me against the rocks. I hung on hard with my bare hands, but the undertow snatched me away again. The skin of my hands was scraped and I was bleeding profusely as the sea dragged me off. The salty water burned my raw flesh like fire. I screamed with pain but did not give up my unending fight against cruel destiny. I swam along the coast to get clear of the reef, seeking a less hostile spot to get ashore, but the light of day was fading and soon it would be night. I was seized by anguish; I realized that if the reef continued at any length I would become lost, my strength would fail me and after so much struggling I would drown. But then I remembered that the coot had brought me a piece of cloth to wrap around my loins; my goddess had wanted me to know that I would be saved.

All at once the sky opened and tattered holes in the clouds let through the rays of the setting sun, allowing me to get a clear view of the coast. The cliffs were lower and the reefs were thinning out, and when the sun was no more than a red slice on the horizon beneath a dark swarm of galloping clouds, a low, sandy beach opened up before me. The limpid waters of a river glistened and flowed into the sea. I could feel fine gravel under my feet, and then sand. I was touching bottom. I began to walk, slowly at first and then more quickly until I was out of the water and on dry land.

I'd been in the water for what seemed like an endless time, but my throat was parched. I put my head into the river and began to drink in long gulps. I felt alive again. I stood up and prayed: 'Oh god of this river that has welcomed me and sated my thirst, you whose waters have saved my life, accept my gratitude and have pity on me, your humble servant, tossed up onto this land by the sea after having lost all I ever had.' I fell to my knees and wept, sobbing, shaken to the very core of my being.

When I got up again a voice sounded in my heart: 'Return what I gave you. Walk backwards to the water's edge, remove the cloth and toss it behind you into the sea!' It was the coot. He had come to take back the miraculous cloth that had led me to safety. I did what my heart ordered. One step after another I walked backwards towards the lapping waves. They had shed their devastating power and were gently dampening the sand. I took off the cloth I'd wrapped around my loins and, without turning, threw it into the water behind me. I heard the cry of a bird, then nothing.

I was naked, like the day I was born in the palace up on the mountainside. I no longer had a single ship, warriors or weapons, nor treasure plundered from a conquered land. I was alone, without a companion and without a rag to cover myself. I was crusty with salt, my beard was long and my hair was tangled, and yet, for the first time in many years, I felt free. As if I had been born into a new life.

I walked to the edge of an oak forest and advanced among

those ancient trees, treading on the thick layer of dry leaves that rustled under my feet and then, when my knees would no longer hold me up, I lay down, covered myself with leaves, gathered more under my head to serve as a pillow and I stretched out to rest on that dark, unfamiliar soil. Just then the moon was rising from the sea.

12

I was awakened by a sudden, shrill scream. I sprang to a sitting position and then to my feet. My hand moved instinctively to the sword I no longer had. Where had I ended up this time? In a savage land? Were more difficulties in store for me, more grief? Almost instantly, the cry repeated itself, but I realized it was many voices, all together, girls' voices, silvery. I walked towards the sound, which had the light-hearted, carefree tone of youth. And I saw a group of girls playing with a ball. The ball had fallen into the river and that's what their cries were about. One of them had waded into the current to fetch it. She tossed it back to the others and they gleefully resumed their play. Anyone who dropped it was out.

At a short distance, hanging from a line stretched between two wild olive-tree trunks, were some linens drying in the sun. Just a bit further away, two mules yoked to a little cart were tranquilly browsing on wild fennel and chicory. Behind them I could glimpse cultivated fields, vineyards arranged in orderly rows on the slopes of mild hills, olive groves glittering in the clear, sharp morning light. The air was fresh and cool and colours shone brightly in the wake of the storm.

Tears came to my eyes. How long had it been since I'd viewed such a scene? Surely not since my boyhood on Ithaca, with her secret little bays, the coloured gravel at the shore, the torrents that carried the island's waters off to the sea. My heart swelled with emotion.

I had been washed ashore in a prosperous, orderly land,

governed by fair laws and wise rulers, a land in which the young could play carefree.

The girls soon tired of running and shouting and went to sit in the shade. One of them began singing a song and the others joined in. The melody was delightful, but there was a melancholic undercurrent to the harmony that reminded me of watching the colours of the sun sinking into the sea. Then they started chatting and telling each other stories.

They spoke a language similar to mine and I realized I could understand it; it was rich and sonorous with an odd, almost musical cadence. A language that seemed very ancient, making me think that the land where I'd been washed up was remote and isolated. The girls' clothing was also different, and quite unusual. I'd never seen such fabrics before. One of them, the lovely, luminous girl who had been singing, was sitting on a boulder and telling her friends about a dream she'd had: 'A girl came to wake me. She resembled a friend of mine who had just got married; it was her voice and it looked like her, but there was something different and strange about her. She said: "What are you still doing lazing in bed? It's time you found a husband for yourself! Your clothing, and that of your brothers and your father the king, have been gathering dust. You know how much those boys like to dance, and how your father prides himself on wearing fresh garments to the council of elders. Why don't you go to the river to wash them? It's a lovely, sunny day. They'll dry in a moment and the breeze will refresh them with the scent of flowers."'

'Really?' one of her companions broke in. 'You mean we're here because a friend of yours appeared to you in a dream?'

'Well, yes, but it was her and it wasn't her. I felt a chill and a strong sensation . . . as if I were in the presence of royalty.'

My heart started at hearing those words, as I watched the face and eyes of the girl telling the story. I knew exactly what she meant: I'd felt the same thing myself, many times, when my goddess, Athena of the blue-green eyes, touched me. It was she who had sent those girls there to the shore, to help me!

The girl who'd spoken was different from all the rest: her gown was striking and made of precious material; she wore golden earrings and bracelets and rich purple sandals. She truly had the bearing of a princess. The girls playing with her must be high-born as well, judging from their mannerisms and the confidence they had with the pretty one who had spoken. Another group of girls, dressed more humbly, were sitting together at a short distance; handmaids, young slaves in the service of the others. Every now and then one of them would get up to check whether the clothing hanging on the line was dry.

I was about to leave the forest, to go and speak to them, but then I remembered that I was completely naked. They would be frightened and start screaming, they'd run straight off to tell their parents who would hunt me down and beat me bloody. I couldn't approach them as I was, but I felt as though I could collapse at any moment. I was starving, exhausted and needed help. I had no choice, I would have to leave my hiding place and ask them for something to cover myself with, at least. I looked around, broke off a laurel branch to cover my loins, and came forward. I must have been a horrible sight: encrusted with salt and seaweed, my hair tangled, my eyes red and lips cracked.

It went exactly as I had imagined. As soon as they saw me, the girls started screaming, terrified, and scattered in a panic. Some of them, perhaps, had run off to seek help.

But not all of them: one alone, the most beautiful one, was left standing, unafraid. She regarded me more with curiosity than with anxiety. I was ashamed of my revolting appearance. I didn't know what to do. Should I embrace her knees, like a supplicant? No, she would take offence at the touch of such a vile-looking stranger. Better to speak to her at a distance.

'I beseech you, hear my words, *wanaxa*, whoever you may be, whether a mortal woman or a goddess who inhabits the heavens. You are so beautiful that only Artemis, the goddess who runs in the forest, could resemble you . . .' I saw the hint of a smile and took a step towards her. One only. 'Do not disdain me for my miserable appearance. I have been at the mercy of sea and storm and fought hard against them. My craft capsized and broke into pieces and I floundered in the waves until last night, when the sea pitched me onto this beach. I lost everything, even the clothing on my back . . .' I bent my head. 'Give me a rag to cover myself, one of the cloths you use to cover the drying linens. That's all I need. I was a powerful man once, the chief of many warriors. Many ships followed mine. Now I have nothing.' The tears falling from my eyes as I spoke were real ones. Hot and bitter, I could feel them at the sides of my mouth. I could not say another word. I stood there, unmoving, a leafy branch my only defence from abjection.

The other girls had begun to creep closer. Perhaps they were ashamed at leaving their mistress on her own, or perhaps they were merely curious to see the foreigner that the sea had thrown up onto the sand.

'Come closer,' she said. 'Don't be afraid.'

I took a few steps forward. From that distance I could not hide my bristly hair and shrivelled skin. I must have looked like an old man.

'I'll have my maidservants wash you. You can put this on.' She took from the line a magnificent white robe of fine linen, and a cloak to cover my shoulders. She added a little jar of clear oil.

'No, *wanaxa*, it's best that girls who do not yet have husbands do not see the nudity of a grown man. I'll wash myself.' I stretched my hand out and took the garment and the oil. Then I drew back until my back bumped against a sandy hard surface, a rock jutting up on the beach. The river curled around it, creating a little pool, before flowing out into the sea. There, sheltered from all eyes by the rock, I washed myself. I held my face under water for a long time so my beard and hair would soften and I sank my fingers into the sand again and again until my nails came out white and clean. There was a lavender bush growing on the side of the rock in the bright sun and I rubbed a spike of it on my chest and my limbs. Then I spread the oil on my skin, which became softer, looking more like a young man's.

I left the pond and leaned against the rock face to dry off, and then I put on the white robe. At that moment I felt a chill, a sensation of cold and then of heat, and I heard the fast beating of wings. I turned just as a coot took flight from the river's surface and disappeared into the forest.

I walked back towards the lovely princess. She was intent on watching a duck swimming down the river with her ducklings and she raised her eyes upon seeing my shadow. An expression of surprise crossed her face. She was looking at a man, not a derelict. She ordered a stool to be brought for me and had me sit at a big flat stone where abundant food and a jug of water were waiting for me. I was famished and I could feel the strength flowing back into my limbs as I ate the bread, roast meat and fruit she'd offered. When I had finished this meal, I asked her:

'What land is this, *wanaxa*? Who lives here? Is there a city I can reach on foot, where I can ask for help? As soon as I can I will give you back these rich garments, which were not meant for a man reduced so low.'

She drew close, close enough to smell the lavender, I think. She'd understood that I wasn't a common man, could see that I venerated her beauty and respected her rank.

'Who are you?' she asked me. She seemed to be struck by the change I'd undergone. Had my goddess, perhaps, enhanced my looks so she would be fascinated by me?

'My name is . . . I don't think my name would tell you anything. I'm nothing more than a castaway who has been sorely stricken by bad fortune. Please, tell me where I find myself.'

'This is an island, foreigner. It's called Scheria and my people are known as the Phaeacians. We are the best and the boldest sailors in the world. There's no land that we haven't reached and none unknown to us. Our island is so distant from any other inhabited land that we've never fought a war since we've been here, but our men are formidable warriors, ready to die for our homeland if necessary.

'The city I come from is close by. It's from there we travelled this morning on the cart you see there, drawn by those mules. It is ruled by my father Alcinous and my mother Arete. I am their daughter, Nausicaa, and I have five brothers, two of whom are married. I'll gladly take you to our palace – you'll see wondrous things there. But listen well: as soon as we enter, throw yourself at the feet of my mother, not of my father. If you convince her, you'll have convinced him as well, and the twelve elders of the council. Tell her the truth.'

I nodded. The girls had finished gathering the dried garments from the line and wrapped them in large cloths, which they loaded onto the cart. Then they all got onto the cart along with the princess. I followed on foot.

We crossed rich pastures with herds of cows and flocks of sheep, vineyards and olive groves, orchards full of trees laden with fruit. Tufts of spiralling leaves rose from tall, luxuriant palm trees, bursting with fruit as well. A couple of wooden bridges allowed us to cross rushing streams like the one that had greeted me at the seashore the night before. Slowly the city began to appear: it encircled a harbour and was surrounded by mighty walls. A citadel stood in a commanding position above the city. Several ships had been pulled aground alongside the road and shipwrights were busy at work planing down oarblades and shaping curved planks for the hulls.

Nausicaa turned to me: 'Don't follow me too closely, I don't want people to talk. They'll say: "Who is that good-looking stranger the princess has in tow? Where did she find him? Where is she taking him? She must have picked him as her husband. She's too haughty to accept a nice boy from her own city." There's nothing they like better than gossip, you know?' In the meantime she was pointing at a wood of oaks, cypresses and olive trees at a short distance: 'See that grove of trees over there?

You can wait there for a while. You'll find shade under the trees, and fresh water. I'll go to the palace first. Let some time go by before you follow. I'll come to welcome you at the gate.'

My heart laughed, because that was Nausicaa's way of telling me that she thought I was a handsome man. Before we parted, she said: 'As you make your way to the palace, don't stop to talk to anyone. It's rare for anyone to come here. As I told you, we're far away from any other land and people here don't tend to like strangers.'

I slowed my pace to put more distance between us so I wouldn't excite the curiosity of the inhabitants and I stopped when I got to the wood that she'd pointed out. I waited there long enough for the princess to reach the palace, counting her steps and measuring her words in my heart. Then, when I was sure sufficient time had passed, I started on my way again. The clothes I wore made me look like one of them and, since I spoke to no one and held my head low as if I were absorbed in thought, no one found me odd enough to stop me.

As I walked up towards the citadel I wondered at the view of the harbour that opened itself up to my eyes: there were hundreds of vessels of every size there, cargo ships and war galleys with curved rostra, bristling with oars. The machines that towered at the end of the wharf were so huge that only Hephaestus, the god of blacksmiths, could have built something so wondrous. I imagined that they had been posted there to defend the port against any outside aggression. I'd never seen such things.

When I was high enough, I noted with surprise something that had remained hidden to my sight until then: a tall mountain rose behind the city and at its peak was a boulder of enormous dimensions, seemingly as big as the city itself. From the road I was on, which led up to the citadel, I could clearly see that it was perched quite precariously; just a small part of its base was touching the mountain. The back of the boulder was completely detached, and it would appear that any tremor, any vibration of the ground, could have jolted it and sent it tumbling down onto the city. None of the passers-by seemed even slightly alarmed, however. I had to think that the immense boulder had, perhaps, always been there. The city's inhabitants had been born under its looming threat, and perhaps their fathers and their fathers' fathers before them. They were not at all frightened by it.

I reached the citadel and found myself standing in front of the palace. I'd never seen anything remotely resembling it. Wide steps led up to an imposing colonnade. The shafts of the columns were ivory in colour and the capitals were painted red and gold. Behind them, in their shadows, stood the entry gate framed by finely sculpted carvings. The same motifs decorated the windows under another colonnaded balcony directly above the entrance, and a magnificent painting graced the walls between them, seeming to portray an entire people migrating from one land to another. A scene of one hundred ships crossing the wide sea. Blue dolphins leapt from the water alongside the long ships with sails bellying in the wind, as though to escort or guide them. In the background was the land the ships were leaving: it was red, with tall swaying palm trees and lions hunting down other long-horned animals.

At the base of the steps were two silver statues, so finely crafted that it seemed Hephaestus himself could have cast and fashioned them using his incomparable skills. I was enchanted: they represented two gigantic Molossian hounds with eyes of flaming jasper and tails curved forward over their backs. I walked towards the steps with the idea of reaching the entrance gate. I had no sooner placed my foot on the first step than the dogs, one after another, turned their heads towards me, opened their mouths full of ivory fangs and let out a terrifying noise, like a bark. Then they began to move their paws and approach me. I stopped in shock, afraid to take my eyes off them, when I heard the ringing of laughter: it was Nausicaa.

I turned towards her as she descended the steps.

I said, still trembling: 'These statues are marvellous. I've never seen anything more beautiful.'

Nausicaa smiled: 'They're not statues, as you've just seen. They are automata.'

I shook my head without understanding.

Nausicaa struck a kettledrum hanging from a pillar and the dog closed their gaping jaws and returned to their guard posts.

'Now we can enter,' she said with a smile. 'Follow me.'

I walked behind her: 'What does the painting of the ships on the porch above us represent?'

'The history of the Phaeacians, my people. We have not always lived here on Scheria, this island. We once lived in the land of Hypereia, near the cyclopes . . . we call the balcony above us the "porch of morning". It tells of our exodus.'

I could not help but grimace at the mention of the cyclopes. The memory of the monster who had slaughtered my comrades was still too fresh and too painful.

Nausicaa noticed: 'What's wrong, foreigner?'

'Nothing. I've heard say that the cyclopes are horrible, ferocious creatures.'

'That they are. They were the reason why King Nausithous decided to abandon our ancestral home and to sail here. We are far away from everything else here but we live well, in peace, and we lack nothing. This island is blessed by the gods.'

Perhaps she read uncertainty in my eyes.

'Why, don't you think that's so? You've seen crowded markets, the port teeming with ships, our cultivated fields, the fertile pastures and fat livestock.'

'This is the loveliest place on earth, without a doubt.'

One of her handmaids, in the meantime, had entered the palace, perhaps to announce our arrival. Nausicaa beckoned for me to follow. We crossed an entrance hall guarded by two tall warriors, armed with weapons I'd never seen before and wearing tunics and cloaks matching in colour.

'Our colours distinguish us from anyone else on the battlefield, should we ever be attacked,' explained the princess.

We continued down a wide corridor with a floor made of

artfully cut stones of different colours. Every now and then there was an inset dolphin carved from blue stone, the same animal I'd seen in the large painting on the facade. I realized they must represent the sea creatures that had guided the Phaeacians in their migration from Hypereia to Scheria. Any population that migrates always has an animal leading them: an eagle, a wolf, a bear. *It must be sad to leave your homeland forever.*

Just a few more steps and I would be entering the throne room where I would find the king and queen. They would surely be more like gods than mortals. The door was open, guarded by two more sentries. They were very young. I wondered whether they had ever seen combat. Perhaps their fathers had, or their ancestors, when their people had been living near the land of the cyclopes, but surely not these youths. The island was so far from the rest of the world, they would scarcely have seen many foreigners, let alone fought them. When I entered, preceded by the princess, everyone turned to stare at me. They followed me with their eyes as if to observe every minimal detail of my mannerisms: the way I walked and the way I moved my hands. They were surely surprised at the clothing I was wearing, which they must have recognized.

Before me were the king and queen, garbed in simple yet precious robes which they wore with grace and majesty. The queen had brown hair and light, amber-coloured eyes with long, black lashes and fine eyebrows. Her slim, harmonious figure was accented by her gown. The king had black hair with a few white threads here and there, a well-groomed beard and dark, deep eyes. He seemed much older than his wife. I was later to learn from Nausicaa that he was her mother's uncle, and that he had married Arete after his brother's death.

I threw myself at the queen's feet and embraced her knees: 'Divine *wanaxa*,' I said, 'I am here to beseech your indulgence. I have suffered great misfortune. My raft was wrecked in a storm and I lost everything. The sea tossed me up onto the beach as darkness was falling, after I had spent a day and a night in the throes of the gale clinging on to a log . . .'

I could sense that the queen was looking at my skinned, wounded hands and then at the robes I wore.

'Not a single thing was left to me, not even a rag. From a distance, covering myself as best I could, I appealed to your lovely daughter who was washing linens at the river with her maidservants. I was truly a horrible sight, and all of the girls ran off except for her. She definitely has the courage of a great race in her heart, the sacred strength of her father and the grace and beauty of her mother.

'It was she who showed me the road leading to the high palace. I beg you to grant me your protection. Have mercy on me.'

Only then did I raise my eyes and I saw that my words had moved the queen. She motioned for me to stand and turned her gaze towards her husband.

I turned to him then: 'Great king, *wanax* Alcinous, I implore you to grant me your help and hospitality because I come in need of everything.'

The king nodded. All of his gestures were slow and measured. This was how I imagined the immortal, celestial gods must move as they sat on their thrones in assembly. 'You've already obtained your wish, for whatever my wife desires I desire as well. And because it is our custom to welcome the poor and derelict. Please join us this evening for dinner. When dusk draws near, we shall take our places at well-set tables and cheer our hearts with fine red wine as we listen to the song of our poet, who tells marvellous stories. Nausicaa will meanwhile show you your rooms and give you more garments, sandals and a belt, and finely crafted clasps for your cloak so it will not slip from your shoulders.'

'My heart is full of gratitude, *wanax*,' I replied. 'From the moment when I began the long voyage of my endless return, I have never been welcomed thus, nor have I ever seen a land more blessed. At first glance, I mistook your daughter for a goddess.'

I bowed deeply, kissed the hand of the king and that of the queen and followed the girl who had taken pity on me out towards the colonnaded porch. The view from the balcony took my breath away, so wondrous were the sights before my eyes. The sun was descending towards the sea and its vermilion light streaked through the passing clouds, scarlet sails flitting above the still, shiny waters of the port.

'Do you like our island? And our city?' asked Nausicaa as the declining sun set her cheeks and hair aglow.

'More than any other place I've ever seen in all my life . . . But there is one thing that burdens my heart.'

'What's that?'

I reached out my hand and pointed to the mountaintop rising beyond the citadel and the palace. 'There, that enormous mass overhanging the city and the port. From below it looks like part of the mountain, but from here it seems that only a miracle is holding it in place on that rocky cliff. It would take nothing to make it fall.'

I was about to say that Poseidon, the blue god, the shaker of land, could make the island tremble with his trident and cause the boulder to come tumbling down, but these words did not leave my lips. If such a disaster were to happen, the blame could only be mine. I couldn't bear the thought of bringing harm to such a beautiful and prosperous land, and to the sweet princess who had welcomed, nourished and dressed me and who was now accompanying me to my rooms inside the palace of her father the king.

Nausicaa's eyes, always so serene, were clouded by fleeting sadness. 'We don't think about it, foreign guest. That boulder has rested there since the beginning of time. Why should it fall now?'

'Forgive me,' I said. 'I should not have spoken. I've upset you over nothing.'

Nausicaa didn't answer, but gestured for me to follow her to my quarters and I did so.

When we reached them, she opened the door for me and bid me enter. Her perfect face seemed serene once again. 'You're wrong,' she said. 'It will never fall. We Phaeacians descend from Poseidon, the blue god, who fathered our first ancestor with a descendant of the Tribe of the Giants, Periboea. Why would he ever cause our land to quake?'

I knew why, but I didn't have the courage to say it.

13

THE DAY FOLLOWING MY ARRIVAL, the king and queen announced their intention to give a reception in my honour. I was already a respected guest; I had already slept in the palace. They could have asked me at that point who I was, but they did not do so. The king asked me only how I had reached the palace. I replied: 'As I've already told you, *wanax*, your daughter allowed me to speak to her and she helped me. My raft had shattered to pieces and I had to swim far and long to avoid being crushed against the reefs. I came ashore at the mouth of your river, miserable and stripped of all my belongings.'

'But it was not she,' said Alcinous, 'who offered you protection. It was you who asked for it.'

Nausicaa clearly kept no secrets from her parents. Alcinous had asked me a question that he already knew the answer to, to show me that nothing happened in his kingdom without him knowing it.

'That's true,' I replied. 'What else could I have done?'

'And the garments you were wearing,' asked the queen, 'where did you get them?' She was perfectly informed about this as well, but she wanted me to know that nothing escaped her.

I bowed my head. 'Your daughter gave them to me, splendid *wanaxa*. I had no choice but to ask her. I had nothing left, not even a rag to wrap around my loins. She showed me where I could wash and she gave me fine oil to rub on my tortured body and the robe that I still wear now.'

The queen smiled with her eyes, for I had told her the truth, and the king spoke again: 'You are welcome under our roof. You have the looks of a strong, courageous, noble man. It is our custom to help those in need and you have shown that you deserve the help you have requested.'

And thus I stayed on at the palace of King Alcinous, Nausicaa's father. There was truly something godlike in that man and in his wife Arete, a woman majestic in her beauty. They reigned over an industrious – and one would say happy – people in a land distant from all others, blessed by nature and by the gods. The inhabitants were long-lived, and for the entire time that I remained on the island, I never saw anyone who was crippled or deformed, no one hunched or limping. They seemed like a race born perfect, or perhaps it was the absence of war and conflict that saved them from ever being injured or maimed.

All five sons lived in the palace and emanated the same tranquil strength as their parents. At times I sensed that Nausicaa's brothers were a bit diffident towards me, but that was natural since they couldn't help but notice how she looked at me and hung on my words. For them I was still a stranger without a name or a homeland.

The sovereign was assisted in his governing duties by twelve elders, the wisest and most venerable in the entire kingdom; each one of them carried a sceptre and was called king. They were the first to be invited to the reception, summoned by the king's herald along with other distinguished guests. Alcinous had also sent for the city's – and indeed the island's – most famous singer: Demodocus, who was blind but gifted with a divine voice and the art of storytelling, accompanying his words with a lyre. He was the only person I ever met on Scheria who had been struck by infirmity, but in this case the gods had been just because he had been compensated by the harmony of his voice and his song. The gods always demand a high price for their gifts. This had been the case with *wanax* Admetus in Pherai and with Cassandra in Troy, and it was thus with Demodocus.

The banquet was rich: bread and meat were served, with

exquisite wine from the palace vineyards. The guests nonetheless showed moderation in eating and drinking and preferred conversation to filling their stomachs. They spoke about their families, the teachers they'd chosen to educate their children, about their dreams and about their adventures in youth. They were unable to count back many generations of ancestors, although they knew that their people had always lived close to the primitive, savage races that Mother Earth and Nature had generated in their attempt to create beings who were more knowing and conscious of their own destiny. The Phaeacians had fled cyclopes and giants and had persevered on their own path to perfection. They spoke of the gods as though they were very familiar with them; they would often notice them participating in sacrifices or catch glimpses of them in the hours when the light of day was most uncertain, in the early morning or at twilight, in the fields or on the sea or along deserted beaches.

When the tables were cleared a servant brought a cup of red wine and placed it next to the poet. He took a sip and then began his song. Seeing him brought to mind the lonely minstrel who had offered to sing for me that sad evening when I had failed in my mission in Troy with Menelaus, and I was contemplating my melancholy return. My heart had had a premonition, and rightly so, anticipating the terrible, unending sorrows I would have to bear in the bloody fields below the sacred walls of Troy.

Thoughts of Troy returned, as we listened to Demodocus' song, with words and a melody so strong and intense that *they have remained with me all these long years.*

> Allow me, oh Phaeacians, illustrious, glorious race
> To sing to you of how a terrible quarrel was born
> Between swift-footed Achilles and perseverant Odysseus
> On how to bring down the proud city of Troy
> Whether through brute force or by deceit.

I could barely remember that happening, but the poet brought it back to life for me. I recalled that argument, in *wanax*

Agamemnon's tent: Achilles believed that only the force of the spear and the sword could win the day. I had told him then: 'You speak that way because you are so strong; you are invincible. For you the war is a source of everlasting glory, for our companions it is nothing but bitter suffering and obscure death. If my mind can find the way to end this interminable war by bringing down Troy, I will make her fall!'

Thus the poet recalled that day long ago and my heart melted in my chest. As he went on with his melodious verses I felt hot tears rise to my eyes and I covered my face with my cloak. I wept without restraint. Those memories were too painful. It was painful too to realize how much time had passed since then if such events had reached the very ends of the earth where they inspired the songs of poets. When the tears on my face had dried I lowered my cloak and I saw that Alcinous had been observing me. He was perhaps trying to understand who I might be, if such a tale had brought me to tears. And perhaps even the poet had noticed, blind though he was. Those who are deprived of the light of day reinforce other senses; they can smell pain like a lion scents fear. I didn't take my leave until much later, although I yearned to retire to my room. I was suffering greatly, but couldn't be disrespectful to the singer and the illustrious *wanax* of that supernal home. I wept again when I was alone, wetting the pillow with my tears.

As HER BROTHERS had already noticed, it wasn't long before Nausicaa's attentions towards me were more doting than dutiful. She was still in the age of dreams, and she thought of the future like a magical place and time where the joys of love and of pure, profound feeling would join to create a golden cloud, a garden of delicious fruits waiting to be picked. I did nothing to stop her from dreaming, but I never encouraged the admiration she had for me after I became aware it was turning into something else. I didn't want my bitter destiny to contaminate hers and also I knew I wouldn't be staying on that island any longer than necessary. I yearned to return to my home and my family but I also feared the mysterious equilibrium that was somehow holding Poseidon's hatred towards me in check. I knew it could break at any time. That was why my name could not be pronounced in the air of Scheria.

Nausicaa told me stories about her people and her ancestors, and she entertained me with her dulcet voice, accompanied by an instrument I'd never seen before: a small bellows, like the one that a blacksmith uses, which blew air into a dozen small silver pipes. The sounds that issued forth were soft and delicate; it was the closest thing I'd ever heard to a choir of girls singing. I saw that there was a lead weight on the bellows and that the little string that lifted it was tied to my princess' foot.

Then one day she asked me the question I could not answer: 'Who are you?'

'I'm . . . no one, a man abandoned by all, a beggar without a rag to cover myself. Not even the sea wanted me; she vomited me up onto the beach. It is not ingratitude that prevents me from answering you, nor am I hard-hearted. You are the sweetest and gentlest creature I've ever met and I would do anything for you, even at the cost of spilling my own blood . . .'

'Don't you trust me? What else do I have to do? How can I make you understand that what I feel for you fills my heart and wounds it at the same time?'

I bit my lip; many words were waiting there but I couldn't let them out. I didn't want her to feel that way about me, didn't want the love of this girl as she blossomed into womanhood. Happy would be the man who covered her with gifts and carried her in his arms to their wedding chamber, a husband in the bloom of youth himself. Not me! He was what she deserved, what her parents deserved, what this people of semi-gods deserved: not me! Not a creature cursed by men and gods, scorched down to the bottom of his heart by war and bloodshed.

'The time will come, my *wanaxa*, luminous princess, but now I have to protect you. I am a man dogged by heartache and misfortune, and saying my name would bring on more of the same. That's not what you want, is it?'

THE POET sang on for another night: of deception this time, of the horse that caused sacred Troy to fall, of the death of Priam and his sons, of little Astyanax thrown over the walls by the savage warrior, flaming Pyrrhus. He sang of the bared breasts of proud Helen, of the weeping of the women taken in slavery along with their children, of the unquenchable flames that devoured the houses and the palace of fifty bedchambers.

I could not hold back my tears this time either, and the king regarded me enquiringly. When the song of Demodocus was over, utter silence fell over the gathering. Alcinous approached and stood squarely in front of me. Nausicaa watched, her eyes flickering light and dark.

'Who are you?'

Once again I remained mute. I didn't say a word and my silence spread over the room, over the guests, the king, queen and princes, lovely Nausicaa, the poet himself. If those white bulbs had been able to see he would have read who I was in my eyes.

Alcinous finally spoke: 'If our foreign guest does not want to reveal himself he must have his reasons. Some men suffer unspeakable horrors and cannot bring themselves to trust their fellow men again, for fear of more suffering. The night is already halfway through its course and the time has come for us to seek repose. May sleep restore strength to your limbs after the labours of the day and refresh you, for tomorrow will be a day of great celebration on the island. We remember and honour the voyage of our forebears who left Hypereia, our ancestral homeland, to seek a new home. We celebrate Poseidon, the blue god who embraces every land. It was he who led our people here, sending his dolphins to show us the path that would bring us to our beloved Scheria.

'Our young men will take part in athletic games and the best will receive rich prizes. Many of them will surely hope to attract the attention of our daughter, who has not yet decided whose wedding gifts she will accept. They are all noble, young and brave, but . . . I would like our guest to be the man she chooses.'

All those present were astonished at the king's words. Nausicaa blushed. There was no way now of stopping the rumours from flying through the city, and I would be hated for this. *I remember the words my grandfather Autolykos used when he came to give me the name I bear*: 'I have come here today nursing hatred in my heart for many a person . . . So the boy's name shall be Odysseus.' I realized, suddenly, that I hadn't met his shade among the pale heads when I called up Tiresias, the Theban prophet, from Hades. Had he been hiding from me?

'He is a man who has suffered greatly,' continued the great king. 'He knows what sorrow is and he cannot desire anything but happy days, for himself and whoever is close to him.'

I dropped my head in confusion. I couldn't speak. Before taking my leave and retiring to my room, I turned my gaze to Nausicaa and saw that her eyes were glittering with tears.

It was difficult for me to fall asleep that night. I kept hearing the automata who guarded the royal palace pacing back and forth, stretching their jaws and barking their metallic warning at the dark presences passing through the night.

As soon as day broke, the bustle of the maids and servants cleaning the floors and staircases reached my ears. Singing and flute playing wafted up from the streets to greet the day of solemn festivities.

I put on a pure white, freshly washed robe and decided to join the king, queen and other guests of the palace in the procession forming in front of the palace steps. We proceeded to the sanctuary, where Alcinous sacrificed a bull to Poseidon while a choir of young maidens raised their voices in a song that celebrated the long voyage of the Phaeacians from Hypereia to a new homeland far away from every other land. The bull was felled by the axe, the priests burned his thighs in honour of the god and the organs and other parts were roasted in preparation for the magnificent banquet that the king would provide for all his people after the games had been celebrated.

I glanced around several times to see if there were any gods participating in the ceremony. Nausicaa had told me that sometimes they could be seen at sacrifices. But I didn't recognize a single one and so was greatly relieved. If the blue god had appeared and laid eyes on me I could not have borne it; it would probably have been the death of me. I never saw my goddess any more. Those few times when I'd felt a hint of her presence were surely just a trick of my own mind; there was no one protecting me any longer.

The procession continued to the great arena in the city's main square, which opened onto the sea. There the king announced the start of the games.

Many young men came forward, shiny with oil, muscular and in high spirits. They seemed like statues sculpted by a god. They competed in bouts of wrestling, jumping, discus- and spear-throwing. Those who were defeated slunk away with heads low. They were ashamed at losing under the gaze of the most noble and lovely maidens of the island, but above all at losing in front of Nausicaa. It was she who shone most brightly, so beautiful, radiant, gentle. The winners filed in front of the spectators to delight in their applause and glory in the looks they got from the girls and, finally, to receive their awards from the hands of Alcinous.

I was sitting at a distance from Nausicaa so that no one would have any reason to carry on about the two of us. The king and queen would turn towards me now and then, and smile, wanting to put me at ease and make sure that I wasn't becoming bored with a spectacle that didn't interest me.

At a certain moment, the youth who had most greatly distinguished himself, winning all the most difficult contests, approached the place where I was seated and addressed me: 'Foreign guest!'

At first I pretended not to have heard him in the general confusion and applause, but the crowd fell utterly silent at his cry, so I could not feign the second time around: 'Foreign guest, word has it that you are a great warrior who has taken part in great endeavours. We Phaeacians are accustomed to welcoming and appreciating a man of great prowess. Why don't you join us in our contests?'

Everyone turned towards me. The king and queen appeared surprised at the invitation, which sounded more like a challenge; Nausicaa could not hide her concern. The games included sword duels, and of course anything could happen in such a match. That proud, lusty young man seemed to know exactly what he wanted and to be just as certain of getting it. It wasn't hard to understand why he'd chosen me to pick on. Alcinous had declared his intentions and Nausicaa's feelings towards me were clearly evident to many in the audience.

I answered: 'I'm grateful for your invitation, but these are games for young men. I'm weary and my limbs no longer have the vigour they once had. My only thought is returning to my home. I beg you to forgive me if I do not accept.'

The youth turned towards the king and queen, and the spectators. Cocky with the victories already under his belt, he continued: 'I understand. So we were wrong about him! We can't expect the guest to boast of deeds he's never accomplished. I don't believe he ever was a warrior, or even a fighter. Perhaps he's merely a merchant who wanders from port to port, one of those men who live off their cunning and are ready to sell the goods they've stolen from shipwrecks or the slaves they've captured, if the opportunity presents itself.'

That was too much. A fierce heat rose from my chest. The flames that had licked at my heart in all those years of savage fighting on the fields of Troy blazed up and set my face on fire. How dare that disrespectful, unseasoned young man insult me thus? How could I sit back and be humiliated in front of the people who had taken me in and honoured me? In front of

Nausicaa who had dressed me and fed me and whose heart swelled with a feeling for me that went well beyond respect or esteem? A blind, unrestrainable fury scorched my throat and, hoarsely, I shouted: 'You are a fool, with no respect for a man older than you with more experience of life. Let's see what's bigger: your tongue or your heart. I'll see you at the sword-duelling ring.'

I threw off my cloak and leapt from my place onto the playing field. Six or seven discuses were lying there where the athletes had cast them. Instead, I grabbed a heavy bronze shield leaning on the fence and hurled it beyond all the markers. All of a sudden, a man appeared near me. He stared at me with penetrating green-blue eyes and with a wide smile said: 'Nice throw!' My heart trembled. He looked just like Damastes, my old weapons trainer, with a few white hairs at his temples. I tried to answer but the figure dissolved. At first it quivered like a mirage in the summer heat and then vanished. I wanted to shout out but I couldn't take time to think. I had other things on my mind.

The expression on the face of my young challenger changed at once. I strode across the field and seized a solid bronze weight of the kind used for long-jumping. I swung it around and let fly in his direction as if it were made of wood. It soared up into the air and then rained down, plunging into the earth with a dull thud. Less than half of it was visible. Then I crossed the javelin-throwing field. I grabbed the first one I saw and held its bitter tip up against the streaming sunlight. It shone with a sinister light. How many times, again and again, had I wielded this arm, how many times had my fist closed around the hilt, had my eye pinpointed my target like a falcon does his prey! I launched it with such force that it rammed into the ground just a few steps away from my adversary. He wasn't laughing any more, nor was he speaking. Green terror gripped him and I could smell his fear as I got closer, until I found myself standing in front of him with a sword in my hand. A deathly silence fell over the arena.

The youth tried to take me by surprise. He hoped that his

youthful vigour might suffice to defeat me, but I was far more expert than one who had perhaps only ever played at fighting. Too often had I inflicted death. I knew only one way of striking: I aimed to kill.

He attacked me with vigour, but his blows wasted his strength and were wielded with too little precision. I responded to one blow out of ten, but always struck my target. In no time, the boy was spilling blood from any number of wounds and the blood made me even fiercer and more violent. I circled around him like a wolf does to its prey. With my last blow I dodged his lunge and surprised him with a great cleaving swing from above. His already aching hand lost its grip and the sword fell from his hand. I pressed my own against his neck, preparing to cut his throat.

The face of a woman with her eyes full of tears stopped me. The anguished expression of his white-haired father made me drop my sword. I could not slaughter the son of such a generous, mild-natured people.

'Don't try it again,' I told him. 'Do not offend a guest who has suffered greatly.' And I led him out of the ring. His head hung as shame welled up inside him. He wept.

I walked to the centre of the arena and cried out: 'So that all of you may be sure that I'm no merchant who buys stolen goods and drags slaves away in chains, know that I am Odysseus son of Laertes, king of Ithaca, destroyer of cities. My fame is as high as the sky!'

A buzz passed through the crowd still seated in the arena. They all exchanged looks, whispered to one another.

Nausicaa hid her tears in the sleeve of her gown.

The king walked up to me: 'That young man insulted you and it was your right to finish him off with your sword, but you showed pity on him, on his parents and on his people. We are all grateful to you for this. Only the greatest men are so magnanimous.'

Hearing this filled my heart with peace and I felt like weeping myself. Just a few words from a rash young man had been enough to awaken the beast. My name had resounded like thunder in the air of Scheria and the blue god had certainly heard it, if he had not already left the land of the Ethiopians. I hoped ardently that my goddess had heard it as well and might come to my aid, but I couldn't sense her, couldn't feel the chill under my skin or hear her voice in the bottom of my heart.

We returned to the palace where the king had laid an enormous banquet for his people. As well as the animal that had been sacrificed, there were sheep and goats and even two white long-horned oxen. The meat had been skewered on spits and roasted and basketfuls of bread were served by the palace baker. Red wine as bright as pomegranate seeds was poured into cups and good cheer began to spread among the guests again. Nothing so terrible had happened, after all. The boy would heal from his wounds, get over his fright and have learned some common sense. Don't challenge a stranger before you know who he really is.

The king spoke again: 'Now I understand your tears when Demodocus sang of the trickery that led to the fall of Troy and the terrible night of the massacre.'

'I thank you, *wanax*, shepherd of the glorious Phaeacian people,' I answered. 'Yes. The poet's song brought me back to the bloodshed and pain that all we Achaians had to bear during the long, endless years of our siege of Troy. We lost our way on our return voyage and since then I've suffered everything that a man can suffer. I saw all the comrades who survived the war perish, even my brave Cephalonians. Devoured by monsters and savage flesh-eaters, strung up like fish by the dreadful Laestrygonians. I lost all my ships, everything. And arrived here beseeching pity at the knees of glorious Arete.'

'Your suffering is over,' replied the king. 'I'll give you a ship that will take you home and this time nothing will happen. We are descendants of Poseidon and we are capable of navigating towards any land in the world, be it the most distant and remote.'

He motioned to one of his guests, a robust man with greying temples: 'Prepare a ship, the sturdiest we have, for fifty-two rowers, twenty-six on each side. Have the hull, the oarlocks, the mast and its housing all inspected. Do you see this man here beside me? You must be prepared to take him to his homeland, to Ithaca.'

I tried to thank him, as my heart commanded, for such great generosity, but he cut me short with a gesture of his hand.

'Now that I know who you are, I feel even more strongly that you should stay and become my son-in-law. How long have you been away from home?'

'In my time,' I said, 'twenty years.'

'There is no other time,' said the king. 'Twenty years . . . I don't think you'll find anyone waiting for you. You'll be returning without your ships, without your comrades. What is left for you there? Here you could generate a new race. The echo of your deeds will live on in the stories of the poets and the songs of the court minstrels and street singers. I'm sure there are many more adventures that you yourself can tell us about. The nights are starting to get longer, a most propitious time for telling tales with a cup of strong wine to fortify your heart.'

'Great king,' I replied, 'every man on this earth would be honoured and fortunate to receive such a proposal from you. Your daughter Nausicaa is a fragrant flower, pure enchantment. But all I desire is to return. I want to see my home, the young bride I left with a child in her arms when I went off to the war.'

'As you wish,' said the king with seeming reluctance. 'As soon as the ship is ready you can leave. But until then, linger here with us, cheer your heart with my wine. Later, if you are willing to indulge us, the queen and my daughter and all of us who rule the Phaeacians, tell us your story. Your name was unknown to us until now and we could not imagine who you were.'

'I will,' I replied, 'even if it saddens me. Every comrade that I lost torments me still. But it is only right for me to repay your hospitality and, perhaps, speaking of all that happened with men and women who have welcomed and comforted me will help me make sense of things that I have not understood.'

EVERY EVENING after that day, when the tables had been cleared, I told of my misfortunes. The unfamiliar lands, the comrades who died but were never forgotten, the ghosts plaguing both my dreams and my sleepless nights, *ghosts who still appear to me as the groaning wind whips through these vast empty spaces, swirling the snow over the icy expanse.*

And yet, somehow, I felt relief in telling such stories in a safe, tranquil place, protected by powerful, wise people who lived like gods on their wondrous island.

When my evening of storytelling was over and everyone had gone to bed, I would often walk out onto the balcony. Sitting on the hard stone I would curl into myself, hugging my knees to my chest, and think, or sometimes weep.

'Why don't you wait for the good weather?' Nausicaa would ask me. 'The nights are longer than the days now; put off your departure until the return of the warm winds. It's only a few months. You've waited so long, can't you wait a little longer?'

'I've made my decision, my lady. I don't want to wait any longer.'

'Are you in such a hurry to leave me?'

I couldn't speak. How could I explain to this young woman in the bloom of her youth what lies in the heart of a man with so much pain, blood, despair behind him? But she'd look at me, expecting an answer.

'You are the sweetest and loveliest person I've ever met throughout all these long years. You are beautiful, charming, as fresh as the first rose of spring: how could I ever wish to leave you? But it's because you've entered into my heart that I want the best for you. You must be free to meet the partner that destiny has in mind for you. You'll meet a man who will give you boundless love, and children as handsome and strong as sprouting palms.

'I'll never forget the day when you stood unwavering before me, seaweed-smeared and brine-encrusted as I was, naked and filled with shame, while your friends ran off to hide. You smiled and the sun started to shine again for me. But I'm tired now, exhausted by all the trials that I have gone through, by the ache of memory, by the nightmares that jolt me awake in the middle of the night. You have to forget me, Nausicaa. Leave me only the music of your name and the light of your eyes. You are young, and bound for life. I can only hope to face my decline with serenity.'

She turned to look at me: in her eyes, tears, on her cheeks, pearls of regret.

14

THE FEW DAYS THAT SEPARATED me from departure filled my heart with melancholy. I should have been serene, even happy. I was finally returning home at the head of an expert crew made up of the best sailors in the entire world, under the auspices of a king who descended from Poseidon himself. But every time I saw the look of dismay in Nausicaa's eyes, my heart plummeted in my chest. I knew that look. I'd seen it in Penelope's eyes every time I'd been about to leave; her counting every instant until we'd finally part. A sense of inconsolable desolation, of dread.

We would walk along the bank of the river for hours, even for days at a time, stopping every now and then in the shade of a palm or willow tree. Plants and trees of every type shared that wondrous land; those from warm climes and cold. We talked together about a great number of things, like the adventures I'd experienced and the wild lands I'd visited. Other times, instead, long silences fell between us, filled only by the remote, mysterious messages whispered in the sigh of the sea.

In the evenings I continued to tell my story at the palace: how I'd met up with the red-flower eaters and then the cyclops, how I had blinded him and then mocked him with ill-conceived words. I was uncertain whether to tell them about the curse he'd hurled at me, how he had called upon his father Poseidon, lord of the sea and the Ocean, to revenge him. I feared that the king might regret giving hospitality to a man who had earned the rancour of a god who was their ancestor. It had already happened once, with Aeolus, the tamer of the winds. He had thrown me out and refused to help me after he'd understood that a powerful god was enraged with me. But the king and his people had been generous and they deserved my sincerity, and so I decided not to hide the terrible words that had come out of the monster's mouth after I had forever deprived him of the light of day.

I watched as Alcinous' face darkened. The Phaeacians knew many things about the cyclopes, since they had once inhabited the land of Hypereia, which bordered the giants' territory. They had often had to defend themselves from that despicable race. But instead of fighting them off as enemies, they had chosen to set off for a new homeland, and thus had remained dear to the blue god, who often manifested himself to them openly, not covered by the clouds which always hide the gods from mortal men.

And I told, barely managing to hold back tears, of how the savage Laestrygonians, eaters of human flesh, had massacred my men, and how they had smashed and sunk all our ships by pitching huge boulders at them. All of them except one.

I was unable to tell them what the Sirens' song had revealed. *So greatly had it wounded my heart that I still suffer now. Not a day or a night passes without me trying to unravel that enigmatic revelation.*

The men who would be accompanying me by ship to Ithaca were among my listeners. They heard me out with fixed expressions, never asking or objecting. Perhaps they didn't understand. I couldn't help but wonder at times: they had sailed all the seas in the world, why hadn't they seen the things that I'd seen? Was their silence due to amazement or disbelief? Where had they been? Which seas had they navigated, which waves? On which lands had they set ashore? I wanted to ask whether they had ever passed the wall of fog . . . did that gloomy barrier truly separate reality from dream or nightmare? I didn't dare. It was better not to lift the veils of that mystery when I was so close to returning to my own world. Even if I found that my world had changed greatly, I would still recognize it, surely. The circle would close.

At least until I received the sign that would force me to leave again.

The night I told the story of Circe there was a new moon. The sky was covered with black clouds and a sighing wind was drifting in from distant lands. I told of how she had urged me to seek out the gateway of Hades, to summon up the shade of Tiresias and to ask him what my destiny held in store for me. A profound silence fell over the hall from my very first words: 'I crossed the sea and entered the deep, boundless Ocean. I set ashore where a white cliff of smooth rock rose as high as the sky, piercing the clouds. The coast was bristling with jagged rocks above the surface and treacherous reefs below and the waves were boiling with white foam.'

I saw the sailors who would be on my ship murmuring something to one another. Had they seen it, perhaps? Had they boldly navigated as well beyond the extreme limits of the land and sea? I did not interrupt my story, I asked them nothing. There would be plenty of time during the long voyage that awaited us to talk about those places. I told the assembly about the fallen comrades I found there, mere shadows of what they had once been. I spoke of their desolation and the infinite sadness that enveloped them. And finally of Tiresias' prophecy: that I would return late, a broken man, that I would find my home violated and invaded. That I would restore order and justice, but not for always. Another long, endless journey awaited me, no longer over the sea, but through mud, snow, ice; a journey of silence and screams.

Even the wind fell still and my words reverberated off the shocked walls. The twelve elders watched me, their faces placid and smooth as wax. *A blade of cold air froze my breath. I saw it condense as I can see it now.*

Reliving these adventures, my misfortunes and my grief, were like opening up wounds that had never scarred over. The loss of my comrades, their bodies mangled, buried in the stinking bowels of cruel savages, unworthy exequies, unworthy burial! I felt it all.

I told my whole story dry-eyed. I didn't want to sadden the king and the assembly. It is thus that a guest reciprocates the kindness of his hosts, who have taken him in and fed him at their table. I ended my story with the night I was washed ashore on their island and it felt like I was still a prisoner of the swells that had flung me against the reefs and sharp rocks. I held up my hands, which still hadn't healed. And, looking Nausicaa in the eyes, I told of our encounter, the scattering of her friends and handmaids as soon as they saw me, the help that she offered without asking for anything in return.

One still afternoon, some time after I had finished telling my story, Nausicaa led me to the sanctuary. Deep in the most secret penetralia of that sacred place was a large painting that represented the gulf, the city and the huge boulder that loomed over it. At the centre of the bay a ship was setting out to sea. Underneath the painting were painted marks, all of the same colour, that stood for words. They looked much like the ones I'd seen long ago on the rim of the shield wielded by *wanax* Idomeneus, king of Crete and Knossos: a perfect weapon that had belonged to King Minos, Lord of the Labyrinth, before him.

'Do you want to know what the marks say?' Nausicaa asked me.

'Yes, I do,' I replied.

'They say that one day a man will show up on the beach and ask for our help to return to his homeland. A man hated by Poseidon, our god and protector. If the Phaeacians decide to take him to his destination, they may do so, but upon their return, their ship will be turned into a rock at the entry to the port, blocking all access, and the boulder will fall from the mountain and crush the city under its enormous weight, destroying its houses and killing its inhabitants.'

Tears streamed from my eyes. 'So there's no escape for me. I'm that man. And this curse has been lying in wait here for me from time immemorial. As has this atrocious dilemma: I can either accept your help and condemn you to annihilation, or forever give up my island, my family, my people.'

My heart rejected this cruel sentence. I even hoped that Nausicaa had invented it all to convince me to stay and forget about returning. But she saw the expression on my face, the tears streaming down my face, and perhaps she took pity on me. She said: 'There's one last phrase. It says: "If the god so wishes." So it may not happen.'

'Your father knows of this prophecy, doesn't he?'

'Certainly, as do my mother, my brothers and the elders.'

'Why would they do this for me?'

'Wouldn't you do the same thing? We are a great people, with a great heart.'

'I would do the same.'

'So you can surely understand the choice of the valiant Phaeacians, uncontested masters of the sea.'

My eyes ran over the painting, poring over every detail, every corner, and then stopping in the middle. 'That ship . . .'

'What about that ship?'

'It has no means for steering.'

'You saw ships like this one down at the port, didn't you?'

'I thought the oars had been stowed away.'

'No. None of our ships have steering oars. They always know the route. The sailors will ask you where your island is and the ship will know how to take you there.'

I was dumbfounded. I realized that mortals could become like the gods and perhaps even better, if we could live according to fair laws and were led by the highest minds. But my heart ached at the thought that by accepting such a generous gift, I would be exposing those people that I had learned to love – that wondrously wise king and queen, and golden Nausicaa herself – to mortal danger. To the possible extermination of their whole people.

How could I accept? Alcinous, who was aware of the

threatening prophecy, had offered me his daughter, certainly his most precious treasure, in the hope of binding me to this land. So that I would stay, forget about returning. After all my stories, he was surer than ever that I was the fatal man, *he who gives rise to hatred*, and he was just as sure that I had nothing to go back to. He knew that my world didn't exist any more, or was dying. We had been away too long. Many kings had died or had gone missing. Others, like me, had been given up for dead. Too many young men in the bloom of their years had left their lives on the fields of Troy.

But I could not give up Ithaca and I already knew in my heart what I would say. I asked Nausicaa if her mother and father would receive me. Nothing penetrated from outside, neither sounds nor voices. Only the light of midday poured in from above like molten bronze, along with the twittering of sparrows.

'They will hear you today,' she replied. That was all I needed to know.

King Alcinous and Queen Arete received me in their chambers before sunset. A golden light streamed in through the window that looked out on the garden. The singing of youthful voices, a girls' choir perhaps, wafted in gently as if carried by the breeze from a distant land.

'You've asked to speak with us,' said the king. 'Why is that? Is something worrying you? Aren't you pleased with what we've promised you? Do you doubt our word, perhaps? The ship that will take you home is ready, the strongest and most seasoned of our young men have been chosen as sailors. And you won't be going home empty-handed. Let no one say you've lost all your ships and men and that you return wretched and poor.' As he spoke, the queen nodded in assent at every phrase.

This is how far they were willing to go! They would cover me with gifts so my dignity would not be called into question.

'Great king,' I said, 'splendid queen, no doubts could arise in my mind regarding your promises. I have had endless proof of your magnanimity. You are like gods for me. You are greater than they – the gods have often been cruel and relentless with me and they continue to be so, despite my sacrifices and prayers. If I acted as I did, it was only to save myself and my comrades from horrible deaths. But today, in your sanctuary, I learned of the woeful prophecy that threatens the destruction of your people and city if you help a man who has come from afar to return to his homeland. A man that the sea has tossed up onto your shores.

'I won't be the cause of your ruin. I beg of you, all I need is a solid boat that I can handle myself. I'll use a steering oar made with my own hands. I have experience in woodworking. In this way, you will not be punished by a god who hates me and who heaps suffering upon me. I will sail alone towards my homeland and if it is my destiny to perish in the attempt, so be it. I don't want others to suffer. I won't let the enormous mass looming over you tear free of its moorings and come crashing down on your beautiful city and the people living here.'

'Glorious Odysseus,' replied the king, 'far be it from us to abandon you after all you have suffered on sea and land! No one can stave off his destiny; if the gods wish to strike us they will find other ways to do so. What I have decided will be.'

'You've made the heart of our Nausicaa beat for you,' the queen continued, 'but you have respected her. It would have been easy for you to revel in a young girl's love, but you have been sincere with her, you've spoken to her using true words and you have guided her towards her future life. This is a great joy for a mother, the greatest of gifts . . .'

'You mustn't feel that you are to blame . . .' continued the king – they spoke like a single person with two different voices, the first deep and resonant, the second gentle. 'No one is obliging us to do what we do. I trust that our father Poseidon will not unleash his anger on us who are his descendants. We always honour him with sacrifices and, when he honours us with his presence, we see his face in the billowing sea. The ship will be loaded by tomorrow, with plenty of water and food and many gifts. My sailors will take you home.'

I was tremendously moved by those words and I wept hot tears as I stood before them: out of gratitude, admiration, at the thought that I might never see them again. I kissed their hands. There were so many things I wanted to say, but the words would not leave the circle of my teeth. A knot closed my throat. I said only: 'You will be always in my heart, great king, sacred force, and you, luminous queen. If there is a god who listens to me, I would beg him to grant you every blessing. May your progeny flourish and may you one day be transported to a blissful land where there is neither cold nor frost, where drought never strikes, where a brilliant light always shines and the soil produces fruit spontaneously without any call for hard labour, for you have had pity on a man forsaken by all.'

'There's no need, Odysseus,' said the king with a smile. 'We're already here.'

'Now go,' said the queen, 'go to Nausicaa. There's not much time left for you to be with her.'

I followed her advice. Before leaving the room, I turned to take a look at them: handsome on their thrones and imperturbable. They looked like gods, and yet they were as mortal as I was, and one day they would have to die, abandoning everything they loved.

I found Nausicaa where I had left her, on the wide colonnaded porch up on the palace facade. I leaned on the parapet next to her, my elbow nearly touching her own, so close I could smell the fragrance she wore, a blend of the mysterious blossoms cultivated in the secret gardens of the queen.

'Nausicaa . . .'

'Has the time come to say farewell?'

'Yes.'

'See? The prophecy doesn't worry the Phaeacians, nor does the unfavourable weather.'

'I didn't want this. I asked your father for a boat I could sail on my own. I would have added an oar for steering. He wouldn't listen to me. He wants to give me a ship and oarsmen and rich gifts that I do not deserve. Your parents are like the immortal gods when they sit on their thrones, and when they speak they show all the affection and warmth of simple men.'

'Nice words. Few people know as many as you do, Odysseus, son of Laertes. You've readied such nice words just to say goodbye! Words for me to remember when I'm lying in bed watching the sea grow grey in the winter.'

'There are no words for this, *wanaxa*. There's nothing but sorrow for me, nothing but heartache.'

'But do you remember what you said to me that day you appeared dirty and naked on the beach, covering your groin with a laurel branch?'

'I do remember. "Pray, my lady, be you mortal or one of the gods who possess the infinite sky? You are so beautiful that only Artemis could resemble you . . ."' Here my voice broke.

'I believed you, do you know that?'

'You were right to believe me. I was saying the truth. You can't imagine what it means to spend days and nights in the dark, in the cold, wholly desperate, on the edge of the abyss, and then to wake up and hear girls laughing and to find an apparition before you . . . like you were, radiant, amber eyes and lips like lotus petals, your voice an enchantment. I really did think you were a goddess, because you didn't run off like the others.'

'Maybe I should have. You're leaving now and I'll never see you again.'

'That is the only truth. I won't tell you honeyed words – they would only hurt you.'

'So you know what would hurt me. But do you know what would be good for me?'

I bowed my head in confusion. Where was my brilliant mind, where was the ingenious Odysseus of old? I couldn't manage to answer a girl who could have been my daughter.

'I'll tell you then, glorious Odysseus, son of Laertes, king of

Ithaca, destroyer of cities. I took you in, alone among my companions who had all scattered away. I gave you food and drink, I washed and dressed you, I welcomed you to my home, I implored my parents to help you.'

'It's all true and you will be forever in my heart for this, as long as I live.' How could she not see in my eyes how my soul was trembling?

'Would you do something for me, then?'

The sun was descending just then into the purple sea and the song of the birds among the cypress and myrtle boughs was softly silenced.

'Anything.'

'Then give me a kiss. The first and the last, the only one. And then go. I don't want you to see me crying.'

She turned and threw her arms around my neck. I kissed her.

'There are moments that are worth a whole lifetime,' she said. 'This is worth everything I did for you. Farewell.'

'Farewell, my adored princess. May the gods grant you happiness for all the days of your life.'

It was she who ran off, and I could hear the sound of her weeping until she disappeared into the dark rooms.

It was time to turn on the lamps. The last flash of fire had gone out on the waves.

15

I DIDN'T SEE NAUSICAA AGAIN. She wasn't present at the final banquet that the king and queen gave in my honour, inviting the elders and the counsellors, but it was better that way. Neither she nor I would have been able to face the evening without distress because every instant would have had us longing to be alone, to talk, or not to talk at all, just to look into one another's eyes. And if my heart was already practised at losing or separating from a loved one, hers was not. It was the first time she'd fallen in love, with a nameless man who appeared out of nowhere on the shores of the island so far away from all other places, and who proved to be none other than the victor of the war that was already on the lips of all the poets.

Despite all that abundant food, between one libation of red wine from the king's own jugs and the next, all I could think of was leaving. The uncertainty of how I would find my wife again, my son, the father who was like a god for me, was agonizing. And an acute sense of melancholy was welling up inside me at the thought that Nausicaa would be sad and alone for who knows how long . . . until a new, real love drew her thoughts to a husband and a family, children to watch grow and to love. My face would fade, then; my features would dissolve into the mist of time. She would forget me.

The rich gifts that Alcinous had heaped upon me were already stowed under the benches on the ship, and he'd asked the elders to add more of their own: urns and craters, cups and jewellery, treasure which put the plunder I had been carrying back from Troy to shame.

The banqueting mercifully drew to a close and the time for my departure finally arrived.

I approached the king and queen for our final farewells: '*Wanax* Alcinous, *wanaxa* Arete, rulers of this magnificent land, perhaps there is nothing that I can wish for you that you don't already have, but I want to say that no matter where I may be, whether I have returned to the homeland I yearn for or whether my destiny has thrust me back again to the ends of the earth, you will always be in my heart. From the moment I leave these shores until the last instant of my life. May the gods protect you and make everything your hearts desire come true.' I kissed the queen's hand as, I think, a tear fell upon it.

The king accompanied me in person to the threshold. Before parting for the last time I said to him: 'There's something I've never dared to ask you, great king, but since I'll never see you again I'll do so now. Tell me, how does it feel to sit alongside a god in his true being?'

Alcinous shook his head slightly and the curls of his long hair danced around his face. 'Your heart groans as if a weight were pressed upon it, your breath quickens, some part of you evaporates like dew when the sun rises. Any number of things seem clear and evident and then they don't. If he looks at you, you perceive innumerable visions in his eyes, some are recognizable, others are not. Truth is revealed in fragments. Many of the things which have astonished you on this island have emerged from these visions and these visits.'

'And when he leaves?'

'Relief, as if an enormous weight had been lifted from you. Mortals are no longer accustomed to the presence of the gods.'

'Farewell, great king,' I said. There was nothing more to add.

'Farewell, glorious Odysseus, great king.'

Eight warriors in bright armour escorted me from the palace to the port where the commander and the oarsmen of the ship that would take me home were waiting. I went aboard and greeted the captain, a dark-skinned, powerfully built young man, and I observed the other members of the crew, the fifty-two rowers sitting at the oarlocks. Under their benches my treasure glittered in the torchlight. The moon was a thin sliver.

We cast off the moorings and the oars dipped into the water. The sail swelled and the ship majestically ploughed the tranquil waters of the port. We soon reached the outlet, leaving a path of foam in our wake.

I turned towards the city and the palace. The door was open and lit from inside. I could see two figures standing next to each other who appeared to be looking in my direction. On the porch above them, under the overhanging roof, lamps lit the painting of their exodus. The balcony was deserted.

THE SHIP swiftly picked up speed and the rowers were able to pull the oars on board. A couple of them laid out sheepskins on the aft deck, topping them with linen covers and an amaranth blanket in woven wool and a pillow. The captain approached me: 'This is your bed, *wanax*, where you'll sleep tonight.' He smiled. 'We have orders to make sure you're comfortable.'

'I don't think I will sleep tonight,' I said, 'I'm too agitated by my thoughts and I'm not tired yet.'

'As you prefer,' was his answer.

'What course have you decided upon?'

'*Wanax* Alcinous our king told us where your island is. The ship will choose its direction.' He raised his eyes to the sky: 'For now, as you can see, we're holding an easterly course, slightly south as well.'

I didn't know how to respond. How could a ship steer itself? I wondered, but I asked nothing. If he had wanted to explain it to me, he would have. I did see the yard rotating around the mast at times, and the sail picking up the wind in a different way, although the hull maintained its direction and speed. Could my long agony truly be ending? Was this the last stretch of sea I'd have to cross before arriving home?

'How many days and how many nights of sailing will be needed to reach my island?'

'That is something I'm not allowed to tell you, *wanax*, forgive me. Our counsellors fear that someone may calculate the course in reverse and manage to sail back to our island from the opposite direction.'

'It's only fair for you to defend yourselves and your freedom. But you'll have to trust me in the end. I can recognize a route and I can count the days and nights.'

'Perhaps, *wanax*. Try to rest now. The voyage will be long. Very long.' He stared at me with his light, piercing eyes and he smiled again.

They had prepared such a cosy and comfortable place for me to sleep that I suddenly felt myself becoming drowsy. It was right for me to show them I appreciated their kindness and I lay down on the bed to contemplate the sky: it was a clear and cloudless night and I could see an infinite number of stars in the dark vault. Brighter and bigger than I'd ever seen them before. I felt flooded by a sense of deep peace and mysterious joy. I had never in my life sailed in such a way, free of responsibilities and exempted from hard toil, stretched out on the deck beholding the myriad stars.

I wanted to keep my eyes open to see if we would pass the wall of fog that I had crossed after the storm on Cape Malea. It had kept me from returning all these long years. But my lids were becoming heavier and the sound of the sail in the wind and the rustling of the sea that never rests brought on slumber.

A RAY OF SUN woke me and I stretched out my hand. The soft sheepskin, still; I was in my own bed. But then I heard a tinkling of bells, like the ones that goats and sheep wear so the stray ones can be found. Could we have already arrived?

I jumped to my feet and I found myself standing on the

pebbles lining the seashore, under the boughs of an olive tree. How much time had gone by? Just one night, no longer than that. Had they abandoned me on the first bit of land they'd run into? 'Why? Why?' I shouted out loud. They'd given me a drug to make me sleep and then they'd robbed me of all the treasure Alcinous had given me. Curse the greed that contaminates everyone in the end, even a fair and happy race like the Phaeacians.

But I was soon to regret having thought badly of them, for behind me, next to the olive trunk, was heaped the treasure of Alcinous, shining in the sun. I couldn't understand. I looked around me and I had no idea of where I was. Anxiety gripped me: whose country was this, who lived here? Would the curse against me never let up? Could I never escape it?

The one thing I knew was that I was not prepared to give up. I would never give up the idea of returning home. Never! Firstly I had to find a hiding place for my valuables. I might be able to trade them for food, or even a ship and crew. I soon came upon a little cave and, one piece at a time, I brought all my treasure there and buried it under the sand. Then I went back to the olive tree.

The bells started ringing again and from behind a hill appeared a herd of goats in the care of a young shepherd boy. At least this time my appearance would not scare him off, I reasoned, so I approached him. 'Hail, young man,' I said, 'can you tell me where we are?'

The shepherd wore a leather tunic and sandals with leather laces and carried a reed flute around his neck.

'Do you mean you don't know where you are? Everyone knows this little island! We grow a bit of wheat but otherwise it's all forests. The pigs are happy with the acorns. There's not much grazing land, but it's good enough for my goats. Even people in Asia, which is so far away, have heard of this island. It's Ithaca!'

Ithaca . . . Ithaca! I wanted to fall to my knees and kiss my soil. My heart was bursting with joy. I was back. I was home!

Those pebbles, the little waves caressing them, the sparkling olive leaves, the olives that were ripening to make good, fine oil, the wild flowers, the smells! How could I not have recognized this fragrance? It was my own land, so often on my lips, so intensely desired in all those bitter, bitter hours . . . But I couldn't say anything. I couldn't shout, or weep, or dance around the olive tree, or run to Penelope and throw my arms around her. I couldn't shout out for my son: 'Telemachus, I'm home, my boy!' I had to hide my feelings, my joy, my memories. I couldn't make a slip. I knew that thanks to Agamemnon's shade, from his words of warning when I'd called him up from Hades. But I was feeling something different as well, a strange uneasiness, a cold wind creeping between my clothing and my skin.

The shepherd smiled: 'If you know nothing of this island that's so famous, where do you come from? Who are you?'

I made up a story. It wasn't the first time, nor would it be the last. I thanked the bloody shade of Agamemnon, who had put me on my guard when he said: 'Trust no one, not even your wife; say one thing and think another . . .'

'Oh, it's a tale of woe like no other,' I began, inventing each word as I went along. 'I had stopped in Crete with the army of *wanax* Idomeneus, lord of that great island and of the Labyrinth. We were returning from the war, and his son tried to rob me of part of my share of the plunder. Can you believe it? With all that it cost me – sacrifice, wounds, sleepless nights . . . understand? He wanted to take it. And he did! I couldn't stand the man and . . .' The shepherd smiled, he never stopped smiling. What did he have to smile about? '. . . and so I decided to ambush him one night. I found him on a lonely road. It was pitch-black and I killed the scoundrel with my sword. He had it coming! Then . . . I escaped to the port and found passage on a Phoenician ship, the same that dropped me off here on the shore just last night . . .' I broke off, distracted. What was that smile?

'What an incurable liar you are! Do you never tire of spinning those yarns of yours? You've come up with so many! You're so good at it you'd even manage to fool a god. But . . . don't you recognize me?' She touched my cheek. That had never happened. Had she missed me?

Her amber eyes changed to green, then blue, a shade so intense it hurt. I prostrated myself with my face to the ground, tears welling up, and then lifted my gaze to hers again: 'Where had you gone to? You abandoned me. I've suffered so much. Why didn't you ever come to my aid? What did I do for you to leave me so alone?' I was reproaching her like a betrayed lover. How did I dare? But there she was, sitting under the olive tree next to me. I couldn't believe it: what a wondrous thing!

She answered with the same tone: 'Alone? It was you who no longer saw me, no longer listened to my voice. Who do you think sent the youth with the sun in his hair to Circe's island, and Calypso's? Who do you think the toad hobbling along next to you in the icy mud of the land of the dead was? And the seagull with its feathers all ruffled on top of the mast? The coot that shot out of the sea to guide you? The same one who flew out of the river waters and gave you the courage to leave the forest and appeal to Nausicaa for help. Who do you think made you look so handsome to the princess? You aren't as good-looking as all that, you know . . .' She wasn't above teasing me.

'Why were you so hard to recognize?'

'Because you were almost always on the sea or on islands surrounded by the sea, where Poseidon, my father's brother, has immeasurable power. I didn't want him to see me or hear me. Who would have been left to help you if he found me out?'

'But we're in the middle of the sea here and you've never appeared to me like now. You've never spoken to me so clearly.'

'It's different here,' she said, flashing her green eyes at me. 'Here we're behind the wall of fog. Here everything returns to how it was before the storm carried you away. That's not saying it's better.'

'Why?'

I was talking to my goddess, after such a long time, as if I were talking to a friend and I couldn't really believe it. Was I still asleep, and dreaming?

But she continued: 'You can't go home looking like that. Your house has been occupied by arrogant young men who are devouring all that is yours. There are many of them, and they are well armed. They want to oblige Penelope, who has remained faithful to you, to marry one of them and they plot to murder your son.' I was shaking with rage. 'Easy, I'm protecting your boy. And now . . . off with this opulent garment that makes you look similar to a god . . .'

I found myself covered in rags like a beggar. The sack I carried was soiled and greasy and hung off my shoulder on a piece of worn rope.

'We'll have to hide those warrior's arms and those powerful thighs . . . and let's add a few wrinkles to that face of yours and more white to that head of hair; it's too dark.'

I felt myself aging as her hand swept over me.

'There,' said my goddess, satisfied. 'That's much better. You can't stay here, too much coming and going. Take that path up that way, it'll lead you to crow's rock and to the shack where Eumeus the swineherd still lives. He's never stopped awaiting your return; you can trust him. Farewell.'

She disappeared.

She'd left me a walking stick.

I REACHED the path and started climbing the steep slope. The sun had risen high in the sky and was causing me to sweat profusely. When I was high enough I turned to contemplate my homeland. I could see where I had disembarked: it was the secret port, hidden between two tall promontories. There was Same, directly in front of me with her beautiful cliffs and woodland. At one side, the cave of the Naiads where I used to go to make sacrifice. So many things were returning to mind! At the end of the channel I could see tiny Asteria, little more than a rocky outcropping. I started to climb again, using the stick to help myself along. When I was nearly at the mountain's top I turned again. On the horizon, I thought I saw a tiny white sail. Could that be the ship that had brought me home? No, it couldn't be. By this time it would have travelled much further away and wouldn't be visible from here.

If Scheria were to be found at just a single night's voyage from Ithaca, my father and I would have gone ashore there on many occasions. Alcinous would have been our neighbour and guest and we his. So that was impossible, as were many other events that I'd experienced on the other side of the wall of fog. Had my helmsman crossed it in the middle of the night while I was fast asleep? Just how fast could that wondrous vessel travel, a ship that could find its own way without even a steering oar! Perhaps in a single night it had sailed a distance that would have taken a common craft ten or twenty times as long.

I had reached the high plain, which was covered with oaks. I could see how much they'd grown in my absence! If I had any doubts that I'd truly landed on Ithaca, that vision alone would have dispelled them. And there was crow's rock . . . how often I'd climbed it as a boy! I'd been ordered to by Damastes, to strengthen my arms and toughen my hands. Now I had to find Eumeus' house. Would he recognize me? No, not in the state I found myself in, not even my mother would have recognized me, not even my nurse, *mai*. I walked along the path, which had narrowed into a goat track, up the final incline, and found myself at a short distance from the stables and pigsties.

As I was approaching, I remembered how one day long ago Eumeus had shown me how a boar mounted a sow and that helped me to understand a lot of things in life. Great gods, I was little more than a child and my father was a hero at the peak of his strength. I'd been away so long! My whole world had changed in the meantime, and I doubted that I'd be able to recognize it.

I was very close now and I prepared to enter the pen. It was well made, a wall of stones topped with bundles of thorns to keep the wolves out. All at once I heard furious barking and two dogs ran out at me. I backed up against the trunk of an oak tree and raised the stick, but I didn't need to fight them off. The swineherd came and, shouting at them and throwing stones, managed to call them off. He called out to me:

'You're lucky, old man. If I hadn't been here they would have ripped you to shreds. Come on, come inside, I'll get you something to eat. Where are you from? I've never seen you around these parts.'

Eumeus . . . my heart leapt in my chest. My old servant! He hadn't changed so much. I could still see that it was him. His hair was thinner and he'd lost a tooth, but he still had those enormous hands, those wide shoulders and big dark eyes. And those bushy eyebrows!

I made up another story. I was used to it by now. 'I come from the continent. I found passage on a ferry. I hear say that there are many princes at the palace and a banquet to be had every day. I was hoping to pick up some alms.'

'Then I wish you good luck! Those aren't there to give, only to take. They eat a whole pig every day and they drink as much wine as they can get poured for them. And when they leave at night, my master's house looks worse than this pigsty. I hardly ever go there myself. I always send one of the hands, I can't stand to see such havoc. It's a terrible shame.'

I entered the pen as he went on grumbling and complaining. The dogs had come back in the meantime but, at seeing me talking to their master, they sniffed at me and went on their way.

'Why does your master allow such a thing? Why doesn't he throw them out of his house?'

'Because he's not there. He's dead.'

'He's dead? Did you see him die yourself? How did it happen?'

His voice seemed to tremble. 'No, although I wish I had. To close his eyes, render the honours he deserved and raise a great mound over his tomb. You see, he left many many years ago for the war, and he never came back. By now he's on the bottom of the sea, if the fish haven't finished eating him yet, or dead in some foreign land, slaughtered by a tribe of savages. He left with a whole army and none of them ever came back. Damned war. Damned war took my master.'

'He was good to you?'

'Good to me? He treated me like one of the family. I would have died for him. Once I had finished as his swineherd and trained another to take my place, he would have given me a fine woman for a wife, tall and shapely, and a house where I would have raised a family . . .' he sighed. 'But I'm happy you've shown up, old man, I'm happy to have your company. Know what we'll do now? We'll take a couple of little piglets and put them on a spit. We'll toast some bread over the embers, down a glass or two of good wine and to hell with these sad thoughts.'

His eyes were bright with tears. Good old Eumeus . . .

'Oh, don't go expecting the best though, that goes to the princes. We'll take a couple of runts, two of the skinny ones that got the last teats, but once they've been nicely seasoned and roasted they'll do just fine.'

'That's even too much for me, my friend. When I'm lucky I get thrown a chunk of dry bread.'

Eumeus tossed some wood onto the fire. 'It's starting to get cold at night,' he said, 'and we'll need the embers to roast our pigs.' He treated me like an old friend and we had just met. At least, that's what he had reason to believe.

I helped him to place the piglets under the sows for suckling and to herd the hogs and the barrows into their separate pens, while he began to cook a couple of small piglets. They looked scrawny, but soon the fragrance of their meat roasting made my mouth water. At least I felt that I had earned my keep.

We sat near the fire and waited for the meat to be done and the bread to toast. The wine was ready and Eumeus poured it into two cups, and then took the spits from the embers and cut off portions for both of us, without skimping. It tasted delicious. I hadn't eaten since I'd woken up under the olive tree. When we'd finished we took the bones out to the dogs, so they could enjoy it as we had. The evening was still young; we poured more wine and went on talking.

'But who was your master?' I asked. 'And what was that damned war you were talking about earlier?'

'Everyone around here knows about the war,' replied Eumeus. 'It's the war that Agamemnon of Mycenae and Menelaus of Sparta declared against Troy. It was all because of Helen. My master had just married, he had an infant son and he didn't want to go, but he was forced to. His name was Odysseus.'

'Why do you keep saying "was"? Couldn't he still be alive?'

Eumeus pulled his stool up close, leaned over and looked me straight in the eye. 'Listen up, old man. My master is dead. Hear that? Dead! And even if he isn't, it's as if he was. Twenty years have gone by. That's too many. Don't get it in your head to go to the queen up at the palace and start telling her stories: that you've seen him, that you've heard he's still alive. She's already heard it from every beggar or tramp who happens by here, hoping to get himself something to eat or to cover himself. Everyone knows that the queen refuses to marry because she hopes that Odysseus is coming back and so these vagabonds take advantage of that and tell her what she wants to hear. I have the feeling that for some new clothes or even a cloak a bit better than that rag on your shoulders you'd do the same.' His eyes shone as he repeated in a tired voice: 'My master is dead . . . dead.'

I had no words in the face of those tears.

'I loved him more than I ever loved my own parents. Not that I ever knew them. Phoenician merchants carried me off when I was just a child and sold me on the slave market.'

At that point I couldn't stay quiet. His loyalty deserved some consolation. 'Now you listen to me,' I said, without moving my eyes from his. 'Odysseus is coming back. Soon. I can promise you that. He'll return before the new moon. At the end of this month or the beginning of the next.'

He regarded me even more suspiciously.

'Listen, we'll make a bet,' I told him. 'I'm willing to wager a new tunic and cloak that I'm telling you the truth. To prove that I'm sincere I don't want them now. You'll give them to me when you see your master back here at home.'

Eumeus shook his head. It had become dark and the only light in the house came from the hearth. He threw another piece of wood onto the fire.

'That won't work with me, old man,' he said. 'You can't play games with me. You'll never earn that tunic and cloak. You'll have to find some other way to get what you need. You aren't bad with the pigs and I could use a helper . . . I have too many problems of my own to sort out. Telemachus, my master's son – a lovely boy, as good-hearted and generous as his father – has got it into his head to go off looking for him. By now he should have arrived in Pylos, Nestor's kingdom.'

'King Nestor is famous for being a just and generous sovereign. I'm sure the boy will be treated well.'

'It's not him I'm worried about – it's these wretched bastards who are occupying the palace. They want Penelope to choose one of them as a husband. They're plotting to ambush Telemachus in the channel as he's returning home. He's the last heir of the house that reigns over Ithaca and the islands and they mean to murder him. His mother suspects as much and is desperate. But there's nothing you and I can do about it, is there? Let us set such sad thoughts aside and trust that Zeus will protect him. We can't always allow anxiety and grief to rule our lives. Tell me about yourself, old man. Where are you from? And how did you fall so low?'

He poured me another cup of wine. The north wind whipped the cloths covering the windows like sails in a storm. My loyal old servant was yearning for a good story, a long one, full of adventures, and I was happy to satisfy him. It wasn't hard to do. All I had to do was weave together bits and pieces of the events I had experienced myself. A difficult return from the war, no more than a month with my wife and son, the impossibility of staying put in a place that may have been my own country but one I didn't recognize any more. An adventure in Egypt, a defeat, a long absence, seven whole years! An escape, a shipwreck, days and nights hanging on to the ship's mast for dear life before being cast ashore in Thesprotia, where the king himself swore that he'd seen Odysseus with his own eyes and that he still had all the treasure he'd piled up in Troy. The king had given him a ship and directed him towards Ithaca. And that was that and here was I, nothing but a sorry beggar at the end of it all, but happy to be warmed by the fire with a cup of good wine, resting at last after fleeing cruel persecutors and plain bad luck. The stars outside followed their courses in the night sky, where a thin sickle moon glittered low on the horizon, casting its pale light on crow's rock.

Eumeus was moved by my retelling of these fictitious events, so similar to what I'd gone through. He was a good-hearted soul. He said: 'You've certainly seen suffering, much more than I! But why try to make me believe that Odysseus will return soon? No, my friend, I know what happened to him. It isn't hard to imagine. We've heard rumours over the years. He was the one who found the way to end the war, but he didn't die in combat. Had it only been so! He would have died a hero, the Achaians would have raised an enormous mound, as they have for all the heroes who fell so far from their homeland, and his glory would have illuminated his son as well. No, he's not coming back. He died because the gods didn't love him enough. The ghosts of the tempest spirited him away and carried him off to some dark death, robbing him of glory.

'And me? Here I remain, among my pigs. If guests arrive, the queen never summons me to the palace. She's tired of hearing me warn her about swindlers and beggars like you. She'd rather be deceived into believing that her husband is still alive, even if it's just for a moment. But when she does invite me I'm happy to go and speak with her, or just look at her, beautiful as she is, so noble and proud. I understand that you're miserable, old man, but you can lay off with your tall tales now. There's no tricking me. And that's not why I've welcomed you under my roof, or why you're warming yourself by my fire, drinking my wine or eating my bread. I've taken you in because I pity you and because I know that any poor man in tatters seeking shelter may be a god in disguise, putting us mortals to the test.'

The wind picked up and it started to rain hard. We could hear it pelting down on the roof. I asked him for a cloak to cover myself, because I'd be cold with the rags I was wearing.

'Here,' he replied, tossing me his own, 'but you'll have to give it back tomorrow, I don't have another.' Then he threw a cape made of sheepskins over his shoulders, girded on a sword and picked up a spear.

'It's nights like these that robbers go roaming under the cover of darkness. They imagine that we're slumbering peacefully alongside the fire, but they're wrong. I'm going to sleep out by the pigsty, with the dogs. There's a spot that's sheltered from the rain. I'll see you in the morning.'

I watched as he left, pulling the sheepskin tight. The wind slammed the door against the jamb several times before he secured the latch. I was alone, in the silence of the hut, with the crackling of the dying flames and the patter of the rain on the roof for company.

Then, in the middle of the night, a shepherd's flute warbled its solitary tune. My goddess was letting me hear her voice.

16

THE NEXT DAY, AT DAWN, Eumeus came back into the hut. I could hear him stamping his feet on the ground to warm them, and rubbing his hands.

'The mountain peaks on the mainland are covered with snow,' he said. 'That's why it was so cold last night.'

Then he blew on the embers and added a small bundle of dry sticks, and the flames were rekindled. At this point he threw a big piece of olive wood onto the fire; it was slow-burning and would last much longer than a softer wood. I got up and walked towards him. 'If your master could only see this, he'd certainly be happy with you. You care for his property and his pigs as if they were your own.'

'I do it because it's my duty. It's the property of Telemachus and the queen I'm preserving,' he answered. 'Who knows where my boy is now?' he added with a sigh. 'It's terrible not to be able to warn someone who's in danger. But what can I do? Send out a ship? Where to? Will he choose to sail along the coast or between the islands? Anyway, if I were to leave from the port on a ship, everyone would know about it in no time. A swineherd fancying himself a sailor wouldn't go unnoticed, I'd wager.'

A flute echoed in the distance. I strained to hear: 'Did you hear that?' I asked Eumeus.

'Hear what?'

'A flute?'

'No, I don't hear anything. You're imagining it.'

But I could hear it quite clearly. A single note at first, followed by others, lower and deeper, and then by more highly pitched ones, and finally the single, tense note again: like a signal. My goddess was close and wanted me to know it. I needn't worry. No one would touch my boy.

'What's he like?'

'What's who like?'

'The prince. Telemachus. What does he look like? Is he a good sort of lad?'

Eumeus peered into my eyes as if trying to make out the thoughts that flitted through my heart.

'He's a handsome boy indeed. You should see him. He's a little taller than his father was and well built with a thin waist and broad shoulders. His eyes are dark and deep like his mother's, and he gets irritated like she does if you rub him the wrong way. I know him well and I can see right away if he's feeling moody. If it's one of those days, I take him over to see Philoetius, if he's got a newborn calf, or we go hunting wood pigeons with a bow and arrow, or he'll help me plant an olive tree. He likes to watch me while I'm working. He's got a generous heart. He thinks of me as . . . I don't know, an uncle. Someone he cares about. Every now and then he'll bring a gift for me, carry it over himself. When he comes to dinner, once or twice a month, he never arrives empty-handed. He has an amphora of special wine from Same or Corinth sent over, or a wheel of goat cheese. The cloak I lent you last night? He gave it to me.'

'So his father would be proud of him.'

'You can say that again, more than proud. That boy is a treasure. What vexes him most, besides what he sees going on in his house, is never having known his father. You can tell he misses him awfully, especially now that he has these arrogant bastards invading the palace. A boy shouldn't have to watch his mother cry without having the means to defend her.'

I turned to poke at the fire so he wouldn't see my face. A cloud of sparks rose towards the opening in the middle of the roof.

'He's never felt so alone as he does now,' he continued. 'The company of a swineherd is certainly not the best you could wish on a prince and a boy his age. His grandfather, King Laertes, left the palace long ago to live on his farm in the country. All told, it's better he did. If he had remained, blood would be spilling.'

'Doesn't he remember anything about his father?'

'He was too young when his father left for the war.'

'Does he ever ask you about him?'

'Oh, sure. What were Odysseus' eyes like, what was his hair like, was he good with a spear and a sword, was he as clever as everyone says, what did he like to eat, did he like hunting wood pigeons . . .' Eumeus went to the door. 'It's better that I go and put the piglets under the sows. I don't trust the farm hands. They get distracted so easily. I don't want any of the sucklings to be crushed.' He went out.

I spent the next few days with him, and every evening we'd stay up late talking and drinking wine for as long as the fire lasted. He recounted the complicated tale of how he'd ended up on Ithaca, one I'd heard ever since I was a child. How he'd been kidnapped by Phoenician merchants as a small boy. The son, back then, of a powerful and respected man, he was betrayed by his nurse, who had taken a bribe from the foreign sailors. I pretended to listen with great curiosity, and urged him on with my exclamations. We were good companions. It was a true novelty for him after the sole company of the stable boys who worked for him.

Then one day at dawn, as soon as we'd got up, I told him that I could stay no longer, that I'd become as bad as the pretenders to the throne, living off his master's bounty.

'I thought I'd go to the palace and make myself useful there. I can serve at table. I know how to mix wine and carve meats . . .'

'Are you crazy, old man? Don't even think about it. Do you want to know what their servants are like? Boys from good families who they've brought along with them: educated, well-dressed, sweetly scented. They'd kick the life out of you, ragged as you are and reeking of the pigsty. Anyone who stays here longer than a day ends up smelling like a pig.'

'All I know is that I've been here for days eating your bread and drinking your wine without being of any real help. I'm not so good at tending pigs. It's like I told you: I was once a wealthy man, with servants and women and a magnificent house. But I want to thank you. I'll never forget your hospitality. You took me in without even knowing who I was, you fed me and sheltered me from the biting cold. I may stink now but that's easily taken care of. I'll just stop at the spring near crow's rock and wash.'

Eumeus was about to answer when he abruptly held his finger to his lips. The dogs outside were signalling someone's arrival.

'Who could it be?' I asked.

'Listen, they're not barking like they did with you. They're yelping, it's someone they recognize. There's only one person they'd be so happy to see: the master's son. It's Telemachus! He's made it back safely! May the gods be praised . . .'

He ran outside. I heard shouts of joy, voices raised in greeting . . . the voice of a young man, strong and deep. It was the first time I'd heard the true voice of my son!

They entered straight away and my heart leapt in my chest. I swiftly rose to my feet but Telemachus said: 'Don't get up, foreigner, Eumeus will find me another stool.' I couldn't believe that my son was talking to me. My son! I started trembling as I never had before and when Eumeus entered with a bundle of sticks and a sheep's skin he looked at me and asked: 'Are you all right, my friend?'

I mumbled an excuse and left them. I couldn't bear for my son to see me in that state. I went out of the small back door, rounded the stables and hurried to crow's rock. There was a stream flowing from the spring where the flocks came to drink. I washed myself and my hair, combing through it with my fingers. As I was about to go back, I spied a long white tunic and a lovely cloak hanging on the branch of an olive tree. Who could they belong to? I put them on and returned to Eumeus' house. My heart was pounding hard enough to suffocate me, even harder than when, biting my lip, I would wait unflinching for the order to attack the enemy army on the fields of Troy.

As I retraced my steps I caught a glimpse of the shepherd boy, among the trunks of the centuries-old olive trees, taking his goats to pasture. It was my goddess, restoring the look and the vigour of a king in me, so I could face my son after twenty years gone.

I entered through the main door so I wouldn't have to bend in two. Eumeus, who was carrying a basket of bread, turned to stone at the sight of me. He regarded me without saying a word. Perhaps he couldn't understand or perhaps he understood too well. But my eyes were for the boy. I needed to fill my heart with the image that I'd so often tried to dream up on those solitary nights in distant lands, in anguished exile, on the vast, insurmountable sea.

'Who are you, foreigner?' he asked me, seemingly amazed at my appearance.

I prayed that my heart not fail me and took a step towards him. I'd been asked that question so many times and had answered in so many ways – a wanderer who has no country and no shelter is everyone and no one. But I – who had always had so many tales ready to tell – could not find a word to break the silence. The boy continued to look at me, curious and perplexed.

I opened my mouth finally and said: 'I am—'

'He's your father,' said Eumeus. 'He could never hide his emotion when he spoke of you – tears glittered in his eyes as they do now that you stand before him. And just before you came in, he mentioned a place that no foreigner new to this island could possibly know: crow's rock. Now that he looks like a king or a god of the heavens, I recognize him without any doubt. He is your father, Telemachus. Your father has returned after twenty years!'

I suddenly found my words: 'It's me, son. I know that you aren't ready to accept me yet, to recognize me. I'm simply a foreigner to you, a stranger. How often I've tried to imagine what you were like. With every year that passed I tried to let you grow inside me, in my heart, in my eyes. And now that I see you I feel that I've never been separated from you. I never wanted to leave you, son, I did everything I could not to leave you. When from my ship I watched the shore becoming more and more distant, your mother holding you in her arms becoming smaller and smaller, my heart broke. I can't believe I'm standing here in front of you.'

I opened my arms and, after a moment's hesitation, he embraced me tightly. We stood there, unmoving, without saying a word. Everything was silent, I could see nothing and no one. Even Eumeus had disappeared. We wept, father and son, in each other's arms.

'There's so much we have to talk about, son!' I said when my tears had run out.

He nodded, smiling. He seemed happy and he was much more handsome than I ever could have imagined.

'Tell me where you've been,' I said. 'And why you left without saying a word. Eumeus tells me that your mother nearly went mad when you disappeared.'

'It was Mentes, chief of the Taphians, who convinced me to go. He showed up here twenty days ago, unannounced. I told *mai* to receive him and we conversed for a while. But my mother's suitors were making such a ruckus, arguing at the tops of their lungs as the servants were taking the animals to the courtyard so they could be slaughtered for the banquet . . . the pigs were squealing under the knife. I was ashamed that there was no place I could talk peacefully to a guest in my house.'

'Mentes . . .' I'd never heard the name before. But I thought of Mentor. Where was he?

'It was he who urged me to leave and seek news of you. I

thought that, if I could be certain that you were dead . . .' he stared at me intensely, 'I would have raised a mound on the seashore and allowed my mother to remarry.'

'You'll have to raise that mound some other time,' I said. 'And then? What else did he say? And what was the chief of a tribe of pirates doing in Ithaca?'

'I don't know. But he tried to convince me that you were still alive and that he was almost certain that you would return. Soon.'

'Did you believe him?'

'No . . . I'm not sure. But I thought his advice was good. I thought that living in uncertainty, without knowing, was worse than finding out bad news. I sailed for Pylos, where I met King Nestor.'

'How is he?'

'His face is ageless but the war plainly left its mark on him. When I tried to confide my anxiety, my sadness, my rage, all he could say was: "Just think of me. I had to watch my son Antilochus die." He told me that he was killed by a black king called Memnon.'

'It's true. On that day long ago when I went to Pylos to call the princes to arms, Nestor claimed that he would never be able to let his son go to war while he stayed behind. He couldn't bear the thought of scanning the sea day after day awaiting the boy's return, and he insisted on coming as well, with the result that he watched Antilochus, his favourite son, die. Destiny always waits for us where it knows we will pass, my boy.'

Telemachus gave me a searching look, as if trying to find the signs of the truth that he had never known in the lines of my face.

'What else did he tell you?' I asked.

'That after the war you and he left Troy with the first group, following *wanax* Menelaus, while the others stayed behind with Agamemnon.'

'And did he tell you that after passing Tenedos I turned back with my ships?'

'He did.' I could tell that each of my words was increasing his certainty that the man before him was his father. 'Why did you do it? Why did you head back?'

'It has to do with the saddest and most bitter moment of my life. Let me enjoy this moment of finding you again after so many years, *pai* . . .' *I called him with the same name my father had used with me and it still warms my heart to think about it.*

'After you turned back, with the wind against you and the sea in storm, he never saw you again.'

'It's true. When I finally started off again, the same north wind carried me far from Cape Malea into unknown waters . . .'

'Go on, please. Don't stop.'

'No, you go on. I'll have time to tell you about my wanderings. What happened after you spoke to Nestor?'

'*Wanax* Nestor urged me to continue to Sparta. Rumour had it that Menelaus had just returned from a journey which had lasted years; he might have had news of you. He had his son Pisistratus take me on a four-horse chariot. We flew like the wind . . .'

'Pisistratus . . . he was barely walking the first time I went to Pylos with my father. And now he's driving a four-horse chariot!'

'Yes. We became friends. He's a good lad, generous as can be, but I wouldn't want to find him against me on a battlefield! In Sparta, King Menelaus welcomed me like a son. He embraced me and told me how greatly he esteemed you, what a friend you were. He said that he'd hoped to give you a city near the sea so that you could spend the last years of your life close to him.'

'Nothing else?'

'He said he'd been to Egypt, where he had consulted the oracle of the Old Man of the Sea. The oracle revealed a prophetic vision: you were alive, but a prisoner in a place surrounded by the sea, without your ship or your comrades. There was no hope that you would return. Great sadness overcame us all, but Queen

Helen had good wine served and that cheered us a bit and helped us to forget our melancholy.'

'What else did Menelaus tell you?'

'I believe he's plotting to avenge the murder of his brother. Perhaps you don't know: no sooner had *wanax* Agamemnon returned from Troy, than he was killed by Aegisthus, Queen Clytaemnestra's lover. Menelaus is helping his nephew Orestes, Agamemnon's son, to avenge his father and reconquer Mycenae. I believe a great war is in the offing.'

His words brought to my mind the great king of the Achaians as I'd last seen him, a sad, angry ghost at the gates of Hades, and my heart froze.

'Queen Helen gave me a finely embroidered peplum to give to my betrothed. When I find one, that is! She was gentle and kind to me, but you can see that she's still tormented by remorse for the war she herself set off by fleeing with Paris to Troy. Before I left, the king showered me with gifts and we returned to Pylos where my ship was waiting for me. I asked Pisistratus to explain to his father Nestor that I couldn't prolong my travels. I knew that if I so much as stepped into the palace, he would never have let me leave! They all showed me such affection. Perhaps they were thinking of you, Father, how you'd never returned, when they showered me with gifts and with kindness.

'Then something strange happened. As my shipmates were about to cast off, a man approached the ship. He was a stranger to me, a fugitive. He blurted out that he'd killed a man and the relatives were pursuing him to get revenge. His name was Theoclymenus and he was asking for passage on our ship. He also told us that he was a seer who could look into the future. I told him he could come aboard, and now he's down at the port with the others.'

'That was rash of you, *pai*, the relatives of a dead man can be very violent with anyone who offers him shelter.' We were both smiling. I'd come back after twenty years and here I was already scolding him.

'Perhaps he'd killed to defend himself or because he was forced to do so. He struck me as a noble person; his eyes were dark and piercing, and I was fascinated by him. During the voyage we talked about many things, except the one thing that really interested me: you. What I wanted to ask him was: Where is my father? Will he ever come back? When? Or has he simply disappeared without a trace? Must I resign myself to the idea that he will never return? The words never came out of my mouth. I suppose I was afraid that the seer would tell me a truth that I didn't want to hear, and I suppose he sensed that.'

We fell silent for a while. From outside came the grunting of the pigs, the laughter of the farm hands and the voice of Eumeus ranting at them.

'Tell me about your mother,' I said.

Telemachus lowered his gaze and turned his head away. The question I'd asked him was hard on his mind and on his heart.

He answered: 'She has always remained faithful to you. At first, when Laertes my grandfather was still living with us, it wasn't so bad. We tried to get used to you being away, we knew you were at war and that the war wasn't over. We had each other. Phemius told me stories, my mother spent a lot of time with us. Grandfather would take me up to the woods on top of Mount Neritus . . . once we got to the peak, we'd sit close and he would cover me with his cloak to protect me from the wind. We would wait for the sun to set, for the sky to turn pink, then red, and the sea the colour of wine, and then we'd make our way back home, guided by the lights behind the windows of the great hall. I wanted so much to ask him: "When will Father be back?" but I knew it was forbidden, a question that gave everyone pain – Grandfather, Mother, even *mai*. I learned to keep quiet.

'Once, from the mountain peak, I spotted a ship in the distance. It was approaching the island, its white sail billowing in the wind. I couldn't help myself, I stretched out my arm and hand to point it out to my grandfather, and shouted:

'"*Atta's* ship, *atta's* ship!"

'He looked at me with shiny eyes the colour of the sea. He answered: "That's not *atta's* ship, my boy. When it comes it'll be from the opposite direction and there won't be one alone, but a great many." That never happened again. Whenever I saw a sail in the distance I'd bite my lip and keep my mouth closed.

'Then news came that the war had ended and the agony of waiting became ever more acute, more painful. Whenever any wanderer happened by the palace or any merchant landed on our shores, my mother would ask if they had news of you. One day a group of ships sailed up and moored at the great port. The warrior who came ashore had powerful arms and a wide chest, and wore a red cloak on his shoulders. I thought it was you, I was certain of it, and I ran to the wharf. But I realized that no one had recognized him and I understood it couldn't be you. But he recognized me. "You're Telemachus," he said.

'I replied: "How do you know my name? I've never seen you."

'"I knew your father, King Odysseus. I was his friend. You look like him, that's how I recognized you."

'"Do you know if my father's coming back?" I asked him.

'"Of course," said he, "and he'll bring you beautiful gifts."'

Telemachus broke off. He couldn't continue his story and my heart was heavy as well.

'What do you remember about him?' I asked.

'He had sad eyes, a grim look and hair the colour of flames. He walked as if he carried a great weight on his shoulders.'

'Diomedes,' I muttered to myself, 'Diomedes of Argus.'

'What did you say?'

'Nothing, *pai*, nothing. Just old memories.'

17

WE WENT ON TALKING until late. Telemachus had a lot to tell me and I had so much to say to him, but I didn't tell him everything. Not all I'd told the Phaeacians and their king. I just couldn't go back.

There was one thing that I hadn't been able to cast from my thoughts since I'd landed on my island: the prophecy that Nausicaa had announced to me, the annihilation that threatened the city and its people if they helped a man who came from the sea to return to his homeland. I continued to hope that the blue god would choose not to fulfil the prophecy. It was in his power and those people were his own descendants. But who can probe the mind of a god? In the past, whenever I'd had a narrow escape or one of my adventures was over, I would manage to tuck away my suffering in a hidden corner of my heart and find the strength to go on. Not any more.

Telemachus picked up from where he'd left off.

'After that, with every day that passed, the hope of seeing you became more remote. But I had never seen you, so it was different for me. It was much harder on Grandfather and on Mother. Grandmother Anticlea sank into a state of such hopelessness that she wouldn't speak. She never left her room, and many times if I went to visit she wouldn't even open the door. If I found it open and went in, I'd see her sitting at the window and watching the sea with her clear, liquid eyes.' Telemachus' voice was trembling. 'I'd ask her if she felt like talking, tell her that I'd been hunting that day. 'Tomorrow I'm taking a boat over to Same. What can I bring you back that you'd like?' I'd say. Never an answer. When the first fruits ripened, I'd bring her something: a fig, some berries, whatever I'd find. But she'd just look at me without saying anything. Sometimes she'd smile like little children do, when they laugh or cry for no reason at all.'

I lowered my head so as not to cry myself. How much pain I'd left behind me, how many disappointed hopes, how many tears . . .

Telemachus stared at the flames crackling in the hearth. 'When she died, Grandfather had a solemn funeral prepared for her. He dressed her in her most beautiful gown. Weepers came from the continent to mourn the queen mother and the flute players sounded their lament. Her handmaids cut off locks of their hair to toss onto the pyre and Mother threw a precious amber necklace that had been part of her dowry into the flames. King Autolykos her father appeared suddenly out of nowhere, his white hair gathered at his neck with a leather tie. He wore a black floor-length cloak with a silver-studded belt and the crowd parted to let him pass. There was utter silence. The flute players and the weepers hushed and the thunder that had been rumbling in the distance hushed as well. Autolykos threw an object of little value onto the fire, a doll or something that looked like one. Later he was seen boarding his ship at the port and sailing west. We never heard from him again.

'The years passed and everyone began to say that you had died. Many of the warriors who had brought down Troy had come back, thousands of them, but none from Ithaca or Same or Dulichium or even Zacynthus. I made sure of this as I travelled among the islands. Perhaps, I thought, my father the hero Odysseus stopped on his return voyage with his men to sack some city, to carry off their wealth and their women. And maybe the inhabitants gathered in great number, filled with rage, and killed them all or took them prisoner or sold them off into slavery. So those men would never see their homes again. What else could have possibly happened?

'I wasn't the only son mourning his lost father. Many other youths on this island were thinking the same things I was.

'The only person who never gave up was Queen Penelope, my mother. She refused to raise a mound on the seashore and celebrate your funeral rites. She said that you had promised her you would return and that you always kept your promises. From that moment on, she became known far and wide as the unyielding protectress of your house and your bed, and her hope in your return became legendary. A great number of vagabonds and vagrants, freeloaders all, took advantage of her over the years. All they needed to do was hint that they'd seen the king of Ithaca or heard that he was alive and they'd be guaranteed hospitality, abundant food and a comfortable place to sleep under the palace portico. They told my mother what she wanted to hear. And even if her hopes were always shattered, she never gave up. She wouldn't miss an opportunity to keep her dreams alive. She has suffered greatly.'

'But now everything has changed, I hear.'

'That's right, for the worse. It was two years ago when the princes came: from Ithaca, all the islands around us and even from the continent. They bore wedding gifts in great quantity. They demanded that my mother declare publicly that she was a widow and that she choose a husband from among them. That was when King Laertes left the palace. He couldn't vanquish them and he couldn't stand them. He left for his farm in the country where he grows olives and grapes. He lives like the poorest of men. In the winter he sleeps in the house next to the hearth but in the summer he sleeps in the fields, wherever he happens to find himself, on a heap of dry leaves. I've seen him myself. Anything is more bearable than living in shame in your own house.'

I watched my son and listened to him, the heart in my chest snarling in rage at what I was hearing.

'Eumeus told me they were planning to ambush me at sea, behind the island of Asteria. They wanted to sink my ship, to see me die with all my men. Well here I am, fine as ever, and so are my comrades.'

With every passing instant, the image and the voice of my son entered my eyes and flowed into my heart, so that I felt that I loved him as though we had never lived a moment apart.

'Tell me more about your mother. How has she managed to put off the suitors?'

'She's the worthy wife of Odysseus, the man of the multi-coloured mind. Did you know that the minstrels call you that? Since they were becoming more and more insistent, she came up with a stratagem. She said she would not make her choice until she had finished weaving a funeral shroud for the hero Laertes. No one would dare to oppose such a request. My mother wove the cloth by day and unravelled it by night . . .'

I smiled at her cunning and I remembered the girl with the deep, bright eyes that I'd fallen in love with so many years ago in Sparta.

'. . . but one of the handmaids, who has become the lover of Antinous, their leader, discovered the trick and she told the suitors, who broke into the women's quarters at night, brazenly violating their seclusion.'

My blood boiled in my veins at hearing those words. 'They'll pay for this. I'll slaughter them all, from the first to the last,' I muttered.

But Telemachus had not finished. 'At that point she could feign no longer. I tried to appeal to the assembly, but the princes are powerful, and they're well armed. No one dares to take a stand against them, and I'm not strong enough to do it on my own . . . Forgive me, Father,' he said, bowing his head.

'You have nothing to be ashamed of. You did what you could.'

'Some of them have even importuned Grandfather Icarius in Sparta, offering even richer wedding gifts to convince him to intervene and declare that his daughter is a widow. If you hadn't returned, I don't think she would have been able to hold them off any longer.'

'It's true. She wouldn't have been able to put off a decision. But why did you return from your voyage so soon? You told me that King Nestor and King Menelaus were willing to extend their hospitality for as long as you wanted.'

'I heard a voice calling me home, and Theoclymenus, the seer, swore to me that you were on the island. The heart in my chest was dancing with joy. Do you believe me?'

'I do, *pai*, and I myself can't wait to see King Laertes my father again, to console him for so many bitter years. But first . . . first the suitors will have to pay. And you will help me.'

'You and I alone? *Atta*, there are fifty of them, sometimes even more; strong, young, armed men. Many of my mother's handmaids are their concubines. They know all there is to know about the palace. *Mai* hates them because they don't respect her.'

'I destroyed Troy. Do you think fifty young men should worry me?'

Eumeus entered. His hair was tousled by the wind and he held two baskets in his hands, with bread, cheese and spits of roasted meat.

'Eumeus,' I asked him, 'would you be willing to do battle?'

'Even now, *wanax*,' he replied, setting down the baskets and laying his two big fists on the table.

'Who else can we count on?'

'Philoetius, the cowherd. He's strong as an ox and with an axe in his hand he's a fury. He'd throw himself into the fire for you.'

'No one else?'

'Maybe . . . but it's better not to take risks. Unless you want to call on your father King Laertes. He may not be as strong as he once was, but I'll wager that he's raring to put on his armour.'

'No, better not. He'll know that I've returned when it's time. Now listen to me, both of you: the plan is clear in my mind. You, Telemachus, will leave tomorrow at dawn. Go to see your mother as soon as you can. She must be going mad with anguish and worry. Let her see that you're alive and that no one has harmed you. Eumeus, you and I will leave later, and go to the palace. I'll remain, to beg for something to eat from the princes. You'll head back after you've paid your respects to the queen. I want to get to know them one by one, watch what they do, how they act, what they're scheming.

'Even if the two of you see them insult me or humiliate me, don't make a move. Don't open your mouths, don't interfere. I'll know what to do.'

'What about my mother?' asked Telemachus.

'Your mother must know nothing until the time is right.' *Trust no one, not even your wife, say one thing and think another . . .* 'My decision may seem harsh to you, but it's necessary. No one in my house can know that I've returned. You'll tell your mother that you went ashore at the secret port and that you spent the night at Eumeus'. She won't ask about anything else. She'll be filled with joy at just seeing you.'

Telemachus regarded me with a bewildered look for a moment, but then instantly regained control over his heart. He nodded to let me know that he'd do as I asked him.

'I love your mother, *pai*. I love her more than I love my own life and I've never stopped thinking about her all these years, every day, every night. But we can't tell her anything yet. Trust me. She could give herself away without meaning to, and that would give me away. A look is all it would take, a gesture . . . We can't make a single mistake or we're lost.'

My words seemed to reassure him. Eumeus passed the roasted meat and the bread, first to me and then to Telemachus. He poured us wine as well, serving himself last. We were all three as tense as a bowstring before the arrow is let fly, but in my heart I felt stronger than ever before because I knew I'd crossed the wall of fog in my sleep as the Phaeacians brought me home in their helmless ship. It had followed a mysterious course of its own making on the pathless, limitless sea, ploughing the waves swiftly, covering an infinite distance in a single night. And it had delivered me here, to the world I knew, governed by human and divine forces. Here there were no inscrutable, hidden forces, no monstrous presences which, real or not real, had been capable of murder, annihilation, devastation in that world. This was my world, where I could count the swords and the spears and the sharp, merciless arrows.

Our hearts were light as we ate and spoke of times past, long ago for Eumeus and I, not so long ago for Telemachus. He seemed so young, so unseasoned in my eyes. Perhaps living alone with his mother for all these years had made him that way.

'Who trained you for combat?' I asked him.

'King Laertes my grandfather. Your father.'

'My father?'

'He was a great teacher.'

'Have you ever been in combat?'

'No. This will be the first time.'

A cold shiver ran under my skin. What if things went badly? Where was the flute I'd heard playing in the night? My goddess had already disappeared from my life once. Could it happen again?

'Aren't you afraid?'

'A little. There are only four of us.'

'Five,' I replied.

'Five? Who have I forgotten?'

'My goddess. Athena will be with us. It was she who called me back here from a remote, unreachable land. I wouldn't have been able to return otherwise. She alone is worth hundreds, thousands of warriors. Perhaps we won't see her, but she will give me the strength I need.'

Telemachus and I finally lay down to get some rest next to the hearth, close to one another, still talking in the dark.

'Mentor. Do you know who he is?'

'Certainly, *atta*. He was the advisor who was your friend while you were in Ithaca, before you left for the war.'

'So he's not here any more? Tell me, how long has it been since you've seen him?'

'It's strange, I don't remember. But he has a seat in the assembly. Sometimes he's there, sometimes he's not.'

A long silence. I could hear the sound of my son's breathing, light and serene. The breath that brings on sleep. Many were the things I still wanted to tell him, ask him, but it was better that he rest. For now.

I wondered whether it was right to lead him into combat, to make him spill blood, but it was too late to turn back now. I remembered what it had been like for me to kill a man for the first time. It was on the fields of Troy. I ran him through from side to side, my bronze tearing into his bowels. I'd never done it before and it felt like I had run myself through. A sense of bewilderment and incredulity. Then pain, and fear, and the sense that I had crossed a limit beyond which the land of horror lay. But I was at the head of many men and twelve ships, and everyone had to see what I was worth, especially those of my companions who had already accomplished great deeds, like Diomedes who had avenged his father at Thebes of the Seven Gates.

In the end, I was alone in the dark, turning over a thousand thoughts in my heart. How would I present myself at the palace the next day? How would my heart bear up at the sight of my wife? How I would surprise the arrogant suitors and kill them all without anyone in the city hearing their cries of agony?

I went outside for a while to look at the sky and to listen to the sounds of the woodland at night. I heard the soft chirping of birds who had come home to their nests and their chicks, the rustling of leaves, and then, a song. It was so soft that it seemed to be drifting in on the wings of the wind from a very faraway place. There were fragments of words, of sounds, and I couldn't make sense of it. The voice of a young boy . . . or of a woman? Yes, a woman, perhaps . . . when the wind picked up I felt it was becoming easier to understand, or was it the opposite? Then, when for a few instants the wind blew in from a different direction, so that the leaves stopped rustling, I could hear it clearly, I could make out the words:

'. . . sting of nostalgia . . . bring him home . . .'

My eyes filled with tears. Was it she? She who still remembered me, hadn't lost hope . . . was that possible? Or was I just bent on believing that, with all my heart? When had I last heard that song? Could I still call it up in my mind? Go back in time? Suffer the pangs of separation again with such intense longing, feel that same passion . . . Could I still feel such passion? The wind dropped and left a sky dotted with a myriad of stars, as bright as the eyes of nymphs in the darkness, like fireflies in the woods on a night in May. I couldn't understand what was going through my heart, how I felt under that starry sky. I knew I was with my son whom I'd left barely talking and who now slept and thought and dreamt close by. It was too much, even for someone who had suffered, seen, experienced as much as I had. I needed to lie down in the dark in a little round hut next to my sleeping son, and there await Dawn.

That's what I did. I passed Eumeus, who was slumbering in the shelter of the rock, crossed the courtyard and went back in. The embers were almost completely covered with ash, and it was sweet to stretch out on the sheepskin, under a cover of woven wool. Sleep descended on my eyelids as well, finally, and the voice of the wind started to sing again, faintly. It lulled me like *mai*'s singing had, when I was just a little boy.

THE LIGHT of dawn woke me. The sun was rising from behind the Thesprotian mountains. Outside I could hear the voices of Telemachus and Eumeus.

'Be careful, son!' my good friend was saying. 'They'll be furious when they realize they've failed to kill you. They'll want to try again. Enter boldly, in the full light of day, after the suitors have all settled in and the handmaids and servants are busy preparing their meal. Go directly upstairs to your mother. She'll hear your footsteps and recognize them and her heart will leap with joy. Let the princes know you knew what they were plotting but don't say anything outright. Stay cheerful. That will increase their consternation. I want them to start feeling afraid.'

'I'll do as you say, Eumeus. My father was still sleeping when I got up. He must have been terribly tired. Let him rest.'

'How do you feel?'

'I don't know. I still can't believe it. It seems like a dream, like the ones I had when I was little. I would dream that he was home and that I could run into his arms.'

'I've prepared a sack for you with bread, roasted meat, cheese and a small skin of wine. The dogs will accompany you for a stretch. Take care. The day of revenge is at hand.'

I could hear the dogs yelping outside. I went to the door, which was half open, and looked out. Eumeus was putting a spear into the boy's hand, and a sheathed sword over his shoulder. The dogs ran alongside him across the courtyard and down the path, until Eumeus called them back with a whistle.

I walked out into the light of a radiant day.

The sun had already warmed the air and my swineherd had me sit down under the shade of a leafy maple. He brought me fresh milk, warm bread and honey from his own beehives.

'I feel like a boy again!' I exclaimed. 'I can't tell you what joy it gives me to taste these flavours from my childhood.'

I took off my white tunic and put on my beggar's rags. I threw the worn, soiled rope that closed the sack I carried over my shoulder and grasped my walking stick, the gift of a goddess. Eumeus took a basket with gifts for the queen and we set off walking.

Crossing woods, fields and groves next to the man who had cared for them for so many years, knowing without believing that I'd be back. It filled me with an intense emotion, like when I would go walking with my father and try to catch up my small steps with his long, heavy ones. We chatted about sowing and harvesting, about lambs and goats and about my people. Eumeus had a lot to tell me: who was still alive and who had gone, carried off by the Chaera of death. How far we were from the seaweed-dark cliffs and the livid waves of Cimmeria where the mouth of Hades was! Those images hadn't vanished from my heart, but what I saw before me was so beautiful that it perfectly matched the dream I used to have in my darkest, most trying hours: this light, these colours. The scents, the look and the sounds of my island.

When we arrived at a fork in the road, Eumeus pointed to the left: 'The king your father's farm is that way. Are you sure you don't want to go and see him? It wouldn't take long.'

I did want to, with all my heart, but I knew it was better that I didn't. What I needed to do was quite clear to me and we turned towards the palace instead. 'When what has to be done is finished,' I told Eumeus. 'Not before.'

The palace became visible on the hillside as we made our way out of the woods and began to cross pastures and cultivated fields. My home!

I stopped to gaze at it, almost afraid that it would disappear from one moment to the next like a mirage, without realizing that we were blocking the way, on the narrow path, of a herd of goats. Eumeus motioned for me to join him on the side of the road. 'That's Melanthius, the goatherd,' he told me. 'He's a troublemaker. Don't talk to him if you can avoid it.'

My wise swineherd was right again. Melanthius walked up beside us, spat on the ground and started railing at us. 'Will you take a look at this. One derelict leading the way for another one. Don't we have enough of our own, Eumeus, without you bringing in foreigners as well?'

He threw a stone that hit me on the shoulder. It hurt, and I was not used to letting an insult ride. My hand fell to my belt where my dagger was hidden. Eumeus became alarmed and shook his head to warn me not to do what I was thinking. In fact, my first impulse had been to fall on the lout and smash his skull against a rock, but that would surely have attracted unwanted attention. Better to hold my fury in check and wait for the day of vengeance. It was coming, and that day all my scores would be settled. Even with him.

'He's their friend,' hissed Eumeus. 'He does everything the princes tell him to. Even spying.'

'Then he'll get what he deserves. In good time. Everything in good time.'

And so we went on. The road began to climb upwards. We arrived at the walled fountain and I stopped to drink some cool water. The palace was close now, and the din coming from inside could already be heard, along with the squealing of a pig that was being butchered. I could feel my blood boiling. I stopped right in front of the entry to the courtyard and took a deep breath and looked over at Eumeus, who nodded back. It was time to go in.

'Will you go alone, *wanax*?' he said in a low voice.

'I know this house well,' I replied.

'I know. I was wondering if you needed help.'

'No. Telemachus will be inside.'

'Then I'll go to the back door, where the kitchens are, to deliver my gifts for the queen. I found some black figs, I know how much she likes them.'

He walked away and I entered the courtyard with a hood over my head, leaning on my stick. A wave of memories hit me. I saw myself as a child, running through that very place, Eumeus a bit older than I was and Philoetius just a little boy, and Mentor . . . Mentor who, years later, I would see appear and disappear, his features shifting and fading mysteriously into other semblances.

I could hear the scolding of *mai* Euriclea, could see the hero Laertes my father departing for his adventures on the sea, clad in bronze, shining like a star . . . and my mother, the queen, sitting in the middle of the room, surrounded by her maidservants, spinning soft yarn, dyed purple or light blue. A lost world that would never return.

But just as I braced myself to enter the hall full of unfamiliar, arrogant voices, I heard a feeble, but unmistakable sound. I would never forget it. The soft yelping of a dog. I turned and my heart filled with tears. He lay on a dungheap, mangy and tick-ridden, his eyes glassy and nearly spent. Argus! My Argus, my hunting companion, who would race carefree through the woods and among the silvery olive trees. He was dragging himself laboriously towards me. He alone, he before anyone, had recognized me, after twenty years.

He'd waited for me all that time, repelling death as she nipped at his heels, to see me one last time and then to die at my feet.

I hid my tears in my worn hood and went in.

18

I THOUGHT, AS I ENTERED the hall, that Telemachus must have already arrived and had probably already spoken with his mother. Penelope would surely be in her rooms upstairs, with the other women and with my nurse. The thought of being so close to her took my breath away. My heart, long resigned to the immense distances that had kept us apart, was pounding hard. The bad luck and misadventures that had schemed for so long to push me to the ends of the earth had been vanquished at last.

And there I was, crossing the threshold. There was the door of solid ash. Without letting anyone see I brushed my lips against the fragrant cypress jamb. The house was beautiful and solidly built by the generations of kings that had reigned over Ithaca and extended their rule over all the islands. There was no opulence, no lavish display of wealth, but it showed strength, dignity and simplicity, the virtues that I had learned from my father.

At the end of the great hall was a door in solid oak, bolted shut: the Hall of the Argonauts! It was there that we had received *wanax* Menelaus, lord of Sparta, who had come to decry Helen's abduction. The walls celebrated the glory of my father, Argonaut and hero, and all of his comrades in arms. Penelope had been wise to make it inaccessible, or Telemachus, if it had been he who made the decision.

But when I'd finally made my way in and looked around me, I wanted badly to close my eyes. Scores of men of different ages, richly garbed, were seated on carved wooden thrones draped with bright woollen cloth and sheepskins. Tables were set in front of them, crowded with trays and cups of bronze and silver, or even gold, and the hearth at the centre of the room crackled under spits laden with big chunks of beef and pork. There was a terrible din. The guests were speaking loudly, boasting, quarrelling, drinking. They must have been armed when they entered, but all their weapons were lined up against the wall at the entrance. Another sign of Penelope's or Telemachus' authority. These were the suitors of the queen of Ithaca, my bride, those who wanted to take my place next to her in our wedding bed!

In a corner, sitting on a bench, I recognized Phemius. He had changed greatly. His hair was thinning and going white at the temples and his beard was turning white as well. He was dressed modestly and his head was bowed as if he were slumbering. Between his knees was the same lyre that he'd had when I'd left for Troy.

He didn't see me then, but Telemachus did, as he descended the stairs from the women's quarters. We exchanged a look and he gave me an imperceptible nod. Then I went to sit at the threshold of the main door while a carver took the spits from the fire and passed among the princes of Ithaca and the islands so they could choose the pieces they liked best. He was followed by a steward who was filling their cups with wine. They were hungry and there were so many of them! So this was what went on every day, this invasion of my home and the devouring of my herds.

Telemachus walked towards me. He called out to Eumeus: 'Give our guest a piece of bread, and give him permission to ask for alms in this house.'

Eumeus obeyed. As he handed me the bread, he asked me softly if I'd heard and then, in a loud voice that could be heard by all, said: 'Telemachus, son of glorious Odysseus and head of this house, gives you permission to ask the princes for something to eat with the bread of hospitality he offers you. Don't be ashamed to ask. When a man is forced to beg, he has to put his pride aside.'

'I thank your generous master, good man, and the gods who protect him,' I replied.

'Who is this scrounger? What hole did he crawl out of?' shouted one of the suitors. They were all wolfing down my meat and guzzling my best wine, but I had to take this, and suppress the rage in my heart.

'I know,' spoke up Melanthius. 'He was brought in by the swineherd, Eumeus, the one who just gave him the bread. I saw them coming up this way.'

'You see?' said another, the finest-looking among them. 'We don't have enough ragged beggars around here. Even the swineherd brings along his own!'

I didn't say a word, but Eumeus walked up to him and spoke without fear: 'Does it surprise you, noble Antinous, that I've invited a mendicant here? Everyone is eager to host great lords, singers or artists, as long as it's not some poor wretch, someone who destiny has reduced to penury. No one wants them. And yet they're the ones who are most needy. What trouble is he causing you anyway? What's more, I don't have to account to you for my actions. Only the queen and Prince Telemachus can tell me what I can or can't do. You're no one to me.'

Antinous . . . so he was the one at their head. He obviously thought he could act the master in my house. There was Telemachus, trying to patch up the quarrel between them; he didn't want it to degenerate into something worse. I understood him, my boy. He was alone, without the support of anyone but his two herdsmen. So this is what the son of Odysseus – famous the world over for the feats he'd achieved! – was reduced to. My heart swelled with bitterness, but I couldn't let anything out. I addressed Antinous, the chief suitor, the one who was sure he had the vigour and the means to win over the reluctance of my Penelope.

'You truly seem better to me than any of the other men here, more noble and handsome by far. Set an example to the others, then, I pray you: give me the best morsel! Be as benevolent as your kingly appearance would suggest and let me taste for once what a king enjoys. I'll tell everyone how generous and magnanimous you are. Look at me. I may be penniless, but I can teach you a precious lesson. One day, not so long ago, I was like you. I lived in a palace, I had servants and women, but that wasn't enough for me, I wanted more. And in the end I lost everything, even myself. I was sold as a slave to the lord of Cyprus. I escaped and since then I've been drifting from land to land, from village to village, until my wanderings brought me here to you. All I'm begging for is a meal fit for a man and not for a dog.

'You know something, great prince? You are like I once was and one day you could end up like I am now. Or even worse . . . By doing good to me, you do good to yourself. Can't you understand that?'

I stared into his eyes and he could feel that I was the stronger. I, the beggar, the derelict, was the hunter and he was the prey. I could smell his fear, sense it coursing under his skin.

He rankled at my words, and couldn't bear up under my gaze. 'Get out of my sight, you lousy tramp, there are plenty of others here to beg from. See if they'll feed you. You disgust me!'

All at once silence settled over the hall like a black cloud. 'So be it,' I answered him. 'That's your kind, the kind that won't part with a crumb, won't give up a grain of salt. You've refused to give me even a piece of the bread that isn't yours and that you haven't earned. With all the abundance spilling here before you!' I turned my back to him and went off to carry on my begging somewhere else.

'How dare you!' he shouted. He grabbed a stool and hurled it at me. It hit me hard on the back just under my neck. Pain shot through me but I didn't move, not a hair's breadth. The young braggart must have realized that it wasn't a decrepit old man he'd hit, but a rock.

When the stool had fallen to the ground, I turned and looked straight into his eyes. 'You are nothing but a coward, noble prince. If a man is struck down while he's trying to rob livestock or precious objects from another's home, he can well expect it, but you hit me because I'm hungry. If among the gods there is one who protects the poor and needful, you will pay dearly for what you have done.'

I said nothing else, but went over to sit down at the threshold.

I looked up at Telemachus. He was overwhelmed at what he had seen: his father smitten and humiliated on the day of his return. But he didn't say a word. All he did was shake his head in disapproval. He was waiting, too. Waiting for the day of vengeance.

I stayed at my place at the threshold and watched everything that was going on, including Eumeus and his movements. Every now and then I'd turn to look out at the still body of my poor Argus. He'd finished his suffering! How I longed to pick up his sad remains and give them a proper burial in the woods, under an oak tree . . . but I couldn't let anyone see me doing such a thing, it would have aroused suspicion. Instead I ate the bread my son had given me, the bread that Eumeus had brought to court in his basket. Melanthius, the goatherd who had cast a stone at me while I walked up the trail, passed very close to me on his way out and it was all I could do not to jump to my feet and tear him to shreds. I repressed the ire in my heart . . . the time would come. His time would come.

I watched the princes. They were arrogant, noisy, disrespectful and reckless. There were a lot of them and they were all quite vigorous. I looked at their weapons lined up against the wall at the entrance: swords, spears, polished shields. I was almost certain that they were ornamental, a mark of prestige rather than truly offensive arms. I didn't think they'd ever been used in battle. It was the killing, running a man through from side to side, that made you different, forever. The ferociousness of that act never left your gaze, your heart.

My Telemachus had never killed a man, either. I knew that

he would soon take part in the bloody fray to be fought here, in the palace, and I feared for him. It's too easy for a man who has never known combat to die.

I watched Phemius, our court poet. He ate alone, without speaking to the princes; there was no mingling with them. What songs would they bid him to sing? The sad story of the kings' return from the war? I wondered if he still remembered me. Did he remember how he would tell me stories when I was a little boy tucked into my bed, or outdoors, in the fruit orchard, sitting under a tree? Had he agreed to submit to this travesty? Did he still remember how my father had treated him? Did he ever go to visit him? Did he ever rise up to defend the queen's honour? I thought not. Singers have other talents, but rarely the gift of courage.

I'd lost Eumeus from sight. Where had he gone?

I still hadn't seen *mai*, my nurse. Nor Penelope . . . did she ever come down to the great hall? Knowing that she was so close and not being able to see her created a huge sense of anxiety in me. At the same time, I never would have wanted her to see me in the state I was in.

I had never asked myself so many questions in so short a time. I was afraid of confusing the dreams I'd had over twenty years of separation with a reality that I no longer knew anything about.

Eumeus appeared as suddenly as he had disappeared. He walked through the hall towards me. The princes were no longer interested in us.

He crouched at my side. 'I've seen the queen.'

'How is she?'

'Much better, since Telemachus has returned. I haven't seen her so light-hearted in a very long time. She even ate one of the figs I brought her.'

'That hasn't changed. She's always liked figs.'

'I told her there was a newcomer to the palace . . .'

'And?' I asked in alarm.

'She wanted to know where you come from, if you had news that might interest her. I told her yes, our guest brings news of Odysseus your husband. He has heard that Odysseus has landed in Thesprotia and that he travels with great riches.'

'Well? What did she say to that?' I asked at once, agitated as a young boy hoping to meet a girl for the first time.

'She answered: "Tell the guest I'd like to talk with him." And she promised that if you told her the truth about what you know and have seen, she will give you a new tunic and a cloak so you can walk among other people without feeling ashamed. I'd mentioned how badly off you were. What shall I tell her?'

I was confused, suddenly struck by doubts and fears. I replied: 'After sunset, as soon as it starts to get dark.'

'You may have to wait much longer than that. She can't receive you in the women's quarters. She has to wait until the suitors go home and the house is empty.'

'I have nothing else to do. I can wait.'

'Good. I'll tell the queen. You'll see her come down as soon as the hall is empty and quiet. She'll sit next to the fire. At that point you can approach her and she'll speak to you. *Wanax*, I must ask you something. If you can, don't hurt her. She has suffered so much.'

I nodded.

'Good. I have to return to my pigs, to make sure everything is as it should be. You can never depend on the stable boys, not unless you keep a close eye on them. I'll let Telemachus know I'm going. I'll come back tomorrow morning as soon as I can. I can see you are controlling your actions and your words, *wanax*, so I leave with an easy mind.'

'Don't use that word – what if someone heard you?'

'I'm sorry,' he said. He gave me a slight nod and left.

I watched as he approached Telemachus, who had appeared at the other end of the hall. He moved his lips to the boy's ear and whispered something. He went out of the rear door and I hunkered down at the threshold. The suitors were still feasting and the clamour was only increasing. They had no worries. But I was the king of Ithaca and I'd already passed sentence on them. They were laughing but soon they would be crying and begging. They were shouting but soon they would be silenced forever. I turned towards the atrium and noticed the figure of a tall, thin man who was gripping a stick as though it were a spear. Behind him a black shadow fluttered in the air.

A voice sounded in my heart: 'Theoclymenus!'

The fugitive who Telemachus had offered to protect, a man who had the gift, like Calchas before him. What was hidden to others was clear to him; the future was present. But I didn't want to know anything more than I already knew. I trained my gaze on the hall again, on what was going on there.

I was so absorbed in my thoughts that at first I barely heard the voice that was screeching something at me. A foot planted in my back caused me to turn. The man who had kicked me was fat, with light, watery eyes. The rolls on his stomach swelled and rippled with every move he made. His arms were as thickset and pink as the haunches of a pig, his hair greasy and yellow.

'Who are you? What are you doing here, you revolting beggar?' he cawed. 'Don't you know that I'm the only one here who can ask for alms? Any leftovers belong to me! Get out of here now before I lose my temper.'

I don't know why I remember this episode so well, maybe because of all the things that ever happened to me, nothing was so humiliating or shameful. I, the king of Ithaca and the surrounding islands, destroyer of the greatest city in the world, I who had measured myself against the mightiest champions under the walls of Troy and at the head of my army . . . I accepted to fight a buffoon, a blood-sucking parasite.

I thought it was necessary. I thought that before I could rise out of the utter abjection that I had embraced, I had to touch bottom. I had to make a spectacle of my wretchedness. Only then would the arrogant suitors be convinced that I was nothing to them, certainly not the son of Laertes who, having destroyed sacred Troy, had returned after all these long years. They had to feel sure of themselves, so numerous and well armed, sure that no one would dare stand against them.

At first I tried to beseech my adversary to forgo a quarrel. We were companions in misfortune, after all, and there was surely enough to go around for both of us. But my sorry appearance must have made him cocky and sure that he would get the better of me. The suitors had noticed and they began goading me into taking him on, obviously looking forward to a lively little diversion. They'd begun to come out into the courtyard, one by one, to urge us on. They promised a prize to the winner: a nice chunk of goat-blood sausage already roasting on the embers. They didn't realize that the mud they were throwing was landing on themselves and their families.

I saw clearly how a glorious race had degenerated in just three generations: the Argonauts had journeyed to the ends of the sea and to the rocky walls of the remotest mountains, to extreme limits for mortal men. I and my men had destroyed and plundered the greatest and most powerful city of the world. Our sons had conquered only the stores and the kitchens of an undefended house where they ate and drank themselves silly, taking advantage of an empty throne, of a woman and a boy. I could also see how these were the consequences of the war: these spoiled young men had never learned respect or humility, for they had grown up without their fathers. But then I thought that my own son had grown up without a father but he was judicious and courageous, and had remained devoted to a memory whose face and voice he could not recall. I couldn't feel sorry for the rest of them. After all, they had plotted and attempted to kill him. Each one of them sought to rest on my bed, the one I'd built in the arms of an olive tree, next to my blameless wife. To make love to her. They had to die.

For now all they wanted was a little fun watching two poor unfortunates shoving each other around. Instead, I made sure they didn't enjoy what they saw. I took off my rags and fought bare-chested against my fat, flaccid adversary. I slaughtered him. I broke his jaw with my first punch and made him spit out his teeth; the second one smashed his nose. He was bleeding like a stuck pig. I grabbed him by the foot and dragged him out of the courtyard, propped him up against the boundary wall and gave him a cane to ward off stray dogs or pigs. I put my rags on again and returned to my place at the threshold, my back to the door jamb. The princes' jeering had been cut short. They wandered back into the hall. I'd ruined their fun.

I was waiting for the sun to set. Waiting for them to sate themselves on wine and food and to leave. I saw Telemachus arguing with them more than once. My boy knew that I was watching and listening and he wanted to prove to his father what he was worth.

The shouting and swearing of my violent guests went on and on, inflamed by the wine. The midday meal became dinner. No one was paying me any mind any more, but nothing of what they did escaped me. I saw the looks and the lascivious caresses they exchanged with the maidservants. There was one in particular, who Antinous shamelessly called Mélantho, referring, I was sure, to the dark flower between her legs. She was the object of his ardent desire.

I saw which girls responded with laughs, kisses and immodest gestures and those who obstinately turned away, loyal to their queen and to their master.

I chose one of these, and addressed her with humility: 'Pardon me, dear. It would be a great privilege for me to gaze upon the queen. Her fame is widespread through every nation, and if tomorrow I find myself in another house on the continent I would like to give praise where it is due. I hear she is wise and beautiful and . . . faithful. Does she never come down into the hall? Has she nothing to say to these insolent princes?'

She looked at me curiously, with a note of doubt. Perhaps she'd seen me laying into the beggar who'd been insulting me and dragging him out of the courtyard half-dead. Perhaps she had a question for me. But she abruptly turned instead and pointed to the stair that descended from the women's quarters. She said: 'Take a look, then. There is the queen of Ithaca!'

My heart jumped in my chest; it was beating so hard I thought it would suffocate me. There was my bride descending the steps. Her bearing was proud, and she was beautiful, dressed in a gown the colour of ripe wheat that hugged her waist and her full breasts. It seemed that time had not passed for her. But as she entered the hall and drew closer, I could see that the light she'd always had in her eyes, the light that had once illuminated my life, was dimmed by a veil of sadness.

I looked down at my worn, ragged clothing, the greasy bag slung on my shoulder, my dusty feet and dry, cracked hands and I was deeply ashamed. Tears sprang to my eyes. It was certainly not how I wanted to appear to my wife after such a long time, but this was what my goddess had decided and this was how it had to be. At least I had the sun at my back, so she wouldn't be able to make out my features. I must have looked like nothing more than a dark heap of smelly rags.

The commotion in the room ceased entirely when she appeared, as if a goddess had descended from the sky and suddenly entered the hall. A hush fell over the room, and everyone's eyes were on her. My queen spoke then, in a full, melodious voice. It was the same voice she'd had as a girl and it touched my heart and made me tremble.

'Proud suitors, imperious princes! You've long occupied this house, taking advantage of a woman alone and a youth who doesn't have the power to oust you. You know well that if Odysseus, glorious king of this island, were to suddenly appear on that threshold . . .'

A shiver ran down my spine. The queen had unwittingly revealed a truth she couldn't know. I admired the fire in her gaze.

'. . . I believe that your arrogance would instantly be replaced with fear and dismay. And this means that you are violating all our laws and our traditions. It's not enough for you to consume the chattels of a man who is absent and cannot defend himself, you have gone so far as to insult the guest that Telemachus himself has brought to this house. Nothing has escaped me; none of your insults, your blows.

'You have no right! You should be ashamed of your behaviour! Since when has it become customary to devour the wealth of the bride you hope to win over, instead of offering her gifts?'

She was still trying to gain time for herself; she didn't want to give in to their demands. She wanted to shame them into changing their ways. Antinous did not respond. On the contrary, he took the queen's admonishment as a sign that she had had a change of heart and might entertain the idea of marrying again. Each of the men hastily sent a herald to his house to fetch gifts for the queen. But when they returned, Penelope had retired once again to her rooms.

The handmaids began to prepare supper. I turned towards the hearth, adding wood to the flames and turning the spits. It was a way to earn my keep but also to overhear what my wife's suitors were saying. There was nothing they said or did that slipped my attention. I watched Antinous' hands stealing under Mélantho's gown, up her thighs, seeking her black flower. The slut! She might have sensed me watching her, for she turned and rudely snapped at me: 'Piss off, you filthy beggar! The princes don't need you, they have us and their own pages as well. Go back to your corner and don't come near us again. You stink like a pig!'

Eurymachus, second in standing only to Antinous, saw his opportunity. 'Don't you see?' he cried out. 'He managed to beat up some poor sod out in the courtyard and now it's gone to his head. He thinks he's some kind of athlete, or maybe even a hero, the sort that wins battles. What you are, instead,' he continued, turning to me, 'is a good-for-nothing old man! It's an easy life lolling here by the fire and filling your stomach with the scraps of meat you steal, isn't it? If you wanted to work, you'd be out in the fields cutting hay or harvesting the wheat, or at least taking the sheep to pasture, now that's not a hard job, is it? That's all we needed here, this louse . . . Telemachus is always complaining as it is that there are too many mouths to feed in the palace! Let's start by throwing out this dirt ball.'

Following his example, more of his fellow suitors started insulting me, poking and pushing at me.

How little had Penelope's words counted! I continued to suffer offence. I bit my lip so as not to lash out and repeated to myself: 'Resist, heart of mine! The time has not yet come . . .'

And thus I managed to endure their taunts the whole evening. Every now and then my gaze would meet Phemius' and I could see a glimmer of torturous doubt in the poet's eyes. Then he would lower his head again as if absorbed in thought, unmoving and hunched over, waiting for someone to bid him to sing. But no one did. They were all too busy eating and making fun of me. I could feel Telemachus suffering in silence, but he would not leave the hall, wouldn't leave me alone. I had to signal for him to go – it was better that way.

Antinous finally proposed the last libation before going to bed and the others all followed his counsel. As if he were the master of the house, he had the stewards pour a cup of red wine for each of the princes. They drank to the gods, and then left, picking up the weapons they'd left outside leaning against the wall. They headed off down the road that led to the city. Phemius was the last to go. He was a permanent guest at the palace, as he had been in my time, and the entrance to his room was off the main courtyard. I was sitting on a stool next to the door and he had to pass directly in front of me to go out. He held his lyre in one hand and a night lamp in the other. He stopped before me for a moment and lifted the lamp to get a better look at me. Strange that he should do so now, when I'd been in the hall all day.

He said: 'I see everything, I hear everything and I forget nothing.'

'I believe it,' I replied, altering the natural tone of my voice so he wouldn't recognize it, 'you're a poet.'

He walked away and I watched as his lamp crossed the court-yard. I could still hear the voices of the princes as they trailed off across the countryside. When I could hear nothing I went back in.

Silence reigned over my house.

19

THE LAMPS DANGLING FROM THE columns and pillars were lit, and the opaque, reddish light they cast danced on the weapons hanging on the walls. They were all still there: the spears, shields, helmets, greaves, in precisely the same place I'd left them, although their gleam had long been dimmed by dust and smoke. My fingers brushed the wooden swords that Damastes had wielded when he was teaching me the art of combat . . . Every object, every scratch on the wall, every beam on the ceiling reminded me of the past I had never forgotten. Now, in that silence and that solitude, the pieces seemed to come alive, hailing from a remote place in my heart, recalling the nights and days, months and years of a time that had been happy for me. I hadn't noticed them before, assaulted by the uproar, the jeers, the insults and the bullying. Now the memories surged over me like the waves of a troubled sea.

I suddenly saw Telemachus appear at the end of the great hall, now deserted. Some maidservants came through another door with buckets and sponges, and began to clean up and to gather the leftovers. Mélantho was with them but she merely watched the others as they worked, smug in her position of privilege. She noticed me of course and began to insult me again: 'What? Still here, you leech? What are you still doing in the palace at this time of night? Weren't you listening when I told you to get lost?'

I swelled with rage and stared back at her. 'You wouldn't treat me with such impudence if your master were here. Beware!

Things may change, and much sooner than you think!' For a moment she seemed flustered by my words. She gave me a startled look, as if an unsettling thought had just crossed her mind. How could there still be someone, after twenty years, who so confidently spoke of the king who had surely died in some distant land? Could that beggar really know something?

She left in a huff and the other servants presently left the hall as well. Perhaps they knew that the queen would soon be descending from her room to meet with the wandering guest to whom her son had given permission to ask for alms from the tables of the princes. Telemachus drew close. 'Father,' he whispered, 'my mother the queen is about to come down-stairs. *Mai* has given instructions to put the seat she favours for receiving guests near the hearth. It's the best one in the house, inset with silver and ivory.'

'This will be the most difficult test for me,' I replied. 'But listen, you must do as I say. Tonight, take down all the weapons hanging from the walls of the hall and close them up in the armoury. Nothing must remain.'

'But don't you think that will arouse the princes' suspicions? They've always been accustomed to seeing them where they are.'

'You'll say you had to turn them over to the armourer for inspection and a cleaning. They've all turned black from the smoke of the hearth. Do you own a suit of armour?'

'I do, Father. Of course I do, it's in the armoury. King Laertes your father gave it to me for my twentieth birthday. I'll do as you ask.'

'This will be your first blood, won't it, *pai*?'

He bowed his head: 'Yes.'

'You'll get used to it, as I did in my time. It's a sad necessity. This is what distinguishes a king from a murderer: he kills only when all the other paths have been precluded. Here comes your mother. I must go to her.'

Penelope had taken her seat and had put her feet up on a

stool inset with the same precious decorations. I got a knot in my throat at the sight of her and my heart started beating faster with every step I took. Would I be able to take this? Would I be able to hold back my tears, would the expression on my face betray me?

I was close to her now, but I stopped at the line of shadow, where the reflection of the flames from the hearth gave way to the darkness of night. Her voice rang out in the dark. A girl's voice. If I had closed my eyes, I would have seen her in an olive garden gathering flowers in faraway Sparta. What I wanted to say was: 'Sing, sing for me, my love, like when we were young!' But instead I had to remain completely impassive, hiding my feelings and my desires.

'Come closer, foreign guest. You are welcome here.' Now she spoke as a queen, accustomed to being obeyed.

'I thank you, *wanaxa*, but I'm in no condition to introduce myself to your presence. I'm dirty and tattered.'

'I don't judge a man by his clothing,' she replied. 'I know well that every mortal is subject to the whims of destiny. Come closer. I want to talk to you.'

'I beg of you, my queen, I am ashamed of the way I look and I would not feel at ease in front of such radiant beauty.'

Penelope sighed and bent her head: 'My face has not been radiant for a long time, foreign guest. Too many tears have poured from these eyes.'

For me her beauty was unchanged. The veil of melancholy made it even more intense and heartbreaking. I watched as the light from the fire caressed her cheeks and shone in her black, black eyes.

I wanted to tell her that from the moment I'd left Ithaca I had always thought of her intensely every time I saw the moon rising from the sea, because I was certain that she would be doing the same thing, at the same time, and that our souls would touch. But I had to hide my thoughts and my face. 'I know the reason for your tears, my queen. Your fame is well known in every land.

You suffer because your husband, the glorious son of Laertes, has never returned from the war, but I can tell you that your troubles are ending. Odysseus will return, and soon. If he's not already here.'

Penelope scrutinized my face in the darkness. 'What are you saying, foreign guest? You don't even know my Odysseus. Are you one of the scores of wayfarers who hope to earn my hospitality by telling me lies?'

'No. I'm telling you the truth. I have seen Odysseus. If I saw him again I would recognize him.'

'You've seen him, or so you say. How did you recognize him?' Her eyes sought mine in the darkness.

'I know him because I first saw him in Crete as he was going to war. The wind had swept him off his course as he was doubling Cape Malea.'

'What did he look like then?' she insisted.

A hoarse wind blew outside and a dog whimpered in the courtyard and scratched his nails against the door. Argus? Where are you, Argus? A chill coursed under my worn cloak. The flames flickered in the hearth.

'That was a very long time ago, it's not easy to remember. A well-built man, I would say, with bright eyes that lit up when he smiled.' Penelope paled. A light sweat broke out on her cheeks. 'Wait, now I remember, he was wearing a red cloak with a beautiful gold clasp. It was in the shape of a hunting dog with a deer in its clutches. It was so finely crafted that you could see the deer was trying to get away. A jewel truly fit for a king.'

Penelope's expression had changed. I could see that my words had deeply shaken her, confused her. 'I wove that cloak for him,' she said, 'and the pin was a gift from me as well.' I remembered that moment so vividly it felt as though I was there again. My heart bursting with the pain of leaving her, little Telemachus babbling in her arms. Only Argus could understand him! The ship pulling away from the shore, pulling away from everything I loved . . . the ship that would never make its way back.

'But how can you possibly remember such a tiny thing? Who are you?' she demanded.

She had drawn closer and for a moment I was close to breaking down. I breathed in her fragrance, saw the tears glittering in her eyes. I felt the air vibrate with the beat of her heart. Had she recognized me?

'I am Aithon of Crete,' I said. 'I am the brother of *wanax* Idomeneus, the lord of Knossos and the Labyrinth. Ill luck has reduced me to this state.'

She seemed to accept this, but tears still ran down her cheeks. Her fingers of ivory curled around the armrests on her chair. She didn't move for long instants, her head low, and I could barely hold back my own tears. I ached with desire for her, I longed to take her into my arms, but I had to resist, could not give in, had to stifle the swell of emotion rising in my heart. The time had not yet come. Not yet . . . not yet . . .

Penelope dried her tears and looked up at me again. 'I'll have your feet washed, and a bed set up for you in the atrium . . . Euriclea!'

That name, her name, waves of memories, *mai* . . . how much time had passed . . . how many tears, how much home-sickness . . .

The voice of my queen again: 'Euriclea, wash the guest's feet and have a bed put in the atrium for him, so he may rest. He was a prince once, in Crete, the brother of mighty Idomeneus. Perhaps your master himself is in just as sorry a state . . . a beggar, covered with rags, the brunt of derision and scorn, forced by hunger to humiliate himself. What you do for this man may be what someone else is doing for your lord.'

She stood up, shot me a last sorrowful glance and walked straight-backed up the stairs that led to her quarters. I bit my lip hard so I wouldn't cry.

Euriclea . . . stooped and white-haired, but still her . . . with that sweet gaze and the rough voice that hid the tenderness of her heart. *Mai* . . .

She filled a washbasin with hot water from an urn and put it on the ground in front of me. She was muttering under her breath: 'Another trickster come to repeat idle tales to my sad little girl . . . good-for-nothings, sluggards, all of you . . .'

I was silent. I didn't say a word in my defence. Her tongue was as sharp as her hands were gentle. They dissolved the weariness in my tormented feet and relaxed my strained muscles. The hot, steaming water reminded me again of my childhood. She was going on and on, and I watched her white head bobbing left and right to accompany her grumbling. My soul swelled with tenderness and it was all I could do not to smile, despite her scolding. Even though her gruff temperament prevented her from using kind words with me, I knew that she was thinking of her master, alone and forsaken, reduced to begging in some far-off land, and that she hoped that others would repay her labour by caring for him, as her mistress had suggested. She spilled out the dirty water and added some more from the urn to wash my legs as well. Then her hand came to a stop just above my knee, on the scar that the sharp tusk of a boar had left so many years ago. She dropped my foot abruptly. Water splashed everywhere and the basin overturned.

'My child! My child, it's you! It's you, you're back!' she whispered in a tremulous voice, as big tears coursed down her wrinkled cheeks. I covered her mouth with my hand, nearly stopping her from breathing. I looked around to make sure that no one had seen.

'Not a word, *mai*, or I'll strangle you!'

My threat made her gasp. She could never have expected such words from me. But when I saw her dismay, I added softer words under my breath: '*Mai*, I love you as I love my own mother, and I am as happy to see you as you are to see me, but I'm here to wreak vengeance upon these arrogant suitors and I must stay hidden. I haven't even revealed myself to Penelope, my beloved bride. You can't imagine how hard that was for me . . .'

Euriclea began scrubbing my feet and legs again to waylay

suspicion. She knew well that many of the maidservants were conspiring with the suitors.

'A great many men frequent this palace and they are well armed,' I continued. 'If they have the merest inkling of who I am in reality, they would not hesitate to murder me, and Telemachus as well. You do understand what I'm saying, don't you?'

'I do, my child, my lord and my king. Not a word will leave my mouth, not even if someone were to torture me. Can I bring you something to eat? There's everything you could want in the kitchens.'

'No, *mai*, I can't eat, my stomach is tied in knots. But I'll take a glass of wine if you'll pour it for me.'

Euriclea hurried to get a clay cup, even though, I am sure, she would have preferred a silver one.

'Let me prepare your bed for you now. In your own house, finally.'

'No, *mai*, I don't want you to do that. It might look odd. They'll wonder: "Why is the queen treating this beggar so well? What's wrong with a little straw under the portico?" No, just give me a blanket, that will be enough for me.'

'I'll do as you say, my son. Rest if you can.' She raised her eyes to mine for a moment, and they were shiny with tears. 'You can't imagine how badly I want to hug you, child. I've thought of you every day, every day! I never doubted that you would return.'

She dried her tears with the sleeve of her tunic and walked away with her basin, only to return a short time later with an oxhide and a thick, warm sheepskin cover.

I went outside and laid them out one on top of the other in a sheltered corner of the portico facing the courtyard. The west wind carried a chill and the clear sky was teeming with stars. They throbbed in the great quiet vault and for a moment I felt like I was still on my ship, searching for the Herdsman or the Great Bear. The earth seemed to move in waves beneath me as if my vessel were rocking on the sleepless sea. I had spent such a long time on the water. I thought of distant Nausicaa. Perhaps her eyes were seeking out the stars, the same ones I was seeing. I thought of the helmless ship that had brought me home: was it back in its well-sheltered harbour or had the wrath of Poseidon turned it into a rock at the entrance to the port?

The moon rose over Mount Neritus and cast a pale glow over the courtyard. I saw Argus' dead body: it had been thrown on the dungheap. I found a shovel, stuck it in my belt and slipped closer, after I'd made sure that there was no one looking my way. I gathered him up into my arms, left the courtyard and walked for a spell down the road that led into the city, until I came across a big holm oak that used to shelter flocks of sheep in its shade during the summers of my boyhood. There I dug a hole big enough to hold my friend, gave him one last pat and laid him inside. I filled in the hole and covered it first with stones, and then with leaves and dried grass so it wouldn't be discovered.

'I couldn't give you the honour of a pyre, my friend,' I whispered inside my heart. 'I can't be found out. But I've given you a worthy burial place. So when my time comes, I hope you'll be waiting for me at the threshold of that foggy world. Farewell.'

I returned to my house and washed my arms and chest at the fountain and then stretched out on the oxhide and sheepskin, hoping to fall asleep. But the eyes of the night see many things that conspire to remain hidden. Two or three of the suitors, one after another, stole inside the palace to take their pleasure with the maidservants, who'd come to open the door for them. The sluts!

I tried to sleep nonetheless. 'Be still, my heart,' I said, 'you've put up with much worse!' But my heart was snarling in my chest like a rabid dog at the sight of such an insult. Later I watched them leave. The palace dogs didn't bark either when they arrived or when they left; they were used to their comings and goings.

Silence finally fell over the palace, very late at night, but not for long. The wall on the far side of the portico was the one I myself had added twenty years earlier to build my wedding chambers. From the window came the soft but unmistakable sound of Penelope crying, and it cut me to the quick. I imagined her stretched out on the bed I had made for her, sobbing. What I had meant to be a haven of rest, dreams and enchantment for her was a place of torture instead.

I couldn't bear the idea and I kept tossing and turning; I could not find peace. That was not the only thought that tormented me. I knew that in the final count it was me alone against scores of strong adversaries in the bloom of youth. Even if I managed to kill them all, how would I manage to escape the fury of their relatives and friends? I was struck with immense sadness to think that I'd already led all the youths who had followed me to Troy to their deaths. Their parents had entrusted them to me and I hadn't brought a single one back. And here I was preparing to exterminate another generation, if I succeeded in my intent.

A chill.

Was it the wind or a mysterious presence? The voice of my goddess sounded in my heart: how could I doubt victory if I fought with a god at my side? Not even an entire army should worry me. *In reality still today I ask myself whether I really had the right to slaughter them. I knew, surely, that all that blood spilled would come round to me. But I don't think I ever had a choice. My goddess drove me to do it, but it was also my prerogative as a king, a husband, a father. I had slain so many men over so many years on the fields of Troy. Now I would do it again. I had conquered the greatest city in the world. Now, once again, I had entered in disguise and I would take my own house by force.*

Weariness finally overcame me and sleep weighed down my eyelids. I rested until the Aurora roused me. The first thing I noticed was that someone, in the middle of the night, had thrown a cloak over me. I got up, folded the skins I had lain on, entered and set the bundle down on a stool near the entrance.

A new day was beginning with a flurry of activity and light chatter, while the day of vengeance was approaching. The women who worked the millstones were arriving to take over from those who had just finished their stint. But there was one who had not yet reached her measure of wheat and she struggled on. She could not be replaced until her work was done. This was a rule I had established myself before I'd left for the war. I didn't want a person who had done too little to enjoy the same rest as one who had laboured with great diligence. But after so many years of strain, misfortune and grief of my own, I reasoned that perhaps that woman had failed to produce her measure of wheat not because she was lazy but because she was frail or unwell. 'Suffering,' I thought, 'is the mother of wisdom.'

A crash of thunder sounded in the clear sky and that thin, frail woman, who was dripping with sweat, cried out: 'Oh Zeus, you who send a thunderbolt out of the blue – a signal for whom I do not know – make this the last day that the suitors feast without pause, obliging me to make so much flour for all the bread they eat, else this toil will be the death of me! May this be the last bread they ever eat!'

I took her words as an omen – my endeavour would be accomplished. Even Zeus, the protector of kings, was on my side.

I saw Telemachus walking towards me. He was dressed and armed and I watched him with pleasure: I would never tire of looking at my boy. I heard him speak to Euriclea: '*Mai*, have you taken care of our guest?'

'Certainly. Your mother ordered me to prepare a bed for him but he refused. He insisted on sleeping outside, under the portico . . .'

A man loses the habit of sleeping in a bed when he's ten years at war, besieging a city, or at sea, at the mercy of storms.

'I insisted, believe me, but there was no convincing him,' she went on. 'He's an odd duck, your guest. I offered him dinner but he would only take a cup of wine. I gave him an oxhide and a sheepskin but he laid them one on top of the other and slept uncovered. I waited until he'd fallen asleep and then I covered him with a cloak.'

She was good at feigning, my dear old nurse, and so was Telemachus. Like father, like son. My heart laughed thinking that neither of the two was aware of what the other knew. Telemachus walked by and nodded at me in passing. He was heading to the city, with a spear in his hand and a couple of dogs at his heels. Beautiful animals. I wondered what breed my Argus had been.

In no time, the whole palace was buzzing with activity, all revolving around the arrival of its customary guests: my wife's suitors. The maidservants were drawing water from the walled fountain outside, to the right of the main gate. Others were sweeping, washing the floors, sponging down the tables, rinsing out the cooking vessels.

And the food that was arriving! Eumeus showed up with three pigs and Melanthius brought two goats. He burst in with loud abuse for me: 'Still here, you miserable beggar? Are you on your way out, you cur, or do you need me to beat you into deciding? My hands are already itching!'

My hands were itching as well, but Eumeus warned me off with a stern look. It was no time for a fistfight. The food was still coming. Philoetius came in with a cow and two or three more goats. He was still wearing the tab at his neck that had bought him passage on the ferry from Same with his livestock. I recognized him despite the fact that he'd changed so much. When I'd left he was little more than a boy and now he was a full-grown man, with a strong, sturdy build. He had a wrestler's arms, a bull's neck and legs that looked like pillars. 'Just what I need,' I thought, 'a single man with the force of three.'

He noticed me but did not recognize me. 'Hail there, old boy,' he said with a tone of affection. 'How's it going? Not too well, from the looks of it.'

Eumeus stepped in: 'Philoetius, leave him alone. This friend of ours has been through more than you can begin to imagine.'

But the cowherd continued undeterred. There must have been something about me that wouldn't let him move on.

'You know, as soon as I saw you, I thought, "He doesn't seem like the poor wretch he seems to be." You may be dressed in rags, but your eyes are sharp and your back is straight, like one of those men who never bend, no matter what. It makes me want to cry to see a man like you in such a sorry state.'

I drew closer and looked straight into his eyes. I wondered whether in some part of his heart or his mind, he wasn't remembering the gaze of his master who had set off for distant lands so long ago, never to return . . .

'I'm telling you,' he continued, 'I got the chills when I saw you. I thought, "Maybe my master is like that poor devil who has to put up with insults and humiliation and beg for a piece of bread." If he's still alive, that is, if he hasn't ended up dead and buried. I still think about him a lot. He made me the keeper of his herds, and here I am slaughtering his animals to feed these arrogant gluttons.'

It was as I'd thought. Without even realizing it, he'd recognized me, and he was moved to think that I might be alive. His loyalty deserved to be rewarded, like Euriclea's, Eumeus' and even Argus'. I looked around to make sure that no one could hear me, and replied: 'You're an honest and faithful man, so now listen carefully to what I have to say. Your master will return while you are here today, in this house, and if you like you'll see him kill those gluttons with his own hands. I swear it by Zeus, in the name of the master who is still in your heart.'

Philoetius' eyes lit up and he flexed his muscles, growling. 'May Zeus will your words to be true, guest. Then you'll see what these are worth,' he said, holding up his huge fists, hard as stone. Eumeus had been nodding as I'd spoken but did not speak himself, waiting for me to reveal myself.

We started hearing the usual commotion that everyone had become accustomed to. The suitors were arriving, like they did every day, and there were many of them. They seemed to be in greater number than the day before.

'Count them,' I said in a low voice to Eumeus, and Philoetius shot me a surprised look.

He hadn't understood entirely yet but he was excited, keen-eyed, looking for a fight. Ire that had lain in wait too long, rage swallowed in silence, had made him impatient. He could feel that the time for settling scores was coming, and soon. I laid a hand on both men's shoulders. 'You'll still need patience,' I told them, 'but not for much longer. He's coming.'

The shriek of an eagle sounded above our heads and we raised our eyes to the sky. The majestic bird of prey was soaring in wide circles over my house, and every time he crossed in front of the sun his black shadow traversed the spans of the portico and the jambs of the great gate like a dark omen of carnage.

20

EUMEUS AND PHILOETIUS WENT to the rear of the palace, where the slaughterhouse and the kitchens were. Melanthius seemed to be keeping clear of us; perhaps he'd understood that the wind was changing. I remained under the portico, observing the suitors' comings and goings, who was doing what and how. I listened to their bluster and bluff until Telemachus returned from the city with the dogs and his spear in hand. I could already see a difference in him, in such a short time. He was growing before my eyes, becoming a man in his prime. He looked strong and resolute.

He turned to me and said: 'Guest, I neglected to hail you this morning. My mind was on other things. Matters I needed to see to in the city and with the assembly. It was not my intent to slight you. I hope that no one troubled you and that you slept peacefully last night.'

'No one has mistreated me, prince, and I rested sufficiently. Some good soul threw a cloak over my shoulders as I was sleeping, and only the Aurora awoke me. I folded the skins I'd been given and put them back in their place.'

'Good. Then you may enter for the banquet. I know there is no love lost between you and the princes. I've had a table set for you apart from the others, but I've told the servants to bring you a cup from the royal service.' He gave me a barely visible wink and continued: 'It's the cup that my father, King Odysseus, would use here at the palace when he took his place next to my mother the queen. It's made of embossed gold, crafted by a skilled artisan on the continent.'

He spoke loudly so as to be heard inside and outside the hall. I replied in tone: 'I'm not worthy of such a precious object, prince, and I'm no longer accustomed to using such finery. A simple clay cup is more suitable to my humble condition.'

'No. I want the princes to see how a guest is respected properly in this house – they should be ashamed of their behaviour.'

I nodded, accepting his decision, and followed him over the threshold. On the far side of the hall were a stool and a dark wooden table. The gleaming cup contrasted greatly with the worn surface. I noticed that the table had been positioned so that the sun's light struck the gold, setting it afire.

Others had not failed to notice the same thing.

In particular, one of the princes who came from the continent. He had no particular merits beyond his wealth, and it was said that he had sent Icarius, my father-in-law, lavish gifts, even more precious than those he'd brought for the queen. He observed with great vexation that Telemachus was having me served first: a plate brimming over with lamb, pork and beef, with chopped rosemary and salt on the side to season the meat. Eumeus poured the wine and Philoetius smiled and nodded at me as if to say: 'Now you look like a king!'

But the rich, fat prince wasn't smiling and he spoke out rudely: 'Friends! Look at how Telemachus has honoured his guest and served him such abundant portions. Can we do any less? I want to give him something myself!' He grabbed a cow's hoof from a basket and flung it at me. I ducked and it barely missed me, hitting the wall behind and falling to the ground. As I twisted to the side, I met Phemius' eyes for a moment, and saw a flash of recognition.

I bit down hard on my lip so as not to react to the provocation, but Telemachus reacted for me. He stood squarely in front of the prince who was as loutish as he was fat. 'Thank your god,' he said, 'that you didn't hit him; that he was faster than you are. Otherwise I would have run you through on my sword like a pig on a spit, and instead of a wedding you would have had a nice funeral!'

My son could use humour to his advantage, I noted with satisfaction; the bite in his sarcasm had hit its mark. My heart laughed bitterly in my chest. While I hadn't let go of the insult, it had already sunk to the bottom of my soul where it added fuel to my mounting fury. I would need it all when the moment came: my rage would tear through the hall like wildfire.

One of the princes asked the others for silence so he could make a proposal.

'Telemachus is right,' he began. 'We cannot disrespect his guests, because this is his house, but it's also true that things cannot go on the way they have been. Odysseus, as we all know, is not coming back. He's surely dead. Twenty years have gone by. What's the use of being so obstinate? Take my advice, Telemachus: give up. Since your father won't be coming back, choose one of us and accept his wedding gifts. Consider them as reparation for what we've consumed in all the time we've been waiting for your mother's decision. You can remain here and enjoy the palace. Your mother will simply take a husband and move into his household. Doesn't that seem like a good solution?'

I was astonished by his words. How could he not be demanding the throne? If he were chosen, would he marry Penelope solely out of love? Or had he and the others hatched some wicked plot to murder Telemachus once a wedding had taken place?

Telemachus replied: 'Surely, the way you tell it, this seems like the most sensible of solutions and there's no reason in the world why I should object to such a thing, but there's one thing you've forgotten. My mother doesn't want to follow any of you out of this house, and I cannot and do not want to force her. Is that clear? I will not ever throw my mother out of this house!'

I'll never forget what happened after my boy finished speaking. I had expected them to reflect on his words, thought that they might be reminded of their dignity as princes and even show an inkling of respect, but no.

They burst out laughing.

Unrestrained, compulsive, insane laughter. They just couldn't stop and to me that hilarity was like the barking of dogs, or the shrill screeching of frightened birds. They laughed and laughed as they stuffed their mouths with bloody meat.

There is a fine line between laughter and tears. How often in my life I'd experienced that myself! In Troy, after the battle, in the shelter of our tents, I'd seen the faces of my friends, glorious heroes, befuddled by the fumes of wine, go from laughing to crying or back again, without rhyme or reason.

Those wretches had eyes filled with tears but they couldn't have stopped laughing even if they had wanted to.

Right at that moment, the guest to whom my son had given shelter appeared in the hall, almost like an apparition: Theo-clymenus, the murdering prophet who had climbed aboard Telemachus' ship at Pylos to escape the rage of the dead man's relatives. His face was pale and his dilated eyes were wells of darkness.

'You scoundrels!' he shouted. 'Your doom is sealed!

'I see your heads wrapped in darkness, the hall rings with your groaning, blood is spattered everywhere on the walls and is pooling, steaming, on the floors. I see scores of shadows crowd-ing the palace and the courtyard, shades of dead men running, shrieking like bats, towards the gates of Hades. The sun has disappeared from the sky, deep night descends on this house. Go, leave now if you can, while there's still time!'

'The bloke's raving mad,' one of the suitors shouted out. 'He says it's dark outside! What kind of guests does Telemachus ask in, anyway? That one,' he went on, pointing at me, 'a worthless beggar who won't even let us eat in peace, a leech, that's what he is! And now this other one wanders in, completely demented!'

They carried on devouring their meat half raw and swilling

wine. I watched them, passing among them without letting myself be seen. Nothing escaped me. I observed their movements, their looks, identified their weak spots. No one would elude his destiny. Their lunching went on and on, there was so much to eat, so much meat and so much wine. But the dinner . . . well, I'd be preparing that for them, and they wouldn't find anything to laugh about.

Once again, I met the gaze of Phemius, the poet, and I was certain, from his expression, that he'd read what was in my eyes and that he realized what was coming. Tears coursed down his bristly cheeks. How many stories he'd sung to me as a child, in the dark, in the silent palace, trying to lull me into sleep. Now, in silence, he was pleading for mercy.

MY WIFE appeared, crossed the hall and went up the stairs which led to the women's quarters, followed by the greedy eyes of the suitors. They offended me. Then I watched as Penelope descended the stairs again, haughtily ignoring their gazes. She held a bronze key in her hand. I knew it well. The key to the underground storeroom. What did she have in mind? Had she perhaps recognized me the night before? Had my longing for her revealed me? If she had recognized me, why hadn't she given me any sign?

'Because you lied to her,' sounded a voice in my heart.

While the eyes of everyone in the hall were on the queen, I slipped out of the hall and went to the atrium where I had seen Eumeus and Philoetius retreating earlier. I motioned for them to come close.

'Your master has returned,' I said. 'And he is here, standing before you.'

'*Wanax!*' exclaimed Philoetius and he fell to his knees and embraced my legs.

'Yes, he is indeed our master,' hissed Eumeus, turning to the cowherd. 'But quiet! No one must know!'

'Listen,' I said to them both, 'if you help me to avenge myself and reconquer my home I promise that you won't be sorry. You'll live close to me all your lives and I'll give you land, flocks, a beautiful wife, whichever one of the handmaids you choose.'

'We're with you, *wanax*,' they replied, 'ready to fight to the last breath.'

'Eumeus, my armour.'

'Here,' he said, 'I have everything ready.' He helped me to put it on and then arranged the ragged tunic and torn cloak to hide it completely. The cold chill of the metal raced from my shoulders down my arms. I hadn't experienced the feel of bronze on my skin in years.

'What about Telemachus?'

'His armour is ready as well. It's waiting for him in the Hall of the Argonauts. He knows that, and he has the key in his belt. When you see him disappear, that's where he'll be going.'

'The queen had a key as well. It looked like the one to the underground chambers.'

'It was, *wanax*,' replied Eumeus.

'What is she looking for down there?' I wondered aloud. I was worried at this unexpected turn: what could she be thinking? Would she ruin everything? But then calmness returned to steady my heart. My goddess was helping me; she was at my side in every move I made, in every thought that came into my mind.

'Now, you and I will go back inside, Eumeus,' I told him. 'I'll go in first and you'll follow. Philoetius, you go to the rear door. Lock it and prop it shut from the outside. No one must escape. Are you armed?'

Philoetius smiled widely and opened his cloak, revealing a huge, two-headed battleaxe. 'I can bring down a bull with this,' he said. 'No one will get out that door.'

'Good. Then I'm going back in. When the slaughter starts, Eumeus and Telemachus will already be at my side. Once you've secured the door, come back in through the front. I'll need you.'

None of the suitors noticed me returning because their eyes were still trained in another direction.

Penelope.

She was crossing the hall, accompanied by two maidservants holding a leather sack, closed at the neck with a leather tie. She went to sit next to my throne, vacant for twenty years, and her maids laid the bag at her feet. Then they opened it and pulled out an enormous horn bow. The bowstring was loose and wrapped around the grip.

My bow!

The bow that has meant my survival on this long, harsh, last journey.

The bow that Autolykos, my mother's father, had given to me as a wedding gift, making me promise that it would never leave this house. It was dark and shining, in perfect condition. Had King Laertes my father taken such care to preserve it all these years? Or ordered one of the servants to do so? Why had Penelope brought it into the hall? Again, my heart was pounding, hard.

Theoclymenus, the seer, had vanished.

Eumeus was near the hearth.

Antinous, the head of the suitors, the most arrogant of them all, was pouring himself wine.

A strange silence had settled over the hall. Everyone was speaking, but in low voices, as if they feared someone would hear what they were saying.

The queen rose to her feet. 'Princes!' she said.

No one, from the moment she had reappeared, had taken their eyes off her for a moment.

'Princes! I have decided to accept your demands!'

What was happening? I gave Eumeus a questioning look, but he merely shook his head. I sought out Telemachus, then, and our eyes met. What was happening?

No one knew. He was as surprised as I was, but he was approaching the throne.

Penelope's voice rang out again: 'I'm here to propose a competition. The man among you who succeeds in stringing this bow and in shooting an arrow clean through the rings of twelve axes lined up one after another, and striking the target, will be the man that I follow out of this house and whose wife I shall become.'

I couldn't believe my ears. What was Penelope doing? I had told her that Odysseus was about to return, that he was close by, perhaps even already on the island, and she was offering herself as a trophy in an archery contest? Was she declaring her willingness to follow one of these arrogant usurpers? Perhaps one of those who had plotted to murder her son, our son? My heart screamed in my chest. The mere thought of her lying next to another man was enough to destroy me. Is this why I had come home?

Four more handmaids entered the hall two at a time, each pair holding a basket containing six two-bladed axes, each topped by a ring which normally served for hanging it on the wall, and six blocks of wood with holes drilled in them to hold the axes in place.

Penelope ordered Eumeus to line them up on the floor one after another, each axe inserted upright into its solid wood block. I looked at him again, a question in my eyes, but the swineherd just shook his head again. He had no choice, he could not disobey an order from the queen.

A voice sounded again in my heart. Mentor's, this time! How long had it been since I'd heard his voice!

'You are a resourceful man, with a cunning, complex mind. Use it. Reflect.'

The task's purpose immediately became clear. The key was the bow. Yet who could string the bow without knowing its secrets?

Eumeus continued to carry out the queen's orders. He set each axe firmly into its rest and lined them all up.

Penelope signalled to her maids and they brought out a soft, glimmering veil and placed it on her head, covering her face.

My heart broke in my chest. It was the same veil that she had used to cover her head when she'd had to face her father Icarius so many years earlier, to show him that she was betrothed to me; that she would become my wife and nothing could ever make her change her mind. Now the veil was for whoever won the contest of the bow. I was no longer so certain that none of the suitors would be capable of doing it, and the thought was killing me.

'Where are you?' my heart called out desperately.

Mentor's voice answered again: 'Here, next to you. Why do you doubt me? Because you feel alone?'

'Because I am alone,' my heart replied. 'Because one of them could win. Because I could be forced to take part in the contest and I don't know that my strength will suffice. So much time has passed, too much. Filled with such harrowing trials, screams and blood and aching wounds, unspeakable pain and never-ending storms . . .'

But my time was coming, it was close now, very close, and so I spoke to my heart: 'Be strong, my heart. This is the last test, the most cruel of all, but only you can succeed, no one else. None of these men have ever watched Damastes, expert at his art like no other, as you have, hundreds of times, planting his knee into the only point where the bow can be flexed, and hooking the ring of the bowstring onto the end of the top horn.'

The princes thronged close and Antinous spoke up: 'Friends, the axes have been lined up and the queen has proposed a contest. We shall accept this challenge and we'll soon know who has been smiled upon by fortune! I will be first, and the rest of you will follow, one by one, from left to right, like when the wine is being served.'

I could not stop my thoughts from bounding forwards and backwards. What had I done wrong? If Penelope had recognized me, she must have realized that I had a plan, a plan that would be compromised by a contest of this sort. Did she want to punish me? Show me that she resented me not confiding in her? And if she hadn't recognized me, why had she chosen that moment to offer herself as a prize to the suitors?

Mentor's voice sounded again in my heart: 'There's a third explanation.'

'Yes. She asked me a question. I answered with a lie. She knows this is the only way to make me tell the truth.'

Telemachus' voice shook me from my thoughts. Like his mother, he was ready to take the initiative.

'Suitors!' he said. 'This is my house, the queen is my mother. And the bow is mine as well. I have the right to be the first to try my hand at this contest. If I succeed in stringing the bow and shooting my arrow through the twelve rings, then my mother will not be forced to forsake this house. She will remain here with me for as long as she wants.' He was a man; what he said was true. It was his right.

No one objected, and Eumeus handed the great bow to the prince. Telemachus planted the lower horn on the ground, leaned his left knee against the bow, gripped the ring at the end of the string with his left hand and the top horn with his right, and tried to bend it down so as to hook the ring. His whole body tensed with immense exertion, copious sweat burst from his brow, his eyes reddened from the strain and for an instant I saw the upper horn flexing. My heart swelled with pride. I wanted to shout: 'You can do it, *pai*! String it and let fly!' but I knew it was impossible. The upper horn straightened, winning over the pull of his young arm. Telemachus had to admit defeat.

A sarcastic grin appeared on Antinous' face.

'You try!' said my boy. 'Let's see what you can do.'

Antinous strode forward. He grabbed the upper horn with his left hand and used his right to grasp the string on the end with the ring that he had to hook on to the end of the bow. He turned red and the veins on his neck swelled up. The ring was getting closer to the tip of the upper horn. He had almost succeeded, but I was looking at his knee. The bow would win and he would lose. He withstood the strain, stalling for as long as he could hold the position, but then his strength began to wane and he could not prevent the upper horn from drawing away from the ring. Antinous flung the bow onto the ground in a fit of rage, and would not look at Penelope. Covered by her veil, the queen seemed a mysterious, impassive goddess.

It was the turn of Eurymachus, after Antinous the most illustrious of the suitors, not incapable of reasoning with his own head, at times, from what I'd seen. But his attempt was futile from the start; he knew that he would never succeed. He had already understood that the contest would be a humiliating parade of impotence in front of the magnificent queen they had plagued and humiliated for years.

It was thus that I came to understand the immense strength and shrewd mind of Penelope. I realized that her plan was a hundred times more potent than my own, and more devastating. By proposing such a trial to the suitors, by watching as they puffed and panted to no avail, by maintaining her silence behind the veil as she looked on, she was saying: 'You want me in your house and in your bed? Then show me what you're worth. I'm accustomed to a man of rare strength, power, ingenuity. Go to it then, string the bow, young lions! Let your arrow fly and hit the target. Can you really not manage such a task?'

Leodes tried next. Among all of them, he seemed the most benign. He was never insolent or offensive. He respected the queen and looked at her with adoring eyes. It didn't matter – his gentle nature would not help him escape the Chaera of death. An instant sufficed for him to understand that the enormous bow had an invincible and nearly magical resilience. Inside it was the grim, vicious soul of a marauder. He let go of it almost at once and I heard him murmur: 'If it becomes impossible to achieve what you've longed for your whole life, it is better to die . . .'

I wanted to feel compassion for him, but there was no room left in my heart for such a feeling. The time for mercy was over.

Antinous seemed to have heard him as well. He said: 'Your mother did not give birth to you so you would become a great archer. But where you have failed, another one of us may succeed.' He turned to the others: 'Friends! What a fool I've been! I'd forgotten that today is the feast day of Apollo the archer. How could we dream of competing with him? We should never have entertained such a thought! Let us give the bow a rest for today and wait until tomorrow. Surely the god will then grant one of us the strength to succeed.'

I scanned the room for Telemachus but could not find him. I sought out Eumeus' gaze and he nodded once, solemnly. My boy was in the Hall of the Argonauts.

I turned towards the suitors then and appealed to them using modest words. 'Strange as it may seem to you, noble lords,' I said, 'I once possessed a bow similar to this one, long ago, when I was a prosperous man, and my hands long to grasp such a fine weapon again. I'm sure that the archer god will give the victory to one of you tomorrow, but in the meantime I beg you, let me have a go! I want to see if there's still anything left of my green years in these tired old arms.'

The words were not out of my mouth before I could feel the eyes of my proud wife upon me, and they burned me like a blazing brand.

'Are you demented, you old fool?' shot back Antinous. 'How dare you even ask such a thing? I would never allow you to touch that bow, and I'll make you deeply regret you ever thought of it.'

Penelope spoke up: 'The guest certainly does not mean to challenge you, nor does he aspire to gain any advantage by handling that bow. I don't see why he can't be permitted to try.'

Eurymachus couldn't keep still. 'Let me tell you why, your highness,' he cried out. 'What would people say if word got out that a beggar succeeded where the most noble youth of the kingdom had failed?' He turned, then, to rail at me: 'And listen up, you ragball, back off! If you dare touch that bow you won't leave this house alive.'

'Enough threats!' cried out Penelope. 'Our guest would certainly not pretend to have my hand in marriage, even if he were to succeed. I don't see why we should forbid him from trying. Eumeus, hand him the bow. Until tomorrow it is I who command in this house.'

She stood, crossed the hall and ascended with a light, majestic step to her rooms. My queen was giving me the time and space to redeem myself in her eyes, the chance to wipe out all those years of solitude and humiliation.

Eumeus obeyed her orders and put the bow in my hands. I greased it with a piece of meat fat and warmed it, passing it again and again over the flames of the hearth, to make it more flexible. The princes were watching my movements with great curiosity. They were beginning to suspect that I was not what I had seemed. The time was right. I grasped the top horn with my left hand and the string with the right and, raising my leg, I leaned my knee into the horn just under the grip, where the two opposing forces met. I pushed hard. The bow bent, moaning. The top horn obeyed my hand and lowered to hook the string. I saw Phemius' fingers running along the strings of his lyre and mine did the same on the bowstring. The cord vibrated. A dull rumble at the centre, shriller and louder higher up.

In the deep silence that followed my gesture, I nocked the arrow and took aim.

I let it fly.

Whistling, the arrow shot through all twelve rings and hit the target.

The men in the hall were looking each other in the eye. They had finally understood, but it was too late. The dusky red sun flooded the hall with bloody reflections. When I turned, Telemachus was there on my right, clad in blinding bronze.

21

I STRIPPED OFF MY RAGS and showed them that I was clad in bronze as well. I was no longer an old man, nor a beggar. I was the king of Ithaca and the beast that had grown inside me on the fields of Troy had been awakened.

Antinous was just bringing a cup full of wine to his mouth. I seized the quiver and dumped its contents onto the ground. Tens of bitter shafts bounced on the floor. I nocked one of them to my bowstring and let fly. It struck him at the base of his neck. He collapsed to the ground, blood spouting from his mouth and nose. He gave the table a kick and all the food rolled off on top of him, soaking up his blood.

The others were struck dumb. They turned to me incredulously, believing I'd made some kind of mistake. 'What have you done, you villain?' one cried out, and then another. 'You've killed the strongest young hero in Ithaca. That's your last try with the bow!' 'You're dead, foreigner,' came another voice. 'We'll chop you to pieces and feed you to the dogs and vultures!'

'No!' I cried out. 'You're wrong. The contest is over and now we're going to start another game: shooting at live targets!'

They had still not recognized me. They were too young when I had left.

'I'm your king!' I shouted. 'You thought I'd never return from the war. You've devoured all my wealth, you've plotted to murder my son, you've gone to bed with my slaves, you've threatened my wife. Dogs! You're dead! All of you! I won't stop until I've slaughtered every last one of you.'

Instinct drove them to the walls where the arms had always hung, but they found only the shadows of weapons. Green terror gripped them.

Eurymachus, the most fast-thinking among them, turned to me, drawing closer: there he was, on my arrow's path. What should I hit? His neck, his breastbone, his liver?

'Stop! Wait! If you are truly Odysseus, listen to my words. We didn't think it possible for you to return after twenty years. No one could have imagined it.' His hands were open, held out in front of him as if to protect himself. He wanted to make me take the time to reflect. 'We insulted you, humiliated you, I can't deny it, but we didn't know it was you! You looked like another. We would never have acted thus had we known, you must believe me . . .'

The bastard was clever – he could talk.

'It was Antinous who thought all this up, who convinced the rest of us. We'll pay you back, we'll make reparation for everything we've consumed and much, much more. Our fathers are rich, powerful men. You know some of them, don't you?'

He was coming closer and closer.

'Antinous is dead. Forgive your people. We beg you, great king!'

But the arrow had already taken flight. I couldn't have called it back had I wanted to. It went through him from front to back. He went down screaming. A man with an arrow stuck in him can suffer for hours. Philoetius put an end to his pain.

I might have stopped, then, because I'd killed the two most insolent, but I saw that the others were reacting, or at least trying to. They had only their daggers, but they must have thought they could outnumber us, and were already grabbing the tables to use as shields. Some of them were trying to drive me away from the threshold. I knew that if they were to get out the door, they would run for the city and come back in force with their fathers, brothers, relatives in tow.

No one could be allowed to escape.

Telemachus brought one of them down with his spear. Eumeus and Philoetius were used to slaughter, the wild splattering of blood. They seemed perfectly at ease.

'Pardon your people, great king!'

Whose voice was that now? Was it Mentor's? Athena's? My own, perhaps? Only my own? I watched as they fell, thrashing in pools of their own blood. They looked paler to me, and much younger than they were in reality.

That image makes me suffer. I can hear their shrieks, still now, after I've fallen asleep. But my goddess had certainly willed it to happen, otherwise how could four men have prevailed over thirty or fifty or . . . how many were there?

Telemachus ran to the armoury and swiftly returned with more spears and shields for the cowherd and the swineherd and even for me. We joined in a tight formation, one alongside the other, and we counter-attacked. The clash raged on and on, for how long I do not know.

Suddenly, as if by magic, we saw that some of them were wielding heavy weapons.

'Where did they get those?' I shouted. 'If they manage to find arms, we're all dead.'

Telemachus pounded his fist against his thigh. 'Forgive me, father!' he cried out. 'In my haste I may have left the armoury door open! Someone must have got in.'

'Eumeus, Philoetius, go there, immediately,' I ordered. 'If you find anyone, capture him.'

They rushed to the armoury while Telemachus and I continued to drive back the suitors from the front door. I thought of Penelope. Where was she? Could she hear the cries of agony and massacre?

I'd run out of arrows, but Eumeus and Philoetius were returning, carrying weapons they'd found in a corridor that had not been used for many years.

'It was Melanthius,' said Philoetius, panting under the weight of the arms he carried and his haste. 'We've strung him up by the legs. He's hanging under the ceiling beams. You'll decide what his punishment will be when this is over.'

We threw ourselves back into the fray. I was relentless, unstoppable, striking down one after another. The princes fought recklessly, with a strength born of desperation, but none of them knew what it meant to measure himself against the fury of a real warrior in the thick of battle. None of them had ever seen combat. They must have known they had no hope. It was only a question of time. Although they still greatly outnumbered us, they had lost their cohesion and were like crazed animals in a slaughterhouse. One of them tried to jump up towards a loophole that promised to get him outside, but Eumeus nailed him to the wall with a blow of his axe. He sank to the floor with a thud.

More screams. Cries of utter agony. They were trying to make themselves heard so that someone outside, anyone, would run to the city and sound the alarm.

A groan.

Eurymachus . . . could he still be alive? Hadn't Philoetius finished him off?

Ghosts, shadows, were already flitting amongst us. Mentor . . . was that Mentor? Had Athena transported his semblance all the way here, to my house? What remained of my old counsellor? He vanished, just as a swallow swooped between us (*was it him, her, a swallow?*) in frenetic, syncopated flight, showing first the white of its belly, then the black of its back. It went to perch on the main beam supporting the ceiling. From there it let out shrill cries. I could see it gasping with its beak open.

The princes tried time and again to unite, using their improvised shields to wall themselves off, shouting to brace themselves: 'All men to the front! We have to push them out the door. If we can get out we can run for help! We're dead if we don't. Move it! Get on with it!'

But their companions continued to fall around them, pierced by spears, hacked by axes, run through by swords. The whole floor was steaming with blood. I'd already seen that scene. I knew it from my nightmares. When I had called up Agamemnon's shade from Hades, this was how he described his shipmates, massacred in his own palace. Was I avenging them as well?

Telemachus was mercilessly wreaking vengeance on the suitors for every humiliation suffered, every jeer, offence, insult. My eyes fell upon Phemius, the singer. His hands plucked away at the lyre strings as though they were moved by their own energy. Each finger was a creature acting on its own, while his gaze was lost in the mists of terror.

I found before me Leodes, the soft-hearted suitor, least odious among them all. I had heard him invoke death for not having attained the goal of his life, the winning of Penelope, but now that the Chaera was looming over him and darkness was about to descend, he scrabbled to escape. He let his weapons fall to the ground and threw himself at my feet. He implored me to spare his life, trembling, declaring that he had never disrespected the queen, that he had always tried to convince his fellow suitors to follow his example, but I didn't let him finish: with a blow of my sword I took off his head. His moaning had not touched me.

We continued in our work until every last one of them lay lifeless on the floor.

I had reconquered my home, avenged my honour and that of my family, taught future generations a terrible lesson.

Phemius was still alive: was it his turn? He had, after all, gladdened the arrogant suitors during their banquets. He had never rebelled. There he was, shaking, leaning against one of the pillars that stood around the hearth and supported the ceiling. He heard my footsteps drawing closer and he came out into the open. He threw himself at my feet and embraced my knees. 'Have pity,' he said, 'my king!' And he burst into tears.

How distant were the days of my childhood, the days in which the cool water of the fountain was enough to wash my innocent hands, and the adventurous stories that Phemius told me were enough to set me dreaming. He was trembling like a leaf and weeping. A long sigh pulled the last of my fury out of my mouth, the last poisonous exhalation from my chest. We stared at one another in the red light of dusk and tears glistened in my eyes and his. In his gaze I saw the days and nights of times past, peaceful images of my island and my family, celebrations and feasts. I don't know what he saw in my eyes, but a voice rang out in my heart: 'No one can raise his hand against the poet. He is sacred, because his song brings relief for all mortal anguish.'

Phemius walked away from me. His head bowed and his shoulders curved, he made his way across the bloody floor. The house turned dark, blackness descending all at once on my house, on the atrium and the courtyard, over the whole island, just as Theoclymenus, the murdering prophet, had foretold.

I called Euriclea, and she came down from the women's quarters with a lantern in hand. When her eyes took in the massacre, the bodies strewn all over the floor, she gave a whoop of joy. She took to dancing, with her lantern in hand, as if prey to delirium.

'Stop that!' I shouted. 'You cannot dance on the dead! These youths do not deserve to be derided. They have paid for their offences with their lives. Respect them.'

Euriclea stopped and her head dropped in shame.

'I need you, *mai*. Call the maidservants and order them to carry out the corpses. Have them laid side by side outside under the courtyard portico.'

Euriclea called the women, who had been upstairs closed up in their rooms. At the sight of the massacre they burst into tears. Sobbing, they dragged the bodies out, and when they saw the black sun sinking towards the horizon, that unreal darkness, they cried even harder. It must have felt like they were taking the dead straight to Hades.

I looked out and my own heart trembled in my chest to see that darkness so long before nightfall, and so different from the night. It was as if a black veil had fallen upon the sun. It obscured the light but did not put it out entirely. The moon was still visible, as were the most luminous of the stars. No one was laughing about Theoclymenus' black vision any more. And there was still so much to do. '*Mai*,' I ordered, 'have them take up the broken plates and wash the floor down, first with brushes and then with sponges, until it is perfectly clean. They'll do the same with the tables. When they have finished, you will pick out those who sided with the suitors, betraying their queen, and separate them from the others. Have them stand in a row outside, in the courtyard.'

The maidservants trembled upon hearing those words, imagining what was to come.

When they had finished their work, Euriclea had all of them line up outside in the courtyard. The sun was back, once again illuminating the island, but its light was dull, dense, bloody. They were wailing their hearts out and shaking in terror as Euriclea raised her finger against them: 'You, you . . .' They knew that that brief word meant a death sentence.

The red sun of twilight had been stripped of its veil, but there was little left of its downward course towards the surface of the Ocean. I turned to Eumeus and Philoetius then, and told them to stretch a sturdy ship's rope from a column of the portico to the pillar at the courtyard's entrance gate, high above the ground, and to tie a number of knots along its length. One for each of the unfaithful, traitorous handmaids: there they would hang, with their hands tied behind their backs. The line was high enough so that none of their feet could touch the ground. When they were finally abandoned to their destiny, dangling from the rope that stretched from one side of the courtyard to the other, they kicked up their heels as their toes strove instinctively to touch ground, but not for long. They soon stopped moving and swung lifelessly from their nooses. All their energies had fled from their bodies and their shades had already descended to Hades, chasing after those of the suitors who had preceded them. I could almost hear their sighs.

'It's Melanthius' turn!' exclaimed Eumeus. 'Let's go and get him.' He ran off, followed by Philoetius. When they returned they were dragging the goatherd with his hands and feet bound. He screamed with pain at every yank. His arm bones had popped out of his shoulder joints as he hung from the ceiling beam and his face was already a mask of pain, but the worst was yet to come. The punishment for a man who betrays his king, in the full consciousness of what he is doing, was well known. Eumeus and Philoetius cut off his nose, his ears and his genitals and tossed them to the dogs. Then they threw him onto the dungheap, where he would bleed to death.

I called Euriclea again and asked her to bring me fire and sulphur so their fumes could cleanse the hall and courtyard of the stink of death, purge the clotted blood. My house must bear no trace of the desecration.

Euriclea called out all the surviving handmaids and the servants who had remained closed up in their rooms during the massacre. She invited them to recognize me and render homage. I was moved by their words and gestures. They surrounded me, kissing my hands and my head, they knelt at my feet and embraced me, many of them weeping with emotion at seeing me again or perhaps with relief at having escaped death themselves.

I could not believe that I had restored the law in my home and had reconquered the throne. But the bottom of my heart was filled with profound bitterness, because I had never before had to wield arms against my own people. My own blood. The victory I had so longed for had turned into poison. My homecoming had brought nothing but great, unending grief. Not a single one of the companions who followed me to war had I brought back to their families, to the heartsick fathers and mothers who had yearned for their return, scanning the sea day after day for a sign of them. And now there was fresh grief to be borne. Yet, a goddess had chosen to fight beside me, the gasping swallow on the ceiling's main beam: reason was on my side and legitimized everything I had done. Justice had been served, and this was a king's most sacred duty. This I had accomplished. Now I could think of my feelings.

Penelope.

NIGHT HAD finally fallen. Phemius, the singer, crossed the hall like a ghost. He passed next to me without looking at me, his eyes staring at images that only he could see. He crossed the threshold and his dark figure stood out against the last faint red glow of the darkling sky. I stopped him. 'Can you stay here for a little while?' I asked him. Someone was lighting the lanterns in the hall and courtyard.

'If you like, *wanax*.'

'Yes, I would. We used to be friends once . . . long ago.'

'Yes, we were.'

'Then don't go yet, I need you one last time. Inside. Then you can leave.'

Phemius turned and walked back into the hall. He sat on a stool next to the wall and put his lyre on his lap. Then he bent his head and wept hot tears, and I felt a knot in my throat. I wanted to weep with him and let out the bitterness that oppressed me, but my heart was made of stone.

I watched as Telemachus entered from the courtyard. His armour and face were covered with blood. My boy, innocent and unseasoned until just a short while ago, had wounded and killed with sword, axe and spear. He had crossed a line and he would never be able to go back again. I realized that I must look much the same as him, if not worse. We regarded each other in silence: one the mirror of the other.

I heard the sound of a step descending the stair and my heart trembled. I turned and saw Penelope, my bride. Behind her was Euriclea, who was pointing at me and shouting: 'It's him, my child! It's the husband you've been waiting for all this time. He was the foreign guest begging for alms in the hall. He didn't want anyone to recognize him.' But my queen stood still, staring at me as if I were a stranger. She sat next to the hearth and continued to regard me with a nearly indifferent look. Euriclea, confounded by the silence, insisted: 'I recognized him from the first, as soon as I saw the scar on his leg when you ordered me to wash his feet.'

'Wait, *mai*,' I stopped her. 'The queen cannot recognize me in this state. Have a bath prepared for me and have me brought clean clothes, the best remaining in the chest.'

As if she had been waiting for that moment all day or all year, perhaps, she prepared a bath for me and had the maidservants wash me. Then she had me put on fine garments, the ceremonial robes I once wore at public hearings, when I reigned over a peaceful Ithaca.

'How handsome you are, my child,' said my old nurse, her eyes bright with tears, 'how handsome.'

I went back to my wife then. I sat opposite her and contemplated her in silence: beautiful and proud, cheeks blushing in the warmth of the hearth. Time had done no damage to my queen.

There was a tension between us, like a thunderbolt that could not explode. Neither of us could ever have imagined that our meeting, after twenty years of dreams, desires, tears, would be like this: dead silence, mute, confused glances.

'But can't you see that he's your husband?' Euriclea urged. 'Is this how you welcome him, after such a long time? After you've called out his name for so many days and so many nights?' At the end of the hall, Telemachus watched in bewilderment as his parents challenged each other in an absurd skirmish of looks and unsaid words.

Penelope shook her head and fiery tears glittered in her eyes. 'It's not him, *mai*. Do you believe for a moment that I wouldn't recognize my husband? The sound of his voice? The way his eyes change colour when he smiles?'

She was right. I had never smiled since I'd set foot in the house, nor sought her help. That was why she was torturing me: for not having understood her, for not having believed her. For not having gone to her first, before anyone else. For not having trusted her. 'My name is Aithon of Crete,' I had told her, when her soulful eyes searched my face in the darkest corner of the room. And so she had proposed the contest of the bow without saying anything to me. She wanted me to understand that she was accustomed to making decisions on her own and that she didn't need me. I would have to be the one to adapt to her decisions, and if I failed, worse for me. I evidently was not worthy of her. I remembered how many times I'd thought of her when the moon rose on the sea, desiring her so intensely it hurt. Now I had her in front of me, and she was treating me like a foreigner come from afar to beg for a piece of bread.

The silence between us was more deafening than any clash between warriors clad in bronze. It was breaking my heart. I couldn't bear it any longer. I was about to walk out, to the courtyard where Eumeus and Philoetius were loading up the bodies of the suitors on a wagon. But it was she who broke the silence: 'Euriclea, if the guest tells us that he is Odysseus, go upstairs and bring down the bed that my husband is accustomed to sleeping in, so that he may rest comfortably.'

I turned to look at her and saw a slight glimpse of irony in her dark gaze. She was giving me a chance, a single chance, to win her back. 'What are you saying, my queen? Your words cut me to the core! No one can move my bed. I myself built it among the branches of an age-old olive tree. I prepared a nest for you among its green leaves, my bride, my only love.'

She rose then. I had offered up the secret that only she and I knew, the secret of the bed where she had first given herself to me, where we had conceived Telemachus, our only child, a bed redolent of old wood, lavender and wheat. She threw herself into my arms, weeping, convulsively pulled me close, and I could feel the beating of her ardent heart, her breasts pushing against my chest. I whispered confused, crazy words as I sank my face into her hair, waves of the night sea, and we cried in each other's arms, like a boy and a girl discovering love's longing for the first time.

For a moment my eyes met Phemius' dumbfounded gaze. He instantly lowered his head, waiting for me to tell him why I'd asked him to return to the hall. I left Penelope's embrace and went to him.

'Have the lanterns lit everywhere,' I told him, 'play and sing . . . and you, handmaids, dance and raise your voices in song. If anyone passes by this house, they must think that a wedding is being celebrated, that the queen has decided to marry one of her suitors. No one must know what has happened here.'

They obeyed, and I remained for a while watching that macabre dance which should have been joyful and instead was pure folly. The maidservants danced as their friends swung from their nooses, the poet played his lyre and sang with tears in his eyes, oppressed by grief and dismay. He would never have thought that the house in which we had lived so serenely, dreaming of adventure, would have become the scene of a massacre. When I went back to the hearth, I saw that Penelope was no longer there. She had gone up to her rooms, accompanied by her handmaids bearing torches to light her way. They would be undressing her now, washing her body and spreading sweetly scented oil over her skin, laying her on the bed as if it were her wedding night.

In the end I went up the stone stair myself, preceded by two handmaids with lit torches.

I entered.

22

DRAPED IN MAJESTIC PURPLE, covered with soft linen woven by expert hands, redolent of olive, our bed waited to take us into its folds. I recognized every stroke of my axe and my plane, every surface smoothed by my pumice. My queen had preserved it like a sanctuary, without ever losing hope in my return.

Penelope's love . . . what was it like, after so many years? Her mouth, her fiery womb, her breasts? And her black, black, black eyes? Beyond any enchantment I could have imagined in the long nights of my exile. The intimacy we had so desired enflamed our looks, our breath. I breathed in her mouth, she in mine. The light of the lantern cast a bronze reflection on her skin. She was no more than thirty-seven now, and her beauty was dazzling.

This was the privilege of a queen: she had never exposed her skin to the merciless sun, never ruined her hands pulling weeds in a field of wheat or barley. Food and pure water were always abundant on her ivory table and in her silver cup. Baths and scented oils had kept her skin soft. I couldn't take my eyes off her, just as her gaze was locked on me. We were both incredulous at being together again and in each other's arms.

When I pulled her close to me, the sounds of the dancing and strident singing in the hall ceased and silence fell over the house, enveloped by the night. Perhaps Telemachus or Euriclea had ordered Phemius to give up the absurd pretence. After all, who would ever be passing along the path at such a late hour? Eumeus and Philoetius had their work cut out for them. They would be at it all night, but tomorrow there would be no trace of what had happened. Not a single stain nor hint of the dense, sweet stench of death.

The frenzy of slaughter had not yet been extinguished in me; its force had not ebbed, but it flowed in a different direction. The fire was still burning, with a different energy but with the same intensity, like a river that had changed course. Only exhaustion stopped us, when the sky was just beginning to pale. We fell asleep and we forgot. The warmth of the bed and Penelope's nude body filled me with life after the cold shadow of death had frozen my heart. Time expanded, infinitely. A wave of memories washed over me and it felt for a moment as if nothing had changed. As if I'd never left, as if our love could continue on its natural course, erasing the chasm of the years.

I felt Athena's veil on us, protecting us. She was not jealous of Penelope, perhaps she loved her as she loved me. But would the ire of Poseidon be appeased? Or was the blue god, from the depths of the sea, meditating on more calamity for me?

When would I have to leave again? After a day, a month, a year? How would I ever find the courage to tell Penelope?

Or should I ignore the prophecy as if I'd never heard it?

How could I be certain that I'd summoned up the ghost of Tiresias from Hades, and that I'd heard those words from him? Might I have been dreaming? Might all of it have been a dream?

In that bed, next to the bride I'd desired so fervently, the woman I'd feared would become grey, worn, lifeless, wrinkled, everything seemed possible and impossible. Her breathing, soft and regular in sleep, was a music that I'd never forgotten. That breathing, along with the merest thought from me, was enough to make me forget everything, to let me believe that none of it had really happened. A dream, like so many that had visited me in my sleep over the years. But the squeaking of wheels drifted in from the courtyard. Carts being pulled over stone. Limbs hanging over the sides, the arms and legs of young men slaughtered.

By me, my son, the cowherd and the swineherd. It was all

horribly real, there was no room for illusion. I begged my goddess to give me a few more hours of serenity. Then I would be able to face a thousand adventures, clashes, duels with men and gods, monsters, nightmares, dreams.

I had fallen, after our lovemaking, into a torpor, neither awake nor asleep. I would open my eyes and find Penelope's, staring deeply.

'I heard you crying,' she said.

I didn't know how to answer.

'I understand. This is not how you imagined your return. Perhaps you thought your people would welcome you with festivities, the noblemen accompanying you to the palace where I would be waiting for you, dressed in my most beautiful gown and precious jewels. I'm sorry that didn't happen and I'm sorry you felt you couldn't trust me.'

'I was wrong and I ask you to forgive me, my love. But my crying wasn't for what I did, and not even for the bitterness I made you suffer . . .'

'I've already forgotten that. I made love to you like a girl, I slept in your arms, I felt your heat after so many years. You can't imagine how that made me feel . . . Why were you crying, then?'

'Because I'll have to leave again.'

She looked as if she'd turned to stone.

I couldn't stop. I had started talking. I had to say it all.

'What I'm about to tell you is unbelievable, I know, but in my ship I crossed the wall of fog that separates our world from a place where anything is possible. I reached the ends of the earth, I ventured into the waves of the river Ocean. I went beyond the jagged cliffs and the rocky towers that are the sentinels of the world of the dead. I sacrificed to the infernal gods and called up the shadows of Hades. Thousands of them came to me.

'The Theban prophet Tiresias was among them. He drank of the blood of the animals I'd sacrificed and he spoke to me. It was a dreadful sight to see, but worse was to hear what he had to tell me. He predicted that I would return, here, to Ithaca, late, a broken man, on a foreign ship without a single comrade. He said that I would find my house invaded by pretenders plaguing my wife and that I would have to kill them all. He said that when I had done this, I would have to leave again, to journey in a single direction away from the sea, carrying an oar on my shoulder. I would have to continue on until I found myself among people who do not know the sea, who do not season their food with salt, who have never seen a ship. Until one day I would find a man who would ask me whether the oar on my shoulder was a fan for winnowing grain.

'"This is the sign," Tiresias told me. '"You can't mistake it. You will plant the oar into the ground and offer a bull, a boar and a ram in sacrifice to Poseidon: only then will you be able to return and reign among happy peoples. Death will come to seek you only when you are exhausted by serene old age. She will come for you softly, from the sea."'

My wife's tears gleamed like pearls on her cheeks. The night was never-ending, beyond any limit that I had ever known. Perhaps the spirits of the dark wanted to allow me a little more time for my night of love and sorrow.

'He said nothing of me?'

'You are always in my heart. But the prophecy must be fulfilled. I challenged a god and have paid dearly for it already. This is the last thing that remains to be done: to end the impossible contest of a mortal against an invincible god. Once and for all.

'The first part of the prophecy has come true in every way, why shouldn't the second as well? When Tiresias named the three animals I would have to sacrifice, I remembered something that happened when I was just a boy. The first time I ever went to the continent was to visit my grandfather, Autolykos, for a hunting party. My mother gave me a message for him, and when he'd seen it he asked me to name three animals, but to be very careful with my answer, because those three animals would mark my future.

'I said without hesitation: "The bull, the boar and the ram."' The same as Tiresias. I cannot escape my destiny. It was all foretold. I know that I'll make you suffer by leaving again, but I have no choice. If I don't bring this conflict to an end, I'll never have a hope of living the last part of my life in serenity, with my family, on my island.'

Penelope held me tightly, curled into my arms. I caressed her face, her body, sought out her black eyes in the darkness. I was thinking, perhaps, that her love could keep the restless shades of the murdered suitors away from me.

'The gods are deceitful, they play with our lives pitilessly,' she cried. 'You are their toy. A little man armed only with an oar who must take on first a bull and then a boar with frightful tusks and then a curved-horned ram, in some remote, solitary place. As they sit on their shining thrones, enjoying the spectacle from the sky.'

'I don't believe that. Tiresias was telling the truth. No one tells lies in the kingdom of the dead.'

She turned away, sobbing softly. I felt like crying as well. And yet, wretched as we were, we made love again and again, locked in a fierce embrace, weeping, each of us breathing in the other's pain. In the heat and the bitter taste of tears, from that total intimacy of soul and body rose a challenge to the sky, more defiant and powerful than any that could be fought with a sword or spear: the call of two mortal creatures who loved each other desperately, enmeshed in a moment of extreme emotion and suffering, beyond anything they had ever experienced. A heartbroken passion whose infinite power no god, no demon, could remotely imagine.

THE LIGHT shifted over our faces and our bodies, and my goddess, perhaps, instilled the thought in my heart of what might happen as soon as news of the suitors' deaths spread. I jumped to my feet, washed and dried myself off, put on a tunic taken from my chest, which Penelope had kept closed all these years, and went to the armoury to don my battle gear: shield, spear and sword.

Telemachus, Eumeus, Philoetius and some of their most trusted companions were already waiting for me, armed to the teeth.

Telemachus spoke, the excitement of combat, his first, still evident in his voice. 'Atta, perhaps it's best that we immediately go to King Laertes, so we can join forces with him and be ready if the relatives of the dead men decide to attack. I don't think the palace, or my mother, will be in danger. It's us they'll be after. When they learn that their sons and brothers are dead, they will either resign themselves to fate or decide to exact revenge. In either case, the corpses will have to be returned to the families.' My boy had already reasoned it all out, and he was acting with the wisdom and foresight of a king.

We set off, covering ourselves with long cloaks that concealed our weapons. Penelope was at the window of our bedchamber, watching us leave. She looked like a goddess.

'Where is Phemius?' I asked.

'He's in the servants' quarters,' replied Telemachus. 'He still does not know whether you've decided to pardon him and spare his life.'

'I had told him he could go wherever he liked, after he'd performed that one last service for me.'

'But where? He has no place to go.'

'Then he'll stay with us.'

'Fine. You'll tell him when we return.'

I nodded.

The closer we got to the fork in the road, the harder my heart pounded in my chest. I remembered the words of my mother's shadow: 'He lies down on a bed of leaves wherever darkness catches him. There he sighs, his heart aching for you.' Contemptuous and scornful, my father could clearly not bear to stay in a house invaded, the place from which he'd reigned over Ithaca.

'There is King Laertes your father, Argonaut and hero,' said Telemachus.

It wrung my heart to see him. It was him, but how he had changed! He was wearing worn, patched clothing, a goatskin cap on his head, gloves of sheepskin on his hands to protect them from thorns. This is what the king of Ithaca was reduced to. The man who had quested for the golden fleece with Jason, the man who'd given me the best days of my boyhood, the best memories of my youth, who'd filled my ardent young heart with dreams and hopes.

When he heard our footsteps, he leaned his hoe against the trunk of a pear tree and walked towards us. He recognized Telemachus: 'Who is this man, *pai*? Why have you come so early in the morning to my house?'

I wished I could delay the moment of recognition. I could have told some fantastic tale, one of the many had already come to mind. But how could I think of putting my father, my king, to the test?

I threw myself at his feet, and kissed his hands. 'It's me, *atta*, Odysseus, your son. I've returned.' I removed the cloak from my shoulders and stood before him in my shining armour.

'Do you recognize me?' I asked him then.

He embraced me, clasped me close to his chest. 'Son, my son . . .' he sobbed, 'how long, what a long time . . . I never would have wanted you to see me in this state.'

'Don't say that, *atta*, don't say such a thing. You don't know the joy it gives me to hold you in my arms. Show me the trees, the ones you gave me as a gift. We planted them together, remember? Are they still alive? Have they grown? Do they bear fruit?'

'Yes, of course, come, come with me.' He dragged me by my hand. 'See that pear? I was digging up the weeds around its trunk. Maybe I was still believing in your return and wanted you to see everything in order, but not like this, I didn't want you to see me like this . . .'

'It's all over, *atta*, they're gone. The ones who humiliated you, laid waste to your house, forced you to live like a pauper. They're all dead. I wiped them out, with the help of my son and a couple of men who are still faithful to me.'

'You killed them? How did you manage, so few of you? And why didn't you tell me? I would have rushed to your side! Old as I am, I can assure you that I would have sent many of them into the mouth of Hades myself.'

'I didn't want you to have to jump back into the fray at your age. It wasn't necessary. I'm about to send Eumeus to the city now. He'll tell their families to come and collect the bodies so they can be given funeral rites. Then he'll go to the port to talk to the crews of the ships and have them transport the bodies of those who were not from Ithaca back to the continent and the other islands. Eumeus, go now.'

The swineherd left and my father insisted that I stay with him so that we could have lunch together.

It was incredible: he knew what had gone on at the palace, I'd told him, but he wanted lunch. He'd give his servants orders to prepare it and to invite Dolius, his neighbour, with his seven sons. His magnificent blue eyes shone with happiness.

I said: '*Atta*, we'll stay. My joy at seeing you again is immense. I won't leave you. Tell me, *atta*, where is Mother buried?'

A shadow descended on his eyes, like storm clouds on the sea. 'Then you know that she's dead . . . Come with me. I've left an empty tomb, a wonder to behold, in the royal cemetery. Her ashes are here close to my house, and when my time comes you'll put me next to her.'

We crossed the olive grove and reached a well-tended meadow, its grass freshly cut, with purple thistle flowers and rosehips red as cornelian. There was a little gravestone in the shadow of a holm oak; in front of it, on the ground, a stone cut from the mountain-side. I looked into my father's eyes and then at the stone, and the words of my mother's spirit, the pale wraith I'd encountered at the mouth of Hades, rang in my heart: 'It was neither Artemis with her arrows nor a malady that wasted me away, but my longing for you, my beloved son, that took my life.'

I gathered the red rosehips, the purple thistle blossoms and placed them on her tomb. A thorn on the thistle pricked me and a drop of my blood spilled on the stone.

'Why didn't you wait for me, Mother, why?'

I got no answer in my heart.

My father's eyes were glistening. 'I miss her still,' he said, 'even now.'

We started back, but hadn't got very far before Eumeus ran up to us, panting: 'Hurry, *wanax*, hurry, they're coming!'

'Who's coming?' I asked.

'The relatives of the dead – their fathers, their brothers. They're armed and they're heading this way to get revenge. They were maddened by the sight of the corpses. They threw themselves onto the ground, onto the lifeless bodies of their sons and brothers, groaning and weeping. Antinous' father was shrieking like a wounded eagle. He demanded that all the others take up arms and rush out to kill you. You'd lost all your ships, he told them, the whole army. You didn't bring back a single one of the men who left with you, and now you'd come to murder all the rest. They fear that if they wait you'll seek refuge at Pylos, in King Nestor's palace.' He was gasping for breath.

'Calm down,' I replied. 'We'll draw up in front of the gate. How many are there?' I asked Eumeus.

'A lot, but not all of them. Some have already turned back and taken away their son's bodies to celebrate funeral rites. Quite a few recognized that you had been wronged, your house and your wife's honour violated. I myself heard one of them say: 'It's not his fault if the army was lost. Wars mow down men in their prime and the sea is rife with dangers. Surely he wanted to bring all his comrades back home. And I'm afraid that what he's done must have been the will of the gods. How else could just four of them get the better of so many strapping youths?'

We hastened to my father's house. Dolius and his seven sons

had arrived, and they armed themselves as well. In all, there were over a dozen of us. I was sorry I hadn't thought to bring my bow. I could have struck down many of the attackers at a distance; I could already see them approaching. But when they were at about fifty paces from us, a wondrous thing occurred. Something swooped down from the sky. A bird of prey, perhaps? And just then, in the middle of the two formations, ours so small and theirs so much more numerous, appeared Mentor! He seemed to hesitate for a moment, then headed towards us. I felt a shiver run under my skin.

Our adversaries were already letting their arrows fly, and we raised our shields. A single spear flew from our side, hurled by my father, the hero Laertes. The same one he'd had when he sailed off to find the golden fleece. The massive rod rose straight and swift, and then the inexorable tip started its descent. It found its mark in Eupites' cheek, easily penetrating the futile protection of his helmet. He was Antinous' father. He collapsed, and his arms rattled to the ground with a dull crash.

His comrades stopped in their tracks, dumbfounded. How could the arm of an old man, sapped by years of hard labour and pain, have flung that weapon with such deadly force? Mentor was very close to us now, he shot me a searing look and I instantly knew what I had to do.

I walked towards the relatives of the men we had killed with my father at my side and Telemachus behind us. The others followed in two rows. When we were at a short span from them, Eupites lying pierced between us, we stopped. The vermilion stream flowing from his body was a line of fire between us: we were sons of the same land.

I had tears in my eyes when I said: 'Peace.' I plunged my spear into the ground and the others, lined up to the right and left of me, did the same.

Our adversaries followed our example.

I ordered Dolius' sons to gather the body of Eupites – to wash it, cover it with a shroud, and lay it in a cart in the shade of an oak tree. I cried out: 'Mentor!' but got no response. A hawk soared high above me towards the sun, wheeling in wide circles in the sky of blinding bronze.

Together, in silence, we consumed a meal of reconciliation.

When I raised my eyes, I saw Phemius, the singer, at the end of the road, advancing slowly towards us. The wind was picking up and he was enveloped in a swirl of dust. He seemed to be floating, raised above the ground, like a ghost.

23

WHEN THE FUNERAL BANQUET WAS OVER, the fathers and brothers of the fallen suitors left, heading down the path to their own homes. Eumeus and Philoetius returned to the palace to deliver the corpses which had not yet been claimed to the ships moored at the harbour, waiting to carry them back to their families on the islands.

A profound sadness flooded my heart, because revenge is always a poison that leaves a bitter taste in your mouth. Fury burns itself out, frenzy melts away and your soul remains ice cold, aching with loss and sorrow. What anguished me the most were the days still to come. Who would I be able to talk to? How would I govern my land, how would I administer justice? How could I ever find joy in the company of my son when I knew that I'd deprived so many of my countrymen of the same joy? How would I find consolation in my wife's arms, knowing how many women of Ithaca were tormented by grief? How would I be able to walk down the paths of my island, knowing that there could very well be an ambush lying in wait behind every bush or tree?

I watched Phemius as he advanced towards us and I realized that the days that inspired the poets were over. What awaited me was nothing but the slow wasting of my soul and long nights with my eyes wide open.

Phemius sat under the oak and watched as the mules were yoked to the cart that would carry the lifeless body of Eupites to his last resting place. My father had killed him and I had killed his son. I approached the poet and said: 'Phemius, my heart is heavy but I had no choice. You saw everything that happened. Could I have forgiven them instead?'

'Don't you remember? Not much time has passed!' Phemius cried out. 'That's exactly what Eurymachus asked you to do: "Forgive your people!" Why didn't you? Is it not a king's duty to be magnanimous? You'd already killed Antinous. How much blood did you need to sate your thirst for revenge? They had offered to pay you back for everything they had consumed in your house, and more. They would have done anything to placate your anger. It's always better to look towards the future when you're contemplating revenge and bloodshed. Think about it. Had you pardoned them, wouldn't you be feeling better now? Wouldn't you be walking down the streets of your island light-hearted, surrounded by the gratitude and admiration of your subjects? Wouldn't everyone's lives be better? Yours, theirs, even mine? And instead, look what's facing us: grief, dismay, bitter cold and emptiness.' He dropped his head and let the tears fall freely onto his bristly cheeks.

'Have you forgotten the days of our youth, my king?' he went on. 'Have you forgotten those happy days? No fury, no blood, no infinite mourning. Hope, that's what we embraced then, dreams, singing and joy. The sun, the sea, the clouds and the flowered meadows, the sunsets over a purple sea, the sails returning home, amazement and wonder at the adventure of the life that was waiting for us. That's what you should have returned to, even if these long years had taxed you so sorely.'

He fell silent again. His chin dropped to his chest, the sea breeze ruffling his thinning hair and drying the tears on his cheeks.

I sighed. A strong urge to cry swept over me as well.

'Do you expect an answer, Phemius? I only wish that an answer existed! But there isn't any. Do you want to know why I didn't forgive? Why I couldn't be satisfied with a single victim? Because for ten long years that's all I did: slaughtered, murdered, gutted whoever challenged me. Could I have gone into hiding instead? Fled? Shirked my destiny?

'If I had been able to come back home after leaving Troy in ruins, none of this would have happened. I would reign now as Nestor does, beloved by his people, surrounded by his children and grandchildren.

'It was not my fault, Phemius. Do you know how ardently I hoped? How I wept, searched, implored? But forces much greater than my own, immense, frightful forces, drove me away, further and further away, to the extreme limits of earth and sea, beyond the boundaries that men are held to by the gods. The longing to return never left me, believe me, but my life on the sea was to be no different than the years under the walls of Troy. I had to keep fighting. Monsters, savage man-eating creatures. I had to keep watching my comrades die, one after another, atrocious deaths. Cut down, strung up like fish, mangled in the jaws of horrendous beasts . . .' Phemius' blue eyes considered mine for the first time; his chin was trembling. 'I had to harden my heart, I would have been defeated had I not nursed hatred and vengeance. I wanted to survive. Should I have let myself drown, sink into the abyss?

'When I finally got here, when I kissed my island, could finally smell it, recognize its clouds, I thought that everything could go back to the way it was.' Phemius' blue tears accompanied my words, dripping onto the dry sandy soil. 'I went to Eumeus' sty and met Telemachus there. He had just narrowly escaped death at the hands of his mother's suitors. I held my son and we wept together. That embrace made me feel that I could reclaim all those lost years, that I could love again, think of the future, of my home, of my wife, of my father, the hero Laertes who had so suffered my absence. But then I was told that my house had been invaded, taken over by insolent pretenders to my throne who were menacing my wife and plotting yet another ambush to kill my son. I knew I had to act in secret. I disguised myself as a beggar and prepared to suffer insult and injury. You saw me yourself, didn't you, Phemius? You recognized me under those rags.

'It was what Tiresias, the Theban seer whose spirit I'd summoned up from Hades, had prophesied. "You will kill them all," he told me, "either openly, with your slashing bronze, or stealthily, with deceit." My goddess exhorted me to do the same.

'And yet neither the prophecy of Theban Tiresias nor the goddess of the green-blue eyes would have led me to massacre them had I not wanted it. What drove me to it was feeling myself surrounded by enemies, feeling the shock of their blows. The ancient fury sleeping at the bottom of my heart awoke all at once and it blazed so bright it burnt my soul. Nothing could have stopped me. There was no mercy to be had. Black night had descended upon my home. The glorious palace of Laertes had become the very mouth of Hades. The sun itself was blacked out. Could I have avoided it? Answer me: could I have avoided it?'

It was only then that I realized my father had been listening to my words. He said: 'You have nothing to blame yourself for, son. Nothing could be more craven than taking undue advantage of the home and honour of a man who is far away and cannot defend himself. You exacted justice and you acted like a sovereign. You pronounced your sentence and you carried it out. No one will ever dare to follow the example of those wretches again.'

Phemius rose to his feet. He said: 'Come, my king. Let's return home.'

IN THE DAYS that followed I suffered no less pain than I had in ten years of war and in my long wanderings beyond the wall of fog. I couldn't go back into my house, couldn't speak to my son or my wife. I barely ate, and when I did, it was alone. The only people I felt like talking to were Phemius and my father. For days and nights, I told Phemius what had happened in the long years I spent away from home. Reliving those events made me feel better. I could see what I was describing so vividly that the images in my head seemed almost real. I could hear the sounds, the voices. I saw the colours of any number of distant, different skies, the light of unknown stars. Phemius listened to me intently without saying a word. He did not interrupt me as I spoke and never asked for explanations afterwards.

What I asked my father was how would I be able to continue living on the island, how could I reign over such a harshly wounded people?

'What you did was your right,' he told me. 'You are the king of this land and the surrounding islands. What else could you have done? If you had pardoned them, many others would have followed their example, even on the continent. You don't know what's happened to the others. Agamemnon was murdered the night he returned along with all his comrades, in his own palace and by his own wife, Clytaemnestra, with the help of her lover Aegisthus. Diomedes was forced to leave Argus or unleash another war. His wife Aegialia was plotting to kill him. The same happened to Idomeneus . . .'

'I know,' I answered. 'I know.'

My father's head dropped. 'Our world risks destruction,' he said. 'The war has mown down the best of our youth, the men who could have been governing Achaia and holding us together now. The most valiant and powerful kings have died or disappeared: Agamemnon, Diomedes, Idomeneus, Achilles, Ajax of Locris and Ajax of Salamis . . .' I trembled upon hearing that name. I could see Great Ajax's vexed spirit turn his back to me and vanish in the mists of Hades.

'Nestor still reigns unopposed,' continued my father, 'but he mourns the loss of Antilochus, his best-loved son. When I first heard that he'd returned, I'd go often to visit him. He was inconsolable. Then, when I understood that you wouldn't be coming back, I stopped. I didn't want to weep over a lost son with him. At least he had others. I only had you. And when I lost your mother, I was alone. Alone in this house. I've been living without human companionship for years.'

'I know, *atta*. You always told me that in war there are no winners. Everyone loses.'

Sometimes we'd go walking through the woods, down the mountain paths, and once, towards sunset, we found ourselves at the boulder that overlooked the palace. The place where, as a little boy, I would toss coloured stones, trying to see my future.

'Remember, *atta*? Remember that afternoon? You'd been hunting, and you found me sitting right here. You stopped to talk to me, you, the Argonaut hero, the king of Ithaca. With a child.'

'With my son . . .'

'What peace, what joy. You can't understand what it was for me to hear you talk, to listen to your adventures . . .'

'And now the tables are turned. It's you telling me about your adventures.'

'You're the best father I could have ever had, *atta*.'

'And you are the son every father would have wished for. We didn't have much time together, did we? But if you still want your father's company, come by whenever you like. I have nothing to do.'

I'd go often. Being with him brought me serenity and Penelope encouraged me to spend time with him. Sometimes I'd take Telemachus with me. I liked the idea of three generations of Ithacan kings talking to each other, telling stories, going hunting in the woods or fishing along the coast.

Night was my torment. Everything took on the shape of a nightmare. My heart ached. I could find no peace. The shadows of the suitors crowded into the courtyard, squeaking like bats. I watched them diving straight into the mouth of Hades. That's how I'd begun to see the well in the middle of the courtyard: as the well of souls.

I wouldn't go to bed until very late at night, when Penelope was already sleeping. Or so I thought. But as soon as I had stretched out next to her, coming so light-footed and silent that she couldn't have possibly heard me, she would sigh, and then turn to me and say: 'Don't torture yourself, Odysseus, don't inflict more suffering on yourself. You've already suffered enough.' She would caress me, press her body close to mine.

'I know you'll have to leave again,' she would say then. 'But don't lose yourself to brooding now. How could it have gone any differently? It's true, you spilled much blood, you gave vent to your anger. But you were right to do so. Your bow had waited many years for you. Your grandfather Autolykos had ordered you not to take it to war with you. Remember? He said it must never leave this house.'

Sometimes she took my head between her arms and whispered softly into my ear. Such a sweet voice. She was trying to get used to the idea that I'd be leaving again.

'Where will you go?' she'd ask me quietly in the dark.

'Far from the sea. That's what the Theban seer told me. That means east. Until I meet a man who asks me a question. That's the sign that I've arrived.'

'And when will you leave?'

'I don't know. I don't really understand when myself. The gods will have to guide me. Ill fate has tainted my every move until now. I was kept from returning, made to suffer more than even I could have imagined. And now another journey looms: the last one. They will have to send me a sign. Athena has always protected me, always inspired me in my heart.'

'Does she still speak to you?'

'No. I haven't heard her voice or seen her since the day of slaughter. If she's still close to me, she's so well disguised that I can't discern her. She wanted to be there at the massacre. She wanted to see me in combat, watch as I struck, slashed, murdered. Now she must be thinking of other things.'

'Don't say that. It's she who brought you back to me.'

'So that I could leave again.'

'But at least I've seen you, embraced you. We've made love, slept together in our bed, the bed you made for me with your own hands when we were still so young. You can't imagine how much this means to me. I didn't want to die without seeing you again. I couldn't believe that destiny, or the gods, would be so cruel with me.'

'After all these long years away from my island, seeing you was bliss. When I watched you come down the stairs, cross the great hall, so proud and so beautiful, I couldn't believe it was true. My heart was full of shame, because I had to cover myself with rags and feign being a wrinkled old man. I wanted to be as handsome as a god for you.'

'You've always been as handsome as a god for me. It's impossible to put out that light in your eyes . . . Will you make peace with your people?'

'I have.'

'No, you haven't. You made a pact to avoid more bloodshed. That was only natural. No one wants to reign over an empty island.'

'I thought you wanted me to avenge you: your honour, your anguish, your fears.'

'I did. But now you must reconcile with your people. A king is a father to his people. You yourself have said so. You've inflicted a terrible punishment on them. Now you have to show compassion and atone for the blood you spilled so that it will not cry out from the earth and call for more.'

I said nothing. I held her close and sought sleep in her arms.

I AWOKE EARLY, took the dogs, put on my sword and left the palace. I was looking for Eumeus. 'What should I do?' I thought, my heart wishing that Mentor were with me.

The wind picked up, blowing eastward from the sea, rustling the treetops on the mountainside. The dogs sniffed at the air as the wind ruffled the tufts of hair hanging over their eyes.

'Is that you?' I asked aloud, looking all around. 'I need you. Can you hear me?'

The branches opposite from where I stood were stirring and

the dogs were barking in that specific direction. My hand dropped to my sword. Out stepped a boy of thirteen or fourteen who threw himself at my feet. 'It's only me, *wanax*,' he said, trembling like a leaf from head to toe. 'Don't hurt me.'

'Who are you?'

The boy was terrified. His eyes were fixed on my hand and then dropped to the ground.

'What are you afraid of?' I asked.

He shook his head as if to show me that he couldn't get a word out. His chin was quivering and he looked as if he were about to cry.

'What's your name?' I insisted.

'My name is Euthymides. I'm Eupites' youngest son. Please don't hurt me, I beg of you!' He tried to embrace my knees, to kiss my hand.

'You're Antinous' brother . . . oh, mighty gods. What are you doing here?'

'I was looking for a place to hide. In the city, everyone is saying there's no man alive who can match your strength and that your rage is without limit. They're saying that no one will be spared. You've killed my father and my brother. I beg of you, let me live!'

I helped him up from the ground and looked into his eyes. 'You've done nothing wrong, Euthymides. You have nothing to fear from me. It wasn't me who killed your father. It was King Laertes whose spear stopped him from attacking us.'

Euthymides burst into tears.

'But it's as if I killed him myself,' I went on. 'I have slain all those who offended the queen my wife, who plotted to murder my son and who gorged themselves on the property of an absent man who could not defend himself or his family. They forced my father King Laertes to flee to the countryside, to live in penury. But you have no blame in any of this. No one will hurt you. I swear it.'

The boy seemed calmer, but his look was still wary.

'Do you want to talk to me?' I asked.

He shook his head, without moving his eyes. He didn't want to talk. His gaze burned into my heart.

'You'd like to avenge your father and your brother. Wouldn't you?'

No answer.

'I know that's what you're thinking. I'm willing to give you my sword so you can exact revenge here, now, on me. But hear me out first. Imagine that you have to leave for a war you didn't want, abandoning your bride, your infant son. You suffer unending grief: wounds, fear, hunger. Horror. You watch as the best of your friends die, one after another. Then, finally, after a very long time, you head back home. But you lose your way, you end up in a forsaken, unfamiliar world where you have to fight horrible, bloodthirsty monsters, where you have to summon the spirits of the dead from the Underworld to try to discover how and when you can ever return home . . .'

The boy's eyes were wide with wonder. He'd never heard such a story.

'Then, after years and years, you finally set foot on your land again. But what is your home like now? Invaded by boastful, violent young men who scheme to devour your belongings, to seduce your wife, to kill your son. How would you have felt? What would you have done? Tell me, and then I'll give you my sword and you can use it on me and avenge your family. Tell me, now,' I repeated.

I don't know what the expression on my face was like as I said those words, but the boy was staring at me in a stupor. He dropped his head and remained mute.

I drew my sword from its sheath and handed it to him hilt first. 'If you think that your brother and your father were in the right and that I deserve to die, your time has come. Take advantage of it. You may not have another chance.'

He ran off weeping, instead, and I continued on my way towards Eumeus' pigsty. I found him there making goat cheese.

He came up to me and kissed my hand. '*Wanax!* Why didn't you let me know? I would have made a good lunch for us, a meal worthy of you.'

He bustled about finding me a chair, stoking up the fire, arranging meat on a spit.

'Don't trouble yourself so,' I said, 'I haven't got much of an appetite. I've come to keep my promises. As of today, you are part of my family. This is your house, the flocks and herds you care for are yours. You can choose a bride from among the hand-maids, the one you like best. I hope she'll give you sturdy children. One day you will tell them that the destroyer of sacred Troy is beholden to you for his kingdom. Tomorrow I will visit Philoetius as well, and I will give him the same gifts as a reward for his loyalty.'

Eumeus fell to his knees, deeply moved. He kissed my hand time and time again, repeating: 'Thank you, *wanax*, thank you. I will be faithful to you as long as I live, and continue to work for you as I always have.'

'Living . . . it won't be easy to live in this place any more. I longed to return for so many years, but now I feel like a foreigner in my own land. I've brought ruin and destruction upon my people. Who will ever want to talk to me again?'

'You're wrong,' replied Eumeus. 'Many, here in Ithaca, be-lieve that you acted with justice, that the suitors deserved the end they came to. Don't say such things. You've returned to your home and your family, try to find peace for yourself. Time takes care of everything. Those who are weeping now will forget their troubles, because no one can suffer forever.'

'What about you? What's it like when you go down to the city? Do you feel threatened? Do they hate you because you helped me?'

'No, no one dares. Everyone, even your enemies, realize that without the aid of the gods, four of us could never have prevailed over more than fifty adversaries, some of whom were armed. Everyone knows that peace has been made.'

'Peace . . . I don't know what that word means any more.'

'Then why don't you talk to your people? Why don't you call for an assembly? Why don't you allow them to see you? You need to understand what your people are feeling, both the good and the bad. When you've done this, you'll know how to go on. You'll stop tormenting yourself and you'll forget the war and your long wanderings.'

'Not now,' I replied. 'Not now. When it's time for me to go.'

'What? You're leaving again?'

'Thus it is written. This is the prophecy of the Theban seer, great Tiresias, who I called up from the kingdom of the dead.'

'Let me come with you, then. I'll follow you anywhere.'

'No. This time I'll go alone. At least I won't have to mourn any more lost comrades or listen to their parents weeping and groaning.'

Eumeus knew why I had come to his house: I wanted to settle my debt with him. Whatever happened, I wanted him to remember me as a man of my word, a man who always keeps his promises.

We went on talking for a very long time, waiting for dusk and the flight of the seagulls, reminiscing on times long ago and forgotten happiness. I had restored law and justice to Ithaca, I had won back my house and my family, but the horizon was bleak, the clouds black and low.

In the end I left my faithful friend and descended the mountain slope, looking for the smoke wafting from my rooftop, seeking the sounds of home.

24

I REACHED THE PALACE as darkness was falling and the maidservants came out to receive me, to wash my hands and feet. *Mai* asked me to taste the roast to see if it was well cooked. Telemachus was outside, standing on the grass near the fountain, intent on planting a young ash tree (*was it the season to be planting trees?*). I was told that the queen was waiting for me in the hall for dinner.

Had I ever really been away? Had I ever left my island? Just then it seemed to me that I had never gone to sea. The sky was the same, the clouds as thin and wispy as they had ever been, the head of the pack looked like Argus (*was it him?*), the house in perfect order. I felt calm and I was enjoying that moment of peace. The sense of time never passing gave me the bittersweet sensation of an everlasting sunset, a lazy twilight that fluttered between evening and night.

Penelope was already sitting in her chair. Her eyes were edged with Egyptian bistre, her lips tinged red; she wore amber earrings and necklace. Her white gown was chequered and gave off golden reflections when she shifted. The neckline was opened in a wide rectangle at the front and back. It made me think of the gown with the ducklings that she was wearing when we first met and my heart was touched.

From the moment when I'd come ashore, I knew that reality would be different from my dreams. I knew that, as Calypso had told me, Penelope's body would be different from the one that filled my imagination, but the light of the setting sun was flooding her with red gold and lighting up her eyes. She got up and came towards me. She kissed me, encircling my neck with her arms, pressing her hips against mine. What I wanted to do was take her up to our bed, nestled in the branches of the olive tree.

Euriclea removed my work tunic, passed her soft sponge over my skin and dried me gently. She dressed me again with a fresh tunic that skimmed my feet; it was purple, with a wide hem of white linen interwoven with golden threads. She wanted me to be happy as only a king can be: in his palace, surrounded by love and veneration, beloved by the gods. She almost made me feel like I was that happy king. Yet I wasn't accustomed to such privileges any more.

I could hear the dogs yelping excitedly outside. Telemachus?

'I've invited King Laertes your father,' said Penelope. 'I thought you'd be glad to see him.'

'Of course, my darling. Is that him?'

She nodded. 'I think it must be him. The dogs are noisier when Telemachus comes home. He always has a treat for them.'

The dogs, my father, my son, the setting sun, my royal tunic, my bride. *Mai* running the household. Every thing, every person, had its own colours, shone with its own light. Could my heart heal its wounds?

'Go to receive the king,' Penelope ordered the maidservants and they scurried to do her bidding.

Outside was Philoetius' voice as he halted the oxen who were pulling the cart. Then my father's voice.

'*Atta!*'

'I couldn't refuse an invitation from the king and queen,' he said, entering.

The maids approached him with a silver basin and two linen towels. I watched as they washed my father's hands and feet. My steward offered him a golden cup and filled it with our best wine.

'I'd forgotten how good the wine is in this palace,' he said, winking. 'I see it hasn't changed. And I'd forgotten what it means to be treated like a king.'

'Why don't you move back here with us?' asked Telemachus, coming in. 'You would be treated with great respect. We'll send someone to work the land on your farm and you can go back whenever you like, on the mule or by cart.'

'I have to think about it,' replied my father. 'Old men have their habits and mine have become quite stubborn indeed, I'm afraid.'

I thought about what my mother's spirit had told me when she appeared to me in Hades. I could see all the marks of that harsh, lonely life in my father's body and on his face. Not much remained of the man I remembered, but I loved him all the more for that. It was my absence that had broken his heart.

We took our places around the table, and after the wine had begun to lighten our hearts and chase away ugly thoughts, it felt as if we'd returned to the old days, when King Laertes would invite the island's noblemen to dinner and Mentor entertained us with his stories late into the night.

Penelope retired, ascending the stairs that led to the upper floor, and I stayed to talk with my father and my son. There was a powerful bond between us: the blood of the kings of Ithaca flowed in our veins. I felt that the moment had come to loosen the knot that had been choking my heart and my throat.

'I've reflected long and hard these past days,' I began, 'and I've spoken to Phemius. He's a wise man and he says what he thinks.'

'And what does he think?' asked my father.

'That I should speak to the people. They haven't seen me since I've returned. Phemius says I should have had mercy on the suitors after I had killed Antinous. I would feel better today, he tells me, everyone on the island and in the kingdom would feel better. Instead, nearly every single house is in mourning. Some of them weep because they know they'll never again see the sons who left for the war with me. Others weep because in returning from that war, I have killed a great many others.'

They fell silent for a while, my father and my son.

King Laertes was the first to speak: 'Phemius is a singer. You are the king. You are the one who brought about the fall of Troy after ten years of siege. We all know that men die in war and on the sea. That's no fault of yours. As for the others, you already know what I think about them. Are you sorry that you killed the men who were humiliating your father, plotting to kill your son, seeking to climb into bed with your wife?'

I had an answer to his words but I bit my tongue. Instead, I said: 'Father, I remember when you would return from one of your journeys. How your people would celebrate! We'd rush down to the port to see you disembark and you would ascend to the palace between two wings of people cheering and clapping. Since my return I've had to avoid meeting up with anyone, and if I do all I see is terror in their eyes.'

Telemachus hadn't said a word. Perhaps the presence of a father he still wasn't used to and a grandfather he had always considered the foremost authority on the island induced him to listen rather than speak his mind.

But then he asked me: 'So what are you thinking, then? What do you want to do?'

'I want to call the people to assembly, affirm my rights as their king and then ask for true reconciliation, offering a sign of reparation that will forever extinguish any ill will.'

I was thinking of the way Euthymides, Antinous' young brother, had looked at me.

'What kind of a sign?'

'You'll see when the time comes. But I want you to know that to do this, I'll need you both: you, Father, and you, my son. The Ithacans will see the dynasty of Arcesius in its full might and authority. We'll enter the assembly dressed in our brightest armour. You, Father, will be at my right, and you, son, at my left. I'll speak to my people and after I've finished, each of you will be able to address them, if you so wish. The assembly will be dissolved at dusk. I will summon the noblemen separately after nightfall.'

'But what can you propose that will be stronger than a sworn pact, like the one you pronounced at the gates of my house?' asked my father.

'You'll see, *atta*. Well?'

'As you wish,' replied the hero Laertes, my father.

'As you wish,' replied Telemachus my son, as handsome as a god.

'Tonight I will sleep in peace for the first time since my return to my homeland, and it will be thanks to you. Your rooms are ready. For the first time since I left my land so long ago, all three of us will be sleeping under the same roof.'

We bid each other goodnight and I went up to the bed-chamber where Penelope was waiting for me, awake. Her big black eyes open in the darkness gleamed ever so slightly in the light of the moon.

I WAITED just two days before I sent out the herald to call an assembly. I had planned out what I was going to say word by word, although I was sure that I'd never manage to make my speech when I was actually faced with the parents of my comrades, their widows and orphans, and the parents of the suitors I had killed. Would they even come? Would they heed the herald's call?

My father remained with us at the palace and I hoped that he would stay forever. The morning of the assembly we left the house together just after sunrise. Our suits of armour had been chosen with care and polished by the servants using ashes until they shone like gold. My father had had his hair washed and combed and it looked like silver. He'd donned his cuirass and greaves, and buckled on his sword. His helmet was under his left arm, while his right hand gripped his spear. On his shoulders was the light-blue cloak he was wearing the day I saw him descend from the ship returning from Colchis.

Telemachus wore the first suit of armour he'd ever owned. A gift from my father, it was the same he'd used on the day of the massacre. The armour I wore was very like what I had worn the day I left for Troy, with a purple cloak on my shoulders. All that was missing was the golden pin Penelope had given me as I was leaving, the one I described to her the night I tried to make her believe I was Aithon of Crete, the brother of Idomeneus.

The three of us met in the courtyard and the hearts in our chests were trembling. Tears were springing to our eyes.

The heralds were waiting for us with twelve young warriors, Telemachus' personal guard. We set off and the news that the king was heading towards the city with his father and his son flew to every corner of the island, so that hundreds of people were soon flocking along our path.

I remember that day as one of the most troubled and difficult of my whole life. None of the onlookers spoke. They watched us in silence as we passed and I couldn't look at them, either. I stared at an imaginary point directly in front of me, so as not to meet their gaze. At times, hostile shouts could be heard from the crowd jostling on both sides of the road, but all we needed to do was draw our swords and all voices were silenced instantly. Those who are willing to die first are always exceedingly rare.

When we finally arrived, the city's main square was thronging with people. The warriors escorted us to the point where the king was accustomed to speaking: a roughly hewn slab of grey limestone, one cubit tall and four cubits wide.

I took my place at the centre with my father and son at my sides, so all could see the three sovereigns of Ithaca: the present, the past and the future.

We were greeted by a low hum of voices and a sensation of consternation that weighed on my heart. I signalled to the herald that I was ready to speak. He asked for, and obtained, silence.

'Ithacans!' I shouted. 'Hear my words! I am Odysseus, son of Laertes, and I've returned to the land of my fathers after many years of trials and affliction. I am the conqueror of Troy and the king of this island and the others that surround it. I have summoned you here to tell you that it was not like this that I wished to return to Ithaca. Not alone, not after so many years and not despoiled of all that was dear to me! You all know that I never wanted the war, and neither did my father King Laertes. We did everything we could to avoid it. I went all the way to Troy with *wanax* Menelaus of Sparta to ask Priam to return Helen to her rightful husband. In vain.

'Thus began a war that lasted ten long years. For all that time, I always took care of the sons you entrusted to me. Many of them were like brothers for me. I was always at the front, in every battle, never behind. I succoured the wounded and anyone in difficulty. I risked my own life time and time again. I was forced to abandon the bride that I had so shortly before brought into my house and my still babbling son, prince Telemachus, the same who shines now next to me in his armour.

'If I had been fortunate, I would have brought back to Ithaca most of those who had left with me, along with immense treasure and the memory of the glory we had achieved. Together we would have mourned the fallen and raised a great mound near the seashore to remember them. That was not to be.

'Instead we struggled on with courage, without ever forgetting our families and our homeland, but storms, hostile gods, bloodthirsty monsters and ferocious, savage peoples scattered my fleet, killed my companions, sunk our ships. I am the only one who survived.

'What could I do? Give up, settle among unknown people in distant lands? Lose all hope of seeing my island, my wife, my parents, my son, my people? Never!

'My heart wept at the thought of having to tell you that all your sons had been lost. When the billows cast me up on the beach of an island which turned out to be home to a noble, just people who promised to help me return, I never stopped hoping that some of my shipmates might have been spared. That someone had escaped death and that I would find him here in Ithaca, awaiting my return along with my people. That was not to be.

'When I arrived I was alone, the sole survivor.'

Burning tears rose to my eyes as I pronounced those words and I felt a strange dizziness, as if I were still at the mercy of the waves, struggling to keep my balance on board my ship. My people were weeping with me. Tears poured down the cheeks of many, as I turned to my father, and to Telemachus, longing for some help from them. I felt like I had a boulder weighing down on my heart.

I forced myself to start speaking again. I still had to face up to the most horrendous event of all.

'And when I finally found my homeland, it wasn't like when King Laertes my father would come back after a long voyage abroad. Do you remember? Everyone would turn out to greet him and escort him to the palace, or take him onto their shoulders if he were wounded or exhausted from rough combat and a difficult crossing. It was as if the sun were back, after a long chill. That was how I dreamed that my own return would be like. That was not to be.

'There was no one waiting for me, and I was filled by sad foreboding. I knew of the fate that had befallen *wanax* Agamemnon, murdered in his own house. Diomedes, flaming hero, forced to abandon his own land because his queen was plotting against him. Idomeneus as well, and others like him. Everything had changed in all those years. Everything was different. I didn't recognize my own land! I had to hide, to disguise myself. A benign deity made me unrecognizable. And it was thus, clothed in rags like a beggar, that I entered my house after all that time away. The queen my mother was dead. My father, who had been forced out of the palace, was living on a farm with no one but a Siculian servant to aid him, sleeping on the ashes of the hearth in the winter and on a bed of dry leaves in the summer. My father, the Argonaut hero, living like a savage. No one, among the many he had helped, stood up to defend him.

'I found my house overrun by arrogant, abusive men intent on consuming all that was mine. They acted as if they were the masters of the palace, insulting and inflicting blows on those who could not defend themselves and even bedding down the maidservants, taking their pleasure with those who were willing and violating those who were not. What's more, they were scheming to murder my son, Prince Telemachus, who I hadn't seen for twenty long years. Were it up to them, I would never have seen him!

'They wanted to force my wife, Queen Penelope, to marry one of them. Desirous to take my place next to her in my bed, taking advantage of the absence of a man who could not defend what was his! Never was there a baser, more vile act!

'Garbed in my beggar's rags, they struck out at me, threw a stool at me, hurled a butchered ox's hoof! They hadn't recognized me? So what? They should have! They were still in time to save themselves.

'But then a god ignited a fury in me. How otherwise could four of us have got the better of fifty men?

'Would any of you present here have done differently? Say so! Say what you think!'

No word rang out in the still air. For a moment I thought I saw Mentor sitting on a stone chair in the middle of the square. But the image instantly faded into mist. 'Where are you?' I shouted in my heart.

'I see that you would have acted the same way I did. I did what was right, but this doesn't mean that I'm happy about what happened. And neither is Telemachus, who fought at my side.

'The next day we had to face the wrath of the families of the men who had been killed. My father dealt the blow that brought down Eupites, Antinous' father, but then a sign from the gods convinced us that we must make peace. A peace without joy. There is no joy in seeing the lifeless bodies of the sons of our land being gathered up by their despairing parents.

'I promise to forget my own humiliation and the wrongs wreaked upon my family. You, if you can, will set aside your grief and forget this calamity. None of this would have happened unless the gods had willed it, unless it had been written in the fates of each one of us.

'As for your sons or brothers or husbands who followed me to war and never came back, many were the victims of cruel, continuous combat which cut short their young lives and cast them into Hades. Others were taken by the blue-locked lord, the god of the abyss, and others still by the Sun who sees all, when driven by their hunger they killed and devoured his heifers. I had implored them not to touch the sacred animals, but my pleas fell on deaf ears. I wept for them all, for each one of them. Not a night passes without me seeing their faces in my dreams, without hearing their voices resounding in my heart.

'I know that you hold me responsible. You are right to do so. I was their king and their commander. And I must tell you now that the endeavour we all began together is not yet over. An oracle ordains that I set out once again to offer sacrifice in a remote land. Only then can I truly make my return. This will bring peace and serenity to all of you and to me. Do not bear hatred towards me. Allow me to depart and to fulfil my destiny and yours.'

Astonishment was evident on many faces and low whispers raced through the crowd.

'Tonight I will meet with the noblemen. I shall await them, alone and unarmed, at crow's rock. But now those of you who accept my pact will come and stand, one by one, before this stone, to render homage to the king of today, the king of yesterday and the king of tomorrow.'

For long, endless moments no one moved and an oppressive silence fell over the assembly. Then one man got up and came towards me. I recognized him: it was Theoclymenus, the seer who had predicted the massacre and forewarned the suitors. Everyone knew him. He kissed my hand and bowed before my father Laertes and my son. He said, 'Farewell, *wanax*,' and walked away. We never saw him again.

That gesture reminded everyone that the gods had sent a warning that had gone unheeded. One after another, those present passed in front of the stone and bowed their heads as a sign of homage. Most of them kissed my hand. I was choked with emotion at the grief I saw in the eyes of my people, but at that moment I was their king and I had to prove that I had acted within my rights and the rights of my family.

When everyone had filed past me and had left the square to return to their fields and their homes, I left the assembly myself, together with my father and my son, escorted by Telemachus' guard. I glimpsed for a moment, at the top of the stairs, a woman garbed in a dark cloak. When she moved I realized that it was Penelope, my queen. She hadn't missed a word of what I'd said. I set off to catch up with her but something stopped me. I couldn't believe that I hadn't seen him earlier: a boy alone, standing in the centre of the square, staring at me.

Euthymides. Antinous' young brother.

He alone had not rendered homage to me, had neither kissed my hand nor bowed his head. It wasn't hate that I saw in his gaze, nor the candid indignation that sometimes flashes in the eyes of an adolescent. His heart had simply suffered all it could. I returned his gaze with a melancholy look of my own and started off towards the palace.

King Laertes and Telemachus were waiting for me there. My father wondered if I had gone mad when I told them that I intended to honour my promise to meet with the noblemen on my own and unarmed, but they let me go.

I made my way to crow's rock alone. When all the nobles had arrived, I told them: 'The King of Scheria, glorious Alcinous, had me accompanied back here to my homeland in one of his ships, and he gave me an immense treasure. He did not want the King of Ithaca to return empty-handed after so many years. When I have returned from my last journey, I will divide that treasure among all of you who have lost your sons, whether at the hand of an enemy or at my own. Until that day comes, remain loyal to my son Telemachus.'

★

FROM THAT day on, I never had to look over my shoulder again. I could stroll through the market or amble down a country path without any worries. As the days and nights passed, my life seemed more and more like it had been before I left for the war. I would go hunting with Telemachus or to my father's grove to prune his olive trees. My father spent long stretches of time with us at the palace. We had dinner together and even Penelope would stay up late to hear us talk of harvests and sowing, of changes we wanted to make in the fields or in the stables. And when I made love to my wife I felt a new sort of energy coursing under my skin. I was beginning to think that fate had forgotten me.

Months passed in this way, maybe years. One or two or more, who can say? One evening when Penelope was at the table with us, my father said to her: 'I've heard about the tricks you once thought up to keep the suitors at bay. Astute indeed, worthy of your husband! Whatever happened to that shroud you were weaving for me?'

'*Atta*, what's got into you?' she asked. 'We've never been so well or so happy, and here we are enjoying the pleasure of your company. There's no need for you to keep working, if you're tired, although you seem stronger than you've ever been.'

'Would you finish it for me? I'd like it embroidered with the *Argo* sailing the waves.'

Penelope's eyes turned shiny. 'You know,' she said, 'why I never finished it? Well, to avoid having to marry any of them, naturally, but mostly because it seemed to me that by unravelling the shroud I was weaving, I could lengthen your life. If you're asking me to do this for you now, I will, *atta*, although it won't be easy for me. I pray to the gods to grant you many more years to live with us in our house, loved and respected as you deserve.'

King Laertes my father stood and gently stroked her cheek: 'Do it for me, my daughter.' He wished us a serene night and retired to his room.

That night, Penelope started to reweave the burial shroud.

25

MORE TIME PASSED and strangely I felt no desire to leave Ithaca. I was reminded of my father's words when I was an adolescent: after a long journey, I would no longer be at ease on my little island. Ithaca would seem too small to me, much like a prison. That wasn't so now. Perhaps because I had desired her so keenly, my homeland, in all those years spent at war and at sea and now I wanted to enjoy what I had. I crossed the forests, took long walks on the seashore, climbed up the cliffs. Looking at her coves and inlets from up above was almost like admiring and caressing Penelope's body.

One day Telemachus joined me at the secret port. Perhaps he'd spotted me from above, from crow's rock, and he felt like spending some time in my company.

'Atta,' he said, 'why don't you and I go to the continent together? We could visit King Nestor in Pylos and King Menelaus in Sparta. I know they'd greatly enjoy banqueting with you, talking and joking, maybe even having a good cry. It would be good for you and for them too. I've sent out messages with the news of your return. They know that you've exacted justice in your home and made peace with your people. But I realized from their responses that many things were already known to them and they were ardently hoping you would make the journey to see them in person. You went through so much together during the war. You fought to save each other's lives, didn't you? Don't you think that seeing them again would be a good thing? It would be like the trip you took with your father when you were young.'

'Yes,' I replied, 'perhaps we should go. There's still so much that needs saying, and it would strengthen the ties of friendship that join us. I'll think about it and I'll set a date for our departure, but not too soon, I don't want to leave your mother alone just yet. She was alone for much too long. I want to wait for all the old wounds to heal. Then we can go.'

Telemachus tipped his head towards me thoughtfully.

'What about my grandfather Autolykos?' I asked him. 'Whatever happened to him? I didn't meet him among the shades of the dead that I summoned up from Hades.'

'He died when I was still very little. Or maybe he just disappeared. No one knows for sure.'

'But I saw my mother's shadow. I spoke to her and she to me. She told me the truth. Why didn't she say anything about him? Why didn't I see him?'

'Maybe he didn't want to make himself seen. You always said he was an irascible, capricious old man. Maybe dying didn't make him any better.'

He smiled and so did I, but that night, resting alongside my wife, I dreamt something different. I thought that my grandfather might still be alive, in some particular, mysterious form. One day, perhaps, I'd go to the continent and pay a visit to his fortress on Parnassus, as sullen and stony as he had always been.

At times my thoughts turned to what I had gone through, what I had seen. At night I dreamt of the storms, the battles, the distant, diverse worlds I had seen. I woke up covered with sweat or shouting. Penelope would hold me and promise in a low voice: 'It's all right now. It's all gone. You can rest easy now, sleep, my darling.' But then I would go for several nights without dreaming at all, and the days that followed seemed empty and monotonous. The images of the past seemed to be fading and, somehow, I mourned for them.

It would happen, every now and then, that sailors landing at the great port would ask if it were true that *wanax* Odysseus had returned. Had he truly wiped out all the queen's suitors? Did he reign unopposed over the island? Sometimes they would ask to meet me, but I would rarely make myself available.

I would often go to the spot where the Phaeacians had left me sleeping on the shore and where I'd met my goddess when I awoke. I dearly hoped I would chance upon the shepherd boy who'd spoken to me then: my goddess, who had disguised herself as the gods are wont to do if they show themselves to a mortal. I missed her greatly and feared she would never appear to me again. Without the sense of her presence I felt very alone.

Then one day, without warning, something happened . . .

It was evening, just after dusk. I was walking along the shore, not far from the secret port. The moon was full and the sky was cold and clear. From the cabins scattered over the mountain slope came the barking of dogs and bleating of sheep, and from the sea the sound of waves lapping. The pebbles at the shoreline shone like precious gems in the light of the moon.

All at once I noticed something coming in slowly on the waves. I waded in up to my knees and pulled the object out of the water: an oar, it was, large and solid, made of ash. Not from a fishing boat, but from a ship!

I felt my heart leap in my chest and my breath stopped short. What wrecked ship had cast off an oar that had made its way to the shores of my island, to my very feet? I ran my hand down the shaft and then up again, to the handle, and my fingers curled around a figure carved into the wood. The light of the full moon was bright enough for me to make it out. I recognized it: a butterfly.

Polites' oar!

Tears sprang to my eyes. How far had that oar travelled? What god had pushed it all the way to where I stood, on a night of full moon, on the shores of the secret port, on my own island? That oar was the last remnant of one of my ships swallowed up by the sea. It had been searching for me for years and it had finally found me, bringing me a mute but unmistakable message.

> *You will depart once again with an oar on your shoulder*
> *And you will journey far into the continent*
> *Until you find people who know not the sea*
> *Who have never seen a ruddy-cheeked ship*
> *Nor the oars which are its wings . . .*

THE TIME had come to resume my journey. The last, the one that would take me to a desolate place at the ends of the earth where I would make a sacrifice to Poseidon, recognizing his victory and my defeat. Only thus would I be able to achieve peace.

I heaved the oar on my shoulder and walked towards home. It was time. Time to leave. Time to tell Penelope, to listen to her inconsolable weeping, to repeat that I'd be returning soon and that we would finally reign over a happy people.

She knew, she said, that it would happen. A lifetime of disappointments had tempered her and she showed great strength of spirit.

'I'll miss you,' she said with quiet sadness.

'I will miss you too,' I told her. 'These are the pains I must suffer to placate the wrath of an unjust god. Once we've made love again, you can start counting the days. Not many. You won't see me leave, nor will I watch you as my ship draws away and you get smaller and smaller and further away from me. I couldn't bear it.'

The second to know was my father.

'When?' he asked me.

'Soon. The sooner the better. There's no reason to put it off. I don't know how long this journey will take, when or where I'll find the man who will give me the signal that I've reached the end of the road. But I'm sure it will be arduous. It won't be so easy to end my quarrel with the god that shakes the earth.'

'Do you know what I think?'

'No, *atta*, I don't, but the look in your eyes tells me it isn't pleasant.'

'It's neither good nor bad. It's only a sensation, or a vision, perhaps.'

'Speak, then.'

'I'm remembering the dream you had at the Sanctuary of the Wolf King in Arcadia. I feel that it has something to do with this last adventure of yours.'

'I will nurse that dream in my heart.'

'If I'm right, I think it's reasonable to believe I won't see you again.'

'Why are you saying such a thing?'

'A presentiment.'

I lowered my eyes without being able to say another word.

It was he who spoke: 'Let us say goodbye now, then.'

His eyes were shining. The hero Laertes, my father. Those marvellous blue eyes. We clasped each other tightly, and wept.

'Farewell, *atta*,' I said. 'It is an honour to have been born of a father like you. The best I could possibly desire. It was worth coming into the world, just to know you.'

'Farewell, *pai*. I want you to know that your return was the greatest joy of my life. I couldn't have died without seeing you again. My only regret is that you didn't come to me first, allow me to fight at your side and perhaps even to die the way I lived: as a king and a warrior. But I understand. You are the most famous of all mortals, you are the conqueror of Troy and you certainly have a plan now, as you did that day. My presence might have compromised it. I'm no longer the man I was.'

'Don't say that, *atta*! It's not true!'

'Now you are departing for your last journey. You'll choose the day and the time. It's better that I don't know, and that I don't see you go. I don't think my old heart could stand it. Follow your fate and the will of the gods. There's no other possible way. My last thought will be for you. My spirit will be at your side forever.'

I left with a swollen heart, but that was the way it had to be.

I walked among the silvery olive trees, along the path we'd travelled so often together.

All at once I heard a scream behind me: the old Siculian servant who took care of him! My heart froze and I ran back as fast as I could. I could see him from a distance: on the ground, unmoving. His old servant was wailing in despair, leaning over him. She was letting out loud, shrill laments, in the way of her people.

My father's voice rang in my heart: 'Best that I don't know and that I don't see: my old heart wouldn't be able to bear it.'

THE PYRE of the king of Ithaca was raised on the tallest height of the northern part of the island. I wanted everyone on the whole island to see the fire that carried the glorious spirit of the Argonaut hero towards the sky. An enormous stack of pine and olive trunks: the first beneath, the second on top.

When I had entered our bedchamber to give Penelope the news, she replied: 'He had asked me to finish his burial shroud. He knew he would die soon and he also knew what would take his life.' She detached the woven cloth from the loom. It was beautiful: you could see the ship, the *Argo*, and you could recognize my father, standing next to Jason and Hercules, by the light-blue cloak on his shoulders.

'I finished it last night,' she said, and wept, hiding her face in her hands.

His body, covered by the magnificent shroud, was carried up to the mountaintop on the shoulders of six warriors. At the start, the only ones following the bier were me, Penelope, Telemachus, Euriclea, Eumeus and Philoetius with their families, the servants and the handmaids, and this filled my heart with sadness. The funeral procession of a king and Argonaut hero like my father should have been very different. But then, as we advanced towards the site of the pyre, others joined us: men and women, noblemen and warriors but also farmers, fishermen and shepherds. The procession kept growing in size, turning into a long snake winding along the path, and I thanked the gods for each person who joined us. Many of them were aristocrats who had lost their sons in my act of vengeance. Their thoughts were not lingering there but on the times of their own youth, when they'd eagerly followed their king in his forays over the waves.

The procession halted when we reached the peak, and the body of my father, covered by the shroud woven by Penelope, was placed on the pyre. Telemachus and I laid his sword on his chest and lit the fire. It blazed the whole night, the wind dragging high licks of flames into the sky and with them the glorious spirit of King Laertes my father. The light emanating from the fire was seen from every corner of the kingdom.

When dawn lightened the sky, Telemachus and I took the king's sword, ritually bent it in two with pincers and threw it into the sea. We put his ashes on his ship and waited until the wind began blowing east and north. We hoisted the sail, locked the steering oar in place and watched until it disappeared over the horizon.

It was the only fitting farewell to an Argonaut and hero.

I SPOKE for a whole day with Telemachus. I swore to him that I would return, that I would teach him the art of governing and the laws of honour, so that he would be a better king than his father and his grandfather. I would become his counsellor, and I would keep a small corner of the palace for Penelope and myself, the part where the royal bedchamber was.

'One day, after we're gone, the chamber will be yours. You'll take your bride there and tell her the story of how it was built and how it became a secret pledge of eternal love and faith between your parents.'

'I want to be the one who escorts you to the secret port, *atta*,' replied Telemachus. 'I will bear your shield and give you the final salute when you are ready to depart. Grant me this privilege, I beg of you. I waited for you my whole life. You wouldn't believe how many times I asked my mother to tell me about you! I wanted to imagine you. I wanted to know what you looked like, what the light in your eyes was like, the speed of your thought, the strength of your arms. I recognized you when you returned and wept as I embraced you. I fought at your side covered with bronze as you slaughtered the shameless, arrogant suitors. Together we put the torch to the pyre of King Laertes your father and my grandfather, together we watched his ship disappear over the horizon. Let me be the one to see you off on your last journey, so that your image remains in my mind, engraved in my heart.'

'I can't. This is not a journey like any other and I must not waver. If I see you, my courage may fail me. Stay at the palace. In my absence you will be the king of Ithaca. You will administer the law, take care of the house and protect your mother. You'll offer sacrifice to Athena for my safe return. You won't need to carry my shield for me. I'll be leaving with nothing but my bow, a dagger, and an oar on my shoulder, as the shade of Theban Tiresias prophesied when I summoned him from Hades. This one.' I showed him the oar.

'Where did it come from?' he asked.

'From one of my own ships. It belonged to Polites. I recognized it from the butterfly carved into the handle. It washed ashore right in front of me. A portent, certainly. A sign from the gods. I knew what it meant: that the time had come.'

Telemachus dropped his head and made no reply.

'Come now, let's go home,' I said to him.

That night Penelope and I made love with consuming passion, and then lay one beside the other, holding hands like two children who are afraid of the dark.

'From today I'll count the days and nights,' she whispered.

I answered: 'Whatever happens, I know we'll continue to love each other forever, beyond life and beyond death. We're not like the others, my love, no two people have ever loved each other so much, rejoiced, hoped and suffered as we have. If I were to be reborn a thousand times, one thousand times would I want my destiny to be united with yours.'

I could hear her crying. I held her close in a long embrace, in heartbroken silence.

ON THE THIRD DAY I rose from my bed before dawn, without making a sound. I could hear Penelope breathing deeply in the darkness. Surely my goddess had showered sleep over her eyes. I descended the stairs, dressed, took my bow and slung it over my shoulder, hung the quiver from my belt, went under the portico and took the oar down from the wall. I was walking towards the door when I found Euriclea standing in front of me. She didn't touch me, but looked at me with eyes full of tears, whispering: 'Child, my child . . .'

I gazed back at her with tear-fogged eyes as well, and I nodded my head as I went out. All those memories, voices, dreams that I was leaving behind as I left her. '*Mai*,' I said in my heart, 'will I see you again?'

I walked past Argus' grave and I imagined that he could see me from the other world. I brushed the mound with my hand as if I were petting him. I was leaving him behind, as I had Euriclea, the servants and the handmaids, Penelope. Had she really been sleeping? Or was she already crying in our empty bed? Telemachus must still be sleeping: *the young sleep so soundly.*

I started down the path that led to the secret port, where the day before I had left a boat that would take me to the mainland. My path took me close to Eumeus' farm. I could see that he'd made many improvements, repairs, had planted a great number of trees. He was the owner of the property now, and you could see that. His dogs didn't bark; they knew me. A strange feeling gripped me. Tears poured from my eyes, but I was seized by intense excitement. The very sound of my footsteps, the thought of another adventure that would take me to the ends of the earth, gave me a small secret thrill that I could not even confess to myself, as shame welled up in equal measure.

Day was breaking and a grey light began to replace the darkness. Dogs barked from the farmhouses, birds practised a few notes as they readied to raise their song to the sun. I walked towards crow's rock and began to descend the steep trail that led down to the secret port. I used the oar to steady myself so I wouldn't fall.

All at once I heard a rustling of bushes alongside the path. An animal?

I pushed on, and continued to hear the same noise, as if someone were following me in the thick foliage. But where from? Uphill or down? Could it be Telemachus after all, coming up from the port? I could half see a ship at anchor.

'Telemachus? Is that you?'

No answer but the sound of branches cracking. All of a sudden, a youth jumped out of the vegetation, wielding something in his hand. A club . . . It wasn't Telemachus, I'd already seen those cold eyes: Euthymides, Antinous' younger brother! He struck me with the club he held and then ran off. I fell to the ground and started to roll downhill, dragging a landslide of stones and pebbles with me. Darkness fell over me. How much time passed? How many days, how many nights? Was I alive? Was I dead?

I heard Telemachus' voice calling me again and again and then a long despairing wail.

I felt at a certain moment that someone was raising up my shoulders and easing me onto a wooden plank. Was I going to my pyre? I tried to call out, to call for help, but I was shouting with no sound.

No. I heard the lapping of waves against the side of a ship, I was lying on the foredeck . . . but why couldn't I move? Why could I hear such weeping all around me? I invoked my goddess from the depths of my abyss: 'Open my eyes, daughter of Zeus, virgin Tritogeneia, let me see!' Indifferent silence was the response.

Finally the ship hit something: the shore? Which shore? I was lifted again and carried up what seemed to be a steep path. I could feel the rays of the afternoon sun on my skin and smell the scents of pine, juniper and, later, of fir. It reminded me of something, that scent. I was familiar with it. From when? My first time on the mainland.

The march continued and I felt my body swaying to the right and left, a dead weight. Then everything stopped. I heard my son's voice: 'Come underground with me, we'll find a doorway with the heads of a bull, a boar and a ram. There my father will sleep, covered by this cloth that the queen my mother has woven, depicting the events of his life. My father is not dead. He will never die.'

I could hear him say closer to me: 'I'll be back, *atta*, you're here in the fortress of your grandfather Autolykos.'

Could that be true? What was happening to me? Telemachus' words filled my heart, but was he saying them? Or was he still sleeping in his bed? Where was I? I thought I could hear the sound of multiple steps ascending the stairs, the clanking of hinges and heavy doors closing. The cold of the stone. And the dark.

26

HOW LONG DID THAT IMPENETRABLE night and that abysmal silence last? Was that my final punishment, a deadly trap that the hostile god had lured me into? To lie immobile for all eternity, alive and conscious, my heart never allowed to sleep? I, who had navigated all the seas, fought against heroes, monsters and storms, against lightning, wind and the screaming sea? Doomed to pass the years, the millennia, counting the beats of my heart? And yet a thread of hope, like a flickering flame, rose from the depths. I was on the continent. Here the blue god, as implacable as he might be, was not so powerful, not more powerful than my goddess. She would hear my heartbeat and she would find me. She would give me back light and strength. Or perhaps she'd send me someone.

I hoped so, intensely. My spirit navigated the night in every direction, searching for a landing place. It expanded like a light mist over an infinite space.

Until the howling of a wolf penetrated into my tomb. It ripped through the silence. Stopped. Growled. Stopped again.

A creaking of hinges.

A footstep descending the stairs.

'Who are you?' screamed my heart, but not a sound came out. The footstep halted.

'Calchas,' a voice answered. The footsteps resumed their descent and came to a halt again, next to me. 'We had a pact.'

Something loosened in my chest, the knot that was holding my voice back lessened its grip.

'How did you find me?' I was shaken with sobbing, as though I'd been freed all at once from heavy chains.

'I was roaming through these mountains and I suddenly felt the beat of your heart vibrating under my feet, from the bowels of the mountain.'

'My goddess sent you. Only she could bring about such a prodigy.'

I opened my eyes and saw a ray of light penetrating from a slit somewhere above me, glancing off steps cut into the solid rock. The light wounded me like a sword.

'The time has come for each of us to tell the other when he will face the extreme moment. We both have the gift.'

'Is that why I can open my eyes and speak?'

'Yes . . . and no. You were hit. Something happened inside you. They gave you up for dead. Still and cold, you were the only one who could hear the beating of your heart. No one else.'

'I thought I was being put on the pyre alive . . .'

'The goddess inspired other thoughts in Telemachus, and others still in me.'

His face was in the shadows and the light was behind him. But his voice was the same one, deep and dark, that had uttered prophecies in the assembly of the Achaeans when the glorious Atreides had bid him to do so.

'Get up,' he said to me.

I tried to get up but my body would not obey me. It had been too long since my muscles had flexed my limbs. Every small movement caused me great pain.

'How long have I been in this place?'

'Only the heart counting its beats could tell you. Months . . . perhaps. Over this time, something has happened to you.'

'Is my grandfather Autolykos buried here?'

'Something has happened to him too.'

IT WAS ALMOST dusk before the pain had ebbed enough to allow me to put my feet on the ground. Calchas dragged me like a dead weight. He pulled at me, braced me, helped me up the stairs. By the time we got to the top it was dark outside. I could breathe!

The moon bathed the peak of Parnassus in liquid silver. A long howl sounded from the fir trees. I trembled.

'Does that remind you of something?'

'Yes,' I replied. 'Now it does. It was a long time ago . . . I'm thirsty . . . I was a boy. The hero Laertes my father was leading me through the valleys of Arcadia, we were heading towards a mountain.'

Calchas drew some clear water from a spring and filled a cup for me.

'I heard howling coming from the mountain, coming from the plains. I dreamed . . . Can you see what I dreamed? I'm thirsty.'

He gave me more water. Then he stared into my eyes: 'Oh, Odysseus, brave heart! I see your dream. The man on the carriage pulled by wolves is you.'

'What does that mean?'

'I don't know. Only you can understand but I don't think you will before it happens.'

Lightning pulsed behind the trees, distant thunder rumbled in the mountains, the clouds hid the moon.

'There's a house here,' I said. 'Help me. A storm is coming up.'

I'd understood where I was. A hidden passage had delivered us into a clearing on the forest floor. I could see where Calchas had removed the stones that hid the entrance, so he could descend into my tomb. With his help I reached the house, familiar to me now. The oar from my ship with the engraved butterfly was leaning against the wall. The door was open but the inside was silent. There were embers in the hearth that gave off a slight glow. Calchas added wood.

'Who lit this fire?' I asked.

'I did,' he answered. 'Something drove me to come here. This is where I slept last night.'

'Do you know whose house this is?'

'I do. It's the fortress of your grandfather, Autolykos. It was a surprise attack – the place was taken by storm. No one is left.'

'What about him? Where's he?'

The thunder sounded closer and closer. The lightning flashed so brightly that it flooded the room we were in and lit up Calchas' face. He looked like a ghost who had come from the distant past.

'He's here. He's close, but I couldn't say where. This place has been abandoned for a long time.'

I began to understand why I hadn't seen Autolykos at the mouth of Hades. I also became suddenly sure that I was being called upon to cross a boundary grimmer and more extreme than the wall of fog. I shivered. I wasn't sure what was giving me that chill: was it the late hour, the cold wind? My exhausted body that could find no warmth, not even next to the fire? Or was it the fear that was flooding me at the thought of leaving my land, my loved ones, my way of being human, yet again? My heart knew what was coming and I was afraid.

'Listen,' I said, 'can you tell me whether Tiresias' prophecy will come true? Will I be able, at the end of this journey, to return to my family and reign in blessed peace until I grow old?'

'The prophet spoke to you from Hades itself. But he might have been lying. All of what he predicted will happen, but I can't say when. I can't see that.'

'When do I leave?'

'As soon as you can. As soon as you can stand on your feet.'

'Then the time has indeed come for you to tell me, and me to tell you, the day and hour our lives will end.'

'Yes. Tomorrow morning we will part ways. I've fulfilled my mission. Tomorrow at dawn we will speak for the last time.'

I struggled for a long time not to give myself up to sleep, so great was my fear of sinking back into impotence and inertia.

But slumber won over and I slept deeply. I saw a myriad of images from my past in my dreams, felt forgotten emotions. And I saw Calchas' end: the time and the place. I understood why the next day I would be able to whisper that terrible truth into his ear while he told me of my last day on earth.

I heard him a few times during the night, getting up and adding wood to the fire, and I heard the wind shrieking outside, hissing under the roof, whistling through the disjointed hinges and the cracks in the walls. Only once, in the silence, did my grandfather's voice sound next to me, and it whispered 'pai'. Then my father's voice, murmuring other words I could not understand. There was no glimmer of joy in my heart, only infinite melancholy.

A pale sun woke me and I felt strong enough to get up. Calchas had gathered pigeons' eggs that he found under the roof and he was cooking them in the embers and the warm ash of the hearth. A pleasant warmth had filled the room we slept in. Everything seemed normal: two people who'd just woken up and were rekindling the fire and making breakfast.

'Where are you from?' I asked him. It seemed to me that such a simple question might dispel the aura of gloom that weighed upon us.

'Argus,' he said, without turning.

'How did you become involved in the expedition to Troy?'

'Agamemnon had heard of my ability as a seer and he asked Diomedes to convince me to come. It wasn't difficult, he was my king.'

'How did you discover that you had the gift?'

'When I was six I foresaw my father's death.'

'That might have been accidental.'

'My mother's as well. I was orphaned in my early adolescence.'

He turned towards me. There was no expression in his eyes or voice.

We ate in silence and then went outside. I didn't close the

door. I wanted the wind, the rain, the snow, to force their way into the ruins of Autolykos' house and fill it with ghosts. That way the memory of the *wanax* of Acarnania would survive his passing.

'There are still many things I would like to ask you,' I said, 'but perhaps it is better that each of us go his own way. You freed me from my prison. I will never forget that for as long as I live.'

'The only way to thank me is to do what we promised each other so long ago in Troy. Come closer.'

As he said this he drew so near me that his cheek was brushing mine. 'When we touch,' he said, 'each one of us will speak into the ear of the other.'

And so it was. A part of me spoke, a part of me listened, in the same moment. I don't know which of the two was the sadder, more bitter or enigmatic sentence. We both had tears in our eyes when we pulled away from each other. And yet, remaining in my heart and his were dark corners that only one day, perhaps, we would ever understand.

We took leave of one another. He set off towards the sea, leaning on a stick to steady his footing. 'Farewell,' I said, 'great seer.'

'Farewell,' he replied, '*wanax* Odysseus, brave heart. I'll see you again, perhaps, in another life.'

'Or in another death,' said I.

I watched as he went off down the path that led to the sea, and for a moment I could see the ghosts that escorted him, bearing shields and gripping spears. Couldn't he see them? Perhaps, I thought, he could feel their presence. Where were they taking him?

The mortal men who eat bread were just awakening in their cabins scattered throughout the wood. They set about milking their animals, taking the flocks out to pasture.

Only he and I were setting off towards a dark destiny.

★

I PICKED up the oar and tried to settle it on my shoulder; it felt terribly heavy, and threw me off balance.

Where was my bow? My arrows? Where was my strength?

'Here,' said a voice that sounded at my left, as a cold, familiar chill coursed under my skin. A man's voice: my grandfather, my father, Mentor, my goddess? They were all present in that voice.

I turned and saw the bow and quiver leaning against the trunk of an age-old oak tree. Had I been dreaming? Perhaps they'd always been there. I was confused, alone and distressed, feeling emotions I'd never felt before. An abyss of solitude, an unearthly chill that nipped at my heart, a trepidation so intense that I would have taken my own life, had I not seen for myself the infinite desolation of Hades and the unhappy souls that inhabited it.

I lifted my bow and nocked an arrow. Before me appeared a roebuck. It was rooted to the spot, staring at me. I killed it and ate meat for two days.

On the third day I started walking, setting off on a long, difficult ascent. Polites' oar was jolted by every rock I stumbled on, until my shoulder was scraped raw. The sight of my own blood comforted me, showed that I was alive, that there was a hot stream of it coursing through me, under my skin, inside my muscles and my heart. I stayed on the crest of the mountains and headed north. I didn't want to meet anybody, I didn't want to be recognized, although I knew that this wasn't likely to happen in any case.

What should I do? Move as far away from the sea as possible, reach a land where people ate foods that weren't salted, where an oar could not be identified as what pushes a ship over the waves but instead as what separates the chaff from the wheat. Wheat . . . grows in large, fertile plains. But where? I'd only seen such fields in Argolis, certainly no other place in Achaia, but where would I find people who had never seen the sea, never heard of a ship? The sea was everywhere.

I didn't understand then that thinking was useless, that my

mind would never get me to where I wanted to go. All I could do was head in the direction opposite to the sea and keep going. That was all. There was no one, nothing, that could show me the way. Nothing human could guide me. There was no destination. The only thing that sustained me was my faith in myself, the certainty that only I could survive the adversities I would find. Only I could keep love alive in my heart, feel the people I'd lost at my side, never stop believing that at the end of the day I would win.

ONE DAY, after having covered an endlessly long tract of land and having watched the sun decline on the horizon, a village appeared in the distance. I had been walking for months without meeting a living soul. I had seen many sunsets, of stunning beauty, and silent auroras over lands which stretched out in a wide expanse before me, where the cold wind in my hair and the light that illuminated every blade of grass aroused forgotten joy in my heart. But never a village.

I decided to enter. I approached slowly. I didn't know whether I would be greeted by men who respected the gods and the laws of hospitality, or whether there might be a young Nausicaa waiting for me on the banks of a river that flowed glittering over the stones and sand, but I made my way nonetheless through the fields and towards the houses, which had walls made of raw bricks and wood. I longed for mortal company, to prove to myself that I was alive, that the world I walked through was real and not the fruit of a dream.

As I approached, I saw instead, in the distance on my right, a fantastic sight: creatures, galloping wild, that I had heard described by the man who trained me to use weapons, Damastes, but which I had never seen with my own eyes: centaurs!

Had I chanced upon another land of monstrous beings? Had I crossed an invisible limit and entered a territory denied to bread-eating men, without realizing it? I set my oar down on the ground and stood still, watching them as they emerged from the cloud of dust that enveloped them and from the red dazzle of the setting sun. They weren't centaurs, but two distinct creatures moving like one alone. Men on the backs of horses!

Once they reached the edge of the village, the men jumped agilely to the ground as if they were weightless, giving the animals free rein. I was getting closer myself now. I continued to advance with the long, heavy oar on one shoulder, my bow slung over the other and the quiver at my side. I realized instantly that the attention of the village people and the centaurs, who had just split before my eyes into creatures of diverse natures, was entirely on me.

Where were you, Damastes? Is this what you'd seen in the wavering light of the sunset, in the deep valleys between veils of fog?

A heavy silence fell between myself and them. No one offered a word or made a sound, not even the children, who were holding on tightly to their mothers. My oar, that I held tightly now in my fist, cast a long and very distinct shadow that crossed the clearing at the centre of the village.

They had completely surrounded me and they were observing me, trying to figure out who or what I was. Then one of the centaurs, who seemed the strongest among them, cautiously drew closer. He stopped where the shadow of the oar ended on the ground; it clearly disturbed him. Then he continued slowly towards me, walking up the shadow's dark path, until we were face to face. He asked me something but I couldn't understand. He insisted, pointing at the oar, and my heart leaped in my chest. Was this the man that Tiresias had prophesied? The one who would ask me about the object I bore on my shoulder? Had I arrived at my destination? Was it there, at the centre of the village I found myself in, that I would plunge the oar into the ground as an eternal symbol of the last journey of the king of Ithaca? Would I find the victims to be sacrificed among the flocks and herds that these people certainly raised? It hadn't been such a long journey, and not a dangerous one. Could I already start thinking about returning to Penelope and Telemachus, once and for all?

I couldn't believe it, and in fact, I shouldn't have. The man suddenly burst out laughing and wouldn't stop. He was pointing to the oar and laughing, and I would have liked to kill him to shut him up.

He bent close to the ground using a stick to draw the outline of a ship. He pointed to it with his finger and then at the horizon to his left as though to say: 'You are seeking the sea and a ship where there are none.'

I didn't stop in that place. I pushed on without delay and with my heart full of sadness. I had fooled myself into thinking that the gods had remitted the terrible penalty to which I had been condemned. I walked away, dragging the oar behind me and listening to the noise it made hitting the stones of the trail. I saw goats, cows, pigs, and even a stray dog who followed me for a while. With every step, the urge to weep grew stronger. Not because I was afraid of a long journey, or of solitude or danger, but because the world I was crossing was insignificant, desolate and empty. Why had the gods driven me to carry out such a useless journey? Why couldn't I make the sacrifice they demanded somewhere on my own island, in a place on the coast, in some sanctuary?

Darkness soon caught up with me. I looked for shelter in the hollow of a solitary oak. I gathered up a heap of dried leaves and laid my cloak on top of them. The purple cloak that Penelope had woven for me so that I would feel enveloped by the warmth of her hands and her arms. I tried to sleep.

The village of the centaurs had long vanished behind me, and the night was animated by rustling, furtive movements, growling, clicking, hooting. They would not disturb my slumber, I was accustomed to much worse. It was they, whoever or whatever they were, who would have to fear me.

And yet that thought wasn't enough to invite sleep. On the

contrary. I was thinking that for days and nights I had done nothing but walk, always north and then always east, without ever encountering anything that was worth remembering, nothing that I could recount one day to my son or my subjects or to Phemius the singer. The only time I had stopped, because I'd felt a desire to mix with other human beings, I'd foolishly convinced myself that my quest was over and I'd been ridiculed.

I was thinking that this would be my torture: nothingness, flatness, stillness, the useless spectacle of nature always repeating itself, always the same. Was I becoming immortal? Had I been assigned the endless empty territory stretching out in front of me, as Calypso and Circe had their islands?

Was this the reason – this infinite solitude – that Hercules, after performing the twelve labours, had thrown himself onto the pyre alive?

Everything had been taken from me: my comrades, my ships, my homeland, my father, my wife and son after I had rejoined them. My house. Must not this, what I was experiencing, be the threshold of immortality? I hadn't asked for it. I'd refused it when it was offered to me on the island at the ends of the earth. I had defied the mouth of Hades to find my future! And I would not allow that endeavour to prove itself futile.

I was sleeping, or perhaps I was in that half-asleep state where dreams and reality are blurred, when I heard a grunting. A sound I recognized: a bear. How could I defend myself? I didn't have a heavy weapon with me and it was dark. I couldn't climb the tree I was using for shelter, because it had been struck by lightning at a short distance from the ground. If I tried to run, over open ground, the animal would catch me instantly. All I had was my dagger. I would fight with that, and almost certainly be killed. I prayed in my deepest heart to my goddess, invoked the shadow of my father, the spirit of my mother and the dark power of Autolykos *wanax* of Acarnania, because I wanted to see my struggle through to the end.

Someone surely listened to me. When I could already sense

the bear's breath close to my face, hear its claws ripping at the dry trunk, I heard the barking of a dog, soon joined by five, ten or even more, and then the growls and snarls and howls of a ferocious fight. Until everything trailed off into silence. Only the penetrating, acrid stench of the beast lingered in the air to remind me that it hadn't been a dream. Then I fell asleep, certain that nothing would disturb me before the dawn.

27

WHEN I AWOKE, I SAW THAT the ground all around the oak trunk was marked by signs of a wild fight, as if not a pack of animals but a horde of demons had been at each others' throats. I got up, slung the bow over my shoulder and fastened the quiver at my side, adjusted the oar on my other shoulder and carried on my way. I decided that from that morning on, I would count the days, and observe the stars and the rising and setting of the sun and moon in order to keep track of what direction I was moving in.

My solitude became greater day by day and melancholy took root within me. I would have given anything, anything at all, for an hour in the company of my son or my wife, yet I avoided contact with any other human being, although I understood that if I continued thus, the prophecy would never come true. I would never meet the man who would ask me the fatal question. But I reasoned that this would force my destiny into revealing itself unmistakably. I knew that in any case the man would turn up when I least expected it, in the middle of a vast plain or on a mountain path or along the banks of a river. *This is the sign. You can't mistake it . . .*

I hunted with my bow, I set traps, I gathered roots, nuts and wild fruits. I carried a small clay jar with holes in its cover to hold the last embers from the night's fire to keep a spark alive for the next day, so I would have light when darkness fell again. So many times, casting my gaze in all directions around me, I saw no light save my own. A solitary flicker on the dark, sleepy earth.

As the days progressed, my body changed. Gone were the days when I'd enjoyed the favours of a goddess, food, wine and precious garments on an island at the ends of the earth. The days of feasting and the long sleepless nights of storytelling in the palace of Alcinous, the divine sovereign of the Phaeacians, those were gone too. My thin skin seemed moulded to my muscles, my sight had become much sharper, I was lighter, more agile and faster, but less powerful. More a hunter and a runner than a warrior. I'd got used to sleeping with one eye open; I would rest without slipping into unconsciousness. I'd learned that abandoning myself to sleep could have very bitter results.

When I hunted and would have to leave my oar behind I took care to hide it well despite the fact that I was always alone. It was, after all, the last memento of my ship and my only hope of making peace with the gods.

I often thought of Mentor – I'd lost every trace of him. Was it my goddess who had taken him, used up his body? Had she snatched his spirit as well? I long invoked her, in vain. I would have given anything to see her as I had that day in Ithaca, the day of my return, when she'd taken on the semblance of a shepherd boy and had touched my face . . . it was the only time I'd ever felt her touch.

I forged on for more than three months, always heading east. I saw hordes of centaurs passing in the distance in clouds of dust, sighted villages with huts made of flayed animal hides. I'd even seen battle chariots that were somewhat like the ones we used. I asked myself how anyone could want to wage war on such desolate stretches of land, where there was nothing beautiful or desirable to be conquered. Only on very rare occasions did I approach small groups of men who were camped on the plains, and I was always welcomed as a guest among them, but these brief encounters only served to confirm my convictions. They were sustained by food that savages, not bread-eating people, ate; they used no fragrant herbs, they had no olives nor the shining oil that gives light in the darkness and nourishment for the body and is a balm for weary limbs. They had no cheeses, no foaming wine that cheers the heart. They ate animal fat and drank milk.

Their women smelled like the animal skins they wore; they had no looms or spindles. Their hair was tangled and dry as straw and they didn't bathe in waters scented with rare and precious essences. I imagined that the only time they got wet was when it rained.

In a particularly poor village, they offered me one as a sign of their hospitality, but her nauseating smell repelled me. I accepted to take her away with me so they would not be offended, but I simply delivered her to the next village, allowing them to believe that I'd found her by chance along my way.

Only once was I forced to fight for my life. I was venturing into a large village when I saw human skulls nailed onto a pole in the middle of a clearing and over the doors of the surrounding huts. The inhabitants must have seen me, and had perhaps interpreted the oar on my shoulder as a weapon, for although I tried to retrace my steps, their centaurs quickly caught up with me and dragged me back to the village.

They subjected me to what must have been a sacrificial rite: I was forced to face off against a gigantic warrior. Although he was surely their champion, he used his sword like a club and not like a weapon with a cutting edge. It wasn't difficult, on my second lunge, to run him through from front to back. The crowd who had been loudly cheering him on were struck dumb. They sent out four more men against me and I took their lives, one after another, with the sword I'd been given, an excellent bronze blade, and I wondered where it had been forged. A moment before sinking it into the chest of the fifth man, I felt a shiver under my skin and was filled with joy. Was Athena back at my side? I thanked her in my heart with such a surge of emotion that my eyes filled with tears. The astonished onlookers allowed me to go then, and I walked off with my oar on my shoulder.

That same night, I found shelter in a small depression in the ground. I lay down wrapped in my cloak on a pile of leaves and fell asleep. Now and then my sleep was torn by emotions very familiar to me in the aftermath of a battle. My hand jerked to my side, searching for the hilt of a weapon. I twisted away, as if to avoid a blow. In this drowsy state I could feel sharp gusts of the north wind chilling my limbs. The wind didn't wake me, but it wouldn't let me sleep.

I don't remember when it happened, whether near dawn or in the middle of the night, but I heard Mentor's voice, calling me. Waking me. I jolted awake and got to my feet. He was standing in front of me, looking at me with that intense expression I knew so well. It surprised me that I could see him so clearly in the dark, as if a fire or a hidden lamp was illuminating him. There was no moon in the sky and everything was dark above and below me.

'Mentor!' I cried out. 'How did you find me in this desolation? Or are you my goddess, posing as my boyhood tutor? She's done that before. I felt her presence today in combat, that cold shiver that tells me she's near.'

He replied: 'I am not your goddess. I am the message that she sends you. Look!' He pointed at my bed of leaves. I did look and saw myself sleeping soundly. 'Now come with me.' Was I moving inside a dream?

I followed him and I realized that we were moving swiftly and covering much ground. Before us was a chain of very high mountains, their peaks capped with snow and ice.

We stopped on one of these majestic crests. 'This is Mount Haemos. The freezing winds that bring snow and cold over all the earth are born here.'

'What will happen to my oar? I left it next to where I was resting!'

'No one will touch it,' he replied. 'You'll find it upon your return. You'll need it.'

'When?'

'Soon, perhaps. I can only tell you that something will

happen next spring. But first you will have to cross the winter, from one side to the other: the freezing cold, the screaming wind. No one has ever survived. You passed the wall of fog: you will have to pass the wall of ice. You will be pierced by one thousand gelid swords. The cold will split your heart. Finally you will cross the last frontier.'

'I want to return to Penelope, to Telemachus! I'm tired, understand? . . . immensely tired . . .'

'You will see them.'

'When?'

'When the moment comes. When you have offered sacrifice, as the Theban prophet you called up from Hades predicted.' As he pronounced these words, the moon appeared between the wind-tattered clouds and lit up three animals on the snowy plain: they were enormous, and they were galloping across that vast expanse, raising clouds of snow, clouds of silver. A great bull with pointed horns snorted clouds of hot steam from flaring nostrils. At his side a tusked swine as huge as the boar of Calydon. On the other side, a gigantic ram, an albino with curved horns. Were they rushing towards the fatal encounter?

Mentor's eyes glowed bright in the dark like those of an owl that see better at night than during the day.

'Calchas has just died. Can you feel him passing in the wind? Just as you had predicted, whispering into his ear. You also have the gift, remember?'

'A snake bite?'

'Yes, just as you had predicted. And Calchas? What did he tell you at that same instant?'

'I can't tell you. It's too hard for me, and it wouldn't be easy for you to hear.'

'What if I showed you where Mentor is?'

'Then maybe I'd tell you.'

'Come, follow me.'

He moved along the mountain ridge without leaving tracks

in the blanket of snow at his feet. I left no tracks either. My body was elsewhere. We found ourselves in front of a cave.

The ghost that guided me let off a dim light, enough for me to make out the cavern walls. I followed him through an enormous room, a petrified forest of pale pinnacles that rose from the floor and hung from the vault above, sweating tears. Some of them looked almost human, or like fabulous beasts, their jaws bristling with stony fangs. Others were joined at the middle to form columns. I'd never seen such a thing in all my life. We entered a tunnel and walked on at length. I felt fear and apprehension. My heartbeat was becoming stronger and faster with each step I took, although my heart was far away in a body sleeping in a hollow in the ground.

The tunnel branched off several times into smaller passage-ways. Was the Labyrinth of Crete that imprisoned the man-bull like this? The narrow passage finally began to widen until we found ourselves in a bigger chamber with a square boulder at its centre. On this stone lay my friend Mentor, stiff and unmoving. The body that my goddess had worn to appear to me or my son, the precious friend who had always been so free with his advice and his chiding, with his help and support. A man of priceless wisdom, so generous that he could not refuse his body, his very person, to the god who loved me and had saved me time and time again.

'In the end,' said the spectre, 'the presence of the green-eyed goddess consumed the fragile husk, and she placed him here in this majestic dwelling, an empty chrysalis, untainted and untaint-able, forever.'

I threw myself, weeping, upon that cold body, caressed his face and kissed his hands. On his chest was a small stone flower – one of those that take shape from the tears of the mountain. 'Allow me, my friend, to wear this on my own chest in your memory. It will protect me as an amulet for as long as I live,' I whispered. But then I shouted out: 'If this is the cost of keep-ing me alive, it would have been better to share the fate of my comrades! A thousand times better to die pierced by an arrow under the walls of Troy or to sink into the abyss with my ship. My death would have quenched the blue god's thirst for revenge and ended his loathing.'

'Don't speak thus!' said the spirit who was guiding me. 'You must not question the gifts and the love of a goddess!'

'I am grateful for her gifts and I miss her terribly. I wish that she were here to give me hope, to tell me the place and time that I will again be able to embrace those I love.'

'This may indeed happen, perhaps, when the time is right. But you and I had a pact. I've showed you Mentor, now you must tell me what Calchas whispered into your ear.'

'I can tell you, but I'm not sure myself of what I heard.'

'Tell me anyway.'

I couldn't understand why my guide insisted on hearing something he should have already known, but I tried to repeat what Calchas had told me, as best I could remember it: '"When you have gathered your victims on the site of the agile oar, you will then have to make a choice: whether to sacrifice them and return to the sea where you will resume your reign and finally meet your death, or whether to take up your journey once again. Forever." How I've struggled to interpret those words! Can you help me?'

I had no reply save a gust of the screaming wind that brings snow and ice over the endless expanse.

I WAS AWAKENED by the cold; my limbs felt numb. I looked all around me, above me. My oar was placed across the hole I slept in and my cloak was arranged over it like a sort of tent, held down at the hem by stones. I didn't remember building such a shelter for myself, nor could I have done it in my sleep. The cloak began to quiver like a sail billowed by the wind and I looked beyond it, outside: it was snowing. There was no use leaving my burrow. I'd be forced to walk through the storm, with the icy sleet stinging my face.

I stayed where I was until the snow had stopped; it was nearing dusk when I emerged. Never before had I seen the land stretch all around me in every direction all the way to the horizon. As flat as the open sea in dead calm, all the same colour of pure white snow. Remembering my father's words in Arcadia, I plunged my hands into it. It felt as soft as the fleece of a lamb, but intensely, bitingly cold. My hands came out red and withered. It certainly wouldn't have taken long to render them completely unfeeling.

I thought of what I had seen and heard during the night. Had it truly been just a dream? It was all so clear and sharp to me, like no dream I'd ever had.

A bit of sun had come out and the air temperature was a little warmer. The wind was still brisk and I could feel it knocking something against my chest. I put my hand to my heart and touched a small, hard object hanging from a ribbon of fabric: the little stone rose from Mentor's chest! What message was that? What was my goddess trying to tell me? That my dream was real, dreams the only truth? Did she want to say that I had to forget the world of the living, the world I loved, the world I'd embraced when I was offered immortality instead?

Grief soon took the place of my astonishment. I realized I was wandering through a Labyrinth with no escape, no Ariadne to provide a thread that would show me the way out.

Calchas was dead. And me? Was I dead as well? I couldn't have given an answer, although I was surely feeling hot and cold, hunger, pain. Perhaps I had reached the second barrier, the wall of cold and ice, after the wall of fog. I set traps around my shelter, hoping to catch myself some food.

The next day I shook the snow off the top of my cloak, lit a fire, gathered the birds captured in my traps and ate them. Then I picked up the oar and started walking again. No trace of a human being, no matter which way I looked.

It was then that the harshest, most painful and arduous part of my journey began. Cold and solitude enveloped me so acutely as to become unbearable. The world I'd lived in was gone; nothing but scraps of it remained in me. I felt empty and yet I continued to seek meaning in what I experienced, what I was forced to face. There had to be a reason, one that was acceptable and comprehensible to my mind.

So I went forward, thinking about nothing but reaching the place I was seeking, at a great distance from the sea. In that place I'd find a man and he would ask me a question: what is that object you carry on your shoulder? A winnowing blade, perhaps? To toss grain into the air, to remove the chaff?

There I would stop, and my goddess would send me a bull, a boar and a ram. There I would make sacrifice to the blue god and I would be rewarded with serenity. My suffering would be over forever.

But the infinite expanse I faced frightened me. I wondered where I would get food, how I would defend myself against the piercing cold . . .

I walked for days and days, gasping for breath, gritting my teeth, imprecating, imploring, cursing, weeping . . . but with every step I took in that endless void, that ferocious wind, I felt courage swelling in my heart, I felt a strength that I'd never experienced before and fear slowly melted away from me.

And when, suddenly, total silence would fall upon me and over the white expanse, the absence of any sound or echo or puff of air made me feel strangely inebriated, not very different from how I remembered feeling on the island at the ends of the earth. It felt like I could expand my being, like water or air or dust or smoke, until I covered the entire space as far as my eyes could see. It was then, in that silence that took my breath away, that I learned to talk with myself, so as not to go mad.

In the end, it would always be the voice of the wind that broke the silence, either with a violent gust or with a plaintive sound that I could barely hear, soft . . . or mocking, like the chirping of a blackbird.

More than two months into my exhausting journey, the wind learned to speak and even to sing.

With the voice of my Penelope, so far away . . .

Epilogue

It took me many more months to cover the last stretch of cruel winter. Every moment of every day was filled with remembering. It barely seems possible that I could relive every instant of my life so intensely, so vividly. It was as though my mind had diffused and expanded my experience to fill that void, so that nothing could exist outside my body. Nothing but myself occupied the limitless space that surrounded me.

I navigated alone, without a single comrade, with only an oar to remind me that I had once crossed the sea, that I had fought impossible monsters and creatures. Nothing on this journey had reawakened the forces that in the past had enabled me to carry out my endeavours; there had been neither glory nor meaning in the only combat I'd been forced to engage in.

I felt like I'd become another person, in another place and in another world, and this pained and alarmed me. I felt my roots being yanked from the earth I knew by a force that I could not defend myself against. Every yank wounded me, spilling blood, not shining sap. My past life seemed alien to me; something that had evaporated with my passing. Changeable creatures, unfamiliar divinities confined to remote, unreachable places . . . places of magical beauty, blissful islands ruled by divine sovereigns, storms of wind and lightning, raging mountains of water: all this faded away in those twilights when the sun never set, in those delusive, tremulous lights that fluttered in the night sky. I was the only thinking animal that could live in that desert of white.

Then this morning, when I opened my eyes and stretched my numb, aching limbs, I found myself immersed in fog. I was lost in a milky fluid that barely let me discern a globe above me that looked much more like a pale moon than the sun that brings light to mortal men. I couldn't even distinguish the features of the ground that surrounded me, nor remember what it looked like before I fell asleep. But then the sun rose high over the horizon, and soon the fog began to dissolve, revealing a tall sparkling rampart beaded with pearls of pure light, and I thought: can this be the wall of ice that Calchas spoke of?

Is what I face truly the last obstacle? Will I overcome this one too? Can I manage to break through this barrier? Suddenly, I'm not sure why, I know that I can.

The wall is in front of me now: blinding glare that stings my eyes. I have to defend them with strips of cloth, ripping the merest slits in them so I can still see. I've had to tie the oar to my belt with shreds of leather and drag it after me. The climb is ever more arduous. The sharp ice lacerates my hands, the trail I leave is of scarlet stains on the immaculate white. How and when will I find the victims to sacrifice to the god of the abyss? When and how will I meet the man who will ask the question that will finally free me of my curse? I look behind me every now and then. My breath is ragged, the prayers I murmur to my goddess a cry of pain and hope. I gaze back at the horizon I crossed so long ago and then move forward again, towards the icy crest.

Slowly, gritting my teeth, I climb up and up. As I near the summit, I'm certain that a revelation awaits me on the other side and I try to imagine what I will see.

I'm just a few steps away from the peak. It's getting harder and harder to breathe. I'm reminded of the snowy mountaintops we glimpsed in Arcadia so long ago, when as a boy I followed the hero Laertes my father towards the sanctuary of the Wolf King.

I'm at the top! I drag the oar towards me and I plunge it into the deep snow so it casts a long shadow. The plain opens wide below, furrowed by raging torrents, blazing in the rays of the sun. I shout with all the voice I have in me, with all my strength, I shout to the men and the gods, to the wind and the peaks I see in the distance. I shout so that someone may hear me and show himself. I can no longer bear this solitude.

But my voice is lost in the silence.

I take up the oar with the butterfly carved into its handle, moulded to the hand of the fallen comrade who drowned long ago in a distant sea. And so I descend the wall of ice, heading towards the plain. The wind starts to blow again, impetuous.

All of a sudden, a roar. The snow in front of me seems to melt and a towering column of water erupts from the ground, rising higher and higher. Behind the transparent column appears a figure wrapped in a vortex. A deafening laugh resounds over all the earth, his eyes inscrutable, locks blue-green like the deepest maelstrom, body liquid as the swirling sea . . .

'Did you really believe that you'd arrived?' Voice of thunder tapering off into a long gurgle, a distant roaring sea monster.

'Did you really believe that you'd reached the end of your long journey? Where is the man, then, who looks at your oar and demands an answer? Where are the victims to be sacrificed to my spirit? Run! Run, glorious Odysseus, crafty and resourceful son of Laertes, run for as long as your breath and your life hold out, run, if you can!'

The earth swallowed him instantly and I can no longer say what I am seeing or not seeing, hearing or not hearing. All that remains is darkest despair. The wind has picked up, ever keener, and a shiver raises my skin under my tattered clothing. Is it the cold that is chilling me to the bone or is it the trembling inside me that I've yearned for so long, the quiver that tells me that my goddess is near?

'Athena!' I shout in my heart. 'Athena!' I'm surrounded by an infinite white expanse. The horizon is deserted in every direction – even the wall of ice has disappeared. The sky is empty, the light unflickering. Perhaps it is morning, perhaps evening. It makes no difference. But there it is, a black speck, far away in the distance . . .

Where have I already seen this? When?

It advances towards me, swiftly, becoming bigger and bigger! I'm certain I've already seen this. Or did I dream it?

I don't know how much time passes before, finally, he reaches me. Him. The Wolf King, on a swift, wheel-less chariot drawn by wolves that seems to fly over the snow . . .

My dream at the sanctuary of Arcadia: this was what I dreamed!

'Oh my goddess who touches me with a shiver, I beg you, reveal the meaning of this vision: is it he who will ask me the question? A hero racing *swiftly on a chariot drawn by wolves?' It stops, all at once and a voice in my heart says to me, 'Draw closer!' There he is, he has stepped out of the chariot and is standing beside it. He is staring at me and my heart leaps in my chest.*

His hair is run through with silver threads, like mine, his beard is like the one that frames my face, on his chest hangs a ribbon of cloth with a little stone rose . . . only his clothing is different: the bracelet he wears at his wrist and the boots he wears on his feet. The mystery opens before my eyes like a black cloud rent by the wind after a storm! The cloak on his shoulders is fastened by a golden pin, shaped like a deer in the clutches of a hound. My Penelope! The desire to weep is huge, I feel the tears leaving my eyes but I see them falling down his cheeks . . .

'Draw closer,' says the voice in my heart, and I draw closer, so close that I am him and he is me and I am no longer. There's only one man on that snowy expanse.

Here come other chariots, drawn by more wolves. They stop next to mine, next to his. Voices shout: 'Commander!' They are the voices of Antiphus, Sinon, Polites, Elpenor, Eurylochus, Euribates!

This is what I've found beyond the wall of ice: another time, another place, another where, another why, and another adventure with other comrades who I know but who don't recognize me. What does it matter? I tie the oar to the chariot as the others laugh: 'What will you need that for, commander? There's not a boat to be found in these parts!'

'What does that matter?' I answer. 'Onward!' And I set my wolves off at a gallop, shouting other words in a language that is different yet similar. Mine, regardless.

What does it matter? I am what I am: a small king of a kingdom I no longer have . . . son of a little island, son of a bitter fate. I, who have faced monsters and invincible heroes without trembling, I, who have been overcome by fear and fled, I, who have shouted the names of my fallen comrades and I who did not hesitate to cast them into deadly danger . . . why? Curiosity, the invincible desire to push on, beyond the last limit and beyond the last horizon. I, who have wept, laughed, rejoiced, suffered, I who have loved and hated. I, who believe in my goddess, in my bride, in my land, and who flee from them all. I who am and who will be until one day, who knows where, who knows when, I'll meet a man who asks me whether what I carry on my shining shoulder is a winnowing blade to separate the wheat from the chaff. On that day I will re-embrace my Penelope for all time, and my son, clad in blinding bronze. And I will reign over happy peoples. I, who am everyone and anyone.

I who am No One.

Author's Note

After *Odysseus: The Oath*, this second volume, *The Return*, covers Odysseus' voyage home after the war of Troy and then his final journey, the one foretold by the prophet Tiresias from the underworld. His story is only one of many '*nòstoi*', the poems of the epic cycle that recount the 'returns' of the heroes of the Trojan War. Odysseus' tale is the only one of these poems to survive; only small fragments of the others remain, mostly as citations in the works of other classic authors. Homer himself includes one of these stories in Book XI of the *Odyssey*: the return of Agamemnon and his murder at the hands of Clytaemnestra, his wife, and her lover Aegisthus. Book IV of the *Odyssey* provides a version of Menelaus' return. Virgil's *Aeneid* indirectly mentions the return of Diomedes, who is forced to leave Argus and forge a new life for himself in Apulia, in the south of Italy.

Today we know that the itinerary of Odysseus' homeward journey is lost to us. Fascinating hints in ancient sources suggest that his original voyage probably took place between the Black Sea and the Aegean. In the 1900s it was believed that the route had been modelled on a Phoenician navigation manual but this hypothesis was dismantled when traces of Mycenaean presence began to turn up throughout the entire Mediterranean. The 'traditional' localizations on the Tyrrhenian Sea (Circe on Mount Circeo, Scylla and Charybdis in the Strait of Messina, etc.) were actually mapped out quite early on, by the first Euboean colonizers who settled on the shores of that sea.

A number of scholars have noted that the hero of the *Odyssey* is a different man from the *Iliad*: Odysseus goes from being a warrior and fighter in the latter to an adventurer in the former, a wanderer of mysterious islands and tempestuous seas who find himself pitted against cyclopes, man-eating giants, sirens, monsters and deadly whirlpools. It is his cunning, not his physical prowess, that allows him to navigate all these obstacles. His adventures are a compendium of the more-or-less stereotypical dangers of a seafaring life that sailors would be well familiar with.

If we take a closer look at the *Odyssey*, we see instead that once our wandering hero has finally made his way back to Ithaca and found his palace invaded by a wolf-pack of suitors, he resumes the role of the avenging warrior who destroyed Troy. No one escapes his wrath; even the faithless handmaids are hanged at his hands. After the suitors have been slaughtered, Odysseus reclaims his full powers as king; he even arranges for the corpses to be returned to their families and with bureaucratic precision has ships prepared for the bodies of those who come from the other islands of his kingdom. Odysseus also acts as king when, faced with the relatives of the men he has killed, who are seeking revenge and intend to exterminate the royal dynasty, he proposes peace instead, forestalling the outbreak of what today we would call a civil war.

What is more important is that the cycle of the 'returns' exposes the dramatic situation of the Mycenaean kings who had taken part in the war of Troy. The fragments we have suggest that the internal equilibrium of that galaxy of small potentates rested fundamentally on two pillars: on one hand, a continuous, sophisticated diplomacy consisting in reciprocal visits, codes of hospitality, exchanges of gifts and matrimonial alliances, and on the other hand, the participation of the kings in 'endeavours' of different sorts. A hunting party to eliminate an exceptionally large or aggressive beast like a wild bull or a boar (like the hunt in Calydon from which Autolykos was excluded in *The Oath*), an expedition across the sea to conquer a treasure (the golden fleece of Colchis) or the pillaging of foreign settlements and territories. The last of these common endeavours was probably the Trojan War itself; it is only by accepting this hypothesis that we can explain the grandiose epic tradition that it generated, unique in all classic literature.

Moreover, if we accept this hypothesis, another becomes plausible. For centuries, scholars have wondered what brought about the collapse of the Mycenaean culture; the blame was long attributed to the Dorian invasion which took place about 1100 BC (even Thucydides reports this in his 'Return of the Heraclidae'). The only problem is that modern archaeology has failed to find any trace of these phantom invaders. A more likely explanation is that it was the Trojan War itself that imploded the Mycenaean system of rule and way of life. The long absence of the kings and aristocrats and the death toll of the war, involving the young men in their prime who could defend their homelands, led to unrest, seizure of power, civil conflict. Some of the returning sovereigns were murdered, or found their kingdoms so profoundly changed that they were forced to flee (like Diomedes) or react (like Odysseus) with ruthless determination, crushing any uprisings in blood. All of these events, and these signals of decline, are present in the epic tradition. It is not by chance that archaeologists do not generally talk about the 'destruction' of the Mycenaean palaces or centres of power, but of their collapse, implicitly accepting the idea that the civilization was extinguished and that its people abandoned the urban structures that they could no longer afford to maintain. Ruins of still-standing ancient structures bear signs of fire which can be attributed to isolated raids on the part of neighbouring tribes; more likely an effect than a cause of the general debilitation of the Mycenaean world.

In the end, the winners came out losers and the '*nòstoi*' paint the sad portrait of a dying world. Homer's voice emerges from the collective, choral song of a great number of court and street poets, from the indistinct assemblage of thousands and thousands of imaginations, like a cathedral which rises from the labour of thousands but from the genius of a single creator.

It has been said that there are two stars in the Homeric firmament: Achilles and Odysseus. But only one of the two survives for all eternity: Odysseus of the complex mind, the wandering hero who wages an unequal war against gods, giants and the forces of nature.

Homer, in Book XI, imagines a second Odyssey, no longer by sea but over land, a journey of mud and dust towards a remote, mysterious place where the hero would have to sacrifice three animals to the blue god, the lord of the abyss. Only thus would he finally make amends for his reckless challenge and admit his inferiority as a man in the face of a god.

No trace has ever been found of this mysterious poem, a true unsolved mystery of universal literature.

VMM

Characters and Places

Anfitea – queen of Acarnania, wife to Autolykos, mother of Anticlea, grandmother of Odysseus.

Anticlea – queen mother of Ithaca, wife to Laertes, mother of Odysseus.

Arcesius – father of Laertes, husband to Chalcomedusa, grandfather of Odysseus.

Argus – Odysseus' dog.

Autolykos – king of Acarnania, husband to Anfitea, father of Anticlea, grandfather of Odysseus.

Chalcomedusa – mother of Laertes, wife to Arcesius, grandmother of Odysseus.

Laertes – king of Ithaca before Odysseus, only son of Arcesius, husband to Anticlea, father of Odysseus. Argonaut.

Odysseus – king of Ithaca and of the Ionian islands, only son of Laertes and Anticlea, husband to Penelope, father of Telemachus. Inventor of the stratagem of the Trojan horse, he thus became known as *ptoliethros*, 'destroyer of cities'. Homer's *Iliad* also calls him 'divine', 'very patient' and 'of cunning intelligence'. His adventures during his long and dramatic journey back to Ithaca give rise to the second Homeric poem, *The Odyssey*.

Penelope – queen of Ithaca, daughter of Icarius and Polycaste of Sparta, wife to Odysseus, mother of Telemachus.

Telemachus – prince of Ithaca, only son of Odysseus and
Penelope.

GODS, GODDESSES AND SUPERNATURAL BEINGS

Aeolus – semi-god, master of the winds. King of the floating
island of Aeolia.

Aphrodite – goddess of love; she convinces Paris to name her the
fairest of three goddesses (Athena, Aphrodite and Hera). In
exchange she promises him he will possess the most beautiful
woman in the world.

Apollo – god of sun and light, an archer. God of prophecy. Sides
with Troy in the Trojan War.

Ares – god of war. On the side of the Trojans in the war.

Athena – daughter of Zeus, from whose brain she sprang directly,
fully armed. Goddess of wisdom and protectress of Odysseus.

Atlas – the Titan who bore the world on his shoulders.

Borea – the northern wind.

Calypso – sea nymph, daughter of Atlas. Lady of the island of
Ogygia

Cerberus – three-headed dog of Hades.

Chaera – personification of death.

Echo – mountain nymph.

Erebus – personification of darkness.

Hades – god of the Underworld. Also, the Underworld itself.

Helios – Sun god, sometimes identified with Apollo.

Hephaestus – the blacksmith of the gods. Forges the armour of
Achilles.

Hera – sister and wife of Zeus. Protectress of the family and
pregnant women. On the side of the Achaians in the Trojan
War.

Hypnos – god of sleep.

Moirai – the three Fates, who control the thread of life of every
mortal from birth to death.

Periboea – Giant who generated the first ancestor of the
  Phaeacians with Poseidon.
Persephone – daughter of Demetra, goddess of nature and the
  earth. Kidnapped by Hades, she lives six months in the
  Underworld with her husband and six months on the earth
  with her mother. Symbol of the seasons.
Poseidon – brother of Zeus, son of Kronos. God of the sea and
  the ocean. Mortal enemy of Odysseus.
Sirens – beautiful and dangerous female creatures with enchanting
  voices who lure sailors to wreck their ships.
Thanatos – personification of Death.
Zeus – father of all the gods, husband to Hera, son of Kronos.
  Personification of thunder and lightning.

CHARACTERS

Achilles – prince of Phthia, son of Peleus and the sea goddess
  Thetis. The greatest hero of the Achaian army. A prophecy
  foretold that he would have to choose between a long but
  obscure life or a short but glorious one.
Admetus – king of Pherai in Thessaly, husband to Alcestis, father
  of Eumelus. Argonaut.
Adrastus – king of Argus, father-in-law of Tydeus, grandfather of
  Diomedes.
Aeetes – king of Colchis, father of Medea.
Aegialia – wife of Diomedes.
Aegisthus – lover of Clytaemnestra. Agamemnon's murderer.
Aeneas – prince of Dardania, son of Anchises and the goddess
  Aphrodite, cousin to Hector. Ally of Troy.
Agamemnon – king of Mycenae, High King of the Achaians, son
  of Atreus, brother of Menelaus, husband to Clytaemnestra,
  father of Iphigenia.
Ajax Oileus – prince of Locris, close friend of Great Ajax.
Ajax son of Telamon (Great Ajax) – prince of Salamis, half-brother

of Teucer, cousin to Achilles. The strongest hero of the
Achaians after Achilles.

Alcestis – queen of Pherai, wife to Admetus, mother of Eumelus.
She accepts to die in her husband's place and is saved by
Hercules.

Alcinous – father of Nausicaa. King of Scheria of the Phaeacians.

Amphiaraus – seer, from Argus. One of the 'Seven Against
Thebes'. Argonaut.

Anaxibia – queen of Phocis, daughter of Atreus, sister of
Agamemnon and Menelaus.

Anchises – king of Dardania, father of Aeneas.

Andromache – princess of Hypoplacian Thebes, daughter of
Eetion, wife of Hector, mother of Astyanax.

Antenor – Trojan nobleman, advisor to King Priam. Mediator
between the Trojans and the Achaians.

Antilochus – prince of Pylos, son of Nestor, friend of Odysseus.

Antinous – leader of the suitors of Penelope. Son of Eupites.

Antiphus – comrade of Odysseus.

Arete – mother of Nausicaa. Queen of the Phaeacians.

Argonauts – Achaian heroes who took part in the expedition of
the *Argo*, led by Jason of Iolcus, to conquer the golden fleece
in Colchis. The sons of many Argonauts would go on to fight
the Trojan War.

Ariadne – Princess of Crete. Helped Theseus to find his way out
of the Labyrinth using a thread of her making.

Asclepius – legendary practitioner of the medical arts.

Astyanax – infant son of Hector and Andromache.

Atreidae – the house of Atreus.

Atreides – one of the sons of Atreus, Agamemnon or Menelaus.

Atreus – King of Mycenae, father of Agamemnon and Menelaus.

Automedon – charioteer to Achilles and to Pyrrhus after Achilles'
death.

Balius – one of Achilles' divine horses, 'the dappled'.

Briseis – beloved concubine of Achilles, claimed by Agamemnon.

Calchas – priest and seer, advisor to Agamemnon.

Characters and Places

Cassandra – princess of Troy, daughter of Priam and Hecuba,
    sister of Hector, Paris and Deiphobus. She was given the gift
    of prophecy by Apollo, who loved her but was spurned by her;
    he thus cursed her so that her predictions would never be
    believed.
Castor – prince of Sparta, son of Tyndareus and Leda, twin of
    Pollux, brother of Helen and Clytaemnestra. Argonaut, with
    his brother Pollux. According to a legend, Castor's real father
    was Zeus, who appeared to his mother in the form of a swan.
Cephalonians – Odysseus' most valiant warriors, coming from the
    island of Same.
Chryseis – daughter of high priest Chryses, taken as concubine by
    Agamemnon. His refusal to return her to her father set off a
    great plague and much strife in the Achaian camp.
Ciconians – a tribe in Thrace.
Cimmerians –mysterious people of uncertain origin. In the
    Odyssey, they live close to the entrance of Hades.
Circe – Sister of Aeetes, King of Colchis. Lady of the island of
    Aeaea.
Clytaemnestra – daughter of Tyndareus and Leda, sister of Castor,
    Pollux and Helen, wife to Agamemnon. According to a legend,
    her real father was Zeus, who appeared to her mother in the
    form of a swan.
Damastes – trainer of Odysseus, a native of Thessaly.
Deiphobus – prince of Troy, son of Priam and Hecuba, brother of
    Hector and Paris, husband to Helen after Paris' death.
Demodocus – blind singer and storyteller on the island of Scheria.
Diomedes – king of Argus, son of Tydeus, husband to Aegialia,
    close friend of Odysseus. One of the strongest heroes of
    Achaia.
Dolius – neighbour of Laertes on Ithaca.
Eetion – king of Hypoplacian Thebes, father of Andromache.
Elpenor – comrade of Odysseus who died on the island of Circes.
Epeius – builder of the Trojan horse.
Eumelus – prince of Pherai, son of Admetus and Alcestis.

Eumeus – swineherd of Laertes, faithful to the royal family.

Eupites – father of Antinous.

Euribates – comrade of Odysseus.

Euriclea – nurse to Odysseus, affectionately called '*mai*' (grandmother) by him.

Eurydice – queen of Pylos, wife to Nestor.

Eurylochus – cousin of Odysseus and his second in command.

Eurymachus – one of Odysseus' comrades in the Trojan horse.

Eurymachus – the second most powerful of Penelope's suitors, after Antinous.

Eurystheus – usurper of the throne of Mycenae, cousin of Hercules.

Euthymides – youngest son of Eupites.

Hector – prince of Troy, eldest son of Priam and Hecuba, brother of Paris and Deiphobus, husband to Andromache, father of Astyanax. Killed in a duel with Achilles.

Hecuba – queen of Troy, wife of Priam, mother of Hector, Deiphobus, Paris, Cassandra, Polyxena.

Helen – queen of Sparta, daughter of Tyndareus and Leda of Sparta, sister of Clytaemnestra, Castor and Pollux, wife to Menelaus, Paris and Deiphobus. According to a legend, Helen's real father was Zeus, who appeared to her mother in the form of a swan.

Hercules – son of Zeus and the mortal Alcmene, cousin of Eurystheus, who condemned him to perform the twelve labours. Argonaut.

Hermione – daughter of Menelaus and Helen.

Icarius – brother of Tyndareus of Sparta, husband to Polycaste, father of Penelope.

Ideus – herald of Priam.

Idomeneus – king of Crete. Member of the expedition to Troy.

Iphigenia – daughter of Agamemnon and Clytaemnestra.

Iphitus – brother of Eurystheus, king of Mycenae. Argonaut.

Jason – prince of Iolcus, leader of the Argonauts, husband to Medea.

Laestrygonians – tribe of man-eating giants inhabiting the city of Telepylus who destroyed Odysseus' fleet.

Laocoon – Trojan priest.

Lapiths – a tribe of Thessaly, renowned for their physical size and prowess.

Leda – queen of Sparta, wife of Tyndareus, mother of Castor, Pollux, Helen and Clytaemnestra. Legendary lover of Zeus.

Leodes – one of the suitors of Penelope.

Lycomedes – king of Scyros, grandfather of Neoptolemus (Pyrrhus).

Makahon – surgeon and warrior of Achaian army, pupil of Asclepius.

Medea – princess of Colchis, daughter of Aeetes, wife to Jason. Enchantress.

Megara – queen of Mycenae, wife to Eurystheus.

Melanippus – defender of Thebes, killed by Tydeus.

Melanthius – a goatherd on Ithaca, faithful to suitors.

Mélantho – maidservant in Odysseus' house, lover of Antinous.

Meleager – king of Aetolia, father-in-law of Protesilaus. Argonaut.

Memnon – king of the Ethiopians who killed Antilochus, son of Nestor.

Menelaus – king of Sparta, son of Atreus, brother of Agamemnon, husband to Helen. He demands that all the Achaian kings and princes honour their oath to defend his honour when Helen is abducted by Paris, provoking the Trojan War.

Menestheus – king of Athens, member of the expedition to Troy.

Mentes – chief of the Taphians.

Mentor – tutor of Odysseus, advisor to King Laertes.

Myrmidons – warriors of Phthia in Thessaly, commanded by Achilles.

Neoptolemus (Pyrrhus) – son of Achilles and princess Deidamia of Scyros. After his father's death, he enters the Trojan War. Famed for his ferocity and ruthlessness.

Nestor – wise king of Pylos, husband to Eurydice, father of

Antilochus and Pisistratus. Also known as the Knight of
Gerene. The great advisor of the Achaian heroes.

Oedipus – king of Thebes. Married his mother and killed his
father. His two sons, Eteocles and Polynices, killed each other
in a duel over the throne.

Oileus – king of Locris, father of Ajax Oileus. Argonaut.

Paris – prince of Troy, son of Priam and Hecuba, brother of
Hector, Deiphobus and Cassandra, husband of Helen after
Menelaus. His abduction of Helen sets off the Trojan War.

Patroclus – cousin and trusted companion of Achilles. Killed in
battle by Hector.

Peirithous – king of the Lapiths, a Thessalian tribe. Argonaut.

Peleus – king of Phthia, husband to Thetis, brother of Telamon,
father of Achilles. Argonaut.

Pelias – king of Iolcus, father of Alcestis. Usurped the throne of
Aeson and sent Jason in search of the golden fleece.

Perimedes – trusted comrade of Odysseus.

Phaeacians – population who migrated to the island of Scheria
from Hypereia, led by King Nausithous.

Phemius – court poet of Laertes.

Philoctetes – king of Malis, famed as an archer. Member of the
expedition to Troy.

Philoetius – a cowherd on Ithaca, faithful to Odysseus.

Pisistratus – prince of Pylos, youngest son of Nestor and
Eurydice.

Polites – comrade of Odysseus.

Pollux – prince of Sparta, son of Tyndareus and Leda, twin of
Castor, brother of Helen and Clytaemnestra. Argonaut, with
his brother Castor. According to a legend, their real father was
Zeus, who appeared to his mother in the form of a swan.

Polycaste – wife of Icarius, mother of Penelope.

Polyxena – princess of Troy, youngest daughter of Priam and
Hecuba. Sacrificed by Pyrrhus on the tomb of Achilles.

Priam – king of Troy, husband to Hecuba, father of Hector, Paris,

Deiphobus, Cassandra, Polyxena and many other sons and
daughters. Killed and decapitated by Pyrrhus on the night of
the Fall of Troy.

Protesilaus – Thessalian king, the first Achaian to die in the Trojan
War.

Pyrrhus (Neoptolemus) – son of Achilles and princess Deidamia
of Scyros. After his father's death, he enters the Trojan War.
Famed for his ferocity and ruthlessness.

Sinon – friend and comrade of Odysseus, persuades Trojans to
pull the horse into the city.

Sthenelus – Argive prince, charioteer of Diomedes.

Taphians – population of pirates, of uncertain origin.

Telamon – king of Salamis, brother of Peleus, father of Great
Ajax and Teucer. Argonaut.

Teucer – son of Telamon and Hesione (sister of Priam),
half-brother of Great Ajax. Famous archer, member of the
expedition to Troy.

Theoclymenus – a seer who fled from Argus after killing a man.
He predicts the Day of the Black Sun and the slaughter of the
suitors.

Theseus – king of Athens, killer of the Minotaur.

Thetis – wife to Peleus, mother of Achilles. Said to be a sea
goddess or nymph.

Thoas – king of Calydon, killer of the boar of Calydon. Odysseus'
comrade in the wooden horse.

Thyestes – twin brother of Atreus.

Tiresias – a seer from Thebes. Odysseus calls up his soul from
Hades to learn about his destiny.

Trasimachus – comrade of Odysseus.

Tydeus – Argive prince, father of Diomedes. Ruthless warrior,
killed in battle at Thebes after slaying Melanippus. Argonaut.

Tyndareus – king of Sparta, husband to Leda, father of Castor
and Pollux, Helen and Clytaemnestra, although according to
a legend, their real father was Zeus, who appeared to their
mother Leda in the form of a swan.

Xanthus – one of Achilles' divine horses, 'the blond'.

Zetes and Calais – the Boreads, sons of the wind. Argonauts.

Geography

Acarnania – region of south-western Greece, facing Ithaca, ruled by Autolykos, Odysseus' grandfather.

Achaia – an area generally corresponding to Greece. Land of the Achaians.

Acheron – river in Ephyra, said to be a gateway to Hades.

Aetolia – region in western Greece ruled by Meleager.

Andros – island lying next to and south-east of Euboea.

Arcadia – mountainous region in the central Peloponnese where the Sanctuary of the Wolf King is located.

Argolis – region of Argus in the eastern Peloponnese.

Argus – city in Argolis ruled by Diomedes, after Adrastus. 'Argus' means 'shining' city.

Arne – city of eastern Greece.

Asteria – small island in the channel between Ithaca and Same (Cephalonia).

Athens – main city of Attica, ruled by Theseus and Aegeus before him.

Attica – region of central eastern Achaia that includes Athens.

Aulis – bay and port in Boeotia where the Achaian army assembles for the assault on Troy.

Boeotia – region of Thebes, where Aulis is located.

Calydon – city of Aetolia, famous for the hunt of the Calydon boar, in which all the major Achaian heroes of the Argonaut generation took part.

Caucasus, Mount – mountain of Colchis.

Chalcis – city of Euboea.

Cimmeria – land of the Cimmerians. The mouth of Hades was said to be found here.

Colchis – region between Caucasus and Pontus Euxinus (the Black

Sea), ruled by king Aeetes. Place where the 'golden fleece' was guarded by a dragon.

Corinth – city on the isthmus that connects the Peloponnese to mainland Greece, between the Gulf of Corinth and the Saronic Gulf.

Crete – island ruled by Idomeneus.

Cythera – island in the south of the Peloponnese, near Cape Malea.

Dardania – region of north-western Anatolia, near Troy, kingdom of Anchises, ally of Troy.

Dulichium – island, part of the kingdom of Odysseus.

Elis – region of the north-western Peloponnese.

Ephyra – place in Aetolia where an entrance to Hades was located.

Euboea – the biggest island of Greece, after Crete.

Eurotas – the river of Sparta.

Gythium – port of Sparta on the Laconian Gulf.

Haemos, Mount – mountain chain in the far north, where storm winds were said to originate. Lately identified with the Carpathians.

Hypereia – ancestral homeland of the Phaeacians.

Hypoplacian Thebes – city south of the Troad, ruled by Eetion, ally of Troy.

Iberia – modern Spain.

Ida, Mount – mountain south of Troy.

Ilium – the ancient name of Troy.

Iolcus – city of Thessaly, ruled by Pelias, port of the Argonauts.

Ismarus – city in the land of the Ciconians.

Ithaca – island in the Ionian sea, ruled by Odysseus, and Laertes before him.

Knossos – capital of Crete.

Laconian Gulf – the gulf between Cape Malea and Cape Tainaron.

Lemnos – island in the north Aegean sea.

Leucas – island, part of the kingdom of Odysseus.

Locris – region in western Greece, homeland of Ajax Oileus.

Malea – cape in the south-east of the Peloponnese, notoriously difficult and dangerous to navigate.

Messenia – kingdom of Nestor in the south-western Peloponnese.

Mycenae – city of Argolis ruled by Agamemnon, after Eurystheus and Atreus.

Nemea – city of Argolis where Hercules killed the Nemean lion.

Neritus, Mount – the tallest mountain of Ithaca.

Olympus, Mount – mountain in northern Thessaly, said to be the abode of the gods.

Ossa, Mount – mountain in Thessaly, said to be the abode of the centaurs.

Othrys, Mount – mountain in Thessaly near Phthia, the city of Achilles.

Parnassus, Mount – mountain in Phocis believed to be the abode of Apollo and the muses.

Pelion, Mount – mountain in Thessaly where the pine tree used to make the keel of the *Argo* was cut down.

Peloponnesus – the Peloponnese, the southern part of Greece.

Phasis – river in Colchis.

Pherai – city in Thessaly, ruled by Admetus.

Phocis – region in south central Greece.

Phthia – city of Thessaly ruled by Peleus father of Achilles, famous for its valorous warriors, the Myrmidons.

Pylos – main city of Messenia, ruled by Nestor.

Rhoetean – promontory of the Troad, where the tomb of Great Ajax was located.

Salamis – small island near Attica, ruled by Telamon, Great Ajax's father.

Same – island, part of the kingdom of Odysseus, probably modern Cephalonia.

Scamander – one of the two rivers of Troy.

Scheria – island of the Phaeacians.

Scyros – island ruled by Lycomedes.

Simoeis – one of the rivers of Troy.

Skaian Gate – the gates of the Trojan citadel, built to be
   unassailable.
Sounion – southern cape of Attica.
Sparta – city of Laconia, also called Lakedaemon, ruled by
   Menelaus.
Stygia – swamp in Hades.
Tainaron – cape of the central peninsula in the Peloponnese.
Taygetus, Mount – mountain in Laconia, west of Sparta.
Tenedos – small island near Troy where the Achaian fleet hides
   while awaiting the signal for the assault on Troy.
Thebes – city of Boeotia, ruled by Oedipus.
Thermodon – river in northern Anatolia, bordering the territory
   of the Amazons.
Thesprotia – kingdom of Autolykos, grandfather of Odysseus, in
   western Greece.
Thessaly – region of north-eastern Greece.
Thrace – region of eastern Greece, north-west of Troy.
Tiryns – city of Argolis, near Mycenae.
Trinacria – land of Helios the sun god.
Troad – region of Troy.
Troy – city of the Troad which controlled access to the
   Dardanelles, capital of the powerful kingdom of Priam, also
   known as 'Ilion' ('Ilium' in Latin), and 'Villusa' in Hittite texts.
   Identified by Schliemann and Blegen with the ruins on the hill
   of Hissarlik in Turkey, recently confirmed by the excavations
   of the late Manfred Korfmann. Ruled by Priam, it was
   besieged for nine years by the Achaians and finally fell thanks
   to the stratagem of the Trojan Horse.
Zacynthus – island, part of the kingdom of Odysseus.